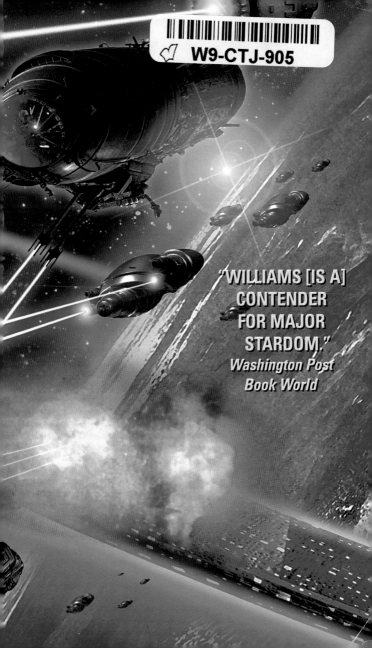

"WILLIAMS [IS A] CONTENDER FOR MAJOR STARDOM."
Washington Post Book World

New York Times bestselling author of

THE PRAXIS
Book One of DREAD EMPIRE'S FALL

"A great read."
Times of London

WALTER JON WILLIAMS

"A first-rate writer."
Washington Post Book World

"One of science fiction's most celebrated names."
St. Petersburg Times

"Williams's writing is always lean, lively, and engaging . . . [He] understands that science fiction can breath life into language."
New York Times Book Review

"With each novel, he tries something completely different."
Seattle Times

"Williams is a skillfully literate addition to the stylish new generation of science fiction writers . . . His fictive universe is grounded in the real possibilities of today."
Chicago Tribune

Also by
Walter Jon Williams

DREAD EMPIRE'S FALL: THE PRAXIS
THE RIFT
CITY ON FIRE
METROPOLITAN

WALTER JON WILLIAMS

DREAD EMPIRE'S FALL

THE
SUNDERING

HarperTorch
An Imprint of HarperCollinsPublishers

This is a work of fiction. Names, characters, places, and incidents are products of the author's imagination or are used fictitiously and are not to be construed as real. Any resemblance to actual events, locales, organizations, or persons, living or dead, is entirely coincidental.

HARPERTORCH
An Imprint of HarperCollins*Publishers*
10 East 53rd Street
New York, New York 10022-5299

Copyright © 2004 by Walter Jon Williams
ISBN 0-380-82021-8

First HarperTorch paperback printing: March 2004

HarperCollins®, HarperTorch™, and ✔™ are trademarks of Harper-Collins Publishers Inc.

Printed in the United States of America

Visit HarperTorch on the World Wide Web at www.harpercollins.com

10 9 8 7 6 5 4 3 2 1

For Kathy Hedges

With thanks to Dr. Michael Wester, for his tour along the hull of a dynamical system, and to Critical Mass for their massive critiques.

DREAD EMPIRE'S FALL

FALL

THE
SUNDERING

PROLOGUE

Warrant Officer Severin avoided the glances of his crew. He had led them into this misery, and now he was unable to lead them out.

The cockpit window of the lifeboat was covered in frost, delicate white clusters of frozen spears that reflected the red light of the Maw, the supernova ejecta that formed a giant scarlet ring which dominated the Protipanu system. The lifeboat was grappled to the nickel-iron asteroid 302948745AF, which was receding from the Protipanu 2 wormhole gate, and from the enemy fleet that guarded it.

The problem was that 302948745AF wasn't receding nearly fast enough. If Severin ordered the lifeboat away from the asteroid, he'd be detected by the ten enemy warships in the system and either captured or destroyed. But if he did nothing, he and his crew would run out of food, or possibly even die of cold.

At the time, his plan had seemed the height of cleverness and high strategic thought. He had been in command of the Protipanu 2 wormhole relay station when Captain Martinez of the *Corona,* fleeing a Naxid squadron, reported that the rebels would enter the system within a matter of hours. Severin had first of all used a trick of physics to physically move Wormhole 2, which caused the pursuing Naxids to miss their target and to spend months of frenzied deceleration trying to claw their way back into the system. Perhaps Severin had been rendered overconfident by this success, because he'd then talked his crew of six into remaining in the system as observers, grappling their lifeboat to the asteroid in order to keep watch on the enemy forces and report their location to any loyalist fleet that might jump through the wormhole to do battle.

Only no loyalist fleet had arrived. That there *were* loyalist fleets was proven by the fact that the Naxid enemy remained in the barren system, barring the most direct route from the capital, Zanshaa, to Third Fleet headquarters at Felarus. If the rebels had won the war, they surely would have left by now, gone to somewhere more useful . . . instead they made a lazy orbit around the Protipanu brown dwarf, and had filled the system with a bewildering array of decoys designed to mislead any force coming to engage them.

And so Severin remained grappled to his rock, and his crew with him. The lifeboat's systems were powered down to avoid enemy sensors spotting a heat signature, and the crew wore several layers of clothing and draped around themselves silvery thermal blankets that made them look like walking tents. Their breath blossomed out before their faces in a white mist, and frost coated the walls and cockpit windows. Frozen white rimed the beards of the men and the eyelashes of the women.

Thus far Severin's crew hadn't complained, and they had offered him no reproaches. Sometimes they were even cheerful, which was remarkable under the circumstances. They had exercise equipment to keep them fit and a full library of entertainments. But Severin reproached *himself*—reproached himself for coming up with the scheme in the first place, and then for failing to provision the lifeboat for as many months as he could. Six months' rations had seemed plenty at the time, but now he was beginning to wonder if he should reduce the number of calories the crew were consuming. And if he did that, the reproaches, both from himself and from his crew, would begin in earnest.

And so Severin avoided the glances of his crew, and counted the days.

No loyalist fleet came.

A pity, because if they ever arrived, Severin could teach them a great deal.

ONE

The defeated squadron was locked in its deceleration burn, the blazing fury of its torches directed toward the capital at Zanshaa. *Bombardment of Delhi* groaned and shuddered under the strain of over three gravities. At times the shaking and shivering was so violent that the woman called Caroline Sula wondered if the damaged cruiser would hold together.

After so many brutal days of deceleration, she didn't much care if it did or not.

Sula was no stranger to the hardships of pulling hard gee. She had been aboard the *Dauntless* under Captain Lord Richard Li when, a little over two months ago, it had joined the Home Fleet on a furious series of accelerations that eventually flung it through a course of wormhole gates toward the enemy lying in wait at Magaria.

The enemy had been ready for them, and Sula was now the sole survivor of the crew of the *Dauntless. Delhi,* the heavy cruiser that had pulled Sula's pinnace out of the wreckage of defeat, had been so badly damaged that it was a minor miracle it survived the battle at all.

All six survivors of the squadron were low on ammunition, and would be useless in the event of a fight. They had to decelerate, dock with the ring station at Zanshaa, take on fresh supplies of missiles and antimatter fuel, then commence yet another series of accelerations to give them the velocity necessary to avoid destruction should an enemy arrive.

That meant even *more* months of standing up under three

or four or more gravities, months in which Sula would experience the equivalent of a large, full-grown man sitting on her chest.

The deceleration alarm rang, the ship gave a series of long, prolonged groans, and Sula gasped with relief as the invisible man who squatted on her rose and walked away. *Dinnertime,* a whole hour at a wonderfully liberating 0.6 gravities, time to stretch her ligaments and fight the painful knots in her muscles. After that, she'd have to stand a watch in Auxiliary Command, which was the only place she *could* stand a watch now that Command was destroyed, along with *Delhi*'s captain and a pair of lieutenants.

Weariness dragged at her eyelids, at her heart. Sula released the webs that held her to the acceleration couch and came to her feet, suddenly light-headed as her heart tried to make yet another adjustment to her blood pressure. She wrenched off her helmet—she was required to spend times of acceleration in a pressure suit—and took a breath of air that wasn't completely saturated by her own stink. She rolled her head on her neck and felt her vertebrae crackle, and then peeled off the medicinal patch behind her ear, the one that fed her drugs that better enabled her to stand high gravities.

She wondered if she had time for a shower, and decided she did.

The others were finishing dinner when, in a clean pair of borrowed coveralls, Sula approached the officers' table while sticking another med patch behind her ear. The officers now ate in the enlisted galley, their own wardroom having been destroyed; and because their private stocks of food and liquor had also been blown to bits they shared the enlisted fare. As the steward brought her dinner, Sula observed that it consisted entirely of flat food, which is what happened to anything thrown in an oven and then subjected to five hours' constant deceleration at three gravities.

Sula inhaled the stale aroma of a flattened, highly compressed vegetable casserole, then washed the first bite down with a flat beverage—the steward knew to serve her water instead of the wine or beer that were the usual dinner drink of the officer class.

Lieutenant Lord Jeremy Foote was in the chair opposite her, his immaculate viridian-green uniform a testament to the industry of his servants.

"You're late," he said.

"I bathed, my lord," Sula said. "You might try it sometime."

This was a libel, since probably Foote didn't enjoy living in his own stench any more than she did, but her words caused the acting captain to suppress a grin.

Foote's handsome face showed no reaction to Sula's jab. Instead he gave a close-lipped, catlike smile, and said, "I thought perhaps you'd been viewing your latest letter from Captain Martinez."

Sula's heart gave a little sideways lurch at the mention of Martinez's name, and she hoped her reaction hadn't showed. She was in the process of composing a reply when the acting captain, Morgen, interrupted.

"Martinez?" he said. "Martinez of the *Corona*?"

"Indeed yes," Foote said. His drawl, which spoke of generations of good breeding and privilege, took on a malicious edge, and it was carefully pitched to carry to the next table of recruits. "He sends messages to our young Sula nearly every day. And she replies as often, passionate messages from the depth of her delicate heart. It's touching, great romance in the tradition of a derivoo singer."

Morgen looked at her. "You and Martinez are, ah . . ."

Sula didn't know why this revelation was supposed to be embarrassing: Lord Gareth Martinez was one of the few heroes the war had produced, at least on the loyalist side, and unlike most of the others was still in the realm of the living.

Sula ate a piece of flattened hash before replying, and when she did she pitched her voice to carry, as Foote had done. "Oh, Martinez and I are old friends," she said, "but my

Lord Lieutenant Foote is always inventing romances for me. It's his way of explaining why I won't sleep with *him*."

That one hit: she saw a twitch in Foote's eyelid. Again the acting captain suppressed a smile. "Well, I hope you're saying good things about us," he said.

Sula fixed Foote with her green eyes and replied in tone-perfect imitation of his drawl. "*Most* of you," she said. She took a drink of water. "By the way," she said, "I wonder how Lord Lieutenant Foote comes to know of my correspondence?"

"I'm the censor," Foote said. His smiling white teeth were perfectly even. "I view every torrid moment of your outgoing videos."

"There's still censorship?" Sula was surprised by the inanity of it. "Doesn't Foote have better things to do?" They crewed a wrecked cruiser, with most of its officers dead, few of its weapons functioning, and the forward third of the ship a half-melted ruin, torn open to the vacuum of space. Surely one of the few remaining officers could find better use for his time than poking into her correspondence.

Morgen's round face took on a solemn caste. "Censorship is more important now than ever, my lady. We've got to keep word of what happened at Magaria from spreading."

Sula hastily washed down a piece of flat bread in order to unleash her reply. "Spreading to *whom*?" she said. "The *enemy*? The enemy know *perfectly well* they massacred forty-eight of our ships! They know we only have six ships left in the Home Fleet, and they've got to know the *Delhi*'s a wreck."

Morgen lowered his voice, as if encouraging Sula not to spread this news to the enlisted personnel, who knew it perfectly well. "We have to prevent panic from spreading in the civilian population," he said.

Sula gave an acid laugh. "No, we can't have the civilians panicking. Not the *wrong* civilians, anyway." She gave Foote a cynical look. "I'm sure our honorable censor's family is panicking *right at this very moment*. The only difference be-

tween them and the general population is that Clan Foote is
going to panic their way into a *profit*. I'm sure their money's
moving all over the exchanges, and it's being converted
into . . ." Her invention failed her. ". . . into, ah, convertible
things, to be carried to the safer corners of the empire to
await a brighter dawn. Perhaps they're even being carried in
the current Lord Foote's very own pillowcase."

"My lord great-uncle," Foote said quietly, "is too ill to
leave his palace on Zanshaa."

"His heir, then," Sula said. "The point of the censorship is
that we Peers are going to have a monopoly on the information necessary to survive whatever's coming. Everyone who
doesn't belong to our order is expected to continue their normal lives, making money for the Peers, right up to the point
where a Naxid fleet shows up and starts raining antimatter
bombs out of the sky. *Then* maybe they'll be allowed to notice that the media reports were less than candid."

The acting captain pitched his voice even lower. "Sublieutenant my Lady Sula, I think this is not a suitable topic for
the dinner table."

Sula felt her lips quirk in amusement. "As my lord
wishes," she said. Probably Morgen's relations were going
to do well out of this, too.

Sula's relations would not, for the simple reason that she
didn't have any. She was in the nearly unprecedented position of being a Peer without any money or influence. Though
the title of Lady Sula made her the theoretical head of the
entire Sula Clan, there *was* no Sula Clan, no property, and
no money save for a modest trust fund that had been set up
by some friends of the late Lord Sula. She had only got into
the Fleet because her position as a Peer gave her automatic
place in one of the academies. She had no patron either in
the service or outside it.

Deplorable though it was, her position nevertheless gave
her a unique insight into how the Peers actually worked. The
alien Shaa, who had bloodily conquered the Terrans,

Naxids, and other species who made up the empire, had created the order of Peers as an intermediary between themselves and the great mass of their subjects. Now that the last of the Shaa was dead, the Peers were in charge—and had managed to land-crash into a civil war within bare months of their last overlord's demise.

Sula was surprised it had taken them that long. So far as she could tell, the Peers acted exactly as one might expect from a class who had a near monopoly on power, their fingers in every profitable business, and who with their clients owned almost everything. The only check on their rapacity was the Legion of Diligence, who would massacre anyone whose avarice became too uninhibited—as, in fact, they had massacred the last Lord and Lady Sula.

The Peers, Sula observed, seemed to act out of naked self-interest. But for some reason it was impolite to actually say so.

Sula finished her flat food, then called a chronometer onto her sleeve display and wondered if she had enough time to look at her mail before suiting up to stand her watch.

She decided she had enough time.

Sula returned to her cabin, one that had originally belonged to a petty officer who had been killed at Magaria, and which still contained most of his belongings. She snapped on the video display with her right thumb, an action that caused a sudden sharp sting. She snatched her hand away, and as the display flashed on she inspected the thick scar tissue on the pad of her thumb. After the battle, in the course of conducting urgent repairs, her thumb had come into contact with a pipe of superheated coolant, and though the wound had healed, a wrong movement could still send pain shrieking along the length of her arm.

She tucked the thumb carefully into her palm and paged through menus with her index finger until she found her mail.

Only one message, from Lieutenant Captain Lord Gareth Martinez, three days in transit via powerful communications lasers. She opened the message.

"Well, *Corona* managed to bungle another exercise," he said wearily. His broad-shouldered figure was slumped in a chair—he, like Sula, had been suffering from many days of high gee, and his weariness showed it. His viridian uniform tunic was unbuttoned at the throat. He had a lantern jaw, thick brows, and olive skin; his provincial accent was heavy enough to send razor blades skating up Sula's nerves.

When they had first met, before the war, they had come together briefly, then came explosively apart. It was all Sula's fault, she felt: she'd been too panicked, too paranoid, too far out of her depth. She'd spent the next several months hiding from him. A conceited son of privilege like Foote was someone she could cope with; Martinez was something else again.

If they were lucky enough to come together once more, she wasn't going to let them blow apart ever again.

"I said by *zero-one-seven!*" Martinez said. "What's the *matter,* there?"

"Sorry, my lord!" Fingers punching the display. "That's zero-one-seven, my lord."

"Pilot, rotate ship." *Corona* was already a little late.

"Ship rotated, my lord. New heading two-two-seven by zero-one-seven."

"Engines, prepare to fire engines."

"Missile flares!" called the two sensor operators in unison. "Enemy missiles fired!"

"Power up point-defense lasers."

"Point-defense lasers powering, lord elcap."

Martinez realized he'd been sufficiently distracted by the announcement of the enemy missiles that's he'd forgotten to order the engines to fire. He leaned forward in his couch to give emphasis to the order; and his command cage creaked as it swung on its gimbals.

"Engines," he said. "Fire engines."

And then he remembered he'd forgotten something else.

"Weapons," he added, "this is a drill."

After the drill was over, after the virtual displays faded from Martinez's mind and the leaden sense of failure rose yet again in his thoughts, he looked out over Command and saw the crew as silent and miserable as he was.

Too many of them were new. Two-thirds of *Corona*'s crew had been on board for less than a month, and though they were taking to their new jobs reasonably well, they were far from proficient. Sometimes he wished he'd had only his old crew—the skeleton crew with which he'd saved *Corona* from capture during the first hours of the Naxid revolt. When he now looked back on that escape—the tension, the uncertainty, the hard accelerations, the terror induced by pursuing enemy missiles—all that now seemed painted in the warm, familiar tones of nostalgia. In the emergency he and the crew had reacted with a brilliance, a certainty that neither he nor they had matched since.

The old crew were still here, among all the newcomers, but Martinez couldn't rely on them alone. The new people all had to be trained, had to fit into their roles and perform as proficiently as if they'd been in their places for years.

There was a whirring in his vac suit as the cooling units cut in, flooding the suit with chilled air and the faintest whiff of lubricant.

"Right," he said. "We'll have another drill after supper, at 26:01."

Despite the fact that the crew were in their white-and-viridian vac suits, he could detect in the angle of their heads and shoulders a slumping attitude of defeat.

In a manual written for officers that he'd found on the frigate's computers, he'd read of the old formula: *praise-correct-praise*. First, the manual recommended, you praised them for what they did right, then you corrected what they did wrong, then praised them for their improvement. In his mind he rehearsed the formula as it related to the current situation.

   1. You didn't screw up as badly as last time.

   2. You still screwed up.

   3. Try not to screw up any more.

The only problem was that his crew had a perfect right to answer, *You first, my lord.*

Martinez, too, was learning on the job, and had discovered that his performance was erratic. Nothing in his training had ever suggested that war was a business filled with such desperate improvisation.

The voice of his junior lieutenant, Vonderheydte, came over his headphones.

"Captain Kamarullah, my lord, on intership net. I believe it's the beginning of the debriefing."

This was all Martinez needed. Kamarullah was the senior captain in Light Squadron 14 and would normally have been in command, all save for the fact that he'd once been blamed for a botched maneuver—and blamed by Junior Squadron Commander Do-faq, who was now in overall command of both the light and heavy squadrons, Faqforce, now heading for Honebar. In an act of pure autocratic malevolence, Do-faq had removed Kamarullah from command of the light squadron and replaced him with the most junior captain present.

Martinez.

Granted that Martinez had accepted the appointment with alacrity. Granted as well that there was some modest justification for this act of despotism: Martinez was the only one of the captains present with actual combat experience. But that experience consisted of stealing *Corona* and fleeing at top speed from the overwhelming enemy force at Magaria; it hadn't consisted of commanding and maneuvering a squadron, the skill sets that Martinez needed at present, and which he was desperately trying to acquire.

It was fortunate that the chance of encountering enemies on this mission was small. Faqforce had been ordered from

Zanshaa to Hone-bar before the disaster at Magaria, and when word of the defeat came they had gone too far to turn around. When Martinez's squadron reached its destination, it would swing around Hone-bar's sun and head straight back to the capital to aid in its defense.

It was *then,* most likely, that *Corona* would need its combat skills.

None of which altered the sad fact that Kamarullah was now on the comm, wanting to exult over his own ship's flawless performance in the drill.

"Tell him to stand by," Martinez said. Instead of speaking to Kamarulla he paged his senior lieutenant, Dalkeith, who had spent the maneuver in Auxiliary Command. While he and his crew in Command had been maneuvering a virtual squadron through an exercise, Dalkeith had commanded the actual frigate *Corona,* keeping it on its steady 2.3 gravity acceleration for the wormhole that led to Hone-bar.

The second-in-command's voice lisped in Martinez's ear. "This is Dalkeith." He had been startled on first acquaintance with his premiere to discover that she possessed a child's high-pitched voice in the body of a middle-aged, gray-haired woman. Lady Elissa Dalkeith was one of the officers who had joined *Corona* a little over a month ago on Zanshaa, and was considered old to have gone so long in the Fleet without promotion, a fact that argued either incompetence or a lack of patronage among her superiors. Martinez hadn't found her incompetent, but uninspired: she performed every task well enough, but without any particular enthusiasm, and without volunteering anything new, efficient, or interesting. He had hoped to have someone younger and more energetic, someone who would relieve Martinez of some of his work, but youth and energy both had been beaten out of Dalkeith over the years of neglect by the Fleet, and Martinez's workload remained daunting.

"The maneuver's over, my lady," Martinez told her. "We will resume command of the ship."

"Very well, lord elcap. We are prepared to relinquish command."

"Stand by." Martinez shifted his channel to broadcast to the crew in Command. "We are taking control of the ship . . . now." His gloved hands tapped his display, and the screens on every board in Command shifted to show *Corona*'s true situation.

"You may stand down," Martinez told Dalkeith.

The crew in Command all reported *Corona*'s situation as it was reflected on their displays, and then Martinez heaved a sigh against the gravities that weighed him down. There was no alternative to Kamarullah and the debriefing.

He told Vonderheydte to patch him into the intership channel and set his display to virtual. The square command room, with its suited figures hanging in their accelerations cages, vanished from his sight, to be replaced at once by Kamarullah's square, graying head. Fortunately Kamarullah was not alone—most of the other captains had joined the link in the meantime, as well as Lord Squadron Commander Do-faq, who commanded the two squadrons that made up Faqforce. Do-faq was a member of the Lai-own species, flightless birds taller than a human. Their hollow bones couldn't stand the heavy accelerations that were possible for humans; but because their ancestors had flown through the sky, their brains were supposed to be better configured for three-dimensional maneuvers, and they were considered a race of master tacticians.

At least the virtual presence of the squadron commander, his bitter enemy, would prevent Kamarullah from being *too* smug in public.

"My lords," Martinez greeted.

"Lord captain," said Do-faq, flashing the peg teeth in his carnivore muzzle. He was young for his advanced rank, as demonstrated by the dark feathery hair on either side of his flat-topped head, hair that Lai-own lost on full maturity. His manner was businesslike without being brusque. Martinez had never actually met him in person, and had little feel for him as a personality, but Do-faq's history with Kamarullah suggested that Martinez would disappoint the avian only at his peril.

The faces of the remaining captains appeared one after another in the virtual display. Do-faq began by summarizing the events of the virtual maneuver in which they'd all participated, and then went on to a detailed critique of each ship's performance. *Corona* was cited for tardy transmission of orders to the other ships in the light squadron, as well as ragged performance of those same orders.

"Yes, my lord," Martinez said. There was little point in offering excuses.

He could see the quiet exultation in Kamarullah's eyes as Do-faq admitted in a brisk tone that his ship had done well.

Do-faq had ordered a maneuver almost every day, the ships flying in close proximity to one another and linked by communication lasers to provide a shared virtual environment. The maneuvers themselves were highly scripted, and taken from the bottomless archive of Fleet maneuvers that went back millennia. Do-faq called for maneuvers in which the heavy and light squadrons battled each other, or fought side-by-side against a computer-generated enemy; or participated as smaller elements in a larger fleet. No independent action was intended, or contemplated: each ship was judged on how well it followed its orders rather than how well it did against the "enemy." The side the scenario intended to win was always victorious, and thus demonstrated the superiority of proper Fleet doctrine against tactics that were less proper, and less doctrinaire.

Corona had consistently ranked low in the standings generated after each set of maneuvers, and the only reason it didn't permanently occupy last place was that other ships were as ill-prepared as *Corona*. Maneuvers weren't very common in the Fleet—they were a dreadful inconvenience, taxing the officers' capabilities and taking the crew away from important duties such as polishing brass, waxing floors, and keeping the engine spaces sparkling clean in the event of an inspection. In a service that hadn't fought a war in thirty-four hundred years, social virtues had come to seem at least as important as military ones, and there were crews in Do-faq's command that had never participated even in a virtual maneuver before joining Faqforce.

Martinez had to give Do-faq credit for realizing that the war had changed everything. He was intent on turning his command into a proper fighting force, and the daily maneuvers and debriefings were a part of it. Martinez commended this industry on the part of a superior even as he winced at his own ship's performance.

"My lords," Do-faq said in conclusion, his golden eyes shifting from one virtual face to the next. "I am pleased to report that the Fleet Control Board has at last agreed to my repeated requests to send me the records of the Battle of Magaria. I am going to transmit them, coded, to each ship under my command. A captain's key will be required to open the file. I admonish you to view these records in private, and to be careful with whom you share them." His transparent nictating membranes closed solemnly over his eyes. "Tomorrow's maneuvers will be conducted by your senior lieutenants from your Auxiliary Command centers. During that time we will confer again and see if we can discover what the battle teaches us."

Martinez felt suspense tingling in his nerves. The government had never officially admitted defeat at Magaria, but instead issued an incessant series of clarion calls that urged every loyal citizen to Do His Utmost in the Crisis, to Repel Seditious Thought, to Uphold the Praxis, and to Unceasingly Fight for the Future of the Empire, a barrage of desperate slogans that argued for considerable panic behind the scenes. Martinez had managed to wangle the raw data out of the Fleet Control Board, and had been stunned by the fact of forty-eight of the Fleet's finest warships blown into radioactive debris along with their commander. What he hadn't known was *how* those forty-eight ships had been lost.

A few hours later, lying in his own bed after supper while the acceleration went on, he called up the overhead display and witnessed exactly that, and he was appalled by the battle's fury. The number of missiles launched by each side was uncountable: whole squadrons on both sides were annihilated at once, or within seconds, by the blazing fury of antimatter warheads.

Particularly useful recordings had been made by a pinnace that had been launched by a cruiser in the lead squadron, and which had somehow avoided destruction for the entire battle, shepherding its barrage of antimatter missiles through the entire fight until they could be used to effect against the enemy, destroying five ships that blocked the retreat of the Home Fleet's six survivors. The pinnace had been in an ideal position to witness most of the battle, from the glorious charge of Cruiser Squadron 2 to the rout of the fleet's battered remains.

Martinez wondered how Caroline, Lady Sula, had felt as she watched the doom of the Home Fleet from her lone pinnace.

Whatever her feelings, they hadn't altered her skill as a pilot. Not only had she destroyed five enemy ships, but she had followed the act of destruction by a broadcast on the all-ships channel, a hoarse-voiced cry of defiance against the enemy:

"*Sula!* It was Sula who did this! *Remember my name!*"

The words sent a shiver up Martinez's spine. He had just wondered how Sula had felt on watching the Home Fleet die—and now he *knew* how she felt. In her words Martinez heard the despair, the fury, and the loss that lay behind the defiant shout.

He felt an overwhelming need to wrap Sula in his arms and lie with her in some silent, unspeaking realm, a place where he could bring peace to the terrors he heard in that desperate, challenging voice.

Which was ridiculous, because he hardly knew her. And when he'd tried to get close to her, she'd fled.

With an act of will he dismissed Sula from his thoughts, and looked through the recordings again. Again and again he watched the squadrons maneuvering against at each other at significant fractions of the speed of light, the missile tracks that connected them, the blossoms of furious radiation in which they died.

A conviction began to harden in him. Martinez reached for his sleeve display and called for the one person on the crew he trusted without reservation.

"Page crewman Alikhan."

"My lord." The answer came quickly, and Alikhan's stern face appeared in the chameleon-weave display on Martinez's left sleeve. Alikhan had retired from the Fleet as a thirty-year man, a weaponer first class, and wore the curling mustachios and goatee favored by many senior petty officers. Martinez had brought him back into the service as his orderly, and as a fund of wisdom and practical information on the service.

Alikhan was wearing his vac suit and helmet, and lying on an acceleration couch.

"Are you alone?" Martinez asked.

"I'm in the weapons bays, my lord, for the maneuver."

Martinez gave himself a mental demerit for forgetting he'd scheduled a drill for 26:01, after supper. He checked the chronometer on the wall and saw that he had a few minutes before the exercise was scheduled to begin.

His presence wasn't strictly necessary: this was a drill he'd scheduled on his own, with *Corona*'s crew alone, in the hopes of sharpening them for tomorrow's fleet maneuver. He'd tell Dalkeith to run it instead, with her crew in Auxiliary Command. She'd be in charge during tomorrow's drill anyway, so she'd need the practice more than Martinez did.

Martinez looked at the image of Alikhan in his sleeve display. "I'd like you to go virtual and look at a file. You aren't to show this to anyone. I want you to look at it closely and see what conclusions you can draw."

"A file, my lord?"

Martinez told him what was in it. Alikhan's eyes widened.

"Very good, my lord," he said.

Martinez then paged Dalkeith and told her that she was in charge of the upcoming drill. "Find something in the files involving two squadrons maneuvering against each other—the sort of thing Do-faq would pick. Give your people some practice, because Do-faq intends that you command in tomorrow morning's fleet maneuver."

One of the advantages of having an unimaginative premiere, Martinez observed, was that nothing seemed to surprise her. Or perhaps all things surprised her equally.

"Very well, lord elcap," she said.

Martinez's left arm had grown very tired of being held aloft in the heavy gravity, and when the chameleon weave of the sleeve display shifted to its normal dark green, Martinez thankfully lowered the arm to his side. He would be more comfortable in an acceleration couch, but the couches were all in public areas, and he wanted the privacy of his own cabin. The scent of tomato and oil wafted toward him from his table, where the remains of his supper waited to be cleared during the next moment of standard gravity. Soft light glowed on the dark wood paneling that had been installed by *Corona*'s previous captain.

That captain, Fahd Tarafah, had been one of the Fleet's most extreme football fanatics, and had gone so far as to paint *Corona*'s hull the lawn green of a football pitch, complete with a white midfield stripe running the length of the ship and a motif of soccer balls bouncing down the ship's flanks. Tarafah's cabin had previously been decorated with sports memorabilia, trophies, pictures of his winning teams and of Tarafah with famous players, along with a muddied pair of athletic shoes preserved by rare gases under a glass bowl.

Tarafah, his winning team, and most of his officers and crew had been captured in the opening moments of the

Naxid rebellion, leaving Martinez in command of *Corona*. Martinez could only hope that wherever Tarafah was, he was taking comfort in the fact that the Coronas, in their last moments of freedom, had beaten the *Bombardment of Beijing* four goals to one.

Tarafah's pictures and other personal effects had been cleared away and sent to Tarafah's family, but Martinez hadn't had time to replace any of them with objects personal to himself. The bare walls now had a desolate look, relieved only by a picture Alikhan had copied from a news report, framed, and mounted: the picture showed Martinez addressing the Convocation, the supreme legislative body of the empire, after he'd been awarded the Golden Orb for saving *Corona* from the rebels.

His great moment in history. It had been all downslope from there.

The final moments of the Battle of Magaria were frozen in the display over his head, an abstract display of blips, traces, heading and speed indicators, all marred by the deadly radio blooms of antimatter explosions. Martinez shifted the display's t-axis to the beginning of the battle and ran the display again. Caroline Sula intruded again on his thoughts, and he found himself unable to concentrate.

Perhaps Sula had sent him a message. He checked and discovered that she had, one that had been three days crossing the empty space between them.

Anticipation sang through him as he called up the video.

Absurd, he told himself. He hardly knew her.

Sula appeared in the air before him. He paused for a moment in appreciation of her pale, translucent complexion, the pale gold hair and brilliant green eyes, elements of a staggering beauty marred only slightly, at this moment, by signs of weariness and pain. And the brain hidden under that remarkable exterior was at least as remarkable as her looks—Caroline Sula had won a First, had scored highest of all candidates in her year for the lieutenants' exams, and had then gone on to blow up five enemy ships at the Battle of Magaria.

Still, it wasn't her mind that Martinez was admiring at the moment. Simply gazing at her was like being hit in the groin with a velvet hammer.

Sula looked at him and spoke. "Another nineteen days of deceleration before we reach—" And then there was the annoying white flash, with the Fleet symbol, that indicated censorship, before Sula appeared again, apparently undisturbed by the interruption. "Everyone's tired. Nobody on this ship bathes nearly enough, and that includes me.

"I'm sorry to hear about your misadventures on the exercise. Working up a new crew can't be any fun." Her lips twitched in a suggestive smile, a flash of sharp white teeth. "I'm sorry not to be there to help you whip them into shape." The smile faded, and she shrugged. "Still, I'm sure you'll manage it. I have confidence in your ability to warp all others to your imperious will."

Well, Martinez thought, *that* was good. At least he *supposed* it was good.

Sometimes Sula's choice of phrase was too ambiguous for his tastes.

"Still," she went on, "you can't be enjoying yourself, not when every other captain in the Fleet is jealous of you and will pounce on your least misstep. I hope you have at least a few friends on board."

Her expression changed subtly, a mask falling into place behind her eyes. "And speaking of friends, an old acquaintance of ours has been given the task of censoring these messages. That would be Sublieutenant Lord Jeremy Foote, who I believe you encountered when he was a mere cadet. So if any pieces of these messages are missing, for instance—" Martinez laughed at the appearance of a white space, knowing that Sula was deliberately filling the air either with military secrets or candid, scatological judgments of superior officers. The long empty moment ended, and Sula returned wearing another of her ambiguous smiles. "—then you'll know it was due to the intervention of a friend." Sula raised her hand to wave farewell, then winced. "The burn is better," she added, "thanks for asking. But sometimes I move too suddenly, and the little bastard *bites*."

The orange End Transmission symbol filled the air.

Jeremy Foote, Martinez thought. A big blond oaf with a cowlick, a rich boy whose arrogance and assumption of privilege skated the line of insubordination and contempt. Martinez had loathed him on first meeting him, and subsequent acquaintance hadn't improved Martinez's opinion.

Foote hadn't bothered with the lieutenants' exams in which Sula had scored her First—that sort of work was beneath the dignity of a Foote. He'd been promoted straight into the *Bombardment of Delhi* by its captain, his yachtsman uncle, and no doubt subsequent promotions were assured by other relations and friends in the service. Perhaps Foote had suffered a setback when the yachtsman uncle had died along with half his crew, but Martinez doubted that Foote's star would fade for very long. The higher-ranking Peers looked after each other very well.

At least Sula seemed as fond of Lord Jeremy as was Martinez, a fact in which he could take comfort.

He squirreled Sula's message away in a file that could be opened only with his captain's key, then told the software he would reply. He looked at the camera and donned what he thought of as his official face, the imperturbable mask of a commander.

"You can only imagine my delight on learning that it was Lieutenant Foote who censors your messages," he said. "I know, of course, that my superior rank means that he can't censor *me,* and that he won't see *this* message unless you show it to him.

"Permission to do this is now granted. As you know, I now command a squadron that is being sent on . . ." He paused for deliberate effect. "A.hazardous mission. I've recently reviewed the records of the battle at Magaria, including the records made by your pinnace. As I may soon be leading ships into combat myself, I'm interested in your assessment of that action."

He gazed sternly—nobly, he hoped—into the camera. "Please reply with your most candid appraisal of our performance, and that of the enemy. You may respond fully, and I hope without censorship—I intend this message should make it clear to Lieutenant Foote that there is no need to keep the facts of the battle from me, as I already know them. I know that all but six of our ships were lost, that *Bombardment of Delhi* suffered the death of its captain and considerable damage, and that what remains of the Home Fleet are returning to Zanshaa in hopes of defending the capital.

"So," he said, looking at the pickup with what he hoped was stern confidence, "I hope that your analysis of the battle will be able to aid my mission and help to restore the rule of the Praxis and the peace of the empire. End transmission."

Let Foote swallow *that* one, he thought.

He queued the message in the next burst of the communications lasers, then turned the display again to the battle at Magaria. Again he watched the Home Fleet fly to its death, and he tried to keep track of the waves of missiles, the increasingly desperate counterfire, the sudden collapse as entire squadrons vanished into the expanding burning plasma shells of antimatter bombs.

A chime sounded on the comm. He answered on his sleeve display.

"This is Martinez."

The face that appeared on Martinez's sleeve was that of his orderly. "I have done as you instructed, lord elcap."

"Yes? Any conclusions?"

"It's really not my place, my lord."

Martinez ignored this disclaimer, a habit with Alikhan. One didn't prosper for thirty years in the weapons bays by telling officers what one actually thought. If Martinez had stated his own opinion first, then Alikhan would have agreed with him and kept his own thoughts to himself.

"I'd very much appreciate your opinion, Alikhan," Martinez said.

Alikhan hesitated for another moment, then caved in. "Very well, my lord. It seems to me that . . . that the squadrons were flying in too close a formation, and for far too long."

Martinez nodded. "Thank you, Alikhan." And then he added, "It happens that I agree with you."

It was useful to know that someone else supported his position, even though the person was not anyone he could bring to a captains' conference.

He signed off and watched the recordings of the battle again. Commanders kept their ships close together in order to maintain control of them for as long as possible, and in order so that their defensive fire could be concentrated on any incoming attack. Though Fleet doctrine assumed that at some point a formation would have to break up—to "starburst"—in order to avoid being overwhelmed by salvos of enemy missiles, the commanders at Magaria had been reluctant to order such maneuvers till the last possible moment, because it meant losing control of their ships. Once control was lost, it would be impossible to coordinate friendly forces in the battle. Each ship would be on its own.

Squadron Commander Do-faq, and Martinez himself, were training their crews in exactly the sort of formations and maneuvers that had brought about the disaster at Magaria.

Now *that,* Martinez thought, bore thinking about.

TWO

Maurice Chen stepped onto the terrace outside the Hall of the Convocation as his nerves tingled with the knowledge that he was about to accept a bribe.

Lord Roland Martinez waited at one of the terrace tables, a cup of coffee in front of him. His dark hair ruffled in a gusty wind heavy with the sweet scent of the blossoming pherentis vines that covered the cliff face below. Spring had come early to Zanshaa City, brightening the gloom of a catastrophic winter.

Above the convocates' hall loomed the Great Refuge, the carved granite structure with its huge dome, from which the Shaa had once ruled their empire, and through the gates of which the last Shaa, less than a year ago, had been carried to his rest in the Couch of Eternity at the other end of the High City. From the parapet the vine-covered cliffs fell away to the Lower Town, the metropolis that spread all the way to the horizon, its boulevards, streets, alleyways, and canals aswarm with members of the sentient species conquered by the Shaa. On the horizon the baroque silhouette of the Apszipar Tower stood plain against the viridian green of Zanshaa's sky. And above all, above even the Great Refuge, was the silver metal arc of Zanshaa's accelerator ring, which served as a home and harbor to the Fleet, to hundreds of civilian vessels, and to millions in population who had chosen to live above planet rather than on it.

As Maurice Chen approached, Lord Roland rose. He was

a larger, older version of his brother, the famous captain of *Corona,* and had the same long torso and overlong arms atop shortish legs.

"Will you have coffee, Lord Chen?" he offered. "Or tea, or perhaps something stronger?"

Chen hesitated. On one side the terrace was the long clear wall of the Hall of the Convocation, and the Convocation, he knew, was in session. Any lord convocate could look through that transparent wall and see Chen in conversation with Lord Roland, and perhaps wonder what the two had to say to one another.

Perhaps he could suggest moving to the convocates' lounge, which would be a little less public.

"Would you mind terribly if we walked indoors?" Lord Chen said. "I don't have the best memories of this place." He glanced over the terrace and shrugged deeper into the wine-red uniform tunic of the lords convocate.

A few months ago he and his colleagues had hurled Naxid convocates from this very terrace, to break their bodies on the stones below. There were now plans to build a monument here, larger-than-life statues of representative members of the non-Naxid species tipping rebels over the brink. Lord Chen's memories of the event were fragmentary and disordered, unclear yet jagged, like a picture painted on shattered glass, a confused series of images with razor-sharp edges that could still draw blood.

"Of course we can go inside," Lord Roland said. "Maybe I shouldn't have suggested the terrace." His provincial accent was as crude as his brother's, and Lord Chen felt a burst of annoyance at himself for the fact that he was about to take money from such a man. The Chen Clan was at the top of Peer society, and even though Clan Martinez were Peers, they were Peers from the far side of nowhere. In a properly ordered society, Roland should be asking Chen for favors, not the other way around.

Lord Roland took a final sip of his coffee and walked with

Lord Chen past the armed Torminel who now, since the rebellion, were posted on the terrace doors. Footfalls were softened by plush carpet as the convocate and his guest walked up a long ramp.

"I hope Lady Terza is coping with her loss," said Lord Roland.

"She's doing as well as we can expect," Chen said. He really didn't want to discuss family matters with Lord Roland. It wasn't as if the man would ever be an intimate of his family.

"Please give her my best wishes."

"I will."

Lord Chen's daughter, Terza, had lost her fiancé at Magaria. She and Captain Lord Richard Li had formed an uncommonly lovely, lively, charming couple, and though Lord Chen's heart warmed whenever he'd seen them together, he had noted other advantages to the match. Clan Li, though a step below the Chens socially, had grown uncommonly prosperous, and an alliance would have done well for the Chens.

Another bit of financial bad luck that had made this meeting necessary.

Bronze doors, cast with a heroic relief of The Many Species of the Empire Being Uplifted by the Praxis, opened silently before them, and the convocate and his guest passed into the building's foyer. There Lord Chen was startled to see a Naxid, in the dark red tunic of a convocate, speed across the foyer, her four polished boots beating at the stone floor, her body whipping from side to side as she hurled herself the even greater bronze doors that led into the Hall of the Convocation.

"Strange to see Naxids again," Lord Chen murmured.

"Stranger still to see Naxid convocates." Lord Roland watched the huge silent doors close behind the centauroid figure. "For a while I thought you'd killed them all."

Lord Chen blinked. "Not me personally, I hope." His

heels clacked on the granite floor with its inlaid semi-precious stones. "But no, it seems they weren't all involved in the plot."

For a while it had been difficult to remember that only some Naxids had revolted. Perhaps not even the majority. The Committee for the Salvation of the Praxis, on the Naxid home world of Naxas, had kept knowledge of their rebellion in as few trusted hands as possible—even half the Naxid convocates hadn't been told, and had fled the violence in the Hall of the Convocation, or stayed in their seats out of fear and confusion.

For some time after the rebellion, it was rare to see a Naxid in public—it was as if a sixth of the population of the empire had simply vanished. Even in Naxid neighborhoods the streets were quiet. But gradually, first by ones and twos, then in small groups, they had appeared in civil society once more.

"We've had a number of Naxid convocates return," said Lord Chen. "Of course, the new lord senior keeps them off committee chairmanships, and any committees to do with the war."

"You can't be too careful, I suppose," said Lord Roland.

"I've observed that the Naxids are careful to vote with the majority on all war measures. And they regularly forward patriotic petitions from their clients."

"Hmm." Lord Roland stroked his chin thoughtfully. "I wonder how their clients are faring in the current climate?"

"Not well, I'd imagine. The Convocation has better things to do these days than to pay attention to Naxid petitions." Resentment rumbled through his mind. "No one will trust a Naxid for generations, believe me."

The two passed through the foyer and into the lounge, then walked along the gleaming dark ceramic bar, with its dashing accents of brushed aluminum, to a booth with plush leather benches contoured to the Terran physique. Lord

Roland ordered another coffee, and Lord Chen a glass of mineral water.

"I'm pleased to report that another two ships have passed through the Hone-bar system on their way to safe areas," Lord Chen reported.

"Excellent." Lord Roland smiled thinly. "I'd like to lease them all, of course."

"Of course," Lord Chen agreed.

The onset of war had hit the Chen Clan hard. Lord Chen's home planet, which he represented in the Convocation, was in the hands of the rebels, as was much of his personal property. Other Chen possessions scattered over many worlds were now controlled by the enemy, and so were at least half the ships belonging to Chen-controlled merchant companies. Much of Lord Chen's remaining wealth was in the Hone Reach, which could be cut off in the event of a Naxid capture of Hone-bar, the Lai-own home world.

Lord Chen was facing ruin. Fortunately he now sat across the table from a man who had volunteered to be his financial savior.

Lord Roland proposed to lease Clan Chen's ships. *All* of them, including those lost in Naxid-controlled space. The lease would be for five years, and specifically exempted Lord Chen or his companies from any nonperformance penalties resulting from war or rebellion—in other words, if the ships were lost, destroyed, or confiscated by the enemy, Clan Martinez would have to pay for them anyway. Insurance would be carried by a company on the Martinez home world of Laredo.

Lord Roland Martinez—or more properly his father, the current Lord Martinez—would subsidize Clan Chen for the next five years.

What Lord Roland wanted in exchange for this was for the most part clear. Lord Chen was a member of the Fleet Control Board, the body that made all major decisions regarding military personnel, supplies, bases, and construction. Lord Roland's home world of Laredo had already been awarded a contract to build frigates to replace those taken by the enemy, and clearly Lord Chen would be expected to arrange more contracts along those lines. Expansion of the yards and the military base, contracts for supplies, appointments for officers belonging to client clans . . . Ultimately, Lord Chen knew, the Martinez clan wanted the opening of two planets, Chee and Parkhurst, to settlement under Martinez patronage.

Lord Chen would be happy to deliver. There was nothing wrong with aiding one's friends. There was nothing wrong with leasing one's ships. There was nothing wrong with letting out contracts that would make the Fleet stronger during a desperate war. And there was nothing wrong with settling new planets, even though there had been no new settlements during the last twelve hundred years of the Shaa overlords' decline.

True, if the Legion of Diligence happened to discover a pattern in this, there might be an investigation with dire consequences. But the Legion of Diligence was now busy rooting out rebels and subversion, and most military contracts were covered by secrecy laws which the Legion was bound to enforce, not to analyze. Lord Chen judged it all worth the risk.

"I have prepared a contract," said Lord Roland, "with names of ships and sums specified. Would you like to review it?"

"Yes, if you please."

Lord Roland held up his left arm. "Shall I send it to your sleeve display, my lord?"

"I don't have a sleeve display," Lord Chen said. Sleeve displays were probably a necessity for busy people such as military officers or office managers, he thought, but for a Peer they were vulgar. He produced a wafer-thin comm unit from an inner pocket, extended the display, and captured Lord Roland's transmission.

While he was doing so, the Cree waitron delivered their order. The scent of Lord Roland's coffee wafted over the table.

"I'm sure there will be no problem," Lord Chen said as he folded away the display. "I'll have signed hard copy delivered to your residence tomorrow."

"Speaking of tomorrow," Lord Roland said, "I hope we can expect you and Lady Chen at tomorrow's party in honor of Vipsania's birthday."

Lord Chen suppressed annoyance. It was one thing to do business with the likes of the Martinez clan, and another to see them socially.

Still, he supposed there was no avoiding it.

"Of course. We'll be happy to attend." A thought struck him. "You have unusual names in your family, don't you? Vipsania, Roland, Gareth, Sempronia . . . are they traditional in the Martinez clan? Or do they have some particular meaning?"

Lord Roland smiled. "Their particular meaning is that our mother is fond of romantic novels. We're all named after her favorite characters."

"That's charming."

"Is it?" Lord Roland's thick eyebrows rose as he considered this notion. "Well," he decided, "we're a charming bunch."

"Yes," Lord Chen said with a thin smile. "Very."

"By the way," Lord Roland said, "I wonder if I might trouble you for advice."

"I'd be only too happy."

Lord Roland glanced over the lounge, then leaned toward Lord Chen and lowered his voice. "My brother Gareth keeps urging the family to leave Zanshaa. I know that you serve on the Fleet Control Board and are familiar with Fleet movements and dispositions." He gazed intently at Lord Chen with his deep brown eyes. "I wonder," he said, "if this would be your advice as well."

Lord Chen struggled to master his thoughts. "Your brother . . . does he give reasons for his opinion?"

"No. Though perhaps he considers the defeat at Magaria a self-evident enough reason."

So Gareth Martinez wasn't handing out military secrets to his family, a breach of discretion that would have set Lord Chen to worrying about how confidential his connection to the Martinez clan was likely to remain.

"I would say," he said with care, "that there is reason for concern, but there is no need to evacuate at present."

Lord Roland nodded gravely. "Thank you, Lord Chen."

"Not at all."

He reached forward and touched Lord Chen lightly on the hand. Lord Chen looked in surprise at the touch.

"I know that you have no fear for yourself," Lord Roland said, "but a prudent man should take no chances with his family. I want you to have the comfort of knowing that should you ever decide that Lady Chen and Terza should leave Zanshaa, they are welcome at my father's estate on Laredo—and in fact they are welcome to travel with my sisters, in our family cruiser."

Let's hope it won't ever come to that, Lord Chen thought, appalled. But instead he smiled again and said, "That's a kind thought, and I thank you. But I've already arranged for a ship to be standing by."

"The fault of the Home Fleet at Magaria," Captain Kamarullah said, "is that they failed to maintain a close enough formation. They needed to mass their defensive firepower to blast their way through the oncoming missiles."

Martinez watched the other captains absorb this statement. The virtual universe in his head consisted of four rows of four heads each, and smelled of suit seals and stale flesh. Martinez couldn't read Do-faq's face very well, or those of his eight Lai-own captains, and the two Daimong captains had expressionless faces to begin with, but the four humans, at least, seemed to be taking Kamarullah's argument seriously. "How close should we get?" one of them even said.

Martinez looked at the sixteen virtual heads that floated in his mind, took a deep breath, and ventured his own opinion. "With all respect, my lord, my conclusions differ. My belief is that the squadrons didn't separate early enough."

Most turned curious eyes to him, but it was Kamarullah who spoke.

"You call for a premature starburst? That's a complete loss of command and control!"

"My lord," Martinez said, "that's hardly worse than the loss of command and control that results when an entire squadron is wiped out. Now, if your lordships will bear with me, I've prepared a brief presentation . . ."

The others watched while he beamed them selected bits of the Magaria battle, along with estimates of the numbers of incoming missiles, missiles destroyed by other missiles, by point-defense lasers and antiproton beams.

"A defensive formation works well only up to a point," Martinez said, "and then the system breaks down catastrophically. I can't prove anything yet, but I suspect that antimatter missile explosions, with their bursts of heavy radiation and their expanding plasma shells, eventually create so much interference and confusion on the ships' sensors that it becomes nearly impossible to coordinate an effective defense.

"You'll observe," running the records again, "that the losses during the first part of the battle were equal, very sudden, and catastrophic for both sides. It was only when both sides had lost twenty ships or so that the enemy advantage in numbers became decisive, and then the attrition of our ships was steady right to the end. Lady Sula's destruction of five enemy cruisers was the only successful attack made by the Home Fleet without equivalent or greater loss.

"My conclusion," looking again at the sixteen heads in their four rows, "is that our standard fleet tactics will produce a rough equivalence in losses, but the unfortunate fact is that the enemy have more ships, and I fear we can't sustain a war of attrition."

There was a long moment of silence, broken by the chiming voice of one of Martinez's Daimong captains. "Do you have any suggestion for tactics that can take advantage of this analysis?"

"I'm afraid not, my lord. Other than ordering a starburst much earlier in the battle, of course."

Kamarullah gave a contemptuous huff into his microphone that sounded like a gunshot in Martinez's earphones. "A lot of good *that'll* do," he said. "With our ships scattered all over space, the enemy could stay in formation and pick us off one by one."

Frustration crawled with jointed fingers up Martinez's spine. That was *not* what he meant to imply, and he couldn't help but feel that if he could only speak to the captains in person, he could bring his points across.

"I don't mean that our ships should wander at random about the galaxy, lord captain," he said.

"And if *both* sides use these tactics, what then?" Kamarullah continued. "Without any formation the battle will just turn into a melee, ships fighting each other singly or in ones and twos, and that's *precisely* the sort of situation where the enemy superiority in numbers will be decisive. The enemy should *beg* us to starburst early." A sly expression crossed his face. "Of course," he said, "if we aren't expected to keep formation or maneuver simultaneously, it will certainly be easier on the ships that are having trouble doing exactly these things."

You'll pay for that, Martinez glowered, and he saw his thought mirrored on the faces of two other underperforming captains. He could feel his hands, in a world he couldn't at present see, clenching in his gloves.

"Our ancestors understood these things better than we," one of the Daimong said. "We should strive to perfect the tactics they've passed on to us. With these tactics our ancestors built an empire."

During which time they fought only one real war, Martinez thought.

Squadron Commander Do-faq fixed Martinez with his golden eyes. "Do you have a remedy for this problem, lord elcap?"

Martinez chose his words carefully. "I think that we need to expand the concept of *formation*. Ideally we would need ships traveling in a much looser arrangement, far enough apart that a single volley of missiles wouldn't destroy all of them, but still able to coordinate their actions against the enemy."

Kamarullah breathed another gunshot-huff into his microphone, and Do-faq gave an annoyed start and a flare of his crest hairs. Do-faq's flag captain, Cho-hal, then asked, "But how do you solve the problem of communication?"

Ships normally communicated via laser, which had the punch to get a message through a ship's raging plasma tail, and which also had the advantage of privacy—no enemy could listen in on a directed beam. The alternative was to use a radio signal, which might not get through the radio interference of a ship's exhaust, and which in any case could be overheard by the enemy. In a civil war, where both sides had started with the same codes as well as the same coding and decoding computers, that was a serious hazard.

"I have some ideas, lord captain," Martinez said. "But they're rather . . . unformed. We can use secure-coded radio transmissions; or perhaps an arrangement whereby, even after starburst, each ship takes a preassigned path so that orders can reach it by laser . . ."

He saw his defeat in the faces of the others, even the aliens whose expressions were difficult to decipher. His idea managed to be both horribly unformed and far too complex—in itself quite an accomplishment, he supposed.

"Lord squadcom," he said to Do-faq, "I beg permission to send you a more thorough analysis when my ideas have had time to . . . to cohere." The disdainful twist on Kamarullah's mouth turned into a smirk at the sound of this.

"Permission is granted, lord elcap," Do-faq said. "I will also have my tactical officer review your analysis of the battle at Magaria and see what comment he offers."

"Thank you, my lord."

"I'm glad that's settled," Kamarullah said. "The least we can do is learn *one* tactical system before we go off inventing another."

The rest of the conference produced little of interest, and Martinez left virtual world with a burning determination to wipe Kamarullah's smirk right off his face.

He invited his three lieutenants to dine with him, then hesitated for a moment and invited Cadet Kelly as well. She was one of *Corona*'s old crew, one of those who had helped him steal the frigate on the day of the mutiny and escape the enemy, and she had been clever and useful on that occasion.

Corona's former captain, Tarafah, had been served at his lonely table by a professional chef he'd brought aboard, given the rank of petty officer, and doubtless kept sweet with under-the-table payments. Despite the war and the edict forbidding Fleet personnel to leave the service, on arrival at Zanshaa the chef had produced a doctor's certificate testifying to a heart condition unable to stand heavy gravities, and Martinez had shrugged and let him go.

Alikhan, who had cooked for Martinez before the war, now continued in that capacity. He'd prepared a meal for Martinez alone, and couldn't alter his arrangements until the ship lowered its acceleration to 0.7 gravities at dinnertime and he could get into the kitchen. Alikhan's last-second improvisations might be less appealing than his usual fare, so Martinez decided to try to provide a convivial reception for the food by opening two bottles of the wine that his sisters had crated up to him when he'd been officially promoted into *Corona*.

"I *do* want to apologize about today's drill, lord elcap," Dalkeith began. "The confusion with the damage-control robots will not be repeated."

"Never mind that," Martinez said, and for once in her life Dalkeith looked surprised. "I've got something else to show you."

He called up the wall display and showed selected bits of the battle at Magaria. He watched the shock as they saw squadrons of the Home Fleet buried beneath waves of antimatter. "Our tactics aren't working," Martinez said. "The best we can hope for is mutual annihilation. And I don't *like* annihilation, not even if we take enemy with us."

His officers looked at him in shocked surprise. "We need something new," Martinez said. "Lord Lieutenant Vonderheydte, the bottle is at your elbow."

"Oh." Pouring. "Sorry, lord elcap."

"My lord?" Cadet Kelly looked at him with wide black eyes. "Are you asking us to invent a new tactical system? Over dinner?"

"Of course not!" Dalkeith poured scorn into her child's voice. "Don't be ridiculous!"

Ah, Martinez reflected, the moment awkward.

"Well," he began, "I'm afraid I'm the ridiculous one, because that's what I hope to accomplish."

Dalkeith's face expressed surprise for the second time that day.

"Very good, my lord," she said.

Martinez raised his glass. "Here's in aid of thought," he said.

The others raised their glasses and drank. Vonderheydte looked appreciatively at the wine, glowing a deep red in the heavy leaded crystal created to stand high accelerations. "This is a fine vintage, my lord," he pronounced.

Vonderheydte, young and small-boned and blond, was *Corona*'s most junior lieutenant. He'd been one of the frigate's cadets when the Naxids mutinied, and as he'd performed well in a number of highly improvised roles during *Corona*'s escape, Martinez had exercised his powers of patronage and had promoted him.

Vonderheydte took the bottle and looked at the label. "We should get some of this for the wardroom." The others agreed.

Martinez let the wine roll over his tongue and found it much like any other red wine he'd ever tasted.

"I'm glad you like it," he said.

"So should we starburst earlier?" Kelly asked as she drew her cuffs forward over exposed bony wrists. "Is that what you're after?"

"Sort of," Martinez said, and explained his vague ideas. Kelly listened, her head tilted to one side.

The lanky, black-eyed pinnace pilot had been weapons officer during *Corona*'s escape from the Naxids, a job at which she'd shown unexpected talent. Subsequently, in flight toward desperate pleasure from a host of incoming terrors, she and Martinez had shared a frantic few moments in one of the frigate's recreation tubes. Those moments had never been repeated—common sense had reasserted itself in time—but they were moments which Martinez, at least, could not bring himself to regret.

"So not a starburst, exactly," she clarified, "but a very spread-out formation."

"I don't know," Martinez confessed. "I know that I don't want to lose the defensive advantages of a formation, and I don't want everyone to get so dispersed the battle will turn into a melee."

"How do you coordinate movement and formation changes?" Dalkeith wondered. "You'll only be guessing where your ships will be, so it will be sheer chance if you hit them with a comm laser. And if you broadcast on radio, the enemy will hear it, and their computers have the same software that ours do, and plenty of computing power, so they might be able to decode it."

Martinez had been thinking about this since the captains' conference. Before the war his specialty had included communication, and he thought he'd worked out the solution. "Using radio's not a problem," he said. "First, you have each ship repeat the message to all others once it's received, to make certain that each ship receives its orders. Then you devise a very thorough code describing any maneuvers necessary for the fleet, and your computers cipher the codes using a one-time system. The one-time system means that even if the cipher is broken, it won't help the enemy read the *next* message. And even if they *can* read the cipher, all they get is a code they can't read without a key." He shrugged. "You can make it more elaborate than that, but that's all that's really necessary."

The others considered this while Alikhan appeared and placed upon Captain Tarafah's mahogany table the first course of his improvised meal, which on inspection proved to be white beans on a bed of greenish-black vegetable matter, with a splash of ketchup for color.

It could be worse, Martinez thought, and picked up his fork.

"How far can we spread out the ships?" Vonderheydte wondered aloud. "Our superior officers like to see smart maneuvers, with every ship rotating and changing course at the same moment. Obviously this is going to be a good deal more ragged."

Martinez cared less about ragged formations than the fact that this would make the new tactics harder to sell to his superiors. A formation in which all orders were not instantly and smartly executed would not be an attractive picture to the average Senior Fleet Commander.

"My lord," murmured Sublieutenant Nikkul Shankaracharya into his wineglass, "there should be a formula, I mean a mathematical set of formulas, that will tell us how far we can safely set our formation."

His voice was so low that Martinez could barely make out the words. Shankaracharya was a shy youth with a lieutenancy of less than a year's seniority, and his posting to *Corona* was the result of direct intervention by one of the few divinities recognized by the service—in this case a clan patron who served on the Fleet Control Board. That *Corona* was then handicapped by the presence of two very junior lieutenants with little time to learn their jobs, who were supervised by a lackluster, nearly superannuated senior in Dalkeith, was beneath the notice of the divinity in question.

A further complication was added by the fact that Shankaracharya was the beloved of Martinez's younger sister, Sempronia. Sempronia, who was, as part of a plot laid by Martinez and his other sisters, engaged to marry someone else entirely.

It seemed unfair to Martinez that he was beset by family intrigues as well as service politics. One or the other were within his realm of competence; but the both together made his head spin.

"Mathematical formulas?" he prompted.

Shankaracharya touched his youthful mustache with a napkin. "There would be three major subproblems, I think," he said in a voice that was barely audible. "Since we know the effectiveness of our point defenses, and since we now have a lot of empirical data on the behavior of offensive missiles, we should be able to calculate the maximum dispersion at which we can place our ships without the interwoven laser and particle beam defenses losing their effectiveness.

"A second subproblem would involve the maximum dispersion for our ships before any massed offense would begin to lose its punch—that number would be a lot larger, I'd think."

Shankaracharya took another sip of wine, and again touched his mustache with the napkin.

"And the third subproblem?" Martinez asked.

"I forget." Shankaracharya looked blank, and during that moment Alikhan brought in his second course, slices of dense pâté, each surrounded by a yellowish gelatin rind that gave off a strong aroma of liver. With this came pickles and flat unleavened biscuits from a can.

The others were looking at their plates when Shankaracharya added, "No, wait, I remember the third parameter. It has to do with the area of destruction caused by a salvo of enemy missiles, so that you can calculate the likelihood of more than one ship being destroyed, but that's not as important as the first two." He cleared his throat. "It should be possible to come up with a single rather complex mathematical statement for all of this, once we calculate all the variables concerning the capabilities of the ships, numbers of launchers and defensive beams and so on, and you'd be able to calculate the most efficient manner of dispersion for a whole fleet."

Martinez crunched a pickle between his teeth. Any solution to the problem would require partial differential equations, which Martinez had studied at the academy, but his memory for all that had grown foggy—since graduation, all he'd been required to do was plug numbers into existing formulae, then let the computer do the work.

But Vonderheydte had been studying for his exams before Martinez made the exams unnecessary by promoting him, and Cadet Kelly had been preparing for her exams when the war interrupted. They'd be much more useful on this approach than Martinez—or, presumably, Dalkeith.

He'd just have to let the younger folk take the lead on this one, preferably without letting them notice that Martinez wasn't exactly in charge.

Martinez shifted the wall screen to the Structured Mathematics Display.

"Right," he said. "Let's begin."

* * *

"My lords," said Junior Squadron Commander Michi Chen, "Chenforce has now arrived in the Zanshaa system. We await your orders."

At the sight of his sister, Lord Chen felt his anxiety begin to loosen its grip on his heart. Which was irrational, since Chenforce consisted of only seven ships scraped together from the damaged remnants of the Fourth Fleet at Harzapid. The Naxid revolt had failed at Harzapid, but only just, with ships blasting each other at point-blank range with antiproton beams. Michi Chen had come to Zanshaa with the few undamaged survivors—the rest had either been destroyed or were in dock for urgent repairs. It would be months before Harzapid could send another squadron.

But at least Zanshaa now had a force to defend it besides the six battered, exhausted survivors of the Home Fleet plus the swarm of pinnaces and improvised warships that would be swept away in the event of any determined attack. Chenforce could now cover the capital while the remnants of the Home Fleet decelerated and docked to take on new armament, and while Faqforce made its U-turn around Hone-bar and returned to Zanshaa.

When Faqforce arrived, Zanshaa would have twenty-eight ships to guard it against attack.

The great terror was that the enemy had thirty-five known survivors of the battle at Magaria. These, by now, had probably been reinforced by the ten ships that had rebelled at the remote station of Comador; and there remained at large another eight enemy ships last seen over two months ago at Protipanu. Those ships might well be on their way to join the enemy force at Magaria, and if that were the case, the defenders of Zanshaa would be outnumbered nearly two to one.

Senior Fleet Commander Tork, chairman of the Fleet Control Board, rose from his seat and absently peeled a strip of dry, dead flesh from his face before facing the cameras. "Reply, personal to Squadron Leader Chen." His Daimong's voice tinkled like wind chimes in the stillness. "Lady Commander, kindly establish a defensive orbit about Zanshaa and its primary. When other forces enter the system, we will match their trajectories to *you*."

This wasn't a dialogue. Michi's message had taken six hours to reach Zanshaa, and Tork's reply would take nearly that long to return to her.

The chairman politely turned to Lord Chen. "Would you like to say a few words to your sister?"

"Yes, lord chairman, I thank you."

Lord Chen rose and looked into the camera, which obligingly panned toward him. "Welcome, Michi," he said. "Your arrival has brought relief to everyone here. We're delighted to have you with us." And then, as he was on the verge of sitting down again, he added, "I'll send you a personal message later."

There's a lot you'd better know, he thought.

He sat, and butter-smooth leather embraced him. His sister's message had arrived during a meeting of the Fleet Control Board, and resulted in a considerable lightening of the meeting's tone. Lord Chen decided that he wasn't the only person here to feel irrational relief.

Still, the old debates continued.

"The Hone Reach must be defended," said Lady Seekin. Her large eyes, adapted for night vision, were wide in the soft light of the room, and she'd taken off the dark lenses most Torminel wore during daylight hours.

"We can't defend the Hone Reach at the expense of Zanshaa," said Tork. "The capital is everything. It's the whole war. We can't afford to lose it."

A whiff of rotting flesh floated across the table from Tork, and Lord Chen lifted his hand to his face and took a discreet sniff of the cologne he'd applied to the inside of his wrist.

"Two ships, my lord," Lady Seekin insisted. "Two ships to defend the whole of the Reach."

"Two ships, yes," said Lady San-torath, the Lai-own convocate. "There will be no confidence in the Reach unless you can protect them somehow."

Useless, Lord Chen thought. When the war broke out he'd been part of a faction insisting that Hone-bar and the Reach had to be defended, but that was before the Battle of Magaria. Lord Chen had given up trying to protect the Reach—now he was just trying to get what he owned *out.* He had to agree with Tork: the capital was more important.

Lose the Hone Reach, he thought, and you have a chance of taking it back. Lose Zanshaa and you lose everything.

The Fleet Control Board met in a well-appointed room of the Commandery, all low-key lighting, polished wood, and pale, spotless plush carpet. Overhead glowed an abstract map of the empire, connected by lines that represented wormhole gates. Hone-bar and the Hone Reach stood out in fluorescent green.

The map was not a star chart: a map of stars would be irrelevant. The wormholes overleaped nearby stars, jumping anywhere in the universe—sometimes to places so remote that it wasn't clear where they stood in relation to anywhere else.

There were three wormholes in the Hone-bar system, one that led to the fourteen systems of the Hone Reach, and two that led elsewhere in the empire. Whoever controlled Hone-bar controlled access to those fourteen worlds where so much of Lord Chen's wealth remained at hazard.

At the opening of the rebellion, Lord Chen and the other members of the Hone Reach faction had insisted on sending Faqforce to the Hone-bar system. Now those two squadrons were urgently needed to defend the capital, and were to make a wide, fast swing around Hone-bar's sun to return as fast as they could.

"It will be close," said Senior Fleet Commander Tork. "The enemy could be here before Faqforce makes its return."

The elderly Daimong, who was twirling in his fingers the dry strip of dead flesh he'd pulled from his pale face, let it fall in silence to the carpet. Tork chaired the nine-member board, which consisted of four civilian convocates and five active or retired Fleet officers, some of whom were also convocates.

"Can we order them to increase speed?" one of the civilians asked.

"No. They're already traveling as quickly as the Lai-own physique permits."

"But, my lord"—this came from one of the Fleet officers—"the light squadron doesn't have any Lai-own ships, does it?"

After a long moment of chagrin, Tork gave orders ensuring that the light squadron, under Captain Martinez, would separate from Do-faq's squadron and return to Zanshaa with the greatest possible speed.

"After the battle the enemy would need at least two months to decelerate, dock with the Magaria ring, and fill their magazines with fresh missiles," Tork said. "Then another two months to accelerate to fighting speed and begin their journey here. And that's if the enemy is willing to push gee forces to their maximum, with their personnel already on the point of exhaustion, and also if they are willing to dock their entire fleet at once, and risk it being destroyed by a raid."

These facts were familiar to all present—all knew almost to the day the moment when they would begin to dread an enemy attack—but all had also learned not to interrupt Tork when the chairman was in the middle of one of his speeches. An interruption only inspired Tork to greater didactic emphasis, not to mention greater length. It was strange how the Daimong voice, normally chiming and bell-like, could at such moments be altered into such an insistent, nagging tone of declamation.

"The Home Fleet will also need to decelerate and take on new armament before they can again build up enough delta-vee to be of use in defending the capital . . ."

Lord Chen wearily reflected that it was entirely like Lord Chairman Tork to refer to the six battered survivors as "the

Home Fleet," as if it still resembled the armada with which Fleet Commander Jarlath had set about the recapture of Magaria.

"I'm concerned for the well-being of those crewmen," Tork said. His round-eyed, startled-looking face was incapable of showing fear, concern, or any other emotion, but from the tone of the fleetcom's voice Chen knew that the concern was real. "By the time their ships are in position to join the defense of the capital, they will have suffered more than six months of high acceleration. The degradation of their mental and physical state will be acute."

"Yet what choice do we have?" asked Lady San-torath. "As you say, the capital must be defended."

"We have sufficient personnel on Zanshaa to crew an entire new fleet," said Tork. "I propose that we move entirely new crews aboard when the Home Fleet comes in to rearm."

"Ships with new crews?" Junior Fleet Commander Pezzini was startled. "But they won't have time to learn their ships before they may have to take them into combat!"

"And all the experienced officers will have been taken off the ships," added the Lord Convocate Mondi, a retired Fleet captain and the second Torminel on the board. "It would be folly to remove the only officers experienced in battle."

"Fleet doctrine is established," Tork said, "and experience should make little difference in how the battle is fought. And as far as the officers go, one Peer is the equal of another— *that* is doctrine, too, my lords." Pezzini tried to interrupt, and Tork's voice took on its dreaded merciless hectoring tone as he outshouted his junior. "The new crews will have a month to shake down before an attack is likely to come! And beforehand, they can accustom themselves to their new ships in virtual!"

There was argument, but in the end Tork had his way. New crews would be assembled on the ring station and would begin training in virtual ship environments immediately. There was more argument as they appointed commanding officers—each board member had clients and favorites—and then a further brisk discussion in appointing a squadron commander.

"We must appoint an overall commander for the defense of the capital," Tork went on. "The two squadron commanders, Lady Michi and Lord Do-faq, are young officers with no experience in maneuvering an entire fleet. We *must* pick a fleetcom."

This was problematical, as most of the qualified officers had died with Jarlath at Magaria. The new commander would have to be Terran, since he would command from one of the Home Fleet survivors, all Terran ships. Again, each board member had his candidates, and when they deadlocked Lord Chen simply suggested they promote his sister to fill the place.

Well, he thought, it seems worth trying.

The motion had no support whatever, and Lord Chen withdrew it. The board reached no agreement, and Tork deferred the matter till the next meeting.

"If one Peer is as good as the next," Pezzini muttered, "I don't see why this always takes so blasted long."

There followed more decisions in regard to the Fleet's logistical support, and this was where Lord Chen began to earn the money that Roland Martinez was paying him. He managed to snag a delivery contract for a shipping concern owned by a Martinez client, and a supply contract for state-of-the-art laser communications systems for a Martinez-owned firm on Laredo.

"Have you noticed how many contracts seem to be going to Laredo?" muttered Lord Commander Pezzini. "I thought the place was a rustic paradise full of strong-thewed woodcutters and bucolic shepherds, and now I find it's some kind of industrial powerhouse."

"Really?" asked Lord Chen. "I hadn't noticed."

"Why did we lose at Magaria?" From the display in his command cage, Caroline Sula gazed at him with her face drawn by fatigue and deceleration. From her gasping voice Martinez could tell she was undergoing three gees or more.

"There were lots of reasons," she said. "They were ready for us, for one thing, and they had more ships. They outplanned us, though I can't fault Jarlath for that, I suppose his plan was as good as he could make it, given what he knew." She drew in a breath, lungs fighting gravity. "The main reason is that we didn't starburst early enough. Whole formations got overwhelmed at once. The enemy's tactics showed the same fault, but they started with more ships, and they could afford the losses."

Martinez was warmed by Sula's analysis and the fact that it agreed with his own. He felt flattered.

When did he start counting so much on Sula's opinion? he asked himself.

Sula took in another breath, and Martinez realized his own breath was synchronous with hers. For he, too, was living through hard gee, and he as well was strapped into an acceleration couch, his body confined in a pressure suit.

It was impossible to share each other's company, he thought, but at least we can share our misery.

Sula breathed again, and for a brief moment Martinez saw mischief flare in her weary eyes. "We had a discussion about censorship in the mess the other day, and about why the government has been suppressing what happened at Magaria. I suggested that the point of censorship isn't to hide certain facts but to keep the wrong people from finding them out. If the majority knew the true facts, they would begin to act as their self-interest dictates, and not *enlightened* self-interest either. If they're kept in ignorance they'll be much more inclined to act as the self-interest of others dictates." She gasped in air. "One of our officers—won't mention names here—said the whole point is to prevent civilians from panicking. But I think it's what happens *after* people panic that should frighten us. We should be scared of what happens when people stop panicking and start to *think*." Sula gave an intense green-eyed look to the camera. "I wonder what *you* think about such things."

She allowed herself a morbid smile. "I also wonder if your old friend Lieutenant Foote is going to let you see any of this, particularly my speculations on the nature and purpose of information control. But I suppose if he chops any of this, it will only prove my point." Her smile broadened. "I'll look forward to hearing from you. Let me know how your next exercise turns out."

The orange End Transmission symbol appeared on the screen. Apparently Foote had tried to disprove Sula's argument by not cutting any of the message.

Clever Sula, Martinez thought.

Martinez saved the message to his private file as he thought about censorship. It had always been there, and he'd never spent a lot of time thinking about it except when it intruded on his time, as when he was ordered to censor the pulpies' mail.

As for official censorship, he'd always thought of it as a kind of game between the censors and himself. They'd try to hide something, and he'd try to read behind the censors' words to find out what had really happened. From an exhortation to Unceasingly Labor at Public Works, it was possible to conclude that a major building project had fallen behind schedule; likewise, a news item praising emergency services often implied a disaster at which emergency services had been employed, but which was too embarrassing for those in charge to admit. An item praising certain ministers could be a tacit criticism of those ministers who were not mentioned, or a criticism of one junior minister could in reality be a disguised assault on his more senior patron.

Reading behind the news was a game at which Martinez had grown expert. But unlike Sula he'd never thought of censorship having a *purpose,* in part because it seemed too arbitrary for that. What was cut, and what permitted, was so capricious as to seem almost stochastic: sometimes he wondered if the censors were amusing themselves by cutting every sentence with an irregular verb, or any news item in which appeared the word "sun."

Sula's notion that censorship was aimed at giving certain people a monopoly on the truth was new to him. But who *were* these people? He didn't know anyone who didn't have to deal with the censorship—even when he'd worked on the staff of Fleet Commander Enderby, he'd discovered that Enderby's public pronouncements had to be reviewed by the censors.

Possibly *nobody* knew what was really happening. Martinez found that more frightening than Sula's theory of a conspiracy of elites.

It would have been hard, for example, to work into any theory of censorship the conversation he'd had the previous day with Dalkeith. They'd had a breakfast meeting about ordinary ship business, and at the end, over coffee, she'd given him a puzzled look, as if she didn't know where to begin, and then said, "You know I'm censoring the other lieutenants' mail."

Censorship, like all tasks that no one really wanted, was a job that tended to fall quickly down the ladder of seniority. The most junior cadets censored the messages of the enlisted; and the most junior lieutenant censored the cadets. Dalkeith censored the two lieutenants junior to her, and Martinez was left free of all responsibility but that of reviewing her messages only—a light task, as they consisted entirely of dull but heartfelt greetings to her family back on Zarafan.

"Yes?" Martinez prompted. "Is there a problem?"

"Not a problem, exactly." Dalkeith lips twisted, as if searching for an entry point to this subject. "You know Vonderheydte has a lady friend on Zanshaa. Her name is Lady Mary."

"Is it? I didn't know." He rather doubted that the lady's name was of any great relevance.

"Vonderheydte and Lady Mary exchange videos, and the videos are of a . . ." She hesitated. ". . . highly libidinous nature. They exchange fantasies and, ah, attempt to enact them for the camera."

Martinez reached for his coffee. "You haven't encountered this before?" he said. "I'm surprised." When he was a fresh young cadet aboard ship for the first time, he had been deeply shocked by both the ingenuity and depravity of the holejumpers whose messages he'd been called on to review. By the end of the second month of this involuntary course in human nature, he'd become a cynical, hard-boiled tough, a walking encyclopedia of degeneracy, incapable of being surprised by any iniquity, no matter how appalling.

"It's not that," Dalkeith said. "I just wonder at the *persistence*. They spend *hours* at it, and it's all very elaborate and imaginative. I don't know where Vonderheydte gets the energy, considering we're under acceleration." Her troubled eyes gazed into his. "There's a relentless quality to it that seems unhealthy to me. You don't suppose he's doing himself actual physical harm, do you?"

Martinez put down his coffee cup and paged through the mental encyclopedia of depravity he'd acquired as a cadet. "He's not getting involved in, ah, asphyxiation?"

Dalkeith shook her head.

"Or use of ligatures? Around, say, vital parts?"

Dalkeith seemed dubious. "Depends on how vital you consider hands and feet. Well, one hand actually." She looked at him. "Would you like to see the next set of outgoing messages?"

Martinez explained to his senior lieutenant that, however much she failed to enjoy watching a young man engage in acts of self-stimulation, he would enjoy it even less.

"I don't care what he's doing so long as it's on his own time, and so long as he remains undamaged," Martinez said. And then he added, "You can fast-forward through it, you know. I very much doubt Vonderheydte is giving away state secrets during these interludes. Or you can have the computer make a transcript and review that."

Dalkeith sighed. "Very well, my lord."

Cheer up, he thought, the reading might be more fun than the watching. All fantasy, without the reality of Vonderheydte's contortions.

After that conversation, the rest of ship's business had seemed very dull.

A chime on the comm interrupted Martinez's remembrance. He answered, and heard Vonderheydte's voice through his earphones.

"Personal transmission from the squadcom, my lord."

Since the revelations of the previous morning, Martinez had found that Vonderheydte's voice, even carrying a perfectly innocent message, seemed filled with libidinous suggestion. The dread scepter of the squadcom that hovered over his head, however, drove all suggestive notions out of Martinez's head. His imagination flashed ahead to a rebuke, as *Corona* had once again fumbled in the morning's maneuver.

"I'll accept." And as Do-faq's head blossomed on the display, he said, "This is Captain Martinez, my lord."

Peg teeth clacked in Do-faq's muzzle. "I have received an order from the Commandery, lord captain. Your squadron is to increase acceleration, part company from the heavy squadron, enter the Hone-bar system ahead of us, and return to Zanshaa at the fastest possible speed."

"Very good, my lord." In truth, Martinez had been anticipating this order for some time. No enemy were expected at Hone-bar, and every ship in Faqforce was badly needed back at the capital. He had considered suggesting the separation himself, but held back for fear of being accused of being greedy for an independent command . . . that, and the fact that by now he quailed from the very idea of harder accelerations.

"You will commence at once," Do-faq continued. "Your official orders will follow as soon as my secretary can copy them. I wish you the best of luck."

"Thank you, my lord."

Do-faq's golden eyes softened. "I want you to know, Captain Martinez, that I have no regrets in regard to choosing you for command of the squadron."

Martinez's heart gave a spasm. "Thank you, lord squadcom." He felt the millstone of doubt, heavy as a couple gravities' acceleration, float weightless from his shoulders.

"You've been handicapped by an inexperienced crew, but they are improving under your direction, and I have no doubt they'll prove as fine as any in the Fleet, in time."

Gratitude threatened to overwhelm Martinez's tongue, but he managed to say, "Thank you for your confidence, my lord. It has been a privilege to serve under you." Another matter entered his mind, and he cleared his throat. "My lord," he began, "perhaps you will recall our tactical discussion the other day. When I . . . suggested some rather unformed ideas regarding fleet tactics."

Do-faq's expression was unreadable. "Yes, lord captain," he said, "I recall the discussion."

"Well, the ideas have grown more, ah, formed."

Briefly, he explained the attempt to encapsule the new formations within a bit of elegant mathematics. "That was Lieutenant Shankaracharya's particular contribution," he said.

Do-faq's answer was instant. "You shared the data from Magaria with your lieutenants?"

"Ah—yes, lord squadcom."

"I very much doubt the wisdom of this. Our superiors have decided that this information must be controlled."

Which superiors? As Sula's theory flashed into Martinez's mind.

"My lieutenants are reliable people, my lord," he said. *Best not mention Alikhan.* "I have every confidence in their discretion."

"They may be disheartened. They may spread defeatism."

But everyone *knows* we got thrashed at Magaria, Martinez wanted to say. But instead he said, "The news seemed to inspire them to greater efforts, my lord. They know how critical our work could be to the outcome of the war."

Do-faq's golden eyes probed at him for a long moment. "Well, it's too late now," he decided. "I trust you will caution your officers not to go about spreading rumors."

"Of course, my lord." He hesitated. "Would you like to see the formula and an analysis, my lord? There are some unexpected conclusions."

Not least of which was that the effective range of a warship's missiles were considerably less than anyone had expected. Even Shankaracharya had confidently predicted that the missiles would have a much greater range than ships' defensive armament; but analysis of the fighting at Magaria showed that while a ship could of course launch a missile at long range, a longer flight time only gave a target's defenses a longer time to track the missile and shoot it down. The missiles that had the greatest chance of doing damage tended to be fired in swarms from fairly close range, and launched behind a screen of exploding antimatter missiles that confused enemy sensors.

"Send the analysis, by all means," Do-faq said. "I'll review it with my tactical officer."

"Very good, my lord."

Martinez briefly reviewed the analysis he'd prepared for Do-faq, gnawed his lip over the phrasing of the analysis, and then sent it personal to the squadron commander just as the tone sounded for reduced gees. His acceleration cage creaked as the gravities came off, and the soft pressure of his suit relaxed its grip on his arms and legs. He felt his chest expand, the sensation of relief and relaxation in his diaphragm, as he snapped up the faceplate and tasted the control room's cool, sterile air.

There would be a twenty-six minute bathroom, recreation, and snack break at one gravity, then renewed acceleration at high gee. And a higher gee than anyone else knew.

"Vonderheydte," Martinez said.

"Yes, my lord."

"General message to the squadron. Inform them that we have received orders to accelerate ahead of the heavy squadron and return to Zanshaa. Tell them we shall accelerate to three point two gravities once the current break has ended, at 19:26."

The brief hesitation in reply told of Vonderheydte's dismay. "Very good, my lord."

Heavier gees should take the zest out of Vonderheydte's fantasy life, Martinez reflected, and he unlocked the cage's displays and pushed them above his head and out of the way. Then he tipped the cage forward till his boots touched the floor, and he released the webbing and stood.

Blood swirled uneasily in his head, and he kept a hand clamped on the cage tubing until the vertigo eased.

He'd have some water, perhaps, or juice. And more meds to help endure the upcoming acceleration.

From this point on, he thought, the joy of command was going to be considerably reduced.

It was reduced by a larger margin four hours later, during the supper break, when a call came from Captain Kamarullah, personal to Martinez. Martinez answered it in his office, where he was nibbling a sandwich while catching up on *Corona*'s administrative work. Around the desk, towering in special racks to brace them against hard accelerations, were the two Home Fleet Trophies won by Captain Tarafah's football teams, plus a second-place trophy and various prizes won by Tarafah in other commands.

Martinez wasn't after trophies himself. If he could just get through tomorrow's maneuvers without a visit from Mr. Calamity, he'd be satisfied.

"This is Martinez," he said, turning on the comm display. Kamarullah's square face appeared, his eyes directed somewhere behind Martinez's right ear.

"Captain Martinez, I'm sorry to interrupt your meal break."

"That's all right, lord captain. What can I do for you?"

Martinez kept his eyes directed toward his desktop, where he was looking at a report in regard to the replacement of an erratic turbopump used in the engine cooling system. The relevant cooling line would be offline for an estimated ten hours while the work was done by robots operated remotely by crew from their acceleration couches; or six hours if the repair were done by hand. Martinez put his stylus to the desktop, and authorized the robotic repair.

Corona wouldn't have six hours under light enough gees to make a hand repair safe.

"My lord captain," Kamarullah said, "I wonder if I might beg from you a clarification."

Martinez gazed at the next report, which had to do with the condemnation of supplies damaged by high accelerations, and said, "How may I be of service, my lord?"

"I wonder who it was who issued the order separating this squadron from that of Lord Commander Do-faq?"

Martinez cast his mind back to the orders he'd received that afternoon from Do-faq. "The orders originated with the Fleet Control Board," he said.

"And not with the lord commander?"

"No, my lord."

There was a moment's silence. "In that case, lord elcap," Kamarullah said, "I must inform you that, as the senior officer present, I am now in command of this squadron."

Surprise sang through Martinez's veins, but his reply was automatic, and quick.

"Not so, my lord."

"But we're now under Control Board orders," Kamarullah said, "and no longer under the command of Lord Commander Do-faq. His order placing you in command is no longer in effect. Therefore the senior officer now commands the squadron, and that senior officer is me."

Martinez tried to set his face in an expression of mild interest as he sorted this out.

With his stylus, he condemned the stores. Another report flashed onto his desk.

"The Control Board knew full well that I had been placed in command of this squadron," he said finally. "They did not countermand the squadcom's order, and therefore I remain in command."

Out of the corner of his eye he saw the frown form beneath Kamarullah's gray mustache. "A countermanding order wasn't necessary," he said. "In the absence of an order from a superior officer, the senior officer is always in command of an independent detachment."

"But we *have* such an order, dating from when the squadron was formed."

Kamarullah affected patience. "But the squadron is no longer part of Faqforce. We're operating under Commandery orders. We've been removed from Do-faq's command, and his decisions no longer apply."

The squadrons had barely separated. Do-faq, at this instant, was only a few light-seconds away. It was absurd to think that Do-faq's orders no longer pertained.

Martinez turned to look directly into the camera. "If you insist," he said, "we can refer this matter to the nearest superior officer."

Kamarullah stared stonily out of the display. "That senior officer's preferences no longer apply." He made a visible effort to seem at ease, to force a highly artificial smile onto his face. "Come now, my lord," he said. "You know as well as I that Lord Do-faq's order superceding my command was arbitrary and a result of sheer prejudice. You have a new command and a new crew, and I'm sure you've got enough work without taking on the job of a squadcom." The effort to maintain a friendly tone grated in Kamarullah's words. "You know as well as I that the strain has been showing. I say nothing against your abilities, but I've been with my crew for almost two years, and surely you can see that I can give the job of squadcom my full attention, without having to spend most of my time whipping my crew into shape. Don't you think the job deserves that?"

Martinez took a bite of his sandwich, tasting the heat of mustard across his tongue, then chewed as he contemplated the merits of Kamarullah's argument. The problem was that the merits were considerable: Kamarullah *had* been treated unjustly, and Martinez *had* been jumped over his head in a piece of rank favoritism. Kamarullah *was* a more experienced officer with a highly experienced crew.

But, he thought. But . . .

Kamarullah had been insufferably superior when it came to *Corona*'s deficiencies in the maneuvers. He had been wrong when it came to the tactical lessons of Magaria, and would never consider Martinez's new system.

Plus, Squadron Commander Do-faq was an officer who obviously knew how to hold a grudge, as witness his treatment of Kamarullah in the first place. If Martinez willingly surrendered a command to which Do-faq appointed him, and furthermore to a man Do-faq despised, Martinez could hardly expect preferment from Do-faq ever again.

Let alone mercy.

And besides, my lord, Martinez thought as he looked at Kamarullah, I just . . . don't . . . *like* you.

"I'm willing to refer the matter to higher authority," he said, "but until that time I will consider myself commander of this squadron."

Anger drew Kamarullah's graceless smile into a snarl. "If that's the way you want it, my lord," he said. "I'll compose a message to the Control Board."

"No, my lord, you will *not,*" Martinez said. "*I* will compose the letter. *I* will send a copy to you and another to Lord Commander Do-faq . . . for his files."

Kamarullah's color had deepened with rage. "I could just *take* command," he said. "I'll wager most of the captains would follow me."

"If you tried, Lord Commander Do-faq would blow you

to bits," Martinez said. "Please remember he's not that far away."

After he signed off, Martinez dictated a letter that stated the situation as simply and baldly as possible, then sent it to his secretary, Saavedra, to attach the appropriate headings and salutations. "Copies to the files, to Captain Kamarullah, and to Lord Commander Do-faq," he instructed, and Saavedra gave a disapproving, purse-lipped nod. It wasn't possible to tell if Saavedra was offended on Martinez's behalf, or on *Corona*'s, or whether he was offended generally with the world. Martinez suspected the latter.

A few hours later came a signal from Do-faq that the heavy squadron was ceasing acceleration temporarily, as the captain of *Judge Solomon* had suffered a cerebral hemorrhage as a result of constant high accelerations. It was the sort of thing that could happen even to young recruits in the peak of physical condition, and Martinez was thankful that no one had yet stroked out aboard *Corona*. In wartime there was very little that could be done for the luckless captain: he'd be taken to sick bay and given drugs and treatment, but acceleration would have to be resumed before long and it was very likely that *Judge Solomon*'s captain would die or suffer crippling disability.

Thus it was that a day and a half later when *Corona* and the light squadron leaped through Wormhole 1 into the Hone-bar system, they were twenty minutes ahead of Do-faq's eight ships. The message sent to the Fleet Control Board had not arrived on Zanshaa as yet, and Martinez was still exercising command.

The Hone-bar system seemed normal. The system was peaceful, loyalists were in charge of the government, and there seemed no immediate enemy threat. Civilian traffic was light, and the only ship in the vicinity was the cargo vessel *Clan Chen*, outward bound through Wormhole 1 at 0.4*c*.

The Hone-bar system even had a warship, a heavy cruiser

that was undergoing refit on the ring, but the refit wouldn't be completed for at least another month, and until then the cruiser was just another detail.

Martinez had no plans to go anywhere near Hone-bar itself. Instead he'd plotted a complex series of passes by Hone-bar's primary and by three gas-giants, the effect of which would be to whip the squadron around the system and shoot it back out Hone-bar Wormhole 1 at top speed.

The crew was at combat stations, as was standard for wormhole transit in times of unrest. Martinez's acceleration cage creaked as the engines ignited, driving *Corona* on a long arc that would take it into the gravitational field of the first of the system's gas giants. He fought the gravities that began to pile on his bones, and tried to think of something pleasant.

Caroline Sula, he thought. Her pale, translucent complexion. The mischievous turn of her mouth. The brilliant emerald green of her eyes . . .

"Engine flares!" The voice in his earphones came from Tracy, one of the two women at the sensor display. "Engine flares, lord captain! Six . . . no, nine! Ten engine flares, near Wormhole Two! Enemy ships, my lord!"

Martinez fought to take another breath.

Oh dear, he thought. Here's trouble.

THREE

Perfect porcelain glazes floated through Sula's mind, the blue-green celadon of *kinuta seiji,* the *gros bleu* of Vincennes, the fine crackle of *Ju yao.* Fine porcelain was a passion with her, and she often drifted to sleep with illustrations of pots and vases and figurines projected in random order on the visual centers of her brain.

The forms soothed her, as the touch of the real objects delighted her fingertips. And the ancient words used to describe porcelain—*ko-ku-yao-lan, Muscheln, Faience, deutsche Blumen, Kuei Kung, rose Pompadour, Flora Danica, sgraffito, pâté tendre*—evoked exotic places and ancient times, the courts and lime-shaded byways of old Earth.

Her tongue silently formed the words, curling itself around each syllable in sensuous delight. Her silent chant evoked a timeless perfection that was removed from her current situation: unwashed, weary, fighting for every breath. The crew of *Delhi* barely spoke: they climbed in and out of their couches only to shovel in nourishment and perform necessary labor, and the rest of the time they lay on their couches, in the stink of their suits, and fed into their minds the mindless entertainment that might lighten their burden, the comedies that were no longer funny, and the tragedies that seemed trivial compared to what they had already endured. The high gravities had gone on far too long.

The deceleration alarm sang, and Sula reluctantly opened her eyes and let the porcelain fade from her thoughts. She dragged herself out of her suit, then to the shower, then into a clean coverall. Supper's flat food was eaten in silence. Foote lacked the energy to gibe at her, and she was too exhausted to provoke him.

Sula stuck a med patch behind her ear to help her through the next acceleration, then dragged on her vac suit while wincing at the sharp scent of the spray disinfectant she'd used to try to scrub out some of the odor. She would stand— or lie—the next watch in Auxiliary Control while her superiors tried to sleep, but unless the Naxid fleet arrived, or the Shaa came again, there would be little for the watch to do except stare at the displays while the preprogrammed work of the ship went on.

Twenty minutes into the next weary watch a message light glowed on Sula's displays, and she answered to discover a message from Martinez in which he unveiled an entire new system for fleet combat.

Her weariness faded as she devoured the contents of the message. The mathematical equations on which the new formations were based was sound. As were the tactics, at least as far as they went.

Sula's impression, though, was that they didn't go far enough. Martinez's ships would fly at a safer distance from each other, and the effective fields of fire of their defensive weaponry would overlap, but their formation was still strict. Martinez had replaced a close rigid formation with, in effect, a looser but still rigid formation. Sula sensed that it could, and should, be looser still.

She gnawed at the problem for long moments, then called up a math display. She started with the equation Martinez had sent her and then elaborated on it, filling the display with figures, symbols, and graphs in her tiny, precise hand, symbols immediately translated into larger numbers on the display.

She let the computer check her work, fed different experimental numbers into the variables to make certain everything computed correctly. As she worked there rose in her a growing sense of power and delight, a joy in the revelations she was making to herself. These numbers and the reality they described, she thought, had waited for ages to be revealed; but it was she who incarnated them, not another. Just as, thousands of years ago, someone had discovered the perfect curves of a Sung vase, a form that had always existed in potential.

When the fever of discovery passed, Sula sent the work to Martinez.

"This is my first pass at it," she told him. "What I've done is add chaos to your formation—chaos in the mathematical sense, I mean. The enemy will see constant formation changes that appear locally stochastic, but instead your ships will be following along the convex hull of a chaotic dynamical system—a fractal pattern—and provided they all have the same starting place, each of your own ships will know precisely where the others are."

Sula had to pant for a few breaths in order to get enough wind to continue, and she vowed to be a little more careful with her air. "What you have to do is designate a center point for your formation. The point can be your flagship, the ship in the lead, any enemy vessel, or a point in space. Your ships will maneuver around that center point in a series of nested fractal patterns, which should make their movements completely unpredictable to the enemy. You can alter the variables depending on what range you find suitable."

She took another few breaths. "I hope Foote's working at his little censorship duties right now and sends this on without delay. The math's beyond him, I'm sure, but it's hardly subversive. I'll send more when I've had time to think, and a little more leisure."

She sent the message, and then took a few more sips of air. The oxygen content had been boosted to keep the mind and body alive during acceleration, and in a world in which a free breath was becoming the most important currency of existence, the taste of it was like alcohol to the drunkard. Sula glanced over Auxiliary Command, which had been quietly humming along while she'd been dealing with Martinez's equations, apparently without having missed her attention.

And then her eyes lit on the flashing alarm lights on the displays of Pilot/2nd Annie Rorty, and annoyance began to bubble in her blood. "Mind that course change, Rorty!" she called.

Rorty didn't respond. Sharing the cage with Rorty was Navigator First Class Massimo, who was probably also asleep.

"Massimo! Give that lazy bitch a shove!"

Massimo gave a start that confirmed that he, too, had been drowsing. "Yes, my lady!" he croaked in his sandpaper voice, and reached to the next couch to shove Rorty's shoulder. "Officer wants you, pilot." He waited for a response, then shoved again.

There was a long moment of silence, and then in a frenzy of frustration and anger Sula called up the life support data that was supposedly being fed into computer memory by Rorty's vac suit. There *was* no data. It wasn't that Rorty had flatlined, it was that there was no input at all.

"I think there's something wrong, my lady," Massimo growled, redundantly.

"Navigator! Make that course change yourself!"

"Yes, my lady." Massimo's gloved hands fumbled to move Rorty's data to his own board.

"My lady," said the communications officer, "I have a query from *Kulhang*. They want to know why we haven't made the scheduled course change."

"Zero gee warning!" Sula called. The alarm rang out. "Engines, cut engines."

"Engines cut, my lady." *Delhi*'s spars groaned as deceleration ceased, as the vibration and distant roar of the engines faded. Sula's cage gave a creak of relief as gravities eased.

"Massimo, rotate ship."

"Ship rotating."

"Comm," Sula said, "inform *Kulhang* that our acceleration will be reduced due to the sudden illness of an officer."

"Very good, my lady."

Sula's calling a pilot second class an officer was less than
truthful, and many commanders wouldn't have halted an acceleration for a life that didn't have a commission attached
to it, but *Delhi*'s crew had been so reduced that any of the
survivors were precious.

Besides, Sula wasn't going to lose any crew she didn't
have to.

Sula's cage sang as it swung, the ship rotating around it.

"New heading," Massimo said. "Zero-eight-zero by zero-
zero-one absolute."

"Normal gravity warning," Sula said. "Engines, burn at
one gravity."

Sula's acceleration cage creaked as the engines fired, and
her couch swung to the neutral position. Spars and braces
moaned, and shudders ran the length of the ship. "Comm,"
Sula said, "page the pharmacist and a stretcher party to Auxiliary Control." And she flung off her webbing and walked
across the deck to Rorty's cage and stared through the faceplate of the pilot's helmet.

The young woman's freckles stood out as the only spots
of color on her pale, dead face. Though she knew it was
hopeless Sula wrenched off Rorty's helmet, revealing the
plug that Rorty had forgotten to attach to the suit's biomoni-
tor that would have alerted the officer of the watch and the
acting doctor to any number of common medical anomalies.

Sula tore off her own helmet and gloves and felt for a
pulse. There was none. The flesh of Rorty's neck was still
warm.

"Massimo! Help me get her on the deck!"

Auxiliary Control had very little room between the cages,
unlike the more spacious control room that had been incin-

erated along with *Delhi*'s captain. Massimo and Sula got Rorty out of her couch and sprawled on the black rubberized deck, arms and shoulders and dangling limbs clanging against the spinning cages. A heave of Massimo's broad shoulders detached the top of the suit, and Sula pulled it off over Rorty's head as Massimo, bulky in his own suit, straddled her thin body.

Without waiting for orders Massimo began chest compressions. Sula flung the suit top away, knelt, tilted the head back, cleared the tongue with her fingers, and pressed her mouth to the dead girl's lips.

As she breathed for Rorty, Sula felt her own heart throb weakly in her chest. She had to pant for her own breath in between forcing air into Rorty's lungs. A wave of vertigo eddied through her skull. She remembered bending over another girl six years before, a girl who fought ineptly but persistently for life in defiance of the logic that proclaimed that she die. Sula remembered her own eyes scalding with hot tears. She remembered begging the other girl to die.

She remembered putting her in the river later, the chill swift water that rose over the pale, mute face, the golden hair that briefly brightened the water before it vanished into the darkness.

Delhi's doctor had died at Magaria, incinerated along with the sick bay and most of the ship's medical supplies, so it was a Pharmacist First Class who answered Sula's call. He was competent enough, though; got a breathing mask on Rorty's face and cut open Rorty's tunic to get an electrical heart stimulator onto the pilot's pale chest. The cottony taste of Rorty's mouth was on Sula's tongue. When the pharmacist got out a med injector to fire a stimulant straight into Rorty's carotid, Sula had to turn away as nausea burned an acid path up her throat.

She hated med injectors. Sometimes injectors figured in her nightmares. That's why she used patches.

The pharmacist unfastened the cap that held Rorty's earphones and virtual array, then put a sensor net over the pilot's head to get an image of her brain. He studied the display for a moment, then began to switch off his gear. "Every beat of the heart," he said, "just spills more blood into the brain." He turned off the respirator. "You did very well, my lady," he told Sula. "You were just too late."

The stretcher party arrived and stood in the doorway while the pharmacist packed away his gear and twitched Rorty's jumpsuit closed over her chest. Sula fought the sickness that was closing on her throat with velvet fingers. When she thought she could stand, she reached for the cage stanchions and pulled herself upright, then retrieved her helmet and gloves and returned to the command cage.

Rorty was put into the stretcher. "Let me know when you've . . . stowed her," Sula said. "Then we'll resume higher gee."

"Very good, my lady," one said.

She looked at Massimo, who stood with arms akimbo, a thoughtful look on his unshaven face as he watched Rorty's body being strapped onto the stretcher.

"Massimo," she said, "that was good work."

He looked at her, startled. "Thank you, my lady. But—if I hadn't dozed off—I might."

"Nothing you could have done," Sula said. "She forgot to connect the helmet monitors to her suit."

Massimo absorbed her words, then nodded. If we'd got warning, Sula thought, Rorty might be a cripple instead of a corpse.

"Can you do both piloting and navigating duties till the end of the watch?" Sula asked.

"Yes, my lady."

"Better get busy plotting our return to the squadron, then." The squadron had altered course to swing around Vandrith, one of the Zanshaa system's gas giants, and they'd have to pull some extra gees to catch the planet in time.

The stretcher-bearers had to tip the stretcher on end to

walk it down the narrow lanes between acceleration cages. Sula thought about erratic blood pressure throughout the squadron, arteries eroding, blood spilling into brain tissue or the body cavity. Rorty had been twenty and in perfect health. Many more months of this and half the ship might be stricken.

Sula looked at the helmet in her hands and realized she absolutely could not put the helmet on her head, that if she couldn't draw free breaths of cabin air she would scream. She stowed the helmet and her gloves in the elastic mesh bag rigged to the side of the couch, and then resumed her seat. With the back of her hand she tried to scrub Rorty's taste from her lips.

She tried to think of vases and pots, of smooth celadon surfaces. Instead she thought of gold hair shimmering, fading, in dark water.

No matter how many pieces of porcelain she piped into her dreams tonight, she knew, they would all turn to nightmare.

The next day, heavy-lidded and ill, Sula declined her breakfast and confined herself to sips of Tassay, a hot milky carbohydrate and protein beverage flavored with cardamom and cloves. The aromatic spices soothed her sleepless, jangled nerves; the nutrition would keep her conscious, if not exactly sparkling.

"Have I mentioned that Lieutenant Sula is exchanging mathematical formulae with Captain Martinez?" Foote said to the acting captain, Morgen.

Morgen didn't appear very interested. There were deep black blooms beneath his eyes, and lines in his face that hadn't been there a month before. "That's nice," he said.

"She and Martinez are trying to reform our entire tactical system based on lessons learned at Magaria," Foote says. "Martinez places great trust in her, it seems."

Morgen raised a piece of flat bread to his mouth, then hesitated. "Martinez is consulting you on his tactics?"

Morgen found it surprising that Lieutenant Captain Lord Gareth Martinez—who after all was *famous*—was consulting *Delhi*'s most junior lieutenant in the matter of maneuvering his squadron.

Sula answered cautiously. "He asks my opinion," she says.

"Well," Morgen said, chewing. "Maybe you'd better share it with the rest of us, then."

Sula didn't feel up to delivering a lecture to her superiors, but she managed to stumble through a brief explanation without tangling up her thoughts too badly. Foote—who listened with great care and seriousness, and managed not to make a single sarcastic or offensive remark the entire time— turned the video wall to the Structured Mathematics Display and surprised Sula by calling up the formula she'd sent to Martinez the previous evening.

"I cribbed this out of your message," he explained.

Morgen's eyes scanned the formula quickly, then slowly went through it again, statement by statement.

"Perhaps you'd better explain in more detail," he said.

Sula gave Foote a sullen glare of weary resentment, then did as her acting captain requested.

Martinez looked in wild fascination at the ten enemy engine flares registered on the display, and took an extra half-second to make certain that his voice was calm when he spoke.

"Message to the squadron," he said. "Cease acceleration at—" He glanced at the chronometer. "25:34:01 precisely."

Martinez returned to calculating trajectories. As Wormholes 1 and 2 were 4.2 light-hours apart, the Naxids had actually entered the system slightly over four hours ago, and were decelerating as if they intended to stay in the Hone-bar system. It was impossible to be precise about their current location, but it appeared they were heading slightly away from Martinez's force, intending to swing around Hone-bar's sun and slingshot around toward the planet. They would, in time, see Martinez's squadron enter hot, with blazing engine flares and pounding radars, and know the new arrivals for enemies.

Martinez's squadron wasn't heading for Hone-bar either, but rather for a gas giant named Soq, on a trajectory that would hurl them toward the system's sun, on screaming curves around three more gas giants, and then back through Wormhole 1 again and on to Zanshaa. They were heading for the sun at a much more acute angle than the Naxids, and if neither changed course Martinez would cross his enemy's trail on the far side of the sun.

But that wouldn't happen. The Naxids would pass behind the sun and swing toward Hone-bar and the squadron, and then antimatter would blaze out in the emptiness of space and a great many people would die.

Gradually, as he studied the displays, Martinez realized that his message had not been repeated back to him.

"Shankaracharya!" he said. "Message to squadron!"

"Oh! Sorry, lord elcap. Repeat, please?" Shankaracharya's communications cage was behind Martinez, so Martinez couldn't see him, only hear his voice over his helmet earphones.

Martinez spoke through clenched teeth, wishing he could lock eyes with Shankaracharya and convey to him the full measure of his annoyance. "Message to squadron. Cease acceleration at—" He looked at the chronometer again, and saw that his original time had expired "25:35:01."

"25:35:01, my lord." There was a pause while Shankaracharya transmitted the message. And then he said, "Messages from the other ships of the squadron, lord elcap, reporting enemy engine flares. Do you wish the coordinates?"

"No. Just acknowledge. Engines." Martinez turned to

Warrant Officer First Class Mabumba, who sat at the engine control station. "Engines, cut engines at 25:35:01."

"Cut engines at 25:35:01, lord elcap."

"Shankaracharya."

"My lord?"

He had deliberately waited for his junior lieutenant to acknowledge before he spoke. He didn't want *this* message to go astray. "Message to Squadron Commander Do-faq via the wormhole station. Inform him of the presence of ten enemy ships just entered the Hone-bar system. Give course and velocity."

"Very good, my lord. Ten enemy ships, course, and velocity to the squadcom."

Corona couldn't communicate directly with Do-faq, not with the wormhole in the way, but there were manned relay stations on either side of the wormhole, all equipped with powerful communications lasers. The stations transmitted news, instructions, and data through the wormholes, and strung the empire together with their webs of coherent light.

The low-gravity warning blared out, the engines suddenly cut out, and Martinez floated free in his straps. His ribs and breastbone crackled as he took a long, deliberate free breath. He saw Vonderheydte at the weapons board casting him a look, and then Mabumba at the engine control station.

Mabumba was one of the original crew who had helped Martinez steal *Corona* from the Naxid mutineers. So were Tracy and Clarke, the sensor operators. Navigator Trainee Diem—now promoted Navigator/2nd—sat where he had during the escape, and so did the pilot, Eruken. Both had been joined by trainees.

Cadet Kelly, who had acted as weapons officer in the flight from the Naxids, had been returned to her original job of pinnace pilot, and was presumably now sitting in Pinnace Number 1, ready to be fired into action. Vonderheydte had replaced her in the weapons cage, again with a trainee to assist, and Shankaracharya had taken Vonderheydte's original place as communications officer, backed up by Signaler Trainee Mattson.

These were the most reliable personnel he had aboard, along with Master Engineer Maheshwari in the engine department, another veteran of *Corona*'s earlier adventures. Martinez regretted extremely the fact that Kelly wasn't a part of his Control staff. He didn't relish her chances in what was to come—only one pinnace pilot had survived Magaria, and that had been Sula.

It wasn't just Kelly he'd have to look after, though, it was all of them. And not just the personnel aboard *Corona,* but the other ships in his squadron.

And then it occurred to him that many of *Corona*'s people didn't yet know they were about to engage the enemy, only those here in Control and presumably those with Dalkeith in Auxiliary Control.

He had better tell them.

"Comm: general announcement to the ship's personnel," he said, and waited for the flashing light on his displays that indicated he was speaking live throughout the ship.

"This is the captain," he said. "A few minutes ago we entered the Hone-bar system. Shortly after passing through the wormhole, sensors detected the flares of a squadron of rebel warships entering the system through Wormhole Number Two. We have every reason to believe that within a few hours we will be heavily engaged with the enemy."

He paused, and wondered where to go from here. At this point a brilliant commander would, of course, inflame his men with a flood of dazzling rhetoric, inspiring them to feats of courage and radiant daring.

A less than brilliant commander would make an address of the sort Martinez was about to deliver. He made a note to himself that, if he survived the coming fight, he'd assemble a stock of these sorts of speeches in case he ever needed one again.

He decided to stress the aspect practical. "With Squadron

Commander Do-faq's force, we will have a decisive advantage in numbers over the enemy. We have every reason to anticipate success. The enemy force will be crushed here, at Hone-bar, and the Naxids' plans will be wrecked."

He glanced over the control room crew and saw what he hoped was increased confidence. He decided to follow with unabashed flattery. "I know that you are all eager to come to grips with the enemy," he continued. "We've trained very hard for this moment, and I have every confidence that you'll do your duty to the utmost.

"Remember," getting on to the rousing finish, "the comrades we've already lost, killed in battle or taken prisoner by the enemy on the first day of rebellion. I know that you're anxious to avenge your friends, and I know that when the Naxids' captives are finally liberated, they'll thank you for the work you'll do this day."

From the reaction of the control room crew—the chins lifted in pride, the glitter of determination in their eyes—Martinez thought he'd done well. He decided to quit while he was ahead and ended the transmission.

That left only the enemy to deal with. He looked again at the display, ran a few calculations from current trajectories. *Corona*'s squadron, after a month's acceleration, was traveling just in excess of a fifth of the speed of light. The Naxids were faster, coming on at $0.41c$. They could stand higher accelerations than the Lai-owns of Do-faq's heavy squadron, or perhaps they'd been in transit for a longer amount of time.

And then Martinez realized what the enemy squadron was, and what they were doing here, and the entire Naxid strategy dropped into his mind like a ripe fruit fallen from the tree.

These ten enemy ships were the squadron that had originally been based at the remote station of Comador, and were heavy cruisers under a Senior Squadron Commander named Kreeku. On the day of the rebellion, they'd simply left Comador's ring station and burned for the center of the empire.

It had been assumed they were heading for the Second Fleet base at Magaria, but the Comador squadron hadn't taken part in the battle there. The Fleet had assumed this was because they hadn't arrived yet, but perhaps they'd always been intended to go someplace else.

Any ship traveling from the empire's core to the Hone Reach had to travel through Hone-bar's Wormhole 3—if another route existed, it hadn't been discovered. Kreeku had all along been intended to cut the Hone Reach off from any loyalists and secure it for the Naxids.

"Comm," Martinez told Shankaracharya, "message to the squadron, copy to the squadcom. We are facing Kreeku's squadron from Comador. End message."

"Kreeku's squadron from Comador. Very good, my lord."

Martinez told his display to go virtual, and the Hone-bar system expanded in his skull, all cool emptiness with a few dots here and there representing Hone-bar's sun and its planets, the wormhole gates, and little speeding color-coded icons with course and velocity attached.

Since the arrival of the Naxids the merchant vessel *Clan Chen* had increased its acceleration and was fleeing the system as fast as the bones of its crew could stand. Martinez could confidently assume that the Naxids, who would not know of Martinez's arrival for another four hours, would continue their course toward Hone-bar's sun, and by now would have traveled a little short of two light-hours' distance. They would travel an equal distance before they would see Martinez's engine flares, and then their blissful ignorance would end.

There would be many hours after that for the battle to develop, and it would pass through a series of obvious stages. Martinez should begin decelerating and let Do-faq's eight heavier ships enter the system and join him. Do-faq could then confront the enemy with sixteen ships to the Naxids' ten, and engage on favorable terms. With the loyalists swinging around Soq, and the Naxids coming around Hone-bar's sun, the two squadrons would be meeting each other almost head-on, in one of those blazing collisions that Martinez had seen in records from the Battle of Magaria. At the end of which a few loyalist survivors would pass through the fire and into victory.

All Martinez's instincts protested against this scenario. Though he had every reason to believe that Kreeku would be annihilated, he would probably take at least half of Faqforce with him. The whole scenario reeked of useless waste.

There had to be some way to make better use of the loyalists' advantages.

And of what, Martinez asked himself with full, careful deliberation, did these advantages consist?

Numbers and firepower. Eight frigates and light cruisers in Martinez's Light Squadron 14, plus Do-faq's eight heavy cruisers, against ten heavy cruisers. An advantage sufficient to crush the enemy, but not decisive enough to avoid casualties.

Surprise. The enemy wouldn't know of Martinez's arrival for another four hours. But that advantage wasn't decisive, either, because it would take the opposite forces a lot more than four hours to engage.

And . . .

Another surprise. Because the enemy *didn't need to know of Do-faq's squadron at all.*

Martinez's pulse thundered in his ears. He called up a calculator and began punching in numbers.

"Vonderheydte!" he called out. "Shankaracharya! Get out your lieutenants' keys! Hurry!"

In order for *Corona*'s world-shattering weaponry to be deployed, three out of its four most senior officers had to turn their keys at the same moment. Martinez feared he'd already lost too much time.

He was currently carrying his captain's key on an elastic band around his neck. He yanked off his helmet—blind, since he was still in virtual—and scrabbled for his collar buttons. He told the computer to cut the virtual environment, then yanked the key, shaped like a narrow playing card, from his tunic and thrust it into the slot on the display.

Vonderheydte, after a similar struggle with his clothing, slid his own key into his slot. "Key ready, my lord."

From the comm cage behind him, Martinez heard only a quiet, "Let me help you with that, my lord" from Signaler Trainee Mattson, followed by the chunk of a helmet being twisted off its collar ring. Then, after a few seconds in which Martinez's nerves shrieked in impotent agony, he heard Shankaracharya say, "Damn these gloves!"

There was another ten-second eternity before he heard Shankaracharya's, "Key ready, my lord."

Martinez tried not to scream his commands at the top of his impatient voice. "Turn on my mark," he said. "Three, two, one, mark."

From his position he could see Vonderheydte's weapons board suddenly blaze with light.

"Weapons," Martinez said, "charge missile battery one with antimatter. Prepare to fire missiles one, two, and three on my command. This is not a drill." He turned to Eruken. "Pilot, rotate ship to present battery one to the enemy."

"Rotating ship, lord elcap." Martinez's cage gave a shimmering whine as the ship rolled.

"Display: go virtual." Again the virtual cosmos sprang into existence in Martinez's mind. With his gloved hands he manipulated the display controls to mark out three targets in empty space between his squadron and the enemy.

"Weapons," he said, "fire missiles one, two, and three at the target coordinates. This is not a drill."

"This is not a drill, my lord," Vonderheydte repeated. "Firing missiles." There was a brief pause in which Martinez's nerves involuntarily tensed, as if expecting recoil. "Missiles fired," Vonderheydte said. "Missiles clear of the ship. Missiles running normally on chemical rockets."

The missiles had been hurled into space on gauss rails—

there was no detectable recoil, of course—and then rockets would take them to a safe distance from *Corona*, where their antimatter engines would ignite.

"My lord." Shankaracharya's voice in Martinez's earphones. "Urgent communication from Captain Kamarullah. Personal to you, lord elcap."

Martinez's mind whirled as he tried to shift from the virtual world, with its icon-planets and plotted trajectories and rigorous calculations, to the officer who wished to talk to him.

"I'll take it," he said, and then Kamarullah's face materialized in the virtual display, and at offensively close range. Martinez couldn't keep himself from wincing.

"This is Martinez," he said.

Kamarullah's square face was ruddy, and Martinez wondered if it was the result of some internal passion that had flushed his skin or an artifact of transmission.

"Captain Martinez," Kamarullah said, "you have just fired missiles. Are you aware that you can't possibly hit the enemy at this range?"

"Main missile engines ignited," Vonderheydte reported, as if to punctuate Kamarullah's question.

"I don't intend to hit the Naxids with these missiles," Martinez said. "I'm intending to mask a maneuver."

"*Maneuver? Out here?*" Kamarullah was astonished. "Why? We're *hours* yet from the enemy." He gazed at Martinez with a fevered expression, and spoke with unusual clarity and emphasis, as if trying to convince a blind man, by the power of words alone, that he was standing in the path of a speeding automobile. "Captain Martinez, I don't think you've thought this out. As soon as you saw the enemy, you should have given the squadron orders to rotate and start our deceleration. We need to let Squadron Commander Do-faq join us before we can engage." His tone grew earnest, if not a little pleading. "It's not too late to give up command of the squadron to a more experienced officer."

"The missiles—" Martinez began.

"Damn it, man!" Kamarullah said, his eyes a little wild. "I don't insist that *I* command! If not me, then stand down in favor of someone else. But you're going to have your hands full managing a green crew without having to worry about tactics as well."

"The missiles," Martinez said carefully, "will mask the arrival of the squadcom's force. I intend to keep the existence of the heavy squadron a secret as long as I can."

Astonishment again claimed Kamarullah. "But that would take *hours*. They're bound to detect—"

"Captain Kamarullah," Martinez said, "you will stand by for further orders."

"You're not going to attempt any of your—your tactical innovations, are you?" Kamarullah said. "Not with a squadron that doesn't understand them or—"

Martinez's temper finally broke free. *"Enough!* You will stand by! This discussion is at an end!"

"I don't—"

Martinez cut off communication, then pounded with an angry fist on the arm of his couch. He told the computer to save the conversation in memory—there had better, he realized, be a record of this.

And then he stared blindly out into the virtual planetary system, the little abstract symbols in their perfect, ordered universe, and tried to puzzle out what he should do next.

"Comm," he said. "Message to Squadron Commander Do-faq, personal to the squadcom. To be sent through the wormhole relay station."

"Very good, my lord. Personal to the squadcom."

Again Martinez waited for the light to blink, a little glowing planet that came into existence in the virtual universe, and he said, "Lord Commander Do-faq. In my estimation, our great advantage in the upcoming battle is that the enemy do not yet know of the existence of your squadron. As we approach the enemy, I will fire missiles in an attempt to screen your force for as long as possible. I will order Light

Squadron Fourteen into a series of plausible maneuvers in order to justify the existence of the screen.

"If you agree with this plan, please order your force onto a heading of two-nine-zero by zero-one-five absolute, as soon as you exit the wormhole, and continue to accelerate at two gravities. This will allow you to take advantage of the screen I have already laid down."

He looked at the camera and realized that he should perhaps soften the effect of having just given an order to an officer several grades superior in rank.

"As always," he said, "I remain obedient to your commands. Message ends."

He fell silent as the recording light vanished from the virtual display, and as he thought of the message flying from *Corona* to Do-faq through the power of communications lasers, a deep suspicion began to creep across his mind. He began to wonder what might happen if his messages to Do-faq weren't getting through. If, somehow, the wormhole relay stations were under the control of the enemy.

The only thing that made his suspicions at all plausible was that the arrival of the Naxid squadron shouldn't have been a surprise. The station on the far side of Wormhole 2 should have seen the Naxids coming hours ago, and reported to the commander of Hone-bar's ring station, who in turn should have relayed the information to Do-faq, whose arrival he'd known for the better part of a month. In fact, there should have been a long chain of sightings, all the way from Comador.

Why hadn't the information reached him? he wondered. Had half the Exploration Service joined the rebels?

If it had, and if his messages to Do-faq hadn't got through, he'd better order that his last two messages be beamed just this side of the wormhole, so that Do-faq would receive them as he flashed into the Hone-bar system.

He was on the verge of giving the order when Shankaracharya's voice came into his earphones. "Message from Squadron Commander Do-faq via Wormhole One station. 'Yours acknowledged. Light Squadron Fourteen to head course two-eight-eight by zero-one-five absolute and commence deceleration at four point five gravities.' "

"Acknowledge," Martinez said automatically, while panic flashed along his nerves. Do-faq's order was in response to his *first* message, and would send Martinez's squadron on a wide trajectory around the Soq gas giant, wide enough to permit Do-faq's ships to take an inside track, closer to the planet, to make up some of the distance between the two squadrons.

The order was perfectly orthodox and sensible. Unfortunately it wasn't compatible with the plan of the battle as Martinez had mapped it out in his mind.

It would take nearly five minutes for the last transmission, with its suggestion for maneuver on the part of Do-faq, and another five minutes for Do-faq's response to come back. But in order for Light Squadron 14 to embark on Martinez's plan, it would have to begin its maneuver before Do-faq's reply could possibly arrive.

In order for Martinez to continue with the plan that he had devised, he was going to have to disobey Do-faq's order.

Suddenly he wished that the Exploration Service *had* been corrupted, that the messages *hadn't* got through the wormhole stations.

"Comm," he said, "message to squadron. Rotate ships: prepare to decelerate on course two-eight-eight by zero-one-five absolute. Stand by to decelerate on my command."

Shankaracharya repeated the order and then transmitted it to the squadron. Martinez gave the order also to *Corona*'s pilot, and the acceleration cages in Command sang in their metallic voices as Eruken swung the frigate nearly through a half-circle, its engines now aimed to begin the massive deceleration that Do-faq had ordered.

He watched the chronometer in the corner of the display and watched the numbers that marked the seconds flash past.

He thought of Do-faq's dislike of Kamarullah, who Do-faq blamed for wrecking a maneuver, and how Do-faq's vengeance had followed Kamarullah over the years and deprived him of command.

How much in the way of retribution could Martinez expect if he disobeyed Do-faq during an actual *battle*?

And yet, within the ten-minute lag, it was very possible that Do-faq would countermand his own order, and agree to Martinez's plan.

Brilliant light flared on the virtual display. Solid flakes of antihydrogen, suspended by static electricity in etched silicon chips so tiny they flowed like a fluid, had just been caught by the compression wave of a small amount of conventional explosive in the nose of each of the three missiles Martinez had launched. The resulting antimatter explosion dwarfed the conventional trigger by a factor of billions. Erupting outward, the hot shreds of matter encountered the missiles' tungsten jackets and created three expanding, overlapping spheres of plasma between Light Squadron 14 and the enemy ships, screens impenetrable to any enemy radar. The screen would hide any number of maneuvers on the part of Martinez's force.

The plasma would also screen the arrival of Do-faq's eight heavy cruisers.

The sight of the explosions made up Martinez's mind, and words seemed to fly to his lips without his conscious order.

"Comm: message to the squadron. Rotate ships to course two-nine-two by two-nine-seven absolute. Decelerate at five gravities commencing at 25:52:01."

Mentally he clung to a modest justification: Light Squadron 14 was not *technically* a part of Faqforce any longer; Martinez's squadron command was *theoretically* independent until Do-faq actually entered the Hone-bar system. . . .

None of that, however, would make the slightest difference to Martinez's career if Do-faq chose to inflict vengeance on his junior.

The order would swing the light squadron through a course change that would shoot it over Soq's south pole and slingshot it toward the enemy at a very narrow angle that would put it on a trajectory to place it between Hone-bar and the oncoming Naxids. This would place the squadron in an ideal position to further conceal the existence of Do-faq's oncoming heavy ships.

Martinez gave the order to Eruken, and again the acceleration cages sang as, in obedience to the laws of inertia, the couches rotated easily within them.

"Let me help you with that, my lord." The murmured comment from Signaler Trainee Mattson snapped Martinez away from his concentration on the tactical display.

"Display: cancel virtual," Martinez said. He reached a hand to the curved bars of his acceleration cage, seized it in a fist, and swung his weightless body to a position where he could look directly at the communications cage.

Shankaracharya was staring at his communications board, his wide eyes ticking back and forth over the displays in apparent bewilderment. Signaler Trainee Mattson, teeth gnawing his lower lip, tapped away at his own display.

"What is going on, comm?" Martinez demanded.

Shankaracharya gave Martinez a startled look. "I'm sorry, my lord," he said. "I—I didn't hear the order. Could you repeat, please?"

"Course two-nine-two by two-nine-seven relative," Mattson said helpfully.

"Absolute, not relative!" Martinez said. "Check the *record*! All commands are recorded automatically! Call up the command display, everything should be there!"

Mattson gave a quick, nervous shake of the head at this reminder. "Very good, my lord."

Shankaracharya was now busy at his own display. Martinez could see that his hands were trembling so severely that he kept pressing the wrong parts of the display, then having to go back and correct.

"What was that time, my lord?" Shankaracharya asked.

"Never mind. I'll take the comm board myself."

He had been communications officer on the *Corona* prior to the Naxid revolt: he could do the job easily enough, and there was no way he could allow such a critical operation to remain in the hands of a trainee and a very junior, suddenly very erratic lieutenant. In the profound silence of the control room, Martinez let go of the cage and called up Shankaracharya's board onto his own display. Mattson had managed to get most of the message onto the board, excepting only the time of acceleration. A glance at the chronometer showed that all the ships might not have time to perform the maneuver in time, so he advanced the time half a minute to 25:52:34.

He sent the message, as well as the time correction to Mabumba on the engines board. Martinez was still minding the comm board when the call from Kamarullah came.

"Martinez," he answered. "Make it quick."

Kamarullah's image was flushed a brighter color red than it had been before. "Are you aware that you've disobeyed a direct order from a superior officer?" he demanded.

"Yes," Martinez admitted. "Is that all?"

Kamarullah seemed staggered by Martinez's confession, and was without words for a few seconds. "Are you mad?" he managed finally. "Is there any reason why I should consider obeying this order?"

"I'm beyond caring if you obey my orders or not," Martinez said. "Do as you please, and we'll see what a court says afterward. End transmission."

A few seconds later *Corona*'s engines fired and delivered a kick to Martinez's tailbone that threw his couch swinging along the inside of a long arc. This was followed by a series of shorter arcs until the couch finally settled, with Martinez's suit clamping gently on his arms and legs to prevent his blood pooling, and the iron weights of gravity stacking themselves one by one on his bones.

Corona groaned, its frame shuddering as the acceleration built, jolting as if a giant were stamping on the deck. The display showed that Kamarullah's ship had, in fact, obeyed Martinez's order, and done so correct to the second. Whatever Kamarullah intended, it wasn't open mutiny.

A few minutes later, Do-faq's squadron appeared through the wormhole, rotated to two-nine-zero by zero-one-five absolute, and fired their engines. Relief bubbled in Martinez's heart like the finest champagne.

Do-faq had done as Martinez had asked. Martinez had not ended his career with an act of disobedience.

Martinez was too drained by the five-gravity deceleration to celebrate, and he knew he had work to do. Fighting against the deadening anesthesia the high gee wrapped about his mind, Martinez planned and ordered another series of missile launches that would, as his original plasma clouds cooled and dispersed, reinforce the screen behind which the loyalist squadrons could maneuver.

If he commanded a larger ship he'd have a tactical officer to make these calculations and suggest solutions to problems, but as *Corona* was only a large frigate he had to do all the work himself.

With gravity dragging at his brain he couldn't be certain that his calculations were completely correct so he added more missiles just to make certain.

Antimatter tore itself to pi-mesons and gamma rays in the solar wind, and plasma fireballs expanded in the darkness. Behind the torn, hot matter, Do-faq's squadron plunged onward, unobserved. Martinez, fighting to think as desperately as he fought for breath, launched more sets of missiles.

A little over two hours after entering the Hone-bar system, *Corona*'s squadron made a furious burn across Soq's south pole, briefly reaching ten gees as every person aboard sank groaning into unconsciousness. When Martinez battled his way to awareness like a punch-soaked fighter swinging wildly at an enemy he could barely perceive, he put all his concentration into forming and sending an order for the squadron to reduce its deceleration to two gravities.

Martinez gasped and rolled his neck as the weight of gravity came off. With the relief of the interminable pressure he could feel alertness pouring back into his brain as if someone had opened a tap. He called up the abstract, perfect virtual display, and watched little burning figures fly across darkness.

Light Squadron 14 had now swung on a course that would cause it to pass close to Hone-bar, inside the most probable course taken by the enemy. The Naxids, for their part, hadn't altered their course, and in fact had no reason to—they were still two hours from learning of the loyalists' existence.

Martinez ordered another missile barrage—and ordered one of his light cruisers to make it, a ship with a greater store of missiles than his own frigate. He gave no orders for the missiles to explode, or where—he just pushed them out ahead of the squadron in the expectation that they would be useful later.

The Naxids were most likely intending to stay in the Hone-bar system—their deceleration flares implied that—but it was possible they intended to slip by Hone-bar's sun and continue on to Wormhole 3 and the Hone Reach. Whatever their purpose, the appearance of Martinez's squadron on their displays might make them change their plans completely. If they had been ordered to avoid battle, they might blaze away for Wormhole 3 even if their original intention had been to stay. And even if they had been intending to pass on, the sight of a weaker squadron might convince them to engage.

In any case, Kreeku would have to make his decision very soon after detecting Martinez's arrival. His squadron would be on the verge of passing Hone-bar's sun when they first saw Martinez's engine flares, soon to be followed by maneuvers completely obscured by a screen of radiation from exploding antimatter missiles. Kreeku would have to conclude that the maneuvers were intended to bring on an engagement—Martinez *might* be intending to obscure a flight for Wormhole 3, but Kreeku couldn't assume that.

So the question was whether Kreeku would fight or not—and given that the Naxids would believe themselves superior in numbers, Martinez assumed that Kreeku would commit to battle. He would sling his forces around Hone-bar's sun at a sharp angle and head more or less for Soq.

And then, three hours later when Kreeku finally saw what course Martinez had taken shooting out of Soq's gravity well, he would have to decide whether or not to react. He would either crowd in toward Martinez, in effect pinning him against Hone-bar, or engage from a distance. *How aggressive was he?*

Martinez called up Kreeku's biographical file out of *Corona*'s data system and saw the career track of a successful officer—a mix of specialties, ship and planetary assignments, staff college. In the public record there were, of course, none of the more candid assessments given by Kreeku's superiors, nothing to indicate whether he was brilliant, stodgy, dull, or a swashbuckler.

Martinez decided that Kreeku probably wouldn't react right away. He wouldn't need to—it would still be hours before the squadrons would clash.

"Message to the squadron," he said. "Alter course to two-eight-seven by zero-two-five relative, commencing at 27:14:01. Deceleration to remain at two gravities."

As his spoken words were transcribed into text by the computer he sent them forth. He had ordered the course change "relative," meaning with relation to the squadron's current heading, rather than "absolute," in reference to the arbitrary coordinate system that had been imposed on every star system by the conquering Shaa.

He gave further instructions to the missile barrage he'd sent out ahead of the squadron, and then decided it was time to send another message to Do-faq. "My lord," he said into the camera, "I am enormously gratified at the confidence you have expressed in me by taking my suggested course. If you will further oblige me by ordering your squadron onto a heading of zero-one-five by zero-zero-one absolute after you pass Soq, I will do my best to provide cover and prevent the enemy from detecting you.

"Thank you again for your trust. I shall try to prove worthy of it. Message ends."

As he sent the message to Do-faq he was aware of a light prickle of sweat on his forehead. He felt a sudden awareness of how much he was taking on himself, the fate of the Hone-bar system, the lives of thousands of crew. He looked at his displays and hoped that Kreeku wouldn't prove to be a genius.

At 27:14:01 the missile barrage exploded, creating a wall of hot plasma in front of the squadron, and the ships commenced their maneuver. If the Naxids had been able to see it, they would have seen the squadron make a kind of diagonal move in front of them, from a course that would pass between the Naxids and Hone-bar to one that would pass outside of both planet and squadron. It might look as if Martinez had changed his mind about how he wanted the battle to develop.

What Martinez actually wanted was an excuse to create the plasma screen in the first place, any reason to hide Do-faq's force. The maneuver itself was secondary.

Some time later the ships passed through the screen they had created, and *Corona* traveled for several minutes in a bubble of hot radio hash, blind to the universe outside, the hull temperature rising. And then they were clear, and the other ships of the squadron appeared, their formation unaltered, their torches burning.

Martinez shifted their heading again, aiming for where he suspected Kreeku would appear after his transit around Hone-bar's sun, and then he rearranged their formation. The Naxids would see them arranged in a wheel, *Corona* at the hub surrounded by a constellation of seven ships. But the Naxids wouldn't see the ships themselves—what they would see instead would be the ships' tails of antimatter fire pointing straight toward them, obscuring anything behind.

What would be obscured behind, Martinez hoped, would be the eight ships of Do-faq's squadron, flying in Martinez's wake and accelerating at a steady 2.3 gravities, the highest acceleration the frailty of the Lai-own physique would permit. Any radiation from Do-faq's engine torches would, Martinez hoped, be taken for his own squadron's engine exhaust.

If Martinez had worked his calculations aright—and if the Naxids' own maneuvers were reasonably conventional—he would lead Do-faq's heavy squadron right onto the enemy without Kreeku's being aware of their existence.

Do-faq, without comment, followed Martinez's suggestion and put his squadron on the course that would enable Martinez to guard the fact of his presence. Hours ticked by. Martinez could spot the moment when Kreeku first saw Light Squadron 14 fly through Wormhole 1—the deceleration burn ceased, and then the squadron reoriented and began a deceleration at higher gees.

When Kreeku burned around Hone-bar's sun and emerged on the track Martinez had most desired, he felt relief melt his limbs like butter. He made some fine adjustments to the positions of his squadron, and sent another suggestion to Do-faq that enabled Martinez to more efficiently screen his force as the angle between the opposing forces changed with their movement toward one another.

Martinez and Kreeku, now four light-hours apart, were approaching each other at a combined speed of nearly seven-tenths the speed of light. They would meet in less than six hours—though by then, of course, a great many people would be dead.

A flower of something like vanity began to blossom in Martinez's heart. He had actually done it—he had smuggled eight large warships into the Hone-bar system without the enemy learning of their existence. He was giving orders to his own superior officer, the formidable and unforgiving Do-faq, and Do-faq was obeying them without comment. Even the *enemy* seemed to be flying in obedience to Martinez's will.

This battle would be studied by generations of Fleet officers, Martinez knew. Even if, as seemed perfectly possible, he was killed in the next few hours, he had assured himself a place in history.

Martinez celebrated by reducing his deceleration to one gravity and sent his crew to supper. Though he felt no hunger himself, he thought his crew would fight better on a full stomach.

Once food was placed before him he found he was ravenous, and he shoveled Alikhan's fare into his mouth at a relentless rate. When his plate was empty he paged the premiere to his office, then explained to Dalkeith his plans for the upcoming battle, which she would need if he was killed and she, by some wild chance, survived.

"Who do you have on your comm boards?" Martinez asked her.

"Yu, my lord. Backed by Signaler/2nd Bernstein."

"Are they satisfactory?"

She seemed unsurprised by the question, but then she was unsurprised by most things. "I have no complaints, lord elcap."

"Good. I want them transferred to Command. Trainee Mattson is too inexperienced, and Shankaracharya—well, he hasn't worked out."

A tremble in Dalkeith's watery blue eyes demonstrated a pattern of thought that she chose not to voice. "Very good, my lord," she said.

Martinez told Shankaracharya as the Command crew returned to their stations following the meal. "You and Mattson will be going to Auxiliary Command," Martinez told the lieutenant. "Yu and Bernstein will serve the comm boards here."

Shankaracharya's face didn't show surprise—instead there was a kind of spasm, a tautening of the muscles of the neck and cheek, and then no expression at all. "I'm, ah, sorry, my lord," he said. "I—I'll try to do better in future."

"I regret the necessity, lieutenant," Martinez said. "I'll do what I can for you, later."

And what he could do would include never putting Shankaracharya in combat again, at least not in a position in which lives could possibly hang in the balance.

The young lieutenant left Command with his helmet under his arm, his body straight and his eyes fixed resolutely ahead, refusing to meet the pity in the eyes of the other control room crew. It was only then that Martinez remembered that Shankaracharya was his sister's lover.

Sempronia's going to really hate me for this.

Yu and Bernstein arrived and settled into their seats. A check showed the crew ready to resume higher gees. Martinez ordered the squadron to increase deceleration to two gravities.

Time passed, and Martinez grew fretful. He wondered if there were a traitor on Hone-bar or some of the other inhabited parts of the system, and if that traitor would see Do-faq's squadron and alert Kreeku to its existence.

In his long hours, isolated in his foul-smelling suit and with death flying toward him at a significant fraction of the speed of light, Martinez began to believe wholeheartedly in the existence of the traitor. In the traitor's messages. In Kreeku's genius, who fully alerted by the traitor was now luring the loyalist squadrons to their doom. Martinez was glad when the shooting started, and he didn't have to think about the traitor anymore.

The approaching forces were still two hours apart when both sides began firing missiles, waves of onrushing destruction that maneuvered in the empty space between the converging warships. When he saw the missile flares on his display, Martinez made a transmission to his ships.

"It's for Lord Squadcom Do-faq to destroy the enemy," he

said. "He's the hammer that will smash them out of the sky. *Our* job will be to stay alive—we should fight defensively and concentrate more on preserving ourselves than on destroying the enemy. Tell your weapons officers to emphasize defense." He gazed into the winking camera light and thought of the fight that was coming, the weaving missiles bearing their radiation fury, the annihilation that could strike at any of them. "See you on the other side," he said.

Martinez waited to make certain that Warrant Officer Yu actually *sent* the message before he went on to think of other things.

Missiles began finding each other in the depths between the squadrons, the brilliant plasma bursts masking the opposing ships from one another's sight. When the bursts had gained a sufficient density, Martinez sent a message to Do-faq.

"I believe that your lordship can begin launching missiles now."

Without waiting for a reply, Martinez ordered his own force to maneuver. The eight-ship squadron was divided into two four-ship divisions, and he ordered the divisions to separate, as if to catch the enemy between two fires. Shankaracharya's work had shown the theoretical maximum separation at which overlapping defensive fire remained effective, and Martinez kept the ships within that sphere. In the meantime, he made certain that *Corona* kept arcing missiles between Do-faq and the enemy, to provide the necessary screen for the heavy squadron's approach.

The missile bursts intensified, a continuous drumroll of flashes and dying matter. Point-defense lasers lashed across the darkness, striking at any incoming threat. Martinez felt his heart begin an inexorable climb into his throat as he watched the hot, opaque cloud of explosions roll nearer and nearer.

"Starburst!" he ordered. "All ships starburst!"

No doubt Kamarullah would consider the maneuver premature, but his ship as well as the others rotated and began to burn heavy gees away from the others, getting as much separation as possible before the onslaught that was about to engulf them.

"Defenses on automatic!" Martinez called as the hand of gravity slammed him into his couch. The display told him the pressure on his chest was nine gravities before his vision narrowed, and then winked out altogether.

After a long moment of darkness Martinez fought his way to consciousness, clenching his teeth and swallowing to force blood to his brain. He saw his displays as if through the wrong end of a telescope, a long distance down a dim tunnel. Gradually his vision cleared, and he gave a gasp as he realized what he was viewing.

Do-faq and the heavy squadron had launched a hundred and sixty missiles, all of them screened from the enemy by the erupting missiles and counterfire of Light Squadron 14. These missiles now raced out of the concealing plasma clouds, converging on Kreeku's force at seven-tenths of the speed of light.

The missile strike was a vast expanding carpet of light, like the phosphorescence on a moving wave, the entire enemy force torn to elemental fire in a few brief seconds. Martinez watched in awe, unable to believe that the Naxids' end had come so swiftly.

But the battle hadn't ended with the death of the enemy. Missiles were still weaving through space, dodging the defensive lasers and on *Corona*'s trail. There were several minutes of suspense before the last threat was destroyed by Vonderheydte's laser fire.

There was silence, and then cheers began to ring in Command. Martinez felt a giddy exhilaration, and repressed the urge to climb out of his cage in the heavy gravity and lead the crew in a delirious stomping dance.

More cheers burst out as other friendly ships emerged from the plasma fog, though it was not for several minutes that it became clear that Martinez had wiped the enemy from existence without a single loss to his squadron.

FOUR

After *Corona* had finished a pair of high-gee turns around Hone-bar's sun and another of the system's gas giants, and after Martinez had reduced his squadron's acceleration to 0.8 gravities in order to aid the repairs of the two ships that had suffered damage, Martinez was invited to dine in the wardroom by his lieutenants. When he entered the small room with its cramped cherrywood table, his three officers rose and applauded.

"Congratulations, my lord," Dalkeith said. She had a broad smile on her face, and Martinez wasn't surprised—the successful action had almost certainly guaranteed her the promotion that had eluded her for the last fifteen or twenty years, all in despite of the fact that her sole contribution to the battle had been to watch from Auxiliary Control and wait for Martinez to die.

He thanked her and sat at the table, and the lieutenants followed suit. The wardroom steward—a professional chef acquired during Captain Tarafah's regime, and who had stayed in his post while Martinez's own chef fled—laid down the first course, a savory soup flavored with bits of smoked duck.

By all rights Martinez should have been exhausted, not having slept in twenty-five hours, almost a full day. But instead of yawning over his soup he felt himself coursing with energy, and his brain bubbled with ideas. He felt a ravenous appetite. The lieutenants were exhilarated as well, and the mood sometimes caught even Shankaracharya, who certainly had reason enough to be cast down.

Some of Martinez's enthusiasm had been prompted by a message from Sula that had arrived mere hours after the battle, a message featuring her elegant formula for fleet maneuvers. Martinez brought the formula with him to the dinner, hoping to stimulate his officers' thought. To this end—after the dinner was over, and the last toast drunk—Martinez suggested inviting Cadet Kelly, who had participated in the original officers' discussions that had led to the new tactical ideas.

Such a suggestion, under the circumstances, was something akin to a command. Kelly came into the wardroom with her brilliant smile blazing. She had spent the entire battle in her pinnace, ready to be launched into space alongside a barrage of missiles. Martinez, for his part, had never for a moment considered launching either of his pinnace pilots into the hell of raging antimatter.

Kelly was brought up to speed with a couple glasses of the wardroom's excellent wine, and Martinez unveiled Sula's formula. Shankaracharya considered it carefully, tested it a few times with variables drawn from the day's battle, and pronounced it worthy of further investigation. The officers were discussing tactical applications when Martinez's sleeve button gave a discreet chime.

He answered, and on the sleeve display saw the face of Warrant Officer Roh, who had been left in charge of *Corona* while his superiors were roistering in the wardroom.

"Message for you, my lord. It's just been deciphered."

"Transmit, then."

A look of caution entered Roh's eyes. "Perhaps you might want to receive this in private, lord elcap. It's personal to you, from the Fleet Control Board."

Martinez excused himself from the wardroom and stepped into the corridor outside. "Go ahead and transmit, Roh," he said.

The message, from the secretary of the Control Board, was brief and to the point. In his musical Cree voice the secretary informed him that the board had decided, on receipt of Lieutenant Captain Martinez's last communication, that Light Squadron Fourteen should from receipt of this message be placed under the command of its senior officer, Lieutenant Captain Kamarullah.

A burble of astounded laughter escaped Martinez's lips. He was far too astonished to feel resentment at this outrageous usurpation. *They're going to really feel silly when they hear about what just happened here,* he thought. He wondered if they would change their minds.

No. Of course they wouldn't. They'd never admit they'd made an error in judgment.

And in any case the order needed to be obeyed. "Message, personal to Captain Kamarullah," Martinez dictated, and tried to suppress any sign of inebriation as he spoke into the silver button-camera on his cuff.

"Orders have just come from the Fleet Control Board placing you in command of Squadron Fourteen. Naturally I will endeavor to comply with any instructions you see fit to issue to *Corona.* I will immediately inform the other ships of . . ." He hesitated, having almost said *my command.* "Of the squadron," he finished. "Message ends."

He had the message sent, and spent a few moments assembling the words he would use to his other captains.

"My lords," he transmitted finally, "I must inform you that the Fleet Control Board has decided to place the squadron under the command of Captain Kamarullah. It has been a privilege to command Light Squadron Fourteen during the last month, and to have led you in an engagement which has done great service to the empire. I believe we may view our accomplishments with great satisfaction. I will be honored to serve alongside you under Captain Kamarullah's command, and I hope that in the future we may score an even greater success against the enemy."

Not that this was very likely under Kamarullah, Martinez thought, but the sentiment seemed worth expressing. He sent the message, and then paused for a moment outside the wardroom door, as he considered the new dynamics of the squadron.

Kamarullah's wish had been granted, and he now was in command. But Martinez, his rival, had just won a bloodless victory over the enemy, and more than justified the confidence that Do-faq had placed in him. He'd brought all his captains through the fight without harm, and earned their trust. He could expect decorations and possible promotion, and Kamarullah could not. Kamarullah had just replaced a man who had made history, a commander who had won a great victory and who had earned fame and the thanks of the empire. Kamarullah's victory could only turn to bitter ashes in his mouth.

The Fleet Control Board had just made Kamarullah an object of ridicule.

Cheered by this thought, Martinez returned to the wardroom, and accepted Dalkeith's offer of another glass of wine.

The lord secretary of the Fleet Control Board was a Cree, and he spoke in rounded musical tones like the chuckling of a spring.

". . . I call to Your Lordships' attention," he read, "Lieutenant Captain Lord Gareth Martinez, commander of Light Squadron Fourteen, who as the first squadron commander on the scene developed the plan of battle which his squadron and mine together followed. I earnestly hope that Your Lordships will consider Lord Gareth worthy of promotion or some other distinction.

"I also call to Your Lordships' notice the following officers, whose service has been exemplary, and whose contribution to the victory at Hone-bar was by no means negligible . . ."

Lord Chen listened to the list of names as relief sighed

through his bones. Captain Martinez had achieved distinction in the action at Hone-bar, something that would make Lord Chen's own dealings with Lord Roland Martinez less open to question. In addition to securing the victory, Martinez had saved the *Clan Chen,* which made Chen's pocketbook less empty and his sense of gratitude more personal.

"Your Lordships' most recent instructions," the lord secretary continued, "required me to leave two ships at Hone-bar in order to secure the system and the Hone Reach. As the recent victory has lessened the threat to Hone-bar, I hope my decision to leave only the *Judge Qel-fan* will meet with Your Lordships' approval. I will bring the rest of my ships to Zanshaa at the most expeditious possible speed."

Lord Chen suppressed a smile. In fact the board's instructions in regard to the defense of Hone-bar had been erratic, and tended to change from moment to moment depending on the persuasive power of those members with interests in the Hone Reach. From one day to the next Do-faq had been ordered to defend Hone-bar with his entire command, with his squadron alone, with a single four-ship division, and with a number of ships ranging from one to five. No wonder Do-faq had decided to take matters into his own decisive hands.

The lord secretary's voice burbled on.

"I regret to report that I have ordered Captain Dix of the Investigative Service to inquire into the breakdown in communication that permitted the Naxids to surprise us at Hone-bar. Wormhole stations should have observed the approach of the rebels many days in advance, and though the captain of Hone-bar's ring attempted to pass off the breakdown as the fault of a negligent tech, the explanation defies reason, and an investigation should be undertaken if only to clear those officers now under suspicion. I trust that this order meets with Your Lordships' approval.

"In the eternal light of the Praxis, I remain . . . Lord Pa Do-faq, Squadron Commander, etc."

The lord secretary looked up from his reader. "Shall I repeat any of the message, my lords?"

"That will not be necessary," Tork said, answering for them all. His round eyes, mournful in his pale, fixed face, gazed around the broad table. "I am sure we are all aware of how this victory lessens our anxieties. I suggest that the lord secretary be ordered to write a congratulatory reply to the lord squadron commander, and that we all append our signatures."

There was a murmur of assent. The lord secretary glanced down at his display and got busy with his stylus.

Lady San-torath, who represented Hone-bar in convocation, spoke first. "I'm delighted to congratulate Do-faq on his victory, but I wonder if he's not gone too far ordering an investigation of what seems to be a simple communications error. Hasn't the squadcom exceeded his authority?"

By which Lord Chen knew that the lapse hadn't been a communications error at all. Hone-bar understood its own strategic importance as well as its own vulnerability, and probably at least some members of the elite were aware of the scale of the defeat at Magaria. They had seen the Naxid fleet coming, and had been prepared to make their own peace with the rebels.

Unfortunately the conspirators hadn't been able to count. They'd known that Faqforce was on its way, and should have known that Faqforce outnumbered the Naxids. That they hadn't cooperated with Do-faq, who after all had the greatest number of missile launchers, did not speak well for their intelligence.

Chen wondered how much Lady San-torath knew of Hone-bar's plans. Enough at least to know that she might be compromised by any investigation.

"Better the Investigative Service," said Lord Pezzini, "than the Legion of Diligence."

There followed a significant silence that allowed Pezzini's audience to shudder. Neither the IS nor the legion were infallible, but the legion's mistakes tended to be a lot more lethal, as were, for that matter, its triumphs.

Pezzini was telling Lady San-torath to shut up and hope for the best. Nictating membranes deployed over her orange eyes, and she fell silent. Chen wondered how much Pezzini knew. Possibly a great deal, since Pezzini's interests also lay in the Hone Reach.

"Should we not send a congratulatory message to Captain Martinez as well?" asked Lord Convocate Mondi. "He was at least technically in independent command." Lord Mondi's diction was very precise, without the lisp common in a Torminel.

Pezzini scowled. "We could make too much of Martinez," he said. "We've already heard far too much of him."

Chen sighed inwardly, and went to work to earn his stipend. "Surely Captain Martinez deserves more than a congratulatory message," he said. "Even Squadron Commander Do-faq admits that it was his strategy that won the battle."

"It was nothing more than any Peer could have done," said Pezzini.

"That does not eliminate the fact that Martinez was the Peer who did it," said Lord Chen.

Mondi scrubbed with the back of his hand the gray fur beneath one eye. Humans had a tendency to think of Torminel as very large round-bottomed plush toys, a perception of harmlessness reinforced by the lisp common to so many of Mondi's species. Millions of human children slept each night with a stuffed Torminel beside them. Torminel, who were actually nocturnal, predatory carnivores who liked their meat raw, rarely understood why humans so persistently underestimated them.

"I don't see why Martinez shouldn't be congratulated," Mondi said. "In fact he should be promoted and decorated."

"It is Do-faq who should be promoted," said Pezzini. "He was the senior officer. And Kamarullah should be promoted as well—it was he the board placed in command of the light squadron, not Martinez."

"Why promote Kamarullah?" asked a bewildered Lady Seekin, the other Torminel member of the board. "What did *he* do?"

"The Board's decisions must be upheld!" Pezzini snapped. "Martinez has had enough! Kamarullah was our choice for command!"

"And now," said Lord Chen, smoothly interceding, "comes our opportunity to rectify that . . . embarrassment." He had argued against the supercession, but been outvoted. The professional members of the board, those who served with the Fleet, had insisted on the importance of seniority in maintaining discipline, and a couple of the civilians had been impressed enough by their arguments to fall in line.

"We could promote Martinez to captain," Chen continued, "which would automatically put him over Kamarullah. It would *not* counter this board's earlier decision," he said to Pezzini's glare, "but reinforce the principle of seniority that this board considers so crucial to the order of the Fleet."

"That seems simple enough," said Lady Seekin. She was one of the civilian members of the board, from Devajjo in the Hone Reach, and the intricacies of military culture often confused her.

"No member of his family has ever risen as high in the service as Martinez," Pezzini said. "Now the Board proposes to break precedent again and promote Martinez to *captain*?" Exasperation entered his voice. "Should we place his ancestors on a plane with ours? Should our descendants compete with his for places in the Fleet? It's bad enough that the Convocation awarded him the Golden Orb, and that we now have to salute him."

"One Peer is the equal of all others," said Fleet Commander Tork. His chiming Daimong voice took on the harsh, dogmatic overtones the other members of the board had learned to dread. "And we do not *compete*. Not with one another." He paused for effect while Pezzini tried and failed to suppress a gesture of frustration.

"Still," Tork said, "it is not good for one Peer to be favored so publically above others. If Martinez is to be promoted, let it be after his return to Zanshaa. Captain Kamarullah may enjoy command of the squadron until that time."

"Martinez will have to leave *Corona* if he is promoted," Mondi observed. "A frigate is a lieutenant-captain's command."

"Perhaps we should give some thought to his next assignment," Lord Chen said. He didn't want to be the one to suggest that Martinez should have another squadron, perhaps one of those now building in the distant reaches of the empire, but he would not object if someone else made the proposal.

"Next assignment?" Pezzini said. "Do you know how many captains are on the list, waiting for commands? We can't jump some junior captain over their heads!"

"He's a very *successful* junior captain," Lady Seekin remarked.

"It will not do to be seen favoring one officer, however worthy," Tork said. "Captain Martinez has already achieved honor enough for one lifetime. There are many posts worthy of an officer of talent, and not all of them involve ship duty."

Lord Chen concealed his dismay. He would have to do some lobbying among the other members of the board.

Lord Roland would expect nothing else.

"How shall we announce the victory?" Mondi asked. "Shall we mention Martinez's contribution as well as Do-faq's?"

Tork raised his long, pale, expressionless head. A whiff of rotting flesh floated on the air as he raised an arm. "I beg the board's indulgence," he said, "but I do not believe an announcement should be made at all."

The others stared at him. "But it's a *victory*," said Lady Seekin. "It's what we've all been waiting for. It's what the *empire* has been waiting for."

News of a victory would give heart to loyalists everywhere, Chen knew. The news would also discourage those inclined to make peace with the Naxids, such as whoever had suppressed those communications at Hone-bar.

"I do not wish the enemy to learn of their defeat at Hone-bar, at least not yet," Tork said. "If they learn that a force exists at Hone-bar sufficient to destroy their squadron, then they learn also that this force *is not defending the capital at Zanshaa.* It might inspire them to attack us *here,* while we are weak. I beg that the board not release this information until such time as the elements of Faqforce arrive here at Zanshaa."

"But wouldn't the Naxids already know?" asked Lady San-torath.

"Not unless some traitor at Hone-bar told them," said Tork. "But if there is treason there, it appears to be at the top. If it hasn't infected the wormhole relay stations, then no messages will go to Magaria or any other rebel stronghold. To the rebel high command it will seem as if their squadron vanished. They may not even see anything wrong with that—they know they don't control communications. It may be some weeks before they grow anxious. And before they know for certain that Kreeku's force was destroyed, I want Faqforce *here,* and guarding the capital."

Lord Chen took a discreet sniff of his perfumed wrist as Tork's vigorous gestures propelled the scent of rotting meat into the room.

"Very well reasoned, my lord," he said. "I agree that the release of the information should be delayed."

That would give Chen a little time to work on the other members of the board in the matter of Martinez's promotion and assignment. Perhaps he could contact his sister Michi and ask for suggestions.

In the meantime, however, the board occupied itself with totting up numbers. Kreeku's ten heavy cruisers could be wiped from the Naxid column of the ledger.

At the moment, Zanshaa was protected by Michi Chen's seven heterogeneous ships from Harzapid, the six bruised survivors of the Battle of Magaria, and several hundred decoys—missiles configured to resemble a large vessel on radar, and which might absorb at least some of the enemy's offensive power before being blown to bits.

But the six battered ships from Magaria were at the moment practically useless, since they needed to dock with Zanshaa's ring station in order to undergo repairs, to replace their depleted missile batteries, and to take aboard Lord Eino Kangas, the new fleet commander the board had finally appointed after much wrangling. Even then *Bombardment of Delhi* was probably too damaged to fight without spending months in dock. That was why Faqforce was crucial: Dofaq's fifteen ships would more than double the capital's defense. But of those fifteen, Martinez's eight ships of the light squadron had likewise expended most of their ammunition at Hone-bar, and would likewise have to decelerate, dock, and replenish.

Once that was done, the defenders would have twenty-five ships—or twenty-six, if you counted *Delhi*—still decisively outnumbered by the thirty-five ships last seen at Magaria. The odds against the loyalists were even worse if the eight Naxid ships last seen at Protipanu joined the Naxid main body—and why wouldn't they? Zanshaa was the whole war. Once the Naxids were in command of the Zanshaa system, the government on the ground would have no choice but to capitulate under the threat of antimatter fire rained from above.

"We *must* win," Mondi muttered, and drew snarling lips back from his fangs.

Lord Chen felt weariness seep into his mind like spring meltwater into the soil, slowing and chilling his thoughts. They had been over these figures meeting after meeting. "This business of replenishing ships' missiles takes far too long," he said. "A month or more to decelerate, time in dock, a month or more to get up to speed so that you're not a sitting duck when the enemy shows up."

"At least the enemy is under the same handicap," Mondi said.

"The Fleet is not designed for this sort of war," said Tork. Despair edged his chiming tones.

The Fleet was designed to sit in space and bombard helpless populations, or to make overwhelming surprise attacks on barbarians whose level of technology was lower than that of the empire. The Fleet had *not* been designed to fight another fleet with the same technology and tactics, let alone one with advantage in numbers.

"Why can't we just load up a big cargo ship with missiles?" Chen asked. "Accelerate it and just keep it in orbit around the system? Any ship needing a supply of missiles could rendezvous with it and resupply. They wouldn't have to drop their velocity to zero to dock with the ring." He thought of *Clan Chen* burning its way toward Zanshaa, just ahead of Faqforce. "I can even supply the ship," he said, then mentally added, *Lord Roland permitting.*

"I've considered this," Tork said. "The enemy will be on our necks before the ship could be modified, loaded, and accelerated to useful velocities."

"We'll have your tender ready in time for the *next* war," Pezzini added, teeth biting down on his sarcasm.

"What if the enemy doesn't come on schedule?" Lady Seekin asked. "What if they attack and we beat them? Wouldn't it be useful to have missile reloads ready at hand, so that we could pursue them?"

Tork's long, mournful face remained, as always, expressionless, but there was a profound silence before he raised his head to gaze at the others. "I can't help but think that this war will change the way the Fleet operates. After this war, I don't see that our ships will spend so much of their time in dock, where they're vulnerable to rebellion and mutiny. Some of them, certainly, must be kept in orbit, where they can be useful in an emergency. And these tenders could be a part of that scheme, even if they're completed too late for the decisive battle of this war."

"We need *warships*," someone said. "If we're going to spend imperial funds, let's buy something that will kill Naxids."

"When a warship is in dock taking on supplies it isn't able to kill *anything*," Lady Seekin said. "I think this could work." She looked up at Lord Chen. "Thank you, my lord, for a very useful idea."

Lord Chen was calculating how much of this work he could shift to the Martinez family shipyards at Laredo. Not many—they were already stuffed with government contracts.

He'd consult with Lord Roland.

And then he'd speak to some other friends. People who might be very grateful for a contract or two.

Kamarullah issued few commands to the squadron over his first few days. When repairs were completed on his two damaged ships, he increased acceleration toward Zanshaa. Orders for minor course changes came after the wormhole transition.

The first attempt by Martinez to make use of Sula's formula, with ships simulated in *Corona*'s computer and programmed to make use of Sula's tactics, succeeded only in crashing the display. Shankaracharya gave the opinion that this wasn't Sula's fault, but the fault of the program, which wasn't flexible enough to absorb Sula's innovations.

Another attempt was made: Martinez, Vonderheydte, Shankaracharya, and Kelly each commanded a ship in a simulation, battling a squadron commanded by Dalkeith and using conventional tactics. The four ships using Sula's tactics had their course changes programmed in by hand rather than by running it through the simulator. This approach showed promise, and the battle was beginning to look interesting when Vonderheydte's ship vanished from its place in the simulation and reappeared clean on the other side of the virtual "universe," having made an unscripted transition of a sort that was not, so far as was known, permitted in nature. The participants had barely recovered from this surprise when Shankaracharya's ship made a similar leap.

The simulation software seemed to have a good many more limitations than anyone had suspected.

"We'll have to try it with actual ships," Vonderheydte said.

Martinez looked down at his supper, one of Alikhan's casseroles a bit the worse for gravity. Macaroni stood up to high gees very well until the point when you cooked it.

"I no longer command the squadron," Martinez pointed out.

"There's another problem," said Dalkeith. "Whoever heard of a fleet maneuver in which the outcome wasn't determined in advance? No commander's going to call for such a thing—they'd look like idiots if the wrong side won."

In silence they contemplated the enormity of a senior officer calling for maneuvers this radical, and the colossal loss of dignity that would result when things didn't go as expected. Dalkeith's seemed a conclusive argument.

"Well," Kelly said, musing on her glass of wine, "what if we don't *say* it's a maneuver? It can be called an 'experiment.' The whole *point* of experiments is that no one knows for certain how they'll turn out."

Martinez blinked. Stale olive oil wafted to him from his plate. "Worth a try," he judged.

He sent a message to Do-faq, along with Sula's formula and a description of the limitations of the standard tactical simulation. He also suggested that an experiment, rather than a maneuver, would be the best way to test the innovations. Do-faq sent a polite reply saying that he and his tactical officer would review the innovations, and Martinez assumed it would end there.

Martinez also sent a copy of the message to Kamarullah. Kamarullah did not reply beyond a routine acknowledgment from his comm officer.

Five days into his tenure, Kamarullah finally called for a maneuver—a maneuver out of the old playbook, the ships flying closely together and linked by laser into a shared virtual environment. Martinez shrugged and assumed that his theories, and Sula's, would remain in obscurity until one or both of them reached flag rank. But no sooner had the maneuver started than Do-faq's ships, some ten light-minutes behind and visible on the navigation displays, began to separate, one division maintaining a rigid formation while the other formed in a looser group at a distance, a group in which the relative positions of the ships were constantly shifting.

"Screens," Martinez told his sensor operators, "I want that maneuver—that *experiment*—recorded."

Martinez didn't believe for a moment that this was spontaneous. Do-faq was proving even more devious a service infighter than Martinez had suspected. Do-faq had waited for Kamarullah to call a maneuver—he must have partisans within the light squadron, among the captains—and then he'd called his own for the same moment. His staff must have been working overtime to put this together, to show Do-faq's commitment to tactical innovation while Kamarullah was putting his squadron through the same old stodge.

Do-faq had placed his bet in history's sweepstakes, and the bet was on Martinez.

Martinez felt the glow in his heart for days.

As if the Battle of Hone-bar had somehow liberated the frigate from a month-long jinx, *Corona* performed flawlessly in Kamarullah's maneuvers. The glow in Martinez's heart brightened.

Reviewing the recordings of Do-faq's experiment, Martinez felt the pulse of triumph along his nerves, a sense that this might be the start of something sensational, that might in fact be perfectly brilliant. Squadron Commander Do-faq obligingly sent Martinez a recording of his maneuver, one that included tracks of the virtual missiles the ships had "fired" during the exercise, and recordings of the equally virtual defensive laser and antiproton fire. Even though the firing had been simulated, they seemed to suggest that the looser, flexible formation gave a decided advantage to the side that used it.

Immensely cheered by this, Martinez turned his mind to another set of recordings entirely, the recordings he'd made of Kamarullah's communications during the battle, those in which he questioned Martinez's judgment and tried to take command of the squadron. There were a number of things Martinez could do with the recordings. He could, for instance, send them to the Fleet Control Board along with a complaint, which he was reasonably certain would result in the end of Kamarullah's career.

He could erase the messages, which would be the generous thing to do. Kamarullah was already an object of hilarity as the man who superceded a successful commander in the hours after a battle: was it quite so necessary for Martinez to push him over a cliff as well?

Or he could simply leave them where they were, in the recordings of the battle that he would in time turn into Fleet Records Office. The messages would become part of the official record, where they would be found by anyone interested in the battle and with the proper access. There might well be repercussions for Kamarullah's career at some point, but Martinez's finger wouldn't be so conspicuously on the trigger when Kamarullah went down.

Martinez debated the matter with himself for some time. He didn't like Kamarullah, but he told himself to put personal feelings aside.

Though personal feelings aside, he *still* didn't like Kamarullah.

If he sent the messages on to the Fleet Control Board, that would be a deliberate act aimed at finishing Kamarullah for good and all. Kamarullah would remain in the service—officers were desperately needed—but he'd be stuck in a desk job somewhere and he'd never see promotion. Martinez couldn't help but be satisfied at the picture.

But what would happen to Martinez? He would become known as the sort of officer who blew up other officers' careers. Kamarullah might have friends or patrons in the service who would be in a position to take revenge on his behalf.

On the other hand, if he erased the recordings, would Kamarullah be grateful? Would he use his influence to help Martinez advance in the service?

Martinez thought not. If Martinez erased the recordings, Kamarullah would continue in command of Light Squadron 14, though it was likely that—if Do-faq's report offered anything like justice—Martinez would be promoted out of the squadron, either to another ship or to a squadron command of his own, and then he wouldn't have to worry about Kamarullah again.

Martinez looked at his options, his uncertainty tipping the balance one way, then another.

And then he asked himself the question: *If we were in combat, would I feel safer if Kamarullah were in charge?*

The answer to that question came very quickly, with a chill and a start of horror.

He would keep his ammunition against Kamarullah in case it looked as if Light Squadron 14 might actually engage the enemy under Kamarullah's command.

But otherwise he would make no move. He would see what developed in reaction to his success at the Battle of Magaria.

And, until then, he would enjoy Kamarullah's silence.

It was four days before Kamarullah ordered another maneuver, and during that time both he and Martinez were privileged to witness a series of daily experiments by Do-faq's squadron. Again Kamarullah's maneuver was a standard exercise out of the textbook. Again *Corona* distinguished itself with a flawless performance.

It was afterward that Kamarullah dropped the bombshell. In a message to the captains of his squadron, Kamarullah in a toneless voice read an order from the Fleet Control Board, requiring all ships to Zanshaa to dock at Zanshaa's ring, at which point both officers and enlisted would debark and be replaced by fresh crews.

"Are they *insane*?" Martinez wanted to shriek. To replace the only crews in the whole fleet with experience of victory and replace them by people who knew *nothing*? Admittedly the squadron's crews were beaten down from their month of acceleration, but the Control Board was throwing away all his men had learned.

And they were throwing away *Martinez*! The only officer who had given them a victory! What could those people be thinking?

On receipt of the message, Martinez stalked to his office and sat in seclusion with a bottle of brandy, but two swallows made him realize he was too angry to spend his time wallowing in misery. He locked the bottle back in its cabinet and instead dictated and sent an angry letter to his brother, Roland.

He doubted it would do any good, but Roland was at least a safe custodian of his rage.

"And here are the two affidavits testifying to my identity," said Sula. She produced the documents, written as law required on special stiff paper that would remain legible in the archives for at least a thousand years. She handed the papers to Mr. Wesley Weckman, the glossy young man who managed the trust department of the bank where Lady Sula's funds had been kept since the execution of her parents.

Now that she had reached her majority at the age of twenty-three, it would normally require only a signature and a thumbprint to release the funds, but the pad of Sula's thumb had been burned away during an accident with one of the

Delhi's heat-exchange pipes shortly after the Battle of Magaria. Testament from higher authority was therefore required.

Weckman glanced at the signatures. "Your commanding officer," he said, "and . . ." His eyebrows lifted. "Lord Durward Li. Well, they should know you if anyone does." His eyes turned to Sula. "Of course, it's a bit redundant after all your appearances on video."

Bombardment of Delhi had at last returned to Zanshaa after fifty long days of deceleration. On docking with the ring station, the old crew had been relieved while a new crew trooped on board, most of them trooping right off again when it was clear to the new officers that *Delhi* was in as bad a state as the old crew had been reporting all along. Under a skeleton crew, *Delhi* pushed off from the ring station and began an acceleration burn for Preowyn, where it would undergo a complete rebuild before rejoining the fleet.

The old crew, leaving the ship, wearily said their farewells and then dragged themselves into their dens like wounded animals. Each had been given a month's leave. Sula spent over an hour drowsing in a hot bath, then ten hours collapsed on a bed in the hostel the Fleet maintained for officers in transit. The next day, her body still staggered with its good fortune in avoiding high gravities for so long, she dropped down the skyhook to the surface of the planet, where she took the shuttle to the capital. Another dormitory room had been reserved for her in the Commandery, where she was to receive a decoration from Fleet Commander Lord Tork as soon as she could replace her borrowed jumpsuits with proper uniforms.

Arrangements had been made with a tailor ahead of time, the tailor originally introduced to her by Martinez and who had once replaced a set of uniforms that had been sent off to Felarus without her, and which had presumably been blown to bits along with most of the Third Fleet. The tailor had all Sula's measurements from the previous visit and the uniforms awaited only the final fitting. Sula was amused to discover that her chest measurement had increased, a result of the extra muscle packed around her ribs to help her breathe against the force of increased gravities.

For the actual ceremony she stood in the Commandery's Hall of Ceremony, braced at attention in her new viridian full-dress uniform. Lord Tork hung about her neck the Nebula Medal with Diamonds, while she fought to keep her face properly stoic as the stench of rotting flesh came off the fleetcom in waves. A pair of Lai-own aides replaced her sublieutenant's shoulder boards with those of a full lieutenant. The citation was vague in its description of the circumstances in which she had destroyed the five enemy ships— no one was yet admitting that, her own actions aside, the Battle of Magaria was a hideous defeat.

As if people hadn't long since drawn their own conclusions.

Because live heroes were rare in this war, the video of the medal ceremony had been repeated almost hourly on all video channels since, and Sula, on her walk to the bank this morning, had received a number of curious looks and a few congratulations from total strangers. If she presented affidavits to the trust manager, it was because the law required it.

While Weckman tapped silently at the glowing characters in his desk, Sula sat in the deep green leather bank chair and inhaled the delicate scent of old money growing even older.

"What will you want done with the balance?" Weckman said. "Unless of course you intend to take it all in cash."

Sula looked at him. "*Have* people been withdrawing their funds in cash?"

Weckman raised an eyebrow. "You'd be surprised at the names."

Converting their fortunes into convertible things, Sula thought, misquoting herself. Taking their assets to the more shadowy parts of the empire to await the bright sun of peace.

She wondered if Lord Durward Li was one of those carrying a fortune in his pillowcase. When she'd visited the Li

Palace the day before to pay a condolence call on the death of his son and to ask him to provide the affidavit, she'd found he had discovered a need to visit family properties in the Serpent's Tail, and was closing his house.

"I don't need the cash just yet," Sula said. "But I'd like the money available."

"Standard account, then." Weckman's fingers tapped the glowing surface of his desktop. "We have other accounts that offer higher rates of interest, should you wish to commit the money for longer periods of time."

She offered him a slight smile. "I don't think so."

He nodded. "You'd know better than I. Personally I'm hoping that my application for a transfer to Hy-Oso comes through within the next few days."

"Hy-Oso's a long way out," Sula commented.

"Bankers must go where the money goes. And a lot of the money is leaving Zanshaa." He touched the desktop, and new lights burned in its surface. "To open the new account we'll need your signature, a password, and the print of your *left* thumb."

Sula complied and bade Wesley Weckman a pleasant farewell. As she left the bank and stepped into the bright spring sunshine, she felt the tension that had followed her for years fall away from her like a long wave.

For she was not, of course, the real Caroline Sula. Lady Sula had died in murky circumstances on Spannan years ago, and another, a girl named Gredel, had stepped into her place hoping that the circumstances would remain forever murky.

And that other, having burned away the thumbprint that threatened to betray her identity, was now in possession of the real Lady Sula's money.

And now the woman called Caroline Sula, decorated and celebrated and now of modest fortune, passed down the sloping street. The touch of the sunlight caused her to smile, and the fresh air of spring, so unlike the canned air of the *Delhi,* to exult.

* * *

Sula walked along the Boulevard of the Praxis, past the famous statue of The Great Master Delivering the Praxis to
Other Peoples. Over the prow-shaped head of the Shaa, his
arm thrusting out a tablet with the text of the Universal Law
graven upon it, was an accidental halo, the thin silver arc of
Zanshaa's accelerator ring, brilliant in the dark green sky,
the same viridian shade as Sula's uniform tunic.

Sula continued past the statue to the ornate mass of the
Chen Palace, all mellow beige stone and the strange winged
gables of the Nayanid style, separated from the street by a
narrow, geometrically perfect formal garden. Sula rang the
bell, then gave the footman her name and asked for Lady
Terza Chen. Sula waited in a drawing room and examined an
exquisite porcelain swan while the footman queried to see if
Lady Terza was present.

Lady Terza, the daughter and heir of Lord Chen, had been
engaged to Lord Durward's son and Sula's captain, Lord
Richard Li, killed at Magaria. The Li family had once been
clients of the Sulas, but after the fall of Lord Sula had become clients of the Chens instead. Both the Lis and the
Chens had been kind to Sula, presumed a penniless, friend-
less Peer who had endured disgrace and the hideous execution of her parents.

She turned at the sound of a quiet step, and saw Terza enter. The heiress of Clan Chen was tall and slim, with wide al-
mond eyes and beautiful black hair that poured past her
shoulders like a lustrous river of sable. She wore soft gray
trousers and a pale blouse, and over that a short dark jacket
with white mourning ribbon threaded among the frills and
fringe.

Terza walked toward Sula with an unhurried grace that
spoke of centuries of quiet breeding, and reached out a hand
to clasp Sula's own.

"Lady Sula." Her voice was low and liquid, and it floated

in the air like a soothing incense. "It's wonderful that you've come. You must be so busy."

"I'm on leave, actually. I wanted to express my condolences over the death of Lord Captain Li."

There was a subtle shift in Lady Terza's eyes, and her mouth tautened slightly. "Yes," she said, "thank you." She took Sula's arm. "Shall we go to the garden?"

"Certainly."

They walked over echoing marble floors. "Shall I ring for tea? Or wine?"

"Tea please."

"Oh—" Terza was startled. "I forgot you don't drink. Sorry."

"That's all right." She patted the arm that held hers. "No need to remember everything. That's why we have computers."

The garden was in the center of the great quadrangle that was the palace, overhung by the winged gables of the main building and featuring a gazebo of glittering crystal facets. Spring flowers—tulips, tougama, lu-doi—were arranged in bright patterns and rows, separated by neat ankle-high hedges. The still air was heavy with the scent of blossoms. Since the day was warm, Terza avoided the gazebo and chose a table that consisted of a single long strand of brass-colored alloy artfully woven into a series of spirals. She and Sula sat on chairs similarly constructed: Sula found hers springy but comfortable. Terza ordered tea with her personal communicator.

Sula looked at her and wondered where to begin. *I saw your fiancé die*, though typical of her style, was nonetheless an awkward opening. Fortunately Terza knew a more suitable way into the conversation.

"I've saw you on video," she said. "I know my father wanted to be present at the ceremony, but there was an important vote coming up in the Convocation."

"Tell him I appreciate the thought."

"And let me offer my congratulations as well." Her cool eyes glanced at the Nebula ribbon on Sula's tunic, with its flashing little diamond. "I'm sure it's well deserved. My father tells me that what you did was actually quite spectacular."

"I was lucky," Sula said, shrugging. "Others weren't." Then, feeling she'd been too blunt, she added, "At least death is quick, in battle. No one on *Dauntless* would have felt a thing. I saw it happen and . . . well, it was fast."

And that, too, was too blunt, though Terza seemed to take it well enough.

"I heard from Lord Durward that you called to give him your condolences," she said. "That was good of you."

"He was kind to me." She looked at Terza. "So were you."

Terza dismissed the compliment with a wave of her elegant hand. "You were Richard's friend from childhood. I did nothing, really, but welcome you as one of his friends."

But for someone, like Sula, who for so many years had no real friends—and who was not in any case the same human being Lord Richard remembered from childhood—the gesture had called forth astounded, unforgettable gratitude.

"Lord Richard was good to me as well," Sula said. "He would have given me a lieutenancy if he could—and maybe I'm not wrong if I think that was your idea."

Terza glanced toward a spray of purple blossoms near her right hand. "Richard would have thought of it if I hadn't."

"He was a good captain," Sula said. "His crew liked him. He looked after us, and he talked to everybody. He was very good at keeping the crew cheerful and at their work." *And his eyes crinkled nicely when he smiled.*

"Thank you," Terza said softly, her eyes still cast down. A servant came with the tea and departed. The scent of jasmine floated from the cups—venerable Gemmelware, she noticed, centuries old, with a pattern of bay leaves.

"How is Lady Amita?" Terza asked, referring to Lord Durward's wife.

"I don't know. I didn't see her."

"She's prostrate, I understand. Richard was her only child. She hasn't been seen since his death." Terza looked away. "She knows that Lord Durward's father will expect him to divorce her and remarry, so that he can father another heir."

"He could hire a surrogate," Sula said.

"Not in a family that traditional. No. It would have to be a natural birth."

"That's sad."

There was a moment of silence while Sula looked with appreciation at the cup and saucer as she raised them in her hands. Jasmine rose to her nostrils. She tasted the tea, and subtle pleasure danced a slow measure along her tongue.

"The Li family is leaving Zanshaa," Sula said. "Going into the Serpent's Tail."

"To be safe, I suppose," Terza said simply. "A lot of people are going. The summer season in the High City is going to be dull."

Sula looked at her. "You're not leaving?"

Terza gave a movement of her shoulders too subtle to properly be called a shrug. "My father has taken a little too . . . *prominent* a part in resisting the Naxids. He knocked down the Lord Senior, you know, in Convocation. He threw rebel Naxids off the Convocation terrace. I'm sure the Naxids have already decided what's going to happen to him—and to me."

Sula looked in surprise into Terza's mild brown eyes.

"If Zanshaa falls," she said, "my father will die, probably very badly unless he cheats them through suicide. I may die with him—or I might be disinherited, as you were, or otherwise punished. There's no point in fleeing, because if Zanshaa falls we lose the war and the Naxids will find me sooner or later." She gave a little shake of her head. "Besides, I want to be here, with my mother. She's . . . a little too high-strung for all of this."

Sula's heart gave an uneasy lurch as Terza, in her calm, low voice, so easily spoke of her own possible annihilation. It bespoke a kind of courage that Sula had not expected—in her former life, as Gredel, she'd known such courage only in criminals, who accepted their own deaths as an inevitable result of their profession. Like Lamey, she thought, Lamey her lover, who was certainly dead by now at the hands of the authorities.

It was not as if she herself hadn't looked at her own death. Everything she'd done since she'd stepped into the soft leather boots of the real Lady Sula had qualified her for nothing but the garrotte of the executioner tightening slowly around her throat. She had publicly claimed the Sula name at Magaria, as she destroyed five enemy ships. "It was Sula who did this!" she'd transmitted. *"Remember my name!"* If the Naxids won the war, they *would* remember. Sula could expect no more mercy than could Lord Chen. The only difference was that she could expect to die in battle, in a blaze of antimatter fire. After all the years of suspense, all the years in which she'd wakened in the middle of the night, clutching her throat in a dream of suffocation, simple extinction was something she didn't fear.

What Terza said next surprised her even more.

"I've admired you," she said, "for the way you've managed to do so well, even though you have no money and no connections. Perhaps—if I'm disinherited instead of killed—you'll have a few tricks to teach me."

Admired. Sula was staggered by the word. "I'm sure you'll do well," she managed.

"I don't have any useful skills like you," Terza judged, and then she smiled. "I could make a living as a harpist."

She played the harp very well, at least insofar as Sula judged these things. "I'm sure you could." And then, more practically. "Your father could give some money to one of his friends—a safe friend—for you to use later. I think that's what my parents did for me, or perhaps their friends just got a little money together and set up a trust."

Terza gave a solemn nod. "I'll suggest that to my father."

"You've discussed this?" Sula asked. A macabre little conversation over evening coffee, perhaps. Or a chat in the kitchen, while Lord Chen brewed up some poison so that he could cheat the public executioner.

"Oh yes," Terza said. She took a deliberate sip from the Gemmelware cup. "I'm the heir. I'll probably be in the Convocation sooner or later, if the war goes well. I have to know things."

And Lord Chen, Sula knew, was on the Fleet Control Board, and knew how the odds favored the Naxids. For over a month he had been staring every minute at his own death and the extinction of his house, the lineage that went back centuries, and then gone about his business.

There was courage there, too. Or desperation.

There was a step behind on the gravel path, and Terza glanced up from her cup. As Sula rose from her chair and turned, her heart gave a leap, and then she realized that the tall man behind Lord Chen wasn't Gareth Martinez after all, but his brother Roland.

"My dear Lady Sula," Chen said as he stepped forward to take her hands. "My apologies. I so wanted to go to the ceremony yesterday."

"Terza explained that you had an important vote."

Chen looked from Sula to Roland and back. "Do you know each other?"

"I haven't met Lord Roland, though of course I know his brother and sisters."

"Charmed," Lord Roland said. He strongly resembled his brother, though a little taller, and he wore his braided, wine-colored coat well. Like Martinez, he retained a strong provincial accent. "My congratulations on your decoration. My sisters think very highly of you."

But not the brother? For a moment bleak despair filled Sula at the fact that Martinez hadn't mentioned her name. And then the hopelessness faded, and she found herself thankful that Martinez *hadn't* told the story of their last encounter, where they had danced and kissed and Sula, thrown into sudden panic by the arrival of a deadly memory, had fled.

"Tell your sisters that I've been thinking of them."

"Would you pay us a call?" Lord Roland suggested. "We're having a party tomorrow night—you'd be very welcome."

"I'd be happy to attend," Sula said. She considered her next comment for a moment, then said, "Lord Roland, have you heard from your brother lately?"

Roland nodded. "Every so often, yes."

"Has something happened, do you know?" Sula asked. "I get a message from him now and then, and—well, the last few messages have been heavily censored. Most of the contents were cut, in fact. But nothing seems to have gone *wrong*—in fact he seems lighthearted."

Lord Roland smiled, and exchanged a glance with Lord Chen.

"Something *has* happened, yes," Chen said. "For various reasons we're not releasing the information yet. But there's no reason to be concerned for Lord Gareth."

Her mind raced. It wasn't a defeat they were hiding, so just possibly it was a victory. And the only reason to hide a victory was to keep the Naxids from finding out, which meant that behind the scenes, somewhere away from Zanshaa, ships were moving, and battles were in the offing, or had already been fought.

"I wasn't concerned, exactly," she said. "Lord Gareth seemed too merry. But the whole business seemed . . . curious."

Chen gave a satisfied smile. "I venture to remark that very soon there may be another award ceremony, and that Lord

Gareth may be in it. But perhaps even that's saying too much."

A victory, then. Joy danced in Sula's mind. Perhaps Martinez had used the new tactics—*her* tactics—to crush the enemy.

"I'll be discreet about the news," Sula said. Who would she tell?

Chen and Lord Roland made their excuses and went to do business. Sula spent an agreeable hour with Terza in the garden, then said farewell and went out into the sun of the High City. Her footsteps took her to the La-gaa and Spacey Auction House, where she spent a few pleasant hours looking at the displays.

The collectible business was booming. People were turning their wealth into, as she'd once put it, convertible things. Jewelry and portable, durable objects—caskets, small tables, paintings and sculpture—were all doing very well.

Porcelain, by contrast, seemed to be dropping in price. Perhaps people considered it too fragile for the uncertain times ahead.

One pot caught Sula's eye: *Ju yao* ware of the Sung dynasty, a pot four palms high, narrow at the base, broad at the shoulders, and a small central spout. Sula's hands lusted to caress the fine crackle of the blue-green glaze. The factory that created the pot existed in Honan for only twenty years before a Tatar invasion wiped it from the Earth. Sula pictured the pot fleeing south before the invaders, packed in straw in a bullock cart, ending in Yangtze exile a thousand li from its place of origin.

The pot had flown much farther in the years since, and was now part of a collection being dispersed. In the current falling market Sula might be able to purchase it for twenty-five thousand zeniths, a sum amounting to perhaps eighty percent of her current fortune.

It would be absurd for her to spend that much. Insane.

And it *was* breakable. The luck that carried it safely from the Tatars, and through the Shaa conquest of Terra, might be run out by now.

But what, she argued with herself, did she have to spend the money on other than herself?

In the end, reluctantly, she withdrew. Sula had decided to be practical.

For the next several days she went hunting for an apartment. So many were fleeing the High City that rates were almost reasonable, and she paid a month in advance for a third-floor place just under the eaves of an old converted palace. The furniture was the bulky, ornate, and ugly Sevigny style, but Sula figured she could live with it till her next posting. The apartment came with a Lai-own fledgling to do the cleaning, and a cook would do meals for an extra few zeniths.

The building was just down a side street from the Shelley Palace, where the Martinez family was staying.

Sula was thinking about Martinez a great deal. Being near him seemed desirable. Having a convenient place where they could retire, a place that was neither a Fleet dormitory nor a palace filled with a gaggle of inquisitive sisters, seemed only practical.

She attended the Martinez's party, and was greeted with cries of welcome. Sula was a celebrity now, a decorated hero, and her presence made the party an occasion. She reacquainted herself with the family—the ambitious Lord Roland, the two formidable older sisters, Vipsania and Walpurga, and the youngest, vivacious sister Sempronia with her absurd fiancé, PJ.

With all their gifts, none of them seemed a patch on the brother who was absent.

That night she lay in the huge Sevigny bed and wondered what it would be like, after all this time, not to be lonely.

The next day, a polite officer from the Courts of Justice delivered the subpoena to her door.

FIVE

Martinez welcomed *Corona*'s new captain with all the grace he could muster, which wasn't much, and then went through the formalities of turning over his captain's key and various other codes. He wanted very much to say, "Try not to get my ship killed," but he didn't. Alikhan had his belongings already packed.

He declined the new captain's civil offer of a dinner, claiming he had an appointment on the planet's surface—and for that matter, he did.

He was going to meet with his brother, his sisters, the Martinez clan's patron Lord Pierre Ngeni—*anyone*, if necessary, up to the Lord Senior of the Convocation, and he would lobby them incessantly until he received an assignment that placed in him command of a ship.

For after a month's leave to recover from the rigors of the journey, Martinez had been told to report to a training school for sensor operators in Kooai, in Zanshaa's southern hemisphere, where he would take command of the post.

A *training school*. The message was infuriating. A warrant officer could do the job as well, probably better.

Martinez intended to get himself into a ship again, if he had to personally hector and lobby everyone going in and out of the door of the Commandery. If he had to personally grab Lord Saïd by the throat and shake him until the old man gave way.

Martinez had already said his farewells to his officers and

crew, so when he left *Corona*'s airlock umbilical he just kept on going. Alikhan had procured him a car and driver, which meant he wouldn't have to wait for one of the trains that rolled along the upper level of Zanshaa's accelerator ring. The car took him to the Fleet Records Office, where he delivered the data foil that contained the log of *Corona*'s journey. The foil contained as well the recordings that might well explode Kamarullah's career, that is if anyone bothered to view them.

Perhaps no one would. Certainly no one seemed very interested in *Corona*'s journey—news of the Battle of Honebar had yet to be released to the public, and the dull-eyed Torminel petty officer who took the data foil seemed far from excited to be meeting one of the Fleet's heroes, and indeed seemed about to drop into slumber as he handed Martinez the receipt.

Martinez, fury warring with his body's pain and great weariness, stuffed the receipt into a pocket and stalked through the translucent automatic doors that led to the anteroom.

And there she was.

The impulse at first was to stare, and then to stagger forward and wrap his arms around Sula's slim body like a shipwrecked mariner clinging to a mast. Fortunately for the dignity of his rank she wasn't receptive to an embrace: she was braced at the salute, shoulders thrown back, chin lifted to expose the throat, the sign of subordination enforced throughout their empire by the Shaa.

He paused for a breathless moment to absorb her beauty, the erect body, the silver-gilt hair worn shoulder-length, framing the face with its pale, translucent complexion and its amused, glittering green eyes. Then he raised the heavy baton of the Golden Orb, topped with its sphere of swirling liquid, and bobbed it in her direction, acknowledging her salute.

"Stand at ease, lieutenant," he said.

"Thank you, my lord." Her brilliant smile showed a de-

gree of conceit, her own smug amusement at the way she'd
surprised him. "You met me, once, when I returned to the
Zanshaa ring. I thought I'd return the compliment."

"It's appreciated." His bodily weariness had vanished under a surge of blood, but his thoughts were still torpid and
his skull was filled with cotton. He was painfully conscious
that she stood before him, brilliant and rested and desirable,
and that anything he said to her was likely to be stupid beyond all credence.

"Shall I join you on your ride to the surface," Sula asked,
"or do you have more business here?"

"My family is expecting me," he said. Stupidly.

"I know," she said. "I've been in touch with them. They
told me when you were arriving."

He and Sula were hovering behind the doors of the Fleet
Records Office, blocking traffic, and then Martinez remembered that he was the senior officer and that it was customary for him to walk through the doors first. He did so. Sula
followed.

Alikhan was already standing by the car, shadowed by the
door flung up like a wing. "To the skyhook," Martinez said.
There was a knowing smile beneath Alikhan's curling mus-
tachio as he handed Sula into the car next to Martinez.

Alikhan and the driver sat in the front, separated by a bar-
rier that one of them tactfully opaqued. Martinez's nerves
tingled with the awareness of Sula's perfume, a scent that
urged his blood to surge a little faster. Sula looked at him as
they settled into their seats. "The rumor—which is pretty
well official, I'll have you know—says that you did something spectacular, and are about to be decorated. But we're
not allowed to know what it was that you did."

Martinez gave a snarl. "It's satisfaction enough to know
that I've served the empire faithfully," he said.

Sula laughed. "I've worked out that you blew up a bunch
of Naxids, and that our superiors don't want the enemy to
know it."

"You'd think the Naxids would have worked it out by now," Martinez said.

"How many enemy *did* you annnihilate, by the way?"

Confident that she would not be broadcasting to the enemy anytime soon, he told her. She raised her golden brows as calculation buzzed behind her eyes. "Interesting," she said. "That means our cause isn't necessarily lost."

"Not necessarily," he said, still glowering with resentment. Sula gave him a curious look.

"Why don't you tell me how you did it?"

So he did. When he finished, he sensed a degree of disappointment behind her congratulations.

"What's wrong?" he said.

"I hoped you'd be able to use my formula."

"Well. As to *that* . . ." He raised his left arm. "Set your display to receive. I'm about to violate another security regulation."

Martinez beamed her the records of Do-faq's series of experiments. "Analyze them to your heart's content," he said, "and let me know what you think."

Sula looked at her sleeve display and smiled. "Yes. Thank you." She gave him a searching look. "You should be pleased as hell about all this, but you're not. So who's pissed in your breakfast?"

A reluctant grin tugged at his lips. "I've lost *Corona.* That's no cause for joy. And then there's my next assignment." About which he enlightened her.

She seemed startled. "What happened? Did you steal some fleet commander's girlfriend?"

"Not that I know of," Martinez said, and then found himself wondering if Kamarullah was by some chance a fleet commander's girlfriend. The mental image caused him to smile. He turned to Sula.

"And *your* next assignment?"

She gave him an annoyed look. "I'm dealing with the ghost of Captain Blitsharts."

Blitsharts had been responsible for their first meeting: Martinez had planned, and Sula executed, a perilous rescue of the famous yachtsman. Who, when rescued, had turned out to be dead.

"Blitsharts?" he said. "Why Blitsharts?"

"The Fleet Court of Inquiry determined his death was accidental. But his insurance company insists it was suicide, and there's a civil trial coming up. I'm to give a deposition, and the Fleet has extended my leave till then." She looked up at him. "After which I will be free. Just in case some celebrated captain wants to request me for his next ship."

Which was an invitation to kiss her if anything was, and he put his arm around her and was about to lean in close when the car came to a halt and the doors popped up with a hydraulic hiss.

Damn. All he had got was a taste of her dizzying perfume and a tingling awareness of the warmth of her skin.

She gave a rueful smile as he withdrew. When he rose from the car, a score of Fleet pulpies snapped to the salute, throats bared. Anyone in uniform—even the Lords Convocate themselves—were required to salute the Golden Orb, which was why Martinez had chosen to carry it. He'd hoped to relieve his feelings of anger and resentment by abusing his privileges with as many senior officers as he could find.

Now the orb was a dreadful inconvenience. He was going to have to spend the day trying not to walk into stiff, braced figures murmuring "Stand at ease" and "As you were," and attracting far more attention to himself and to the beautiful and celebrated Lady Sula than he wanted.

Sula and Alikhan following, Martinez progressed through the stone-stricken mass of Fleet personnel to one of the cars of the train that would take them to the ring station's lower level—a lower level that, just to make things confusing, was actually above Martinez's head.

The Fleet areas of the ring, resolutely unattractive but functional with their docking bays, storage facilities, barracks, schools, and shipyards, tended to obscure the fact that the accelerator ring was one of the great technological miracles of all time. It had been drawing a sun-silvered circle about Zanshaa for nearly eleven thousand years, a symbol of Shaa dominion visible from nearly everywhere on the planet. The lower level of the accelerator ring moved above the planet in geostationary orbit, tethered delicately to the world of Zanshaa by the six colossal cables of the planet's skyhooks. Built atop the lower level was the ring's upper level, which rotated at eight times the speed of the lower in order to provide its inhabitants with normal gravity.

Eighty million people lived on Zanshaa's ring, housed for the most part in areas considerably more attractive than the Fleet districts, and there was room for hundreds of millions more. To these denizens of the upper level, pressed by centrifugal force to the outside of the station ring, the lower level was actually above them. In order to ascend, they boarded a train that was then accelerated down a track in time to be scooped up by a massive ramp and track that dropped with exquisite timing from the geostationary level. Once there, humming electromagnets braked the train to a stop, and the passengers, bobbing in one-eighth gravity and aided by a series of handrails, made their way along a series of ramps to the giant car that would soon drop through Zanshaa's atmosphere to the terminal on its equator.

Without shame Martinez barged into the compartment reserved for senior officers—it was the Golden Orb, not Martinez's modest rank, that provided access. The hoped-for privacy did not materialize. As Martinez entered he saw the baleful look given him from over the shoulder of the other passenger already strapped into his couch, and his heart gave a lurch as he recognized the hawk-nosed visage of the lord inspector of the Fleet, one of the most feared men in the empire.

"Forgive me if I don't stand," said Fleet Commander Lord Ivan Snow in a sandpaper voice. "I don't fancy unwebbing right now." He was in the first row, with a brilliant view through the huge glass window that made up most of the outside wall.

"That's quite all right, my lord," Martinez said. Ducking beneath the low ceiling, he and Sula took couches as far removed from the feared lord inspector as the modest compartment permitted.

"The day isn't working out well," Sula murmured in Martinez's ear as she bent over his couch.

"Part of a ongoing pattern," Martinez answered softly.

"It may interest you to know," said the chief of the Investigative Service, "that the cause of the breakdown in communications that occurred at Hone-bar has been discovered. At the same time that *you,* Captain Martinez, are being decorated and promoted in two days' time, seven traitors will die screaming." Martinez could hear the quiet satisfaction in the lord inspector's voice. "Die screaming," Lord Ivan repeated pleasantly. "I arranged the timing myself."

Martinez was for a moment at a loss for speech. *Promoted?* Finally he managed words.

"Congratulations on . . . a successful investigation, lord inspector," he said.

"And congratulations to you, lord captain, on a timely and successful combat."

Promoted? He had known about the decoration, but this was the first time a promotion had been mentioned.

Then Martinez felt his ire rising. The training school in charge of a full captain was even more absurd than in the hands of an elcap.

He wondered if he dared mention the matter to the lord inspector. The words *die screaming* returned to his mind, and he decided he didn't.

"There's not a lot of point in our talking," Sula said quietly, as the huge elevator car was locked onto the cable. "Why don't you sleep? You look about dead."

"I feel . . ." He was about to say "fine" but he realized that the ease of low gravity, and the comfort of his couch, were about to make a liar out of him. So instead he said, "Good idea," and closed his eyes.

He was asleep before the car dropped out of the accelerator ring and into brilliant sunlight. The growing acceleration that pressed him into his couch was much less than he'd been enduring for the last two months and it failed to wake him. Below, the land blazed with color: brown mountains tipped with white, the light green of the land contrasting with the deeper, more profound green of the sea. The atmosphere was a faint blurring on the edges of the world. The whirlwind of a tropical storm, its white gyre of cloud edged with blue, was thrashing southward from the equator.

Calculations spinning through her mind, Sula watched Do-faq's tactical experiments on her sleeve display.

Martinez woke, his mind fresh, just as the car settled feather-light into its terminal, and the couch swung into its rest position, inverted from where it had been at the start of the journey. He and Sula stepped onto what had, when they'd boarded, been the ceiling, and let the fleet commander precede them from the car. He nodded civilly as he passed.

"And congratulations to you as well, Lady Sula," he said.

"Thank you, my lord."

Martinez, as he followed the old man from the car, suspected that the congratulations may not have had anything to do with Sula's decoration.

Reunited with Alikhan and Martinez's baggage, they took another train to the shuttle terminus, where they boarded the supersonic for the city of Zanshaa. Martinez traded the ticket he'd already reserved for an entire four-seat first-class compartment. Alikhan retained his original seat in second class.

With the Golden Orb, which like a device out of a fairy tale had the power to turn others to stone, Martinez marched to his compartment, installed himself and Sula, and drew down the shades.

Privacy at last.

He sat next to her and tried not to melt beneath the gaze of those green eyes. Martinez took her hand.

"I'm afraid to speak," he said.

She tilted her head. "Why?"

"Because I'm not at my best right now, and I might say something wrong. And then . . ." He sought for words. "And then everything would be spoiled, and you'd walk out of this compartment and I'd never see you again."

He saw the blood rise in her translucent pale skin. Her perfume whirled through his senses. "I forgive you," Sula said. "In advance."

He kissed her hand, her palm, her wrist. He leaned close to kiss her lips, then hesitated.

"I'm not running away," she said.

He laid his lips to hers for the space of three heartbeats. She raised a hand to lightly cup the side of his head. He kissed her again, then had to break away because he realized he'd been holding his breath, and that his dizziness wasn't entirely a result of Sula's nearness.

"What *is* that perfume?" he asked.

Her lips turned up in a smile. "Sandama Twilight."

"What's so special about twilight on Sandama?"

She ventured a little shrug. "Some day we'll go there and find out."

He inhaled deliberately. "I wonder how many pulse points you've applied it to."

Sula tilted her head back and with her hand swept a strand of golden hair from her throat. "You're welcome to find out," she said.

He feasted on her throat for a long, luxurious moment. A shiver ran along her frame. He kissed a path to her ear— bright and flaming—and reached up a hand to lazily undo the top button of her viridian tunic.

Martinez heard the low chuckle as he kissed the hollow of her throat. "Make the most of it," she said. "I think that's the only button you get to open today."

He drew back and looked at her at close range, so close that her long lashes fluttered against his. "Why? It's such a promising start."

Her speech warmed his cheek. "Because you've already admitted that you're not at your best. And I deserve the best."

"That's fair," he admitted, after consideration.

"And besides," she said practically, "I see no point in losing my virtue in a train compartment when I've gone to all the trouble of acquiring such a nice large bed."

Martinez laughed, then kissed her again. "I'll look forward to the bed. But in the meantime I hope to convince you that train compartments have their advantages."

She smiled. "You're welcome to try."

He caressed her with his lips, brushing her cheek and mouth and throat. The train began a smooth acceleration, without bumps or lurches, that would take it to supersonic speed on its way to the capital. His hands floated over her body, and he was rewarded with a sudden intake of breath, a shuddering gasp, and she clutched his hand with her own. And then, as they lay side by side with the warmth of her white-gold hair soft against his cheek, he felt tension enter her body.

"What's the matter?" he asked.

She turned away, took his hand, and lay against his shoulder, placing his hand around her waist. Through the window he could see improbably green equatorial countryside blur past. "Forgive me," she said. "I'm very nervous. I thought if I could meet you and . . . sort of take charge—"

"It would be easier?"

"Yes."

Martinez nuzzled her hair. "Take your time. I don't want you to run out that door."

She raised his hand to her lips and kissed it. "That's not it.

I promise I won't run again. But I've realized that you *are* going to have to take charge sooner or later, because I'm not going to know what to do."

His start of surprise was so violent that she sat up and turned to him. "You're a virgin?" he said.

"Oh no." Her tone was amused. "But it's been years. A very long time since I had a . . ."

"A man?"

"A boy." Sadness entered her eyes. "A boy I didn't love. I think he's dead now." She slowly turned away from him, and settled back against his shoulder. He caressed her hair.

An intuition flashed along his nerves. "You were drinking then?" he asked. On their last disastrous outing she'd told him that she once had a problem with alcohol.

There was a hesitation before Sula answered. "Yes," she said. "There are things in my past that I'm not proud of. You should know that."

Martinez kissed the top of her head and contemplated her history and his own responsibilities. Her parents had been executed—skinned alive—when Sula was on the verge of adolescence, her family's homes and wealth confiscated by the State, and Sula herself had been fostered out on a remote provincial world. Certainly any one of these incidents constituted a traumatic enough shock to send her reeling toward the erratic solace of alcohol and sex. It was a tribute to her character that she'd been able to draw herself out of the sink of despair into which she'd been swept.

But that meant that her only knowledge of love was confined to drunken adolescent couplings, perhaps with boys who had deliberately made her drunk for the particular purpose of coupling with her. Sula had apparently never known the ease and pleasures of bed, the give and take, the gift of laughter and the fire of a proper caress . . .

Did not know love at all, he realized.

And the boy, she said, was probably dead. So even that attachment, whatever it was, had ended badly.

Martinez took a long breath. She *did* deserve his best. He would have to try to give it to her, in that big bed of hers.

And then a realization struck him and he laughed.

"What's so funny?" Sula asked.

"I'm just realizing that I've lost one of my chief weapons," he said. "I can't slip you a few drinks to get you relaxed."

Her laughter rose bright in the air. He kissed her ear, and they sat for a while, her head on his shoulder, while mountains rose on the other side of the window and danced jagged along the horizon, then fell away again. They chatted of entertainments, of a video they had shared, the comedian Spate in *Spitballs!* They laughed over their memories of Spate's famous Mushroom Dance, and rejoiced in their mutual taste for low humor.

Martinez ordered a meal, and the attendant arrived to set the small table in place, adding white linen, silver, a small vase with flowers, and—to judge by Sula's expression—some rather inferior porcelain. Sula sat opposite Martinez, her tunic properly buttoned. With the meal, Martinez shared Sula's bottle of mineral water.

The train raced on, through forests and over broad rivers; its flanges, placed with precision along its flanks, pulsing out interfering sound waves that canceled its sonic boom. More mountain ranges rose and then fell behind, and the train began slowing as it approached its destination.

Sula and Martinez embraced, kissed, and watched as Zanshaa's Lower Town, the huge expanse radiating on all sides of the High City, sped past the window. After the machine came to a halt in the station, Martinez folded Sula in his arms one last time before leaving the privacy of the compartment.

The terminus was within easy walking distance of the funicular railway that took them to Zanshaa's acropolis. As they rose to the High City, Martinez looked through the funicular's transparent walls at the blue stained-glass dome of the old Sula Palace, lost now to the Sula heir, and wondered what passed through Sula's mind when she viewed it.

"Why don't you take me home in your taxi?" Sula suggested. "That way you'll know where I live."

If Martinez hadn't been so weary, he probably would have thought of that himself.

To his delight, Martinez found that Sula lived just behind the Shelley Palace, the colossal old pile his family rented in the capital. He suspected that was not an accident.

"When you have a free moment," Sula said, "come up and see the bed."

She kissed him quickly on the cheek and slid from the taxi before he could put his arms around her. Martinez restrained the impulse to lunge after her, and instead let the Cree driver swing around the corner to halt in front of the Shelley Palace, where Martinez's family were waiting.

Martinez's brothers and sisters had realized that he would be exhausted, and hadn't planned anything more elaborate than a simple family supper for the night of his arrival. Roland, his older brother, placed Martinez at the head of the table, in the place of honor. He was pleased to be wearing civilian dress for the first time in months. Vipsania and Walpurga, handsome and impeccably dressed even on this informal occasion, sat next to each other on Martinez's right hand, one in a red gown, the other in sea-green. The youngest sister, Sempronia, sat next to Roland on the left.

At the far end of the table, next to Sempronia, was her fiancé PJ Ngeni, a cousin of Lord Convocate Ngeni, whose family represented Martinez interests. PJ was suspected of having lost his money in a series of debaucheries, and his engagement was a stratagem on the part of Clan Ngeni to relieve themselves of an expensive and useless relation. One stratagem deserved another, Martinez had felt, and had devised a plan of his own. Sempronia and Lord PJ were engaged, to be sure, but the engagement would be a *long* one—there would be no marriage as long as Sempronia stayed in school, and Sempronia would be in school for as many years as was necessary for the Martinez family to use the access granted by the Ngenis to wedge themselves into Zanshaa's highest strata of Peers. And once that happened, PJ would be returned to whence he came, there to remain a debit on the ledgers of his clan.

PJ had not yet realized, apparently, that the engagement was nothing more than a ruse, and throughout supper he paid Sempronia a series of elaborate courtesies, courtesies to which Sempronia replied with a graceful inclination of her head and a kind, condescending smile, a smile that vanished whenever she glanced down the table at Martinez.

Sempronia hadn't forgiven Martinez for shackling her, even temporarily, to this human debacle. Especially when her affections appeared to be genuinely engaged by Nikkul Shankaracharya, *Corona*'s former lieutenant.

Martinez found himself uninterested in Sempronia's problems. She, after all, only had to put up with one imbecile. He had the whole Fleet Control Board.

"You'll be decorated and promoted in two days' time," Roland said. "At the same time your victory at Hone-bar will be announced throughout the empire." He gave a sardonic smile. "It'll be Do-faq's victory officially, and he'll be promoted and decorated too—but the people who matter will know who's really responsible, and since Do-faq is still with his squadron, *you'll* be the one seen on video in the Hall of Ceremony. . . ." Roland gave a pleased nod. "After that, we can start pressing to get you a command. It will seem special pleading until everyone realizes you're the only officer in the Fleet to be decorated twice for actions against the enemy. Then giving you a real job will only seem good sense."

Martinez, who personally thought that the special pleading should have started ages ago, nodded as if he agreed, and then realized that his brother had no post whatever within the Fleet or the government, and shouldn't be aware of any of these details at all.

"How do you know this?" he asked.

"From Lord Chen. He and I have been . . . associated in an enterprise."

Martinez looked at his brother. "So how porous *is* the Fleet Control Board?"

Roland shrugged. "*Everything's* porous. If you're on the inside, you can find out anything you want."

"And you're on the inside now?"

Roland looked down at his plate and drew his knife delicately across his filet. "Not quite. But we're getting there."

"If you're so well connected," Martinez said, "perhaps you can let me know why I don't have a new command *now.*"

Roland paused with his fork partway to his mouth. "I haven't bothered to inquire. But I imagine it's the usual story."

"Which is?"

"You're better than they are." While Martinez stared in surprise Roland popped the filet into his mouth, chewed, and swallowed. "You know the tale—Peers are supposed to be, well, peers. Equals. When one stands out above the others it demonstrates that there's something wrong with the system, and the people in charge of the system don't care for that. Remember, the nail that gets hammered down is the one that sticks out.

"You see," reaching for the wine and refilling Martinez's glass, "while you were at the academy preparing for your career as a hero, father and I put our heads together and worked out why he failed when *he* came to Zanshaa. And the answer seemed to be that he was too rich and too talented."

"He's richer now," Martinez pointed out.

"He could buy the whole High City and barely notice the loss. But it's not for sale . . . to *him*." Roland gave his brother a significant look. "He was the nail that stuck out. He got hammered, and the people here dusted their hands of him and forgot that he ever existed. So now his children are here, and we're being a lot more quiet about our gifts than he was." Roland filled his own glass and raised it, glancing over the dining room. "We could have our own palace here, a brilliant house built and decorated in up-to-the-instant tastes, first-rate all the way. But we don't, we rent this old heap."

He gave Martinez a penetrating look. "What we need to avoid aren't so much errors of judgment, but of taste. We could have a ball every week, and sponsor concerts and plays at the Penumbra, and I could wear the latest cravats and our sisters the most extravagant gowns, and we could get into the yachting circuit and sponsor charities and . . . well, you know the sort of thing."

"I'm not sure I do," Martinez said. "I'm only the nail that sticks out."

Roland smiled thinly. "But you're sticking out in war-time—and *that,* I think, is all right. The family can move fast now, because the war is so big that no one's paying attention to the likes of us. And when the war is over, we'll be a part of the structure here, and that will be all right, because we'll have got in without anyone noticing us at all." He frowned. "There may be a backlash after the war, of course. We'll have to be prepared to ride that out. That's why you'll want all the rank and honor you can achieve now, while they still need you."

Martinez glanced down the table at PJ, who was as usual paying elaborate court to Sempronia, and presumably un-able to hear the low conversation at the opposite end of the table. "Clever of you to use Sempronia the way you did," Roland said in Martinez's ear. "And PJ is, well, so *perfect* in his way . . ."

PJ apparently heard his name spoken, and he looked up— long-headed, balding, dressed with perfect taste, and on his face an expression of amiable vacuity. Roland smiled and raised a glass.

"So glad you could come tonight, PJ," he said.

A bright smile flashed across the table, and PJ raised his own glass. "Thank you, Roland! Happy to be here!"

Martinez raised his own glass and pretended he couldn't see the face that Sempronia was making at him.

It was Sempronia who took his arm just after he'd excused himself and began trudging up the main stair to his bed. He turned to her with pleasure: she was his favorite sister, with fair hair and gold-flecked hazel eyes, features so unlike the dark hair and brown eyes of the rest of the family. She was lively and outgoing, unlike her sisters, who had adopted a premature gravity that made them seem older than they were.

"Haven't I been good to PJ tonight, Gare?" she asked. "Haven't I been a good girl?"

Martinez sighed. "What do you want, Proney?"

She looked at him brightly. "Can't you take PJ off my hands tomorrow?"

He looked at him. "I've just got back from a *war,* for all's sake. Can't you get someone else to do it?"

"No, I can't." Sempronia leaned close to him and spoke in a whisper. "You're the only one who knows about Nikkul. *He* just got back from a war, too, and I want to be with him."

Through his weariness he managed a glare. "What if I have an assignation of my own?"

She gave him a look of amazement. *"You?"* she asked.

No man, Martinez reflected, is a hero to his sister.

"You just lost points, Proney," he warned.

"Besides," Sempronia said, "PJ *wants* to see you. He admires you."

"Enough to give up an afternoon of your company?"

She squeezed his arm. "Just once, Gare. That's all I ask."

"I'm very, very tired," Martinez said. Which was why, in the end, Sempronia beat him down. A few minutes later, he called PJ's number from his room and left a message asking if PJ would like to join him tomorrow afternoon for, well, whatever.

"I was so glad you called," PJ said cheerfully. "I'd been hoping to speak to you, actually." He and Martinez were dining in the Seven Stars Yacht Club, one of the three most exclusive yacht clubs in the empire.

The club was the sort of place that would almost certainly have blackballed Martinez had he attempted to join, but which accepted PJ without question even though he'd never once flown a yacht. In the foyer was a glass case containing mementoes of Captain Ehrler Blitsharts, the yachtsman that Martinez and Sula had attempted to rescue—*had* rescued, though Blitsharts was dead by the time Sula finally grappled to his *Midnight Runner.* Among the pictures, trophies, and oddments of clothing was a studded collar belonging to Blitsharts' celebrated dog, Orange, who had died with him.

The club's restaurant was famous, fluted onyx pillars supporting its tented midnight-blue ceiling, its surface perforated by star-shaped cutouts behind which gold lights shimmered. Scale models of famous yachts hung beneath the side arches and gleaming trophies sat in niches. The waitron, a Lai-own so elderly she shed feathery hairs behind her as she walked down the lanes between the tables, visibly shuddered at the sound of Martinez's barbarous accent.

"I thought seriously about becoming a yachtsman," Martinez told PJ, glancing at the gleaming silver form of Khesro's *Elegance* as it rotated beneath the nearest arch. "I'd qualified as a pinnace pilot and was doing well in the Fleet races. But somehow . . ." He shrugged. "It never seemed to happen."

"I'd put you up for membership if you ever changed your mind," PJ said. "That would have to be after the war, of course. No races being held at present."

"Of course," Martinez said. He doubted any amount of

heroism and celebrity could offset the disadvantages of his provincial birth. If he couldn't even impress a *waitron* . . .

He looked at PJ. "So how did you become a member? You haven't raced yachts, have you?"

"No, but grandfather did, ages ago. He put me up for membership." PJ sipped his cocktail, then swiped at his thin little mustache with a forefinger. "And it's useful, you know," he nodded, "if you like to wager. Listening to the conversation in the club room, you can pick up a lot of information about which pilot is off his game or who's having a run of luck, who's just had his maneuvering thrusters redesigned . . ."

"Did you make a lot of money that way?"

"Mmm." PJ's long face grew longer. "Not much, no."

The two contemplated PJ's financial state for a moment, one gloomy and the other lighthearted, and then the elderly waitron brought their plates, the meal that would have been called "dinner" on a ship but was "luncheon" here. The summery flavor of a green herb—Martinez didn't know which one—floated up from his pâté. The waitron departed, leaving behind a cloud of floating hair.

PJ dipped into his soup, then brightened and looked at Martinez.

"I wanted to say that I think you're just the most brilliant person," he said.

Martinez was surprised by this declaration. "That's good of you," he said, and put a bit of the pâté on a crust of bread.

"You've done wonders in the war, right from the first day. From the first hour."

Martinez straightened a little as vanity plucked up his chin. Praise from an ignoramus was, after all, still praise.

"Thank you," he said. He popped the bread into his mouth. The colossal fat content of the pâté began to melt thickly on his astonished tongue.

PJ sighed. "And I'd like to be a part of it somehow. I'd really like to do my bit against the Naxids." He looked at Martinez, his brown eyes wide. "What do you think I should do?"

"You're too old for the service academies, so the Fleet's out," Martinez said, hoping very much that this was true—the thought of PJ in the Fleet was too alarming. They'd probably give him command of a ship or something.

"And I'm not qualified for the civil service," PJ said. "And the civil service isn't exactly on the front lines of the war, anyway. I thought for a moment about becoming an informer . . ."

"A what?" Martinez was thunderstruck.

"An informer." Fastidiously, as he dabbed his mustache with a napkin. "You know, the Legion of Diligence is always urging us to inform on traitors and subversives and so on, so I thought I'd join a subversive group and try a bit of the informing line."

Martinez was enraptured by the idea of Lord Pierre J. Ngeni, Secret Agent. "Have you *told* anyone of this plan?" he asked, smearing sauce on bread.

"No I worked it out myself."

"I thought so." He scooped up pâté. "The idea has all the hallmarks of a incomparable mind."

PJ was pleased. "Thank you, Lord Gareth." A frown intruded onto his face. "But I ran into a problem. I don't *know* any traitors, and all the traitors seem to be Naxids anyway, and since I'm not a Naxid it would be difficult to join any of their groups, wouldn't it? So the plan hasn't worked out."

Martinez chewed thoughtfully through this, then swallowed. "Oh. Sorry."

There was a moment of silence, and then PJ asked, "You wouldn't know any subversive groups I could join, would you?"

Other than the Martinez family, you mean? "I'm afraid not," Martinez said..

"Too bad." PJ was downcast. "So I'm still looking for something to do, to help with the war."

Martinez reflected that he'd been on a ship for the whole war and had no idea what it was that civilians *were* doing, and so he asked.

"Well, we're urged to Uphold the Praxis and Repel Seditious Rumors," PJ said. "And I *do*. I repel rumors like anything."

Martinez drew a feathery hair off his plate. "Very commendable," he said.

"And we're told to Enhance War Production and Conserve Precious Resources," PJ continued, "but I don't really have anything to do with production or resource management, so there's nothing I can do in that line, I'm afraid."

Martinez considered urging PJ to acquire some resources and then conserve them, but that didn't seem to be the sort of thing PJ was aiming at.

"I want to do *more*," PJ said. "It's—these are *critical times,* they call for . . ." He flapped his hands. "For *action*."

"Well," Martinez said, "you could sponsor a benefit show at the Oh-lo-ho or the Penumbra. Proceeds going to Fleet Relief or somewhere useful."

PJ looked abashed. "I'm afraid—well, the current state of the finances does not permit that sort of thing."

Martinez had suspected they might not. "Perhaps a jumble sale," he said. "Urge your friends to clear out their attics for a good cause."

PJ seemed to be considering this for a moment, and then shook his head. "It's useless, isn't it?" He slumped. "*I'm* useless. Here we are in stirring times, and I can't contribute a whit." He looked at Martinez, and genuine desperation shimmered in his eyes. "I want to prove myself worthy of Sempronia, you see. She's *your* sister, and that makes it hard. She's used to having heroes loitering around the house, and when *I'm* loitering instead of *you*, I'm sure she can't help but make comparisons."

Martinez listened in astonishment. *Worthy of Sempronia?* What, he wondered, could have prompted this? Had the poor sap actually fallen for his sister?

His sister, who at this very moment was loitering, if the

word could be said to apply, with one of the heroes of Hone-bar?

"Ah. Well," said Martinez. "Perhaps you could consult with Lord Pierre." Referring to Lord Pierre Ngeni, who was handling Clan Ngeni business on Zanshaa while Lord Ngeni was serving as governor of Paycahp.

"What's the use?" PJ cried. "The only thing I'm good for is buying Fleet officers lunch."

"It's appreciated," Martinez said. He tried to sound as cheerful as possible, but he feared he was unable to succor, or for that matter much care about, PJ's agony of spirit. He was more worried, given that discretion had never been one of Sempronia's prime attributes, about the Ngenis finding out about Sempronia's attachment to Shankaracharya.

"Sorry to bother you with all this," PJ apologized. "But I thought perhaps you might have some suggestions. Or connections you could bring into play." He brightened. "Maybe I could serve on your next ship, as, I don't know, a volunteer or something."

Martinez tried not to recoil in horror from this suggestion. "I'm afraid that's not possible. You'd have to go through one of the training academies first."

"Ah." PJ shook his head. "Thanks anyway." He sighed. "I appreciate your talking to me like this."

"I'm only sorry," Martinez said, "I haven't been able to help."

Afterward, walking home, he passed by an antique store, hesitated, and stepped inside. After tapping it to find if it had a satisfactory ring, he purchased a broad-mouthed porcelain vase, creamy and translucent, with a light relief of chrysanthemums, which he sent to Sula at her apartment. *Here's a vase for your flowers,* he wrote on the card.

Then he went to a flower shop and sent to Sula a huge spray of gladioli. *Here are some flowers for your vase.*

The next hour was spent with a skilled Torminel masseur, having some of the pains and kinks of two months of acceleration poked, squeezed, and beaten out of him. Exhausted but with his skin aglow, he returned to the Shelley Palace and to his bed.

He was awakened by the chiming of the comm. He opened his eyes.

"Comm: voice only. Comm: answer."

"Where's the picture?" came Sula's voice. "I wanted to show you your flowers."

Martinez swiped gum from his eyelids. "I'm trying not to send you screaming for the exit." He rolled over, reached to the bedside table, and aimed the hood of the comm unit in his direction. "But if you insist . . . Comm," he commanded. "Video and audio both."

The flowers sprang into life on the screen—oranges and reds and yellows—and with them Sula's smiling face. Her eyes widened as she took in Martinez's bed, tousled hair and undershirt, then a skeptical tone entered her voice.

"You thought *this* would send me screaming?"

He swiped again at an eye. "It hasn't failed yet."

"At least I get to see what *your* bed looks like."

"Feast your eyes." He looked at the screen, at the pale, golden-haired figure. "And I'll feast mine," he added.

Even on the small screen he saw the flush mantle her cheeks. "I see you're still on ship time," she said, a bit hastily.

"Somewhat." The Fleet's twenty-nine-hour day contrasted with that of Zanshaa, which was 25.43 standard hours. If the twenty-nine-hour day imposed on the empire by the Shaa corresponded with that of any planet, the planet had yet to be discovered.

Sula looked at the vase. "How did you know I liked Guraware?"

"Innate good taste, I suppose. I saw it in a shop and thought it should belong to you."

"If you ever feel a similar impulse, don't restrain yourself. This is some of the best porcelain ever made on Zanshaa." She ran the pads of her fingers over the curves of the vase, and Martinez felt a shiver run up his spine at the sensuality of the protracted caress.

"I'm getting decorated and promoted tomorrow," Martinez said. "09:01, Zanshaa time, at the Commandery. Will you come?"

She returned her attention to the video. "Of course. If they'll let me in."

"I'll add your name to list of guests. I'll be in the Hall of Ceremony."

"It's a nice room." She smiled. "You'll like it."

"There will be a celebration tomorrow evening here at the palace. Will you come?"

"Your kind sisters already invited me, though I wasn't aware of the party's purpose." She looked thoughtful. "I hope you don't think I'm greedy, but . . ."

"You want a matching vase."

"Well, *yes.*" She laughed. "What I meant to ask was whether you were free tonight."

"I'm not. Sorry. And besides . . ." He looked into her green eyes. "I'm not yet at my best."

She held his gaze for a moment, then looked away. "And tomorrow night?" she asked.

"You be the judge."

At that moment the thick teak door thundered open and Sempronia entered screaming. *"What did you do to him?"*

Martinez turned to Sempronia and tried to speak around the heart that had just leaped into his throat. "What?" he said. "Who—?"

Anger flushed Sempronia's cheeks and fury blazed in her eyes. *"I'm never going to forgive you for this! Never!"*

"Well," came Sula's cautious voice from the display, "I can see you're busy . . ."

Martinez's attention whipped from Sempronia to Sula and back, in time to avoid being brained by his own Golden Orb, which Sempronia had just flung at him. He cast Sula a desperate look.

"See you later."

"Comm," said Sula, "end transmission." The orange End symbol flashed on the screen, and then it darkened. By that time Martinez was on his feet, fending off a hairbrush, his shaving kit, and a bottle of cologne, objects that Sempronia found atop the bureau and sent his way.

He snatched the cologne out of the air and dropped it to a soft landing on the bed.

"Will you tell me what this is about?" he shouted in an officer's voice calculated to freeze a member of the enlisted class in his tracks.

Sempronia was far from frozen, but at least she ceased to throw things. *What did you do to Nikkul!*" she cried. *"What did you do to him, you rat!*"

Martinez knew precisely what he had done to him. Into Shankaracharya's record he had written:

This officer possesses great intelligence coupled with imaginative gifts of a high order. He has demonstrated an ability to solve complex technical problems, and would be of outstanding utility in any position requiring expert technical or technological knowledge, or any position in which abstract reasoning or scientific skills are required.

This officer participated as communications officer in the Battle of Hone-bar. Based on his performance therein, it is not recommended that this officer be employed in any capacity in which the lives of Fleet personnel depend on his effectiveness in action against an enemy.

Shankaracharya had frozen in action not once but twice, first at the initial sighting of the enemy, and second when the first missile barrage had gone off and spread its hellfire plasma through the reaches of space. Martinez hadn't given him a third chance.

It was possible that Shankaracharya would have overcome his shock and surprise and given exemplary service for the rest of the battle, his career, and his life. But Martinez, with the lives of hundreds of people under his immediate care, had not been able to take that chance.

After the battle, in the days that followed, he had asked himself the same sort of question he'd asked concerning Kamarullah: *Would I feel safe knowing that I had to depend on Shankaracharya in combat?*

With Martinez's comments on his record, Shankaracharya would be put in charge of a supply depot or a laundry or a data processing center till the end of the war, and then his career would be over.

"What *happened*, Proney?" Martinez shouted in reply. "Can you just tell me what happened?"

Sempronia clenched her fists and shook one of them in Martinez's direction. "Nikkul had it all arranged! Lord Pezzini arranged it for him—he had a place on one of the new cruisers they're building in Harzapid. He and the other officers were going to leave in twelve days' time. And this afternoon the captain called him and told him that his services would no longer be required, and that his place was going to someone else!"

She narrowed her eyes. "Nikkul said his captain must have read your report. So *what did you write in it to wreck Nikkul's career?*"

"What did *Nikkul* say was in it?" Martinez countered.

"He *wouldn't say*," Sempronia raged. "He just said you'd done the right thing." Her lower lip trembled. Tears began to fill her eyes. "He was *ashamed.* He turned away. I think he was crying." Anger returned, and again she brandished a fist. "You were his hero! He pulled strings to get on your ship!" Tears burst out again, and her voice became a wail. "You promised to look after him. *You promised.*"

"He shouldn't have pulled strings," Martinez said softly. "He shouldn't have got Pezzini to put him over the heads of more experienced officers. He was too young and he wasn't ready."

Her voice was a soft, anguished keen. "You said you'd *help* him. You should have *helped* him." Sempronia took a step toward Martinez, but her knees wouldn't support her and in slow motion she coiled down onto his bed, turning away, her fair hair falling into her face. Sobs shuddered through her. Martinez, his mouth dry, put out a hand to touch her shoulder. She shook it off.

"Oh, go *away*," she said. "I *hate* you."

"It's my room," he pointed out. "If anyone leaves it's you."

"Oh shut up."

There was a moment of silence, and then Martinez decided that he was *not* going to shut up. "Shankaracharya is a good man," he said. "But he's not an officer. He can succeed in any path but the one he's chosen. Help him choose another path." He made a helpless gesture. "*You* have to help him now. I can't."

Sempronia rose to her feet and ran for the door, hurling over her shoulder one last blaze of anger. "You bastard! You're so *useless*!" And then the heavy door slammed shut behind her.

Martinez stood for a moment in the sudden thundering silence, then sighed.

He looked at the bed. He decided it was unlikely that he was going to get back to sleep, so he put on his shirt and trousers and civilian jacket, and the half-boots that Alikhan had polished to a mirror gleam just that morning. With proper military concern he tidied the objects that Sempronia had flung about, then went downstairs to the ground floor.

The parlor and drawing room were deserted. Perhaps everyone was in a back room discussing Sempronia's explosion.

In the parlor Martinez poured some Laredo whiskey into a crystal tumbler, and he sipped it as he continued his search.

He found Roland just outside his office, dragging a piece of furniture down the hall toward a storage room.

Martinez looked at the specialized couch that would hold two humans comfortably enough but which was better adapted to a reclining four-legged body the size of a very large dog.

"You've just had a visit from Naxids?" Martinez asked in surprise.

Roland looked up. "Yes. Give me a hand with this, would you?"

Martinez set down his drink on the ancient, scuffed parquet floor and helped Roland carry the couch to the storage room at the end of the hall, where it was placed with other furniture adapted to the specialized physique of the various species living under the Praxis. Then he and Roland carried a second couch from Roland's office, after which they replaced the Terran-scaled furniture that had been taken from the office for the convenience of Roland's guests.

"I could have the servants do this, I suppose," Roland said, "but they'd gossip."

Martinez got his drink from the hall, returned to Roland's office, and made a note of the private entrance that led to the alley on one side of the palace, a discreet way for members of the empire's most suspect species to pay confidential calls.

"Why are you seeing Naxids?" he asked.

Roland gave him an amused look. "I'm not conspiring against public order, if that's what you suspect. These are perfectly respectable Naxids, Naxids that the conspirators never told about their rebellion, and who were as surprised about it as we were."

Martinez sipped his drink as he considered this. "And that doesn't make them *less* trustworthy?"

"I'm *not* trusting them. I'm just helping them do their business." Roland, eyeing Martinez's glass, stepped to the glass-fronted cabinet behind his desk, opened it with a key, and poured himself whiskey. "Freshen yours?"

"Yes. Thank you."

Crystal rang against crystal as the decanter touched the lip of the tumbler. "Naxids have been so cut out of the picture since the rebellion," Roland said, "that they and their clients have really begun to suffer. All the money that's going into military contracts and supply contracts for the Fleet—the Naxids are seeing it go right past them."

"Good," Martinez said.

The whiskey flooded his tongue with its peaty flavor. Roland returned the decanter to the cabin and locked it securely. "Naxids like my guests—Lord Ummir, Lady Convocate Khaa—are prepared to live under suspicion for the rest of the war," he said. "They understand that's inevitable, and their families have the resources to survive the downturn. But the position they're in makes it hard for them to get business for their clients, and their clients *aren't all Naxids*."

Martinez gave a slow nod. "Ah. I see."

Roland smiled. "We're getting the Naxids' clients a share of all the good things, the things they'd be getting anyway if it weren't for their patrons' unfortunate racial affiliation."

"And in return?"

Roland shrugged. "We'll turn a profit, but mainly it's for after the war. I want to earn the Naxids' gratitude."

Martinez felt anger flare. "And why should we want the Naxids to be grateful to us?"

"Because after we win the war they'll be allowed a share of power again, and that power can be turned to good use. And also . . ." He stepped close, and touched Martinez's glass with his own. As the chime of the crystal faded, Roland said, "If we *lose* the war, their gratitude just might keep *you* from being executed. Not to mention the rest of us."

Martinez, his defused anger thrashing in the void, followed his brother out of his office to the parlor, where Vipsania had begun to make cocktails.

The evening's guest was Lord Pierre Ngeni, who arrived at the appointed hour, neat in the wine-colored uniform tunic of a lord convocate. He was a young man with a round cannonball head and a powerful jaw, and in the absence of his father represented Martinez interests in the capital.

In manner Lord Pierre was the opposite of his cousin PJ, being businesslike and a bit brusque. "I've been speaking with people in hopes of getting you an appointment," he told Martinez. "I've prepared the ground. Tomorrow's announcement will provide some impetus. And if necessary"—he looked uncomfortable—"I can raise the matter in open Convocation. The Control Board declining to give the Fleet's most decorated captain a meaningful posting *should* be a matter for discussion."

Though you'd *hate to be the one who sticks his neck out by bringing it up,* Martinez read.

"With any luck it won't come to that," Roland said. He turned to Martinez. "One of the members of the board is very much with us on this matter. Tomorrow's announcement should give his arguments some extra weight."

And that was all that Lord Pierre and Roland had to say concerning Martinez's plight. They had much to say about other business, though—it appeared there were many other schemes afoot, contracts to be awarded, leases to be signed, delivery dates to be met. Vipsania and Walpurga arrived as Roland and Lord Pierre began to get into details, and seemed as familiar with the subjects as Roland. Martinez was surprised by it all, and a little bewildered—*I wonder if Lord Pierre knows about Lady Khaa and Lord Ummir.*

If he did, Martinez concluded gloomily, he'd probably be far from outraged, just demand a share of the spoils.

That was how it seemed to work.

SIX

Sula walked to Martinez amid the throng in the Shelley Palace and watched his eyes go wide as she offered him her congratulations.

"I've never seen you out of uniform," he said as he took her hand.

Clattering in her blood was the anxiety that drew her smile taut. "I thought I'd give you a surprise."

"I hope it won't be the last surprise you'll give me tonight." He put her arm in his and drew her toward the refreshments.

Sula had worn a uniform all those years because she hadn't been able to afford to do otherwise. To compete with the women of the Peer class, each raised from the cradle in obedience to laws of beauty, of fashion, and of courtesy, with wardrobes that changed every season to conform with rules that were understood but were never written down . . . her allowance would never have permitted it, and in any case the idea was too daunting. The danger of making a mistake was always present, and fortunately a uniform was always correct attire for Fleet personnel.

Once she'd been at the center of a kind of whirlwind of modish style. She'd had a lover—a linkboy, the sort of person described in melodramas as a "crime lord," though of a minor kind—and he'd enjoyed dressing her in the most outrageous and expensive stuff he could find. He'd bought a new outfit every few days, and her closets overflowed with clothing. She'd given a lot of it away to her friends just to make room for the new. And then another person had come into her life—a person she didn't want to think about—who also enjoyed dressing her. She'd abandoned almost all of the clothing when she became Lady Sula and left Spannan for the service academy, and since then confined herself to Fleet-approved uniforms.

The binges in the boutiques of Spannan would in any case have been of little use on Zanshaa. The clothing here was richer, more expensive, and worn in accordance with a different notion of style.

For the evening she had purchased a black dress of the kind described as "timeless." She dearly hoped that was the case, since by the time she'd added shoes and a matching jacket she was scandalized to discover she'd spent a little over one-twentieth of her entire fortune. At this rate her simple black dress was going to have to last a good many years.

Certainly it didn't compete with the peacock colors she saw about her, the ruffles and flounces and brocade. Fashion was going through an ornate phase, perhaps in defiance of the grim standards of war. Even the Torminel, who were heavily furred and wore little clothing in order not to fall to heatstroke, sported vests and shorts heavily encrusted with beadwork and gems.

She should have looked out of place, but she'd received several compliments on her appearance from people since she'd arrived, some of them from people who had no motive for pleasing her.

And the look on Martinez's face when he'd first seen her had been priceless.

"Are those beads porcelain?" Martinez asked, his gaze straying to her neck.

She tilted her head to let him see them. "Blown glass." Layered with brilliant color, each bead an individual, swirling masterpiece of art, and inexpensive compared to the rest of her turnout.

"Very nice." His nostrils flared, just a little. "And is San-dama Twilight another part of tonight's ensemble?"

"It is."

He smiled happily. "I'm so pleased you could attend my party, Lady Sula."

She gave a formal nod in acknowledgment and felt the tension flutter in her chest like a caged bird. "I'm pleased to be here," she said.

For the party, pocket doors had been rolled into the walls, turning two parlors, a drawing room, and a formal dining room into one long reception room. Martinez took her the length of the room to the buffet and offered to fill a plate for her. Sula was too nervous to have an appetite, but she managed to swallow a pair of the little bow tie–shaped pastries.

Do not destroy this night, she told herself. Remember that this one actually likes you. Remember that he's giving you a second chance after you wrecked the last one.

Martinez brought her sparkling mineral water.

"I laid in a stock of this just for you," he said as he poured from the violet-colored bottle.

"You think of everything."

"Yes." A tight little self-congratulatory smile. "I do."

Martinez wore the viridian dress uniform of the Fleet. At his throat was the badge of the Golden Orb, a circular sun disk on a gold-and-black ribbon, which he wore instead of carrying the heavy baton. His two decorations sparkled on his chest, the Medal of Merit First Class, for his part in rescuing Captain Blitsharts, and the Nebula Medal with Diamonds, for the Battle of Hone-bar.

She had watched Lord Chen pin the latter on his tunic that morning. Lord Tork, the chairman of the Control Board who had presented to Sula her own medal, had not been present, and neither had any of the other board members. She presumed they were occupied with urgent meetings concerning their fellow board member Lady San-torath, who had been arrested the previous night on charges that she had conspired to suppress information concerning enemy movements at Hone-bar. She had been subjected to a midnight trial before a judge of the High Court, and sentenced to die at the exact moment at which Martinez was being decorated.

Die screaming. Sula remembered the satisfaction in Lord Ivan Snow's voice when they met two days before. He had already known what San-torath's fate would be—to have her fragile, hollow arms and legs broken with steel bars, after which her limbs were amputated with a special hydraulically operated cutting tool and the still-living torso thrown off the acropolis from a site near the great granite dome of the Great Refuge. The new laws specified being flung from a height as the punishment for treason, in imitation of the Naxid convocates who had been thrown off the terrace of the Convocation after proclaiming the rebellion. Executions were no longer performed on the terrace, presumably because it might put the Lords Convocate off their feed, and the Shaa who had once inhabited the Great Refuge were dead, and could hardly object.

The news of the conspiracy, released that morning, also gloated over the fate of the conspirators captured at Hone-bar, who were thrown from a greater height—they were to be stuffed into vacuum suits and hurled with some force from Hone-bar's accelerator ring. Their air supplies had been carefully calculated: they were to burn alive in the atmosphere before they could suffocate. It would take a little over three days for the video images to reach Zanshaa, after which they would be broadcast repeatedly on the news programs and on the channel reserved for punishments.

All very imaginative, Sula thought. If only the imagination applied to torture and executions had been applied to the running of the war.

Sula stood with Martinez's family on the gallery overlooking the Hall of Ceremony, and applauded as Lord Chen took Martinez's hand and murmured some carefully chosen words while a pair of aides strapped on Martinez's new captain's shoulder boards. After which Dalkeith, Martinez's premiere, received the Medal of Merit Second Class, and her step to lieutenant-captain. Other officers likewise received recognition or promotion.

Quite a number of *Corona*'s crew turned up for the ceremony. There was a little blond lieutenant, very young, a half-dozen cadets, and a number of senior petty officers with truly magnificent mustachios. Sula noticed that Lieutenant Captain Kamarullah, who had wrested command of the squadron from Martinez, was not present and was not receiving awards. Also absent, more oddly, was Lady Sempronia Martinez.

While Fleet officers were receiving their promotions and while conspirators died in pain and terror, on his flagship in orbit around Zanshaa's primary the official victor of Hone-bar, Do-faq, was decorated and jumped two grades to senior squadron commander. Various of his officers were likewise honored. The whole circus, trials and deaths and glittering medals, had been carefully staged to maximize the value of the news to the government. With the video of Do-faq's promotion coming in from five light-hours away, and the video of the executions on Hone-bar coming in three days, the honors of the righteous and the degradation of the corrupt would occupy public attention for some time to come.

Sula reached a hand to Martinez's chest and adjusted the sparkling new decoration. "It looks good on you," she said.

"It does, doesn't it?" Martinez said, pleased. He took her hand, and his expression changed. "Your hand is cold," he said.

"Yes. I'm—" She took a breath. "Very nervous."

Concern entered his face, and again he put her arm in his and walked away with her, toward the hall. "Let me take you to a place where we can be private," he said, and then he looked at her. "Unless that would make you more nervous rather than less."

"I think . . . I'll be fine, whatever you decide."

She had decided to surrender to the man with more experience. Martinez adopted an air of firm authority that kept others from approaching him while he marched off with Sula. Suddenly she could imagine what Martinez had been like in command of *Corona*—incisive, intense, and very stern. He led her out of the reception room, then down a hall, through a parlor, and through another hall to a small room, quietly furnished.

"Roland's office," Martinez said. With the back of his knuckles he brushed the walnut desk's gold inlay and silent inset, the access to the palace's various cyber systems, then he sat on the edge of the desk, took her mineral water from her hand and placed it on the table. Drew her to him. She could feel the warmth of his body on her bare shoulders and face.

"Will it help the nervousness if I just kiss you now?" he asked.

An anxious titter escaped her lips. "It wouldn't hurt," she said.

He drew her closer and touched her lips with his lips. They were pliant and not too insistent, both qualities that she appreciated. Her jangled nerves began to ease.

Martinez drew back. "I'm beginning to see what's so special about twilight on Sandama," he said.

She barked another nervous laugh. The brown eyes beneath his heavy brows were half veiled, frankly appraising, but somehow appraising without the insolence she saw in the eyes of other men. A nice trick, she thought.

"You are the most beautiful thing here tonight," he said, breath warming her cheek. "And I'm the luckiest man in the empire—which you once pointed out to me, I remember."

Sula felt herself flushing. She looked at her feet. "I never know what to say at these moments," she said.

"You could try working up some praise of *my* looks," Martinez said, "but if the insincerity would be too challenging, you could just say 'thank you' and blush as prettily as you're doing now."

"Thank you," she said in a small voice.

He folded her in his arms and kissed her again. Her skin seemed to blaze with heat. On sudden impulse she cradled his head in her hands and drove her kiss against his, and felt his surprise and pleased response. Fire scorched her veins. He gasped free of the kiss and buried his head at the juncture of her neck and shoulder, and Sula felt a shudder run up her spine at the touch of his lips in the hollow of her shoulder, just above the subclavian artery with its pulsing blood. She ran her hands through his wavy brown hair.

He gasped again, then drew back and looked at her. "There's a private door in this room," he said. His voice was urgent and feverish. "Let's leave the party and go somewhere. We don't have to go to that famous bed of yours, not if you're not at ease, but for all's sake, let's get away and be together. Anywhere you like."

She looked at him in dawning surprise. "I can't take you away from your party. You're the guest of honor."

"If it's my party, I can leave anytime I want." He began to kiss her throat again, and she gave another shudder and held him there against him for a long moment. Then she placed her palm against his chest and firmly pushed him away.

"No," she said. "You're not going to be rude to your guests."

"They're not *my* guests!" Martinez protested. "They're *Roland's* guests! And Walpurga's guests, and Vipsania's! I hardly know any of these people."

"Stick with them a couple hours," Sula said, "just for politeness. And then," she took the disk of the Golden Orb between her fingers and drew him close to her, "I want a hundred percent of your attention for the rest of the evening."

"You'll have it," he said. "I'm feeling at my absolute best, I want to assure you."

"In two hours or so," *when I can't stand the suspense any-*

more, "I'll thank you politely for a good time, and then leave. I'll expect you at my apartment within the hour."

His face took on a hopeful look. "Suppose I get there *ahead* of you . . ."

"No." Sternly. "For once follow the operational plan without improvising."

"But—" His sleeve comm chimed. "Damn it!" he said, and answered as Sula released his medal and stepped back out of range of the camera button.

Roland's voice came out of the display. "Where are you? I've got an important announcement to make."

Martinez sighed. "I'll be right there."

Sula wanted to laugh at his chagrin. As soon as he switched off the comm she stepped to him and kissed him fiercely. When his arms came up to embrace her, she stepped back and began the adjustments to her appearance that would allow her to appear once more in public without embarrassment. Martinez cleaned her cosmetic from his face with a handkerchief.

"I'm glad I was able to help with that nervousness problem," he said. "I see you've got it under control again."

For the moment. "Thank you. That was very well . . . handled."

He gave her a look. She picked up her drink and Martinez took her arm and led her back to the party. No sooner had they stepped into the reception room than the crowd opened up and revealed the one person who could send Sula's renewed confidence draining out of her like stuffing from a torn rag doll.

Sula didn't know the woman's name, but she recognized the glossy chestnut hair and the spectacular hourglass figure. The newcomer had solved the problem of what to wear to a gathering of high-caste Peers by wearing practically nothing, just a shining, shimmery, form-fitting sheath that restrained her in certain dimensions while allowing her to blossom in others. She was taller than Sula, and her shoulders were tawny while her smile was brilliant and white.

Sula had seen her once before, with Martinez at the Penumbra Theater, shortly after Sula and Martinez had their explosive parting. Sula remembered the wrenching jealousy she'd felt at that moment, and the envy she'd felt at the other woman's abundant charms. Martinez was reputed very successful with women, and she couldn't imagine him not being successful with this one.

The duty cadets at the Commandery, with whom Sula had once served, had been dismissive of Martinez's luck with women, claiming that he preyed exclusively on women from the lower orders. Whatever order this dark-haired goddess was from, it didn't seem lower exactly, more like another plane altogether.

Martinez was smilingly correct. "Warrant Officer Amanda Taen, may I present Lieutenant, the Lady Sula."

"Oh," said Warrant Officer Taen, eyes widening, "you're *famous*. I've seen you on video. I think you're wonderful!" Sula felt her skin prickle, as if in answer to the pheromones that seemed to pour off Amanda Taen in waves, like warm surf rolling off some lush tropical shore.

"And where are you stationed?" Sula managed.

"Zanshaa ring," said Amanda Taen. "I command a cutter that does satellite repair and maintenance."

"Command?" Martinez said. "You got your promotion?"

"I'm Warrant Officer/First now." Smiling brilliantly.

"Congratulations." The word forced itself from Sula's tightening diaphragm.

"But I should be congratulating *you*," Amanda Taen cried. "The *both* of you. All *I* did was pass an exam, but *you*— you're brilliant! You've done great things!"

A gong sounded, and Sula gave silent thanks that she wouldn't have to continue to manage conversation with this living, breathing incarnation of gonadal male fantasy.

Everyone turned to where Roland stood with a mallet in his hand. He rang the broad antique gong again, enjoying the effect, and then hung the mallet from its thong and turned smiling to the crowd.

"I realize that we've all assembled here in honor of my brother, Gareth"—with a glance at Martinez—"and of his brilliant exploits against the Naxid rebels. But I'd like to briefly take the spotlight from my brother in order to make another announcement of importance to the family."

He gestured toward Vipsania, who stood in her beaded gown next to a smiling man in the dark red coat of a convocate. "I'd like to announce the forthcoming marriage of my sister Lady Vipsania to Lord Convocate Oda Yoshitoshi."

Yoshitoshi was a broad-shouldered, glossy-haired man with temples going spectacularly, theatrically white. He smiled and took Vipsania's hand as the audience broke into applause.

Sula sensed Martinez' surprise. "You didn't know this was coming?" she murmured.

"Not a clue," Martinez said. "I don't even know who he is, precisely."

Sula didn't, either. There was a Senior Captain Lord Simon Yoshitoshi who had died at Magaria commanding *The Revelation of the Praxis*, one of the big *Praxis*-class battleships, but that was as far as her knowledge of Clan Yoshitoshi extended.

Martinez might have been baffled by the nature and even the existence of his proposed brother-in-law, but when the applause died he nevertheless raised his glass and was the first to offer a toast to the couple. Sula sipped her mineral water. More toasts followed, and then a rush to congratulate the pair.

When the mob around Vipsania and Yoshitoshi finally cleared, Sula found herself across the room from Martinez, and seemingly attached to Martinez was the abundant figure of Amanda Taen. The two were talking to one another and displaying every nuance of intimacy.

Profoundly cast down, Sula found herself in a corner of the room talking to PJ Ngeni, who was leaning against a bronze statue of an armored warrior maiden, and who seemed depressed himself. "Where's Sempronia?" she asked. "I haven't seen her tonight."

PJ contemplated the floating ice in his highball glass. "She's been ill for the last two nights, and has confined herself to her room. I haven't even been allowed to pay her a get-well visit."

"It must be serious, then."

He gave her a doleful look. "Quite." He returned his attention to his drink. His face was a mournful image of what Sula felt in her own despondent heart. "I must say that engagement to Sempronia hasn't worked out quite the way I intended. I thought, well, a lively girl like that, she'd be fun to take around the city, we'd have weekends in the country, we'd be seen in all the clubs. And instead I see her only rarely, and when I *do* see her there are such *crowds,* it's hard to get her alone."

Sula cast a glance at Martinez, still with Amanda Taen wrapped around his arm. "I know what you mean," she said.

I was the one who insisted on returning to the party. This is what I get for not seizing the moment.

PJ surveyed her gloomily. "You're looking very well, if you don't mind my saying."

"Thank you." She glanced toward the buffet and the open bar. "I'm considering drinking myself unconscious."

"That would be splendid," PJ said. "I think you should. You have the *right.*"

Sula realized that PJ was himself colossally drunk, and if the bronze maiden weren't holding him up he would probably be sprawled across the marble tiles.

"You've earned the right to do anything you want, my

girl," PJ said. "Anything at all. Not like me—I haven't earned *anything*. I haven't killed any Naxids, I haven't managed to become a spy, I haven't even had a jumble sale."

Sula suspected that she would have to be drunk herself to follow this train of thought. "It's not too late," she said hopefully.

"I trust not," PJ said fervently. "I trust not. I desire nothing so much as to be worthy."

He followed this with a rambling monologue on the subject of wanting to participate in the war, and of his general unworthiness until this occurred. He praised Sula extravagantly. He praised Sempronia. He praised Martinez. He spoke of his own misery.

"All I do is give lunches!" he cried. "And what I really want is to be an informer!"

Sula was unable to follow the lurches of PJ's misery, so she confined herself to making the occasional remark and sharing the all-round despairing atmosphere. Somehow Sula got through the next two hours, trying not to watch Martinez as he got Amanda Taen a drink, as he introduced her to other guests, as he laughed at something she said in his ear. Eventually she gathered the shreds of her dignity and gave her thanks and goodnights to Roland and his sisters. Then, heart in her mouth, she approached Martinez to tell him she was leaving.

"Wonderful meeting you!" said Amanda Taen, her eyes bright. "I hope I see you again!"

He won't come, Sula thought as she turned the corner that led to her apartment. Why would he? She was irascible and difficult and uncertain—she wasn't even the person she pretended to be—and Warrant Officer Taen was . . . was so *there*. So *available*.

Nevertheless when she reached her apartment she lit the scented candles she had ready and adjusted her hair and her cosmetic, actions performed with a growing sense of unreality, as if these rituals were unconnected with her or with anything else.

How pathetic am I? she wondered as she walked through the silent, scented room with the light of the candles fluttering on the walls like nervous butterflies.

He won't come, she thought. Her nerves were so taut they seemed to sing.

And then there was a chime on the comm from the Daimong doorman, informing her that a Captain Martinez had arrived to see her.

A moment later he stood in her doorway. His tunic collar was unbuttoned and the ribbon of the Golden Orb hung from his breast pocket where the decoration had been casually stuffed.

Sula wondered if she could possibly manage words. "That wasn't very long," she said, by way of experiment.

"I waited three minutes. That was all the time I could stand." Martinez stepped into the room and revealed what he'd concealed behind his back, a mate to the Guraware vase he'd given her the previous day, filled with a tangle of daffodils.

"You said you wanted another one," he said. "I had it sent from a shop in Tula. I pinched the flowers from the party."

Sula stepped forward, put her arms around him, and pressed her cheek into his shoulder. His warm scent surrounded her. The anxiety poured out of her in a long sigh.

"Three minutes was too long," she said. "I kept picturing you with Miss Taen."

He stroked her back with his free hand. "Amanda's a jolly girl, but when I'm with her I see you. When I'm with *any* woman I see you." He gave a rueful laugh. "I'm glad my mother isn't on this planet."

She choked back laughter. He kissed her nape. His fingers brushed the delicate hairs over her spine, and she shivered.

"May I come in?" he said. "The carpet in the hall is distracting."

"Wait till you see the bed," she said, and drew him inside.

In the darkness of the front room he placed the vase on the first horizontal surface he came to. Wanting his taste, she opened more of his tunic buttons and licked his neck. His large warm hands enveloped her scapulae. He bent to her lips, kissing her forcefully, and she remembered the last time she'd been with a man. It had not been rape exactly, but it had been violent. Sula remembered Lamey's stunning slap against her cheek, the fist sunk into her solar plexus, the frantic business on the bed afterward. The money pressed into her hand.

"What's wrong?" Martinez asked suddenly. He had felt her tension. His eyes were wide in the flickering darkness.

"Nothing," she said quickly, and then, "Bad memories."

"We should go slow," he said. His hand traced the outline of her shoulder. "I don't want you to have those memories when you're with me. I don't want you to run away."

She took his hand in hers, raised it to her lips. "You've been patient enough. I'm the one who's been unfair."

"I—" He began a protest, but she silenced him with fingers on his lips. She took his hand and pulled him into the bedroom. His eyes took in the Sevigny bed, the dark wood pillars carved with capering primitive figures, each dancing with perfectly rounded parted lips and spiky hair; the four arching figures, two with bulbous breasts and two with erect carved phalli, that held up the canopy of woven grass.

"The apartment came furnished," Sula said.

"Good grief," he said, "*they're* going to be watching us all night?"

"Keep your eyes shut and you won't see them," Sula said.

"Ah," he said, his eyes returning to her, "but then I won't see *you*."

Her veins ran with flame at the intensity of his glance, but she forced a more practical mood. Methodically she disrobed him, revealing the long, powerful torso balanced atop the shortish legs, the features which, with his big hands and long arms, had caused the duty cadets in the Commandery to nickname him "Troglodyte."

The jealous bastards.

With her tongue she tasted Martinez again. This was not Lamey's taste. This was not Lamey's scent. These were not Lamey's hands caressing her, or Lamey's lips on hers.

She felt his hands unfastening the collar of her dress, and still in her practical mood she said, "You know, I'm not wearing much under this dress. Just stockings and—"

"You can keep the stockings on," he said a little forcefully, and she felt a spasm of wicked glee at having, so early, triggered one of his fetishes.

Sheets crackled beneath them as they lay on the bed, Martinez unclad and she in her stockings. She pressed herself to him, kissing moistly, ardently. His hands floated over her flesh.

This is not Lamey's bed, she thought. These are not his lips. These are not his hands.

It was becoming impossible to ignore the concrete evidence of Martinez's arousal.

And this is not Lamey's either, she thought.

"I should warn you." There was evidence of strain in his voice. "You should know that there will be a point beyond which I can't stop."

"Oh." Sula looked into his eyes, a shimmering diamond brilliance in the candlelight. "I was hoping we'd passed that point ages ago."

Martinez groaned and threw himself on her. His lips devoured her throat, his tongue licked along the flesh of her shoulder. His hands kindled fire as they touched her. She gave a gasp and thought, against the throb of panic that beat in her chest, this is not Lamey.

And he wasn't. His hands brought her first pleasure, then joy, then wild acceptance. This was unlike anything she had experienced in her old life. Lamey had been a boy, a wild desperate savage boy, but this was a grown man, certain of his powers, with a sharp, calculating mind and with experience and a willingness and a desire to bring pleasure . . .

And yet a boy after all, after the percipient mind sank beneath the tide of lust—and Sula felt the joy of command, that she had brought him helpless to this state. But then her own power vanished, poured away like dust streaming into the ocean of desire, and need claimed her and sent her crying aloud into the starry pavilion of night.

SEVEN

Martinez was amused that Sula kept getting up during the night to plunder the kitchen. "Didn't you eat at the party?" he asked.

"No. Want anything?" Smiling over her shoulder.

"No thanks."

They weren't actually dressed till noon, when they breakfasted on whatever food was left in the kitchen, plates and food strewn over a table ornamented by some distressed daffodils and supported by Sevigny caryatids with sagging breasts, knock knees, and goggle eyes. Sula commanded the windows to open, letting in the spring breezes.

Martinez always delighted in the first breakfast with a lover. From a state of pleased satiation, he could contemplate his companion in light of the fact that his knowledge of her had increased by a factor of six or eight or even a hundred. He knew where she was bold, where reluctant, where shy, where exuberant. He would know at least some of the secret places where she liked to be touched. He would learn how she liked to spend the time in between the courses of a night-long banquet of love—and in Sula's case, that seemed to be with her head in the refrigerator.

And in the morning he would learn what a lover liked for breakfast. Alikhan knew to serve him strong coffee and smoked or jellied fish—he liked protein to start his day—but Sula preferred carbohydrates and sweets, flat wroncho bread with a chutney of plums and ginger, fried sweet goat cheese with a topping of strawberry jam, and coffee turned into a near-syrup with golden cane sugar.

Martinez was buoyant. Energy cascaded through him. He wanted to address the Convocation, command a battleship, write a symphony. He felt capable of doing all three at once.

Perhaps, he thought, he would sing an aria instead. *Oh, the woman on the strand . . .*

Sula's comm chimed just as Martinez was on the edge of bellowing the first note. Sula spoke to the doorman, then went to the door to sign for an envelope from a uniformed functionary. She returned to the dining room and broke the seal.

Martinez's nerves prickled at the possibility that a posting might take her away. "Orders?" he asked.

"No. The Blitsharts trial." She stepped toward the open window and tilted the document toward its light. "I'm giving my deposition in three days."

Martinez observed something glistening below Sula's lower lip, a smear of the strawberry jam. He considered licking it off.

She slowly lowered the thick legal document. Her bright eyes had grown sober. "There *will* be a posting after the deposition, though. My month's leave is almost gone."

"Maybe it will be in the capital." He grinned. "And if it isn't, well, *I* have a month's leave. I'll just follow you."

As she looked at him he saw the hint of sadness in her eyes. "If the Naxids don't come," she said.

"If the Naxids don't come," he repeated. She knew the odds as well as he. Thirty-five ships to twenty-five, with two of the loyalist squadrons being scratch forces, ships thrown together that wouldn't normally serve in the same division. And the eight Naxid ships last seen at Protipanu were still unaccounted for.

"Do-faq was practicing the new tactics—*our* new tactics," he said. "Maybe he can convince Michi Chen. Maybe the two of them can convince the new fleetcom."

"Do you think new tactics are enough?" Sula said. "Enough to overcome the odds?"

Martinez thought about it, then drew a breath. "We'd have to be lucky."

Her jade eyes seemed to gaze through him into some deep abyss of time. "I wasn't scared of the Naxids till just now," she said. Her voice was strange, the languid Zanshaa consonants replaced by sharper accents. There was a flicker across her face, as if she'd just realized where she was; and her eyes focused on him, on the present. "I'm frightened of losing what we've just found," she told him, the Zanshaa voice back. "I'm frightened of losing *you*."

A slow, sad thrill rang through him like a chime. He rose from his chair and embraced Sula from behind, holding her close, her head lolled back against his shoulder. He licked the jam from her lower lip.

"We'll get through it," he said, making an effort to fight the tone of hopelessness that threatened to invade his voice. "I'm going to get a ship, and I'll request you as a lieutenant. We'll spend half each day plotting strategy in the recreational tubes, and the crew will spit with jealousy."

A smile drew taut the sadness on her lips. The soft warmth of her hair touched his cheek like a caress. "I don't even know why they're trying to hold Zanshaa," she said. "Not when there's every reason to give it up."

Martinez felt his mouth go dry. Cold, calculating energy sang through his nerves as he gave the expected reply. "Zanshaa is the capital. It's the government. If Zanshaa falls the empire goes with it." Even as he said the words he knew where the flaw in the argument lay.

"But none of that's true." Sula turned to give him a serious look. "The capital is *not the same as the government*. The government—the Convocation and the senior officials—they can be *anywhere*. We should put them on a ship and get them out of the way of the Naxids.

"Right now the Fleet is nailed here defending Zanshaa

against a force we can't defeat. More ships are being built to replace our losses, but they need time." She tapped a finger against his chest. "Time, in war, is the same as distance. If we draw our forces in toward our source of supply, we're falling back on our own reinforcements. If the Naxids come after us, they'll strain their lines of supply." Her lips drew back to reveal her sharp incisors. "Particularly if we make certain that they can't draw support from here, from Zanshaa."

He looked at her. "How would you prevent that?"

Sula shrugged. "Blow the accelerator ring."

Martinez gave an involuntary glance toward the ceiling, toward the silver accelerator ring that had encircled the planet for over ten thousand years.

"They'll never go for that," he said. "Zanshaa is the *center.* All the Great Masters lie in the Couch of Eternity here in the High City. If we start dropping bits of the ring onto the planet, that's *desecration.* The government would lose all legitimacy—no one would follow them."

Martinez felt Sula's muscles grow taut. "If we won the war, they damn well would," she said. "It's not as if we'd give them a choice." She gently detached herself from his embrace and reached for her cup of coffee. "But that wouldn't happen anyway. The ring is *built* to be detached from the planet."

"You're joking," Martinez said.

"No. I found that out when I was sent to guard a ring terminus just after the rebellion began—I checked the records to find out where the vulnerable bits of the terminus were. And I found out about the fail-safes built into its structure." She sipped her coffee. "The engineers weren't stupid—they wanted to be prepared in case something went wrong. They didn't want the whole mass of the ring to come crashing down on the planet, particularly with antimatter on board. So the accelerator ring was set into an orbit where, if the cables were broken, the release of centripetal force would gently carry the ring away from the planet, not toward it."

"But you'd have to break the ring into pieces."

"Right. The engineers calculated exactly where the scuttling charges would have to be placed. And scuttling charges *were* there, heavily guarded, for years—until the Shaa were satisfied that the ring would stay where they put it."

"What about the cables? If the ring slipped off the sky-hooks, the cables would wrap themselves right around the planet . . ."

Sula dabbled plum chutney onto her flat bread. "The engineers were *smart*. The cable termini are built with release mechanisms *here,* on the planet's surface. The cables would be drawn up into space and we'd never see them again." She took a bite, chewed, swallowed. "Imagine the Naxids' surprise. They'd come expecting to land their government on the ring and take the elevator down to the surface—and they wouldn't be able to get down to the planet! All their officials would be *stuck* up there, issuing decrees they couldn't enforce, at least until they brought enough shuttles from Magaria to land their government."

By this time Martinez had recovered from his slow surprise at this unorthodox notion and his mind had begun to grapple at its implications. "A hot reception could be arranged for them on the ground. I'd have thousands of soldiers guarding Zanshaa city."

Sula seemed puzzled. "What good would it do? The Naxids would just flame your army from orbit."

Martinez felt a triumphant smile split his face. "That's exactly what they'd do—they'd flame any city—*but not Zanshaa.* They wouldn't hit Zanshaa for the same reason that *we* couldn't drop a piece of the ring on it—it would be a desecration of the most sacrosanct place in the empire. Flame the Couch of Eternity? The Convocation? The Great Refuge? The original Tablets of the Praxis? *They wouldn't dare.*"

A wild mirth brought blood mantling the surface of Sula's face. "Your soldiers could hold out in the capital *forever!*"

He shrugged. "For a long time, anyway. The Naxids would have to shuttle in enough troops to defeat them. . . ."

". . . And in the meantime the Fleet would be building its power off in the reaches of the empire." Sula's grin was gleeful. "Ready to come back."

"Ye-es . . ." Further calculations shrank Martinez's smile. "Except that the Naxids are building, too. They'd have to be." He looked at her. "What will the Naxids *do* if we don't fight for Zanshaa? If we blow the ring and withdraw? What could they do? Come after us?"

The green fire of calculation burned in Sula's eyes. "They couldn't."

"Why not?"

"Because they wouldn't know where the fleet's gone. Zanshaa has eight wormhole gates. If the Naxids plunge on ahead toward where they *think* we are—even if they get the right wormhole—our fleet could still double back through another gate and retake Zanshaa. If they leave a smaller force behind to hold the capital, that force could be destroyed. They'd have to stay here." She took a thoughtful nibble of her bread. "Yes," she nodded, "they'd be stuck here."

"In which case," Martinez said slowly, "our forces wouldn't have to just fall back and stay put. They could go on the offensive."

Her face was a mask of concentration. "Yes. They could bypass Zanshaa and strike into the areas the Naxids already control. Disrupt trade, hinder resupply . . ."

". . . destroy reinforcements and anything building in the shipyards," Martinez added.

"While the main Naxid force is stuck at Zanshaa trying to find a way to fight *your* army and secure the High City," Sula said.

". . . And after suitable havoc is wreaked, and the new loyalist elements assemble . . ."

"We rendezvous, return to Zanshaa, and take back the

capital!" Sula almost shouted out her triumph. And then her exhilaration faded.

"But who listens to the likes of us?" she asked. "So far as we know, the Fleet is nailed to Zanshaa to defend or die."

Martinez was mentally adding up the people who might be useful. Lord Chen, he thought, perhaps Lord Pierre Ngeni, the recently promoted Do-faq. Perhaps he could get Shankaracharya to contact his patron Lord Pezzini on his behalf.

And if necessary he could go to Lord Saïd. The Lord Senior had been present when he'd been awarded the Golden Orb, and they'd exchanged a few words—Martinez knew that the head of the government was a busy man, but he suspected that the Golden Orb might be able to win a few moments of the old man's time.

"We should put together a proposal," Martinez said slowly. "A formal proposal, listing all the options." He didn't want to spring an idea prematurely, before it was developed . . . he'd made the mistake of doing that with the new tactics, only to encounter ridicule.

Sula's look was skeptical. "But who will ever read it?"

"I'll think about that later. Proposal first."

They cleared away the breakfast dishes, made another pot of coffee, and ordered the surface of the Sevigny table to brighten with its cybernetic options.

They would have to pare their ideas down to a manageable few.

It didn't pay to be too imaginative in these matters.

Martinez, with Sula's farewell kiss still tingling on his lips, walked toward the Shelley Palace at midafternoon, his mind saturated with a kind of awe. It was as if his brain had just discharged all its energy like a capacitor, and would require several hours to recover. He and Sula had been so perfect together, their minds working as if in tandem, one filling in details while another leaped ahead to the next point, then the two combining to collaborate on a particularly knotty problem. He no longer had any recollection which idea had occurred to which of the collaborators, it was all one smooth, perfect, ecstatic interface.

It was like wonderful sex. And this was in *addition* to the wonderful sex.

He bounded up the stairs of the Shelley Palace as he hummed to himself *Oh, the woman on the strand*, and as he entered the foyer he encountered his brother. Roland was preparing to go out and gave Martinez a saturnine look as he shrugged into his coat and twitched the lapels into place.

"I've been working on family business all day," he said, "and here you come loitering into the house in the middle of the afternoon reeking of sexual satiation."

"It's the uniform," Martinez said. "The uniform works wonders on the ladies."

"It seems to have worked its magic on that Amanda person, sure enough," Roland said. "But you might oblige me by considering a more permanent liaison, as your sister's done."

Martinez, smiling to himself, decided not to correct Roland's misapprehension about the woman with whom he'd spent the night.

"Where *is* the happy bride-to-be, by the way?" he asked.

"At our lawyer's, where I will soon join her." Roland moodily studied himself in a glass, then twitched at his lapels again. "A few last little wrinkles of the marriage contract need to be ironed out."

"I've been assuming the wrinkles on the contract are the whole point of the marriage," Martinez said, "since I hadn't till last evening actually seen the joyful couple together, or heard the groom so much as mentioned."

"You would if you hadn't spent so much of the last few days asleep." Roland stepped to the front door, put a hand on the polished brass knob, hesitated, and then turned to Martinez. "But why be surprised that they don't know each other particularly well? Why be surprised that marriage is about money and property and inheritance? Why else bother with it?"

"That carefree, fey romantic spirit of yours," Martinez said, "will get you in trouble one day."

Roland gave a grunt of annoyance and launched himself out the door. Martinez followed.

"So what gems are going to fall into our collective laps as a result of this alliance?" he said as he fell into stride with his brother.

"Lord Oda is the nephew of Lord Yoshitoshi," Roland said, his eyes fixed forward. "Lord Yoshitoshi had two children—the eldest, Lady Samantha, has been disinherited for reasons that have never been disclosed publicly, but which are assumed to be . . ." He searched for words.

"The usual," Martinez finished.

"Yes. The usual." Roland frowned. "The youngest child and heir, Lord Simon, died at Magaria. That leaves Lord Yoshitoshi's brother Lord Eizo as the heir. And Lord Oda is *his* eldest child."

"And the presumed heir to Clan Yoshitoshi. Very good. But presumably Lord Oda's increased prospects didn't escape the attention of other clans with eligible women. How did we happen to land him for Vipsania?"

Roland's stolid face took on an expression of grim satisfaction. "Lord Oda's only the *presumed* heir," he said. "The elder Yoshitoshis are very strict—remember the disinherited daughter?—and Oda's got some younger siblings who want the title. Oda also has some debts he preferred his father and uncle not know about—"

"Debts?" Martinez began to choke on laughter.

"The usual." With a sidelong smile.

"So you bought up his debts, and . . ."

"The debts will be canceled after the marriage ceremony," Roland said. "The only thing holding us up was that Lord Yoshitoshi insisted on interviewing Vipsania personally. He let us know just yesterday that she passed her audition." He smiled. "Now we'll see how Vipsania runs a video company."

Martinez tried to stifle his rising hilarity. "Video company?"

"Clan Yoshitoshi and its clients own a majority interest in Empire Broadcasting. That's two entertainment channels, four devoted to sports, and one to information, broadcasting in all of forty-one solar systems not counting the ones the Naxids currently occupy. We're going to ask Lord Yoshitoshi to let Vipsania run it. We think he will—he considers broadcasting a plebeian pursuit, nothing like the high culture here in the acropolis that really matters to him."

Surprise quelled Martinez's laughter. "Vipsania knows how to run a major broadcasting corporation?"

"She'll *hire* people for that." Irritably. "The point is that she'll be in a position to influence the public about . . ." He made an equivocal gesture with his hand. ". . . about whatever we think suitable. As, for example, why you aren't being given a meaningful command." He shot Martinez a shrewd glance from under his heavy brows. "You won't have a problem with an adulatory documentary about your exploits, will you?"

Martinez felt a waft of pleasure at the idea, immediately followed by caution. "Perhaps," he said. "But it won't be the public who decides my assignments."

"I'd prefer something more subtle myself, but we can always keep the broadcast in reserve." Roland nodded to an acquaintance passing on the street. "The wedding will be very soon, by the way—we're starting to get the point where I want to get as many of my kinfolk off the planet as possible."

"I've been telling you that for over a month."

Roland chose to ignore the comment. Passing down the walkway, he and Martinez negotiated their way through a pack of glits—fashionable, decorative young people who chattered their way past, leaving behind a waft of laughter and hair pomade. Glits had been in the mode before the Naxid revolt, but the seriousness of the war seemed to have suppressed them: these were the first Martinez had seen since his return.

"If only we can get you and Walpurga married before the time comes to leave," Roland continued, after the glits had passed.

Martinez only smiled. Roland gave him a sharp look. "Do you actually have someone in mind? Someone who isn't a *warrant officer,* that is?"

Martinez increased what he hoped was the mystery of his smile. "Perhaps I do. How are Walpurga's prospects?"

"Nothing concrete, though there are a number of possibilities."

"Get her and Vipsania and Proney and yourself off the planet. Do it *now,* whether they're married or not." He tried to put all his urgency into the words. "Bad things are going to happen here. I think the Fleet's going to get another pasting."

Roland gave a grim nod. "Yes. I think you're right."

And where do your schemes go then? Martinez wanted to ask. But the words never passed his lips: he was afraid that Roland might admit that had been betting on the Naxids all along.

"Which brings us to the reason I'm following you down the street," Martinez said. "I need an interview with Lord Chen, and I need it as soon as possible."

Roland gave him a frowning look. "This isn't about your posting, is it?"

"No. It's about . . ." Martinez realized how absurd this sounded even as he said it. "I have a plan to redeploy the Fleet and save the empire."

To Martinez's surprise, Roland stopped dead on the pavement, then raised his arm and engaged his sleeve display.

"Personal and urgent from Lord Roland Martinez to Lord Chen," Roland said. "I need you to meet my brother, and the meeting must be at once. Please respond."

He lowered his arm and looked up at Martinez.

"Right," he said. "Now it's up to you."

* * *

"And you developed this plan yourself?" Lord Chen asked. He had received Martinez—graciously, under the circumstances—in his garden, amid the scent of the purple lu-doi blossoms growing on either side of the walkway. The afternoon was well advanced, and the garden largely in shade, overhung by the sunlit, winged Nayanid gables. It was growing chilly.

"I—" Martinez hesitated. "I developed it with Lady Sula."

Lord Chen nodded. His dark eyes were thoughtful. "Our two most celebrated officers," he said. "That speaks well for these ideas. But you realize that this isn't simply a military decision. It's political, and of the highest possible order."

"Yes, my lord." It *had* occurred to him that the government leaving Zanshaa for the first time in twelve thousand years was very possibly an act of some significance.

Chen frowned. "I'll send the plan to my sister, for comments."

Martinez had hoped he would. Squadron Commander Chen had been orbiting the system for over a month now, staring into the oblivion of Wormhole 3, through which the Naxids would come from Magaria with annihilating force and missile batteries blazing. It was very possible that she would welcome any plan that would enable her to evade that confrontation.

"I'll presume on Squadcom Do-faq's patience and send the plan to him as well," Martinez said.

"Very good, Lord Gareth. Ask him to copy any comments to me."

"I'll do that."

A subtle smile played about Lord Chen's lips. "Blow up the ring," he said, half to himself. "The idea has a certain barbaric vigor." He rose. "And now, if you'll excuse me, I have several clients waiting."

Martinez pushed back the chair, made of a long spiral of

wire, and stood. "Thank you for seeing me on such short notice."

Chen waved off the inconvenience with a movement of his hand. "I was happy to oblige your brother. Give him my best wishes when you next see him."

Martinez turned at the sound of soft footsteps on the gravel walkway. He saw a young woman holding a tray with teacups and a teapot. She was tall and black-haired and wore a soft, nubbly suit of an autumnal orange, with a white rosette and its dangling mourning ribbons pinned with pleasant asymmetry to one shoulder.

"I didn't mean to bother you," she said in a soft voice. "But I heard you had company, and so I thought . . ."

She made a subtle movement that called attention to the contents of her tray.

"That was very good of you," Chen said. He turned to Martinez. "May I present my daughter, Terza? Terza, this is—"

"I recognize Lord Captain Martinez, of course," she said. Her dark eyes turned to Martinez. "Would you like tea, my lord?"

"I . . ." Martinez hesitated. His meeting with Chen was clearly over, and it seemed absurd to stop for a cup of tea now.

"I can't remain," Chen said, "but if you'd like to share a cup with Terza, by all means stay." He looked at Terza. "I have Em-braq waiting in the office."

"I understand." She turned to Martinez again. "By all means stay, if you have the time."

Martinez agreed to remain. "I'm sorry for your loss," he said. He had no idea who exactly had died, but there were many Peer families who were wearing white after Magaria.

She poured tea, the movements of her hands pale and elegant in the shadowed courtyard.

"Thank you," she said. "I'm told that he was very much admired by his crew."

"I'm sure he was, my lady," Martinez said.

"I see from the morning reports that your sister is marrying Lord Oda. Please give her my congratulations."

"Oh. Do you know Vipsania?"

"Of course. Our families have been acquainted for some time now, while you've been off-world making your name." She smiled. "Under the circumstances, we can't expect you to know all your sister's friends."

Martinez raised the fragile tea cup with its leafy decoration—Sula would be able to tell him its lineage, he knew—and breathed in the smoky fragrance of the tea. He was about to remark that he hadn't seen Terza at last night's party, then realized she wouldn't have attended, she was in mourning.

He sipped the tea to give himself time to think of an appropriately neutral remark.

"Lovely tea," he managed.

"From our estate in the To-bai-to highlands," Terza said. "It's a first cutting."

"Very nice." He sipped again, the tea warming him in the growing chill.

Martinez left after half an hour with a vague memory of pleasant twilight conversation with a graceful, soft-voiced woman amid the fragrance of smoky tea and sweet lu-doi blossoms.

Had he met Terza a year ago, he reflected, he would have made a point of calling on her again. But now, as soon as the door of the Chen Palace closed behind him, his mind turned at once to Sula.

He had made plans to join Sula for dinner, then a show or a club. After which they would return to her apartment, the bed, and the scent of Sandama Twilight.

Once back at the Shelley Palace, Martinez started the water steaming into his bath, added a hops-scented bath oil, and then remembered that he intended to send a message to Squadron Commander Do-faq. Since there was a degree of urgency involved, he thought he'd better turn to the message immediately.

He brushed his hair and buttoned his uniform tunic, and faint alarm rang through him as his fingers missed the disk of the Golden Orb from its place at his throat. He checked his pockets, then remembered where he'd last seen the disk—dangling on its ribbon from the erect phallus of one of the Sevigny figures arched over Sula's bed.

Well. It had seemed funny at the time.

Martinez decided to send the message without the medal. He sat at his desk and activated the camera set into the mirror, and composed a deferent, mildly flattering message to go along with the plan. "We would be interested in any comments you may care to make," he said.

He watched his words print themselves across his desk, and he made a few changes, then rerecorded the whole thing, without the hesitations and with more polished phrasing. He appended a copy of the plan he downloaded from the sleeve memory in his tunic, then sent the message on. It would take three or four hours for the transmission to reach Do-faq where his squadron was zooming around the other side of Shaamah, and that there would be no reply till morning at the earliest.

His duty toward the salvation of the empire complete, Martinez stripped and settled himself into his bath. The scent of a hops floated to his nostrils. Steam rose. Heat soaked into his limbs.

He thought of Sula, the candlelight glowing on the curves of her body. The touch of her lips. The fine, mad frenzy in her eyes as she helped him draft the operational plan.

He wondered if it were possible to live any longer without these elements in his life.

The comm chimed, a two-tone effect in his bedroom and bathroom both. Martinez thought about answering, but didn't. He decided he deserved a few peaceful moments in his bath.

The chime ceased. There were a few moments of silence, and then his sleeve comm chimed, a higher-pitched tone than the room comm. Martinez decided that whatever the message was, it wasn't worth climbing out of the bath, let alone getting his tunic sleeve wet while answering.

There were another few minutes of silence. Martinez told the tap to turn on again and added more hot water to the bath. He'd closed his eyes and was on the edge of slumber when the heavy teak door of his room slammed open. The house trembled.

"Damn it, Proney, I'm in the bath!" he roared in his captain's voice. These interruptions from Sempronia were becoming annoying.

If she started throwing things again, he thought, he'd make a fine sitting target in the tub.

"I'm not Sempronia," said a frigid voice. Martinez looked up in surprise from his bath to see Vipsania standing in the door.

"Don't you ever answer a page?" she demanded. "There's an urgent family conference downstairs. It's a crisis—a bad one."

Vipsania turned and stalked away. "Marriage contract not going well?" Martinez asked after her, but there was no reply.

He toweled, threw on some casual clothes, and bounded down the stairs to find Roland, Vipsania, and Walpurga in one of the parlors. Roland turned his head as Martinez entered. His expression was grim. "Close the door behind you," he said. "I don't want anyone outside the family hearing this."

Martinez slid the heavy door shut and dropped into a plush chair. Vipsania and Walpurga sat on satin cushions on an ivory divan, and Roland sat like an uncrowned king in a massive, hooded leather armchair. Vipsania turned to Martinez.

"I've just got a hysterical call from PJ Ngeni," she said. "He's received a message from Sempronia that she's broken the engagement and run off with another man—*with the man she loves.*"

Martinez felt the slow, cold toll of doom sound through his blood. "Did she say who?" he managed.

"Apparently not," Vipsania said. "We've been cudgeling our brains trying to think who it might be."

"It hardly matters," Walpurga said. "Sempronia isn't of an age to marry without the family's permission."

Roland gave a furious little jerk of his chin. "So she's run off with a man and *can't* marry him," he scorned. "Is that supposed to make it any better?" His voice turned thoughtful. "If we sent police or private detectives after her, that would only make the scandal worse. Our only hope is a private appeal." He turned to Martinez. "Do you have any idea—*any idea*—who it might be?"

"I'm thinking," Martinez said, and what he thought was, *Shankaracharya, you little bastard.* He turned to Vipsania. "How was PJ?"

"Grief-stricken. In tears." Her tone was disapproving. "It seems he's made the mistake of caring for her."

"We *all* made that mistake," Roland said grimly. He passed his hand over his forehead, as if swiping away any inconvenient sympathy. "We can't afford to make enemies of the Ngenis," he said. "They're our patrons and are too critical to everything we hope to accomplish." He turned to Walpurga. "I'm sorry," he said, "but you're going to have to marry PJ, and soon. We can't drag out your engagement as we could with Sempronia."

Walpurga took this news with a long breath and a hardening of her dark eyes. "Very well," she said.

Roland took on a calculating look. "The marriage won't have to last long, I think. And then"—he offered a reassuring smile—"then we can pay off PJ and find you someone more to your liking." With one hand he thoughtfully brushed the soft leather of his chair arm. "I'll contact Lord Pierre and make the arrangements."

Martinez felt his anger rise. "Now wait a minute," he said. "The whole engagement to PJ Ngeni was a *fraud*. I *know* it was a fraud—it was *my* fraud, I *thought* of it." He turned to Walpurga. "This was never intended to be a real marriage. You don't have to do this—not to pay for Sempronia's mistake."

"Someone has to pay for it," Vipsania said levelly. "Otherwise we're disgraced in the eyes of all the highest Peers and of the Ngeni family."

"The Ngenis will get over it," Martinez said. "So will everyone else. They all know how much PJ is worth. All they have to do is get PJ drunk and *he'll tell them himself.*" He pointed at Walpurga. "I *forbid* you to marry PJ Ngeni. You're worth twenty of him and you know it."

A light flush dappled Walpurga's cheeks. She looked down at her hands. "No," she said. "It's necessary. I'll marry PJ."

Martinez slammed his fist on the arm of his chair. The sound boomed against the paneled walls. He turned to Roland. "If you think PJ is worth so damn much," he said, "then *you* marry him."

A soft smile played over Roland's lips. "I don't think PJ has the proper hormonal bias." He looked at Martinez. "You've got to stop thinking like a military officer, Gare. You can't carry the High City by storm. You have to *infiltrate.*"

Martinez rose to his feet and took an angry step toward his brother. "What prize are you playing for? What is there in Zanshaa High City that's worth selling your sister to PJ Ngeni?"

Roland's chin lifted. "We're playing for our proper place in the order of the empire," he said. "What else is worth the game?" His mild brown eyes rose to gaze at Martinez. "And what about yourself, Gare? I haven't noticed that you're free of ambition. *You* devised this sham engagement in part to benefit yourself—and now it's Walpurga who pays when it goes wrong."

Fury blazed in Martinez's blood. He took another step toward Roland and raised a fist.

Roland made no move, and he regarded Martinez with a kind of dispassionate, studious interest. Then Martinez turned to Walpurga, and he slowly lowered the fist.

"I'm not going to fight for you if you won't," he said.

Walpurga said nothing, just turned to Roland. "Make the call," she said.

"You're all insane!" Martinez offered, and stormed from the room.

He bounded up the stairs to his room, still humid with the scent of hops, and stalked for a long moment in a tight angry circuit at the foot of his bed. Then he raised his arm and triggered the comm display.

"Urgent to Lieutenant Lord Nikkul Shankaracharya," he said. "This is Captain Martinez. You are to contact me immediately."

The answering call came in a few minutes, and it was from Sempronia. Her narrowed eyes looked at him from out of the sleeve display.

"Too late," she said.

"It's not," Martinez said. "Your arrangement with PJ was a joke—no one ever intended for you to go through with it. I don't care what you do with Shankaracharya, and maybe even PJ doesn't—but now that you've run off, Walpurga is actually going to have to go through with *your marriage*."

Sempronia gave a contemptuous little puff of anger through pursed lips. "Good," she said. "Walpurga had no problem with PJ when *I* was engaged to him—now let *her* entertain him for a change."

"Proney—"

"I'm not your pawn any more, Gareth!" Anger came hissing off Sempronia's tongue. "*You* shackled me to PJ! And *then* you wrecked Nikkul's career!" The display whirled, and Martinez saw a flash of ceiling, of floor, of a table behind which sat the wide-eyed, meek figure of Shankaracharya. There was the sound of something crumpling near the sound pickup, and then Sempronia flickered back into the frame, holding a large, official certificate, all gold ink and elegant calligraphy, that she brandished before the camera.

"There!" she said. "We've both been to the Peers' Gene Bank! Our visit will be posted in the official record tomorrow. We can get married now." She offered the camera a defiant glare. "You told me to help Nikkul choose another path. That's what I'm going to do."

"You can't marry without permission," Martinez said, fearing as he said it that this would only provoke another storm.

"Then the family will give permission," Sempronia said. "Or if you won't, then we'll just live together until we can marry on our own." She dropped the certificate out of frame. "The one thing you won't do is stop us. Because if you interfere with our arrangement, people will start to hear about some of Roland's dealings, particularly with the likes of Lord Ummir or Lady Convocate Khaa."

Perfectly respectable Naxids, as Roland had called them. Martinez suspected others might disagree with Roland's description.

"May I speak to Lieutenant Shankaracharya?" Martinez asked.

He heard Shankaracharya murmur something in the background, but Sempronia was quick to answer. "No. You may not. He actually respects you, but I know better. Comm: end transmission."

The orange end-stamp appeared in the display. "Comm," Martinez said grimly, "save transmission."

He called Roland. "Sempronia's with a Lieutenant Lord Nikkul Shankaracharya."

Roland's brow clouded. "Isn't he one of *your* officers?"

"He's Sempronia's officer now," Martinez said. "I'm forwarding you the recording of the conversation I just had with her. I suggest you pay particular attention to the threat she made at the end."

He sent the recording, then erased it from his own array's

memory and blanked the display, the chameleon-weave fabric returning to its normal viridian green.

Martinez stood in the silence of his room for a long moment, his anger burning. *Isn't he one of* your *officers?* It was becoming clear who was going to get the blame for Sempronia's defection.

He decided not to stay around to wait for the blame to descend on his head. He changed into civilian evening dress, brushed his hair, and descended the stair in silence. The doors to the parlor were still closed, he saw; the family conference was still going on, with marriages and condemnation being assigned on every hand.

Martinez felt his spirits lift the second he was outside of the palace and into the mellow twilight. In the pre-dinner hour there was little traffic on the streets, and few walkers. A scattering of stars were visible in the darkening sky, and Zanshaa's shadow had cut a wide slice out of the silver accelerator ring. A ship's antimatter torch blazed directly overhead, brighter than anything in the sky, and heading—Martinez guessed—for Wormhole 4 and Seizho. Thoughts of Sula set his nerves tingling.

Martinez bought an armful of flowers from the Torminel pushcart vendor on the corner—a carnivore selling blossoms—then turned the corner and walked on to Sula's building. She met him at the door of her apartment, fading surprise still in her eyes.

"You're early," she said. She wore a green Fleet fatigue coverall, apparently her usual dress at home.

"Sorry," Martinez said. "I couldn't wait." He offered her the flowers. "I thought I'd replace those stolen daffodils."

Sula looked at the extravagant bouquet with bemused pleasure. "You're going to have to give me a lot more vases at this rate," she said.

He stood in the hideous Sevigny extravagance of the front room while Sula busied herself filling some vases, equally hideous, that had been sitting empty on stands, intended apparently as objects of admiration. Fleet officers, raised in a tradition in which every object had its proper drawer or bay or locker, were a tidy breed, but Sula's room was preternaturally neat: even papers with arithmetical jottings, worksheets from her hobby of mathematical puzzles, were squared neatly on a table, slightly offset so that the numbers on the upper right corners were visible. Aside from the vases with their flowers there was no indication that Martinez had ever been present in the room at all, something that sent a waft of depression sighing through him.

"I was just about to take a bath and change," Sula said as she returned a vase to its stand.

Martinez brightened. "Would you like company in the bath?"

"Good grief, no," she said. Martinez blinked in surprise. And then, as if Sula had begun to suspect she'd been too blunt, she stepped close to him and put her arms around him. "My baths are for me alone," she said. "It's one of those things I'm fussy about. Sorry."

"That's all right," Martinez said. How Sula's standards of privacy could possibly have been maintained in the Fleet was something he couldn't imagine.

He kissed her. "Would you mind terribly if I left my family and joined yours?"

She gave him a curious look. "My family's dead," she said.

"There are advantages to that," Martinez said. "And in any case it's you I want to join."

Her expression softened. He kissed her again, and her hands cupped the back of his head to hold his kiss to hers.

Join Sula's family? he thought.

He could. He believed he could.

EIGHT

Sula watched as the juggler spun and danced in the center of a whirl of blades. Torchlight glowed on keen-edged steel. The knives were attached by elastic to the juggler's wrists, ankles, and hips, and snapped back as she threw them out over the heads of her audience. To control them she had to catch them and throw them again, or let the elastic wrap around her limbs or body or head, and then cast the knives off with a jerk of the head or a spin of the body.

The timing was exquisite, and breathtaking. One slip and the girl would be cut, or if the elastic was cut instead someone in the audience could get a knife in the eye.

Sula's breath frosted in the chill midnight air. Martinez's arms coil around her from behind, and she leaned back against his warmth.

He had taken her to a series of clubs in the Lower Town, and on their return had encountered a group of street performers presenting their act on the wide apron before the lower terminal of the funicular railway. Surrounded by torches, Cree drummers had beaten a rhythm while Daimong acrobats balanced atop chairs or barrels or each other; and nocturnal Torminel, huge eyes wide in the semidarkness, had performed a slapstick routine. The air was heavy with the scents of roasting chestnuts and ears of maize produce shipped up from Zanshaa's southern hemisphere, sold by vendors from portable charcoal braziers. Now a Terran girl barely in her adolescence was mastering the flying knives with an intent stonefaced courage that left Sula dry-mouthed with admiration.

"Here," Martinez said. "Try one of these."

In one hand he held a crystalized taswa fruit just purchased from a vendor. Sula bit down on it, and bright sparks of sugar exploded on her tongue, followed at once by a tartness that flooded her mouth with flavor.

"Thank you," she said as the acid puckered her lips.

The juggler was a blur of motion now, the bright knives whipping around her. Sula could hear the sound of her soft leather soles on the flagstones. The juggler bounded into a twisting somersault, landing on her feet just outside of the knives' danger zone. Her hands were a blur as she snatched the steel from the air. Metal clacked on metal. And then the girl was motionless, the knives bunched in her hands, and in the absolute silence she drew her feet together and bowed.

The audience, a hundred or so drifting toward the High City from their evening in the Lower Town, burst into applause and cheers. Sula cheered wildly with the rest, applauding till her palms grew red, and when one of the Torminel came by with a little portable terminal for contributions, she keyed in a generous contribution.

Another act followed, a mournful-looking Terran whose performance consisted entirely of bouncing a ball on the pavement, but doing it in surprising ways. Martinez's arms were still around Sula. She took another bite of the candied taswa fruit.

I am sitting in a circle of torches watching a grown man bounce a ball, Sula thought, *and I am feeling . . . what?*

Happiness . . . The surprise was so strong that she took a sudden astonished breath of the charcoal-scented air.

Happiness. Bliss. Contentment.

The thought that she might be happy was so startling that she had to probe the thought carefully, as if it might explode.

She found herself suspicious of the very idea. Moments of happiness had been rare in her life, and nonexistent since she'd stepped into the role of Lady Sula. She had not thought happiness possible, not when her whole life was an imposture and when she had to remain constantly on guard against the lapse that could expose her.

The man with the ball reacted to an unexpected bounce, and Sula laughed. She hugged Martinez's arms to her. Lazy pleasure filled her mind.

Happiness.

What a shock.

"No," said Lord Tork. "Never. Abandon the capital? Such a thing can never happen."

Lord Chen feigned a curiosity he did not feel. "Both my sister and Lord Squadcom Do-faq have endorsed the plan. What is your objection?"

"Zanshaa is the heart of the empire!" Tork chimed. "The capital cannot be surrendered!"

"To defend Zanshaa is to stake everything on a battle where the odds are against us from the start," said Chen.

"If the government *can* be moved—" began Lady Seekin.

"The government will not move," Lord Tork said. "Lord Saïd would not permit such a radical step."

We'll see about that, Lord Chen thought grimly. He would seek a personal appointment with the Lord Senior.

The eight members of the Fleet Control Board sat around their broad black-topped table in their large, shadowy room in the Commandery. Someone had forgotten to tell the staff to remove the ninth chair, the one suitable for cradling the long breastbone of a Lai-own, and it sat empty as a reminder of Lady San-torath, flung from the rock of the High City two mornings ago.

"I would like to further remark," Tork continued, "that it is not the place of a junior captain to submit these kinds of memorials to the Board. It is the task of junior captains to carry out the tasks assigned them in silence, and to spare us their opinions."

Lord Chen suspected that he was stepping into a trap, but a need for clarification demanded he speak. "I beg your pardon, lord fleetcom," he said, "but it was not a junior captain who submitted this plan to the board. It was myself."

Knowing there was prejudice against Martinez on the board, he had told them only that it was the product of two officers who had brought it to his attention.

Tork turned his white, round-eyed face to Lord Chen. A strip of dead flesh dangled from his chin like a large, twisted whisker as he spoke. "Squadron Commander Do-faq submitted the memorial to me this morning, and identified Captain Martinez as the author."

"Martinez!" cried Junior Fleetcom Pezzini, as if some terrible private theory had just been confirmed, and slapped his hand on the table in annoyance.

Lord Chen would have mentioned Lady Sula as the co-author, but he suspected he would only blacken her name.

"Captain Martinez has a habit of submitting memorials to his superiors," Tork continued as disapproval rang in his words. "He has offered a radical tactical theory to Do-faq, and Do-faq has given it to your sister. Now they are both engaged in maneuvers that are detrimental to the traditions and practice of the service."

"Will his interference never cease?" Pezzini said, just as Chen was about to reply. "Just a few days ago he blackened the name of a client of mine, a perfectly sound young man who revered him—revered him against my advice, I must point out."

"I fail to see where any of this is improper," Lord Chen said. "Captain Martinez submitted his suggestions to his superiors with proper regard for rank and with all deference. And now *your own commanders* see merit in these proposals."

"The rot has spread far," Tork said. "I trust that Lord Fleetcom Kangas will halt the infection and restore discipline. Only the tactics of our ancestors, adhered to with utmost inflexibility, can possibly save the capital."

"Let Martinez rot in his damned training school," Pezzini said. "That should cool his ambitions."

Chen, his face expressionless, felt his insides twist with growing contempt. *You people know nothing but how to lose a war,* he wanted to shout. *You've been offered a way to win, and you can't see it.*

But he kept silent. He knew that protest was useless in the face of Lord Tork's rigidity, and his private lobbying with other board members hadn't yet reached the stage where they would support a vote against the chairman.

He would send the Lord Senior a message requesting an immediate meeting. And then hope for the best.

Martinez, in high heart, stepped into the foyer of the Shelley Palace twirling the ribbon of the Golden Orb medal around his index finger. As he prepared to bound up the stairs to his room, he was approached by one of the maidservants—a thick-legged, homely woman, the type his sibs hired so that the Martinez sisters would always be the most beautiful women in the room.

"Captain Martinez," the woman said. "Lord Roland asked me to tell you that he'd like to see you in his office."

In his memory, a girl snatched flying knives from the air. Martinez caught his medal in his hand with a sigh and said, "Very well, thank you."

He found Roland behind his desk, talking to someone—a Torminel—on his display. "We hoped you could attend," he said, "as you've been so kind to us since our arrival."

The Torminel, whomever she was, accepted the invitation, whatever it was, with pleasure. Roland signed off and looked up.

"I hope you'll be able to take time off from your carnal adventures," he said, "to attend your sister's wedding tomorrow, at sixteen and one."

Martinez dropped into a chair. "Which sister are we talking about?"

"Vipsania. After which she will be joining Lord Oda and his family on a visit to their clients on Zarafan."

Martinez put his feet up on his brother's desk. He was in a buoyant mood, and not simply because he'd spent the night in Sula's arms. In the morning had come the communication from Do-faq saying that he approved Martinez's plan and had sent it on to the Fleet Control Board. Do-faq had also sent the results of his latest series of experiments in the new tactics, and he and Sula had analyzed them over breakfast. He couldn't help but be buoyed by physical satiation followed by useful mental exercise, and all with a partner whose imagination and wit more than matched his own.

Poor Vipsania, he thought.

"Sounds like a delightful honeymoon," he said, "stuck on a ship with a pack of her desiccated in-laws. Will she be running her broadcasting empire from Zarafan?"

"Probably, unless Zarafan in its turn becomes unsafe."

Roland folded his hands on his desk and looked at Martinez from over the glossy toes of the shoes. "If Sempronia tries to contact you, I'd be obliged if you don't reply."

Martinez only raised his eyebrows.

"She's to be disinherited," Roland said. "No money, no communication, no contact. When we have the time to pack them all up, her belongings will be given to charity."

"Charity," Martinez repeated, as if the word were a stranger.

"Walpurga insisted on banishment for Sempronia, and after the threat she made I can't say I have any objection. Oh, did I mention this?—Sempronia agrees." Roland gave a smile filled with grim satisfaction. "I spoke to her last night, and again this morning. She'll be given permission to marry, but she'll be a Shankaracharya from now on—he'll have to support her fancies, not us."

"I believe he's rich," Martinez pointed out.

"Clan Shankaracharya is heavily invested in pharmaceuticals and biochemicals." *Trust Roland to know these details.* "Nothing on Zanshaa, though—we expect she'll relocate after the war."

"No doubt a crushing blow," Martinez said. Roland seemed to have forgotten it was their father, he thought, who did the disinheriting—that was one task he couldn't delegate to one of his offspring. Martinez might be able to influence that decision with a personal message, perhaps not to Lord Martinez, but to his lady, a woman to whose romantic nature an elopement might appeal . . .

Roland gave Martinez a curious look. "What did you do to enrage Sempronia so totally? I've never heard her use such language."

Martinez was silent. Roland shrugged, then continued with his news.

"Lord Pierre and I have fixed Walpurga's wedding with PJ for three days from now. It won't be a very elaborate affair, but we hope you'll be present."

"You don't mind if I wear mourning, do you?" Martinez barely had to search his mind for the cutting reply.

Roland's eyes were level beneath his heavy brows. "You know the wedding's necessary."

"I know nothing of the sort." Martinez tossed the Golden Orb medal into the air, then caught it. "You want the Ngenis because they give you access to the highest circles of the capital. Very well." He drew his feet off the table and leaned forward, letting his gaze meet that of Roland. "Suppose I give you all that myself? Suppose I sacrifice myself in place of Walpurga?"

Roland's gaze was unblinking. "You're offering to marry?"

"Yes." Tossing the medal again.

Roland drew back, his frown thoughtful. "I would have suggested it myself if I hadn't known how much you enjoy being a bachelor—I assumed you'd turn me down flat."

"Perhaps I would have. But with all this romance in the air, how can I resist?"

Roland's look grew abstract. "I can suggest a number of young ladies—"

"I already have one in mind."

Roland's eyes narrowed. "This isn't your Warrant Officer Amanda, is it? Because my patience is—"

"Lady Sula," Martinez said, enunciating the words with passionate clarity.

Roland blinked, and Martinez rejoiced at his surprise.

"I see," Roland said slowly. "It's not Miss Amanda you've spent the last couple nights with, it's—"

"None of your business."

"Quite." Roland fingered his chin. "She has no money, of course."

"Only the Sula title, which is of the highest. You can't find a more formidable ancestry in the records. And it's the ancestry and the title that opens the doors to all those drawing rooms and ministries, the ones that won't open to mere money."

"True." Roland still gazed inward at his own calculations. "Still, we'd have to lay out a fortune to set the two of you up in the High City. Provide you a palace here, a place in the country—she can ride, yes?"

"I've no idea." Martinez grinned. "But what *will* be necessary is an empire-class collection of porcelain."

"Porcelain?" Roland was frank in his amazement. "What does porcelain have to do with anything? Has she made it a condition?"

"No, but trust me to know my bride."

A thought occurred to Roland. "Have you even asked her yet?"

"No, but I will tonight." Martinez suppressed a grim laugh. "How can she resist a family like ours?"

"I doubt she will," Roland murmured. "She must be sick of being poor in a rich world."

Martinez clapped his hands and made as if to rise. "So! Walpurga's off the hook?"

Roland snorted out a condescending little laugh. "Of course not. Don't be ridiculous. I can't go back on my word to Lord Pierre."

Martinez gave his brother a long, angry look. Roland held his gaze for a moment, then gave a snort of irritation. "Don't give me those Command-room eyes—your shoulder boards are too new, and I'm not one of your snotty cadets."

"I thought we had a deal."

"Not for Caroline Sula we don't." Roland gave his fingernails a fastidious inspection. "The Ngenis are rich, they're already in place in the Convocation and the ministries, and haven't lost their influence. Rehabilitating Lady Sula would be a years-long project—it would pay off eventually, but the Ngenis are paying off *now*." He looked up from his fingernails. "But don't let me discourage your matrimonial ambitions. Sula's beautiful and bright, and that's one more advantage than *you've* got."

"Damn you," said Martinez. Roland shrugged.

Martinez rose and left the office.

She's the heir to a title, he thought, *and I'm not. And thankfully all my children will be Sulas.*

"No," said Lord Saïd. "That is out of the question. The empire has been ruled from the High City for twelve thousand years, and will for ten million more."

The Lord Senior's office, unlike the gloomy board room in the Commandery, was brilliant with light. One transparent wall showed the great granite dome of the Great Refuge, from which the Shaa had ruled their empire, and beyond that a spectacular view of the Lower Town. From his seat Chen could see the private gallery by which Lord Saïd's predecessors had once traveled to the Great Refuge to receive orders from their masters. But the Great Refuge was closed now, with the death of the last Shaa, and vague plans to make a museum of the place had been ended by the war. The first man in the empire sat before him, comfortably disposed in a huge domed chair with a kind of flaring hood that overshadowed the Lord Senior's face.

"The High City and the government aren't the same thing," Lord Chen said, paraphrasing Martinez's memorial. "The government can be anywhere—it *should* be somewhere else, where a stray missile can't wipe it out. Where it won't be trapped on the planet if the battle goes against us."

"What is a more glorious death than one in service to the Praxis?" asked Lord Saïd. He was over ninety, with close-cropped white hair and mustache and a beaky nose that age was drawing ever closer to his prominent chin. His clan was known for their fierce conservatism, and he had been placed at the head of the government on the very day of the rebellion, when he had denounced the Naxid Lord Senior from his seat in the Convocation, and led the resistance that had ended with the rebels being flung from the High City to the rocks below.

Chen looked at him. "The government is determined to die, then?" he said.

Saïd seemed a little surprised by Chen's words. "We are determined to preserve both the capital and the Praxis." His eyes darkened with thought, and then he said, "I shall tell you a secret, lord convocate, and trust that you shall repeat it to no one. Since almost the very beginning, we have been in communication with the rebel government on Naxas, their so-called Committee for the Salvation of the Praxis."

Chen stared at the Lord Senior in profound shock. "My lord?" he said.

"The chain of wormhole relay stations between Zanshaa and Magaria has never been cut," Saïd said. "We can speak to each other if we need to. They have demanded our surrender, and we have refused . . . officially."

Something in Saïd's tone sent a cold waft of suspicion through Chen's thoughts. "And unofficially?"

"Since the failure at Magaria the Naxids have been contacted by what claims to be a dissident organization within our government. They claim a base of support both within the Convocation and the Fleet. They have been pleading for time while they organize an overthrow of my," Saïd smiled, "inflexible government. And our false traitors are also using the conduit to feed them false information—for instance that the Fourth Fleet is in a much better state than it actually is, and will be here from Harzapid at any time."

"And the Naxids believe this?"

The Lord Senior gave a subtle shrug. "They show every sign of belief. We hope to delay long enough to bring reinforcements to Zanshaa."

"This game is very dangerous, my lord," Chen said. "You can never be certain who is deceiving who. And they may decide to force the issue by coming anyway."

Saïd gave a thoughtful nod. "True, lord convocate," he said. "But what choice do we have?"

Chen left the Lord Senior's office with his mind on a thoughtful, rolling boil. He was a Peer of the highest caste, and until the previous day he had felt himself ready to meet a Peer's fate, dying for the Praxis beneath the fire of Naxid antimatter bombs, or with a pistol to his head as Naxid gendarmes broke down the door of the Chen Palace.

If he had thought the situation completely without hope, he would have shot his wife and daughter first, and he would have expected them to show the same indifference to fate as he hoped to display himself.

But that determination had ended the previous afternoon, in the quiet garden amid the scent of lu-doi blossoms, when Martinez had spoken to him, and Chen had seen new possibilities open before him like a flower.

Now, Lord Chen realized, it was possible that his wife and daughter would survive, and that very possibly he would live as well. And in order for this to happen, he would have to convince enough members of his own caste of the virtues of a plan developed by their social inferior.

Mere days ago, he would have laughed at this idea. But that was before he had spoken to Martinez.

He already had a mental list of people to talk to, people both in Saïd's administration and without it.

He stepped into his own office and told his secretary to contact the first person on the list.

A singer stepped onto the stage. She was dressed in the traditional flounced skirts of the derivoo, her hair was drawn severely into a forward-tilting pile atop her head, and her face was whitened, with a perfect circle of red on each cheek.

The audience fell into an expectant silence. Accompanied only by three musicians, the derivoo began to sing. It was a song of love and longing, and despite her antique appearance the singer's voice was a wonder, caressing each syllable with the silky care of a languid lover. The singer's hands, whitened like her face, fluttered in the air like doves, illustrating the words as she sang. At times the singer paused, letting the suspense mount, and Sula found herself holding her breath until the singer released the tension with her voice.

At the end, the applause was ecstatic. Sula had seen derivoo before, but only on video: she hadn't realized how powerful a live performance could be.

"She's a wonder, isn't she?" Martinez said.

"Yes," Sula agreed. His hand slipped across the table and took hers. His hand was large and warm and not over-moist. On the whole, Sula decided, a good hand.

The singer began again. It was a song about death, a mother pleading with the unknowable for the return of her child. The voice that had formerly caressed now took on a desperate, raw tone of perfect emotional desperation that cut like a razor. By the end of the performance, the singer's whitened face was furrowed by the track of a single tear.

Sula retrieved her hand to applaud. Listening to the singer was like having her nerves scorched with acid, but for some reason it felt *good*. The songs of mourning and love drew aside the curtains from a charged, elemental fact of the universe, something true and primal and grand. These, the songs said, were death and longing, the unchangeable facts of existence. This, the songs said, was what it meant to be human.

Derivoo was almost wholly a human art. Though one of Terra's great contributions to imperial civilization was tempered tuning, few of the great composers or performers to make use of this discovery were human. Because the faces of the Daimong were expressionless, their chiming voices communicated all emotion, nuance, and context; they were born into what was essentially a musical environment, and lived in it all their lives. They were capable of enormous brilliance and subtlety in musical interpretation, though their performances were best appreciated in recording: the scent of rotting flesh tended to limit the appeal of concert appearances, and the best place to appreciate one of the magnificent massed Daimong choirs was from far upwind.

Whereas it was generally agreed that the Cree *were* music. Their primitive eye-spots were balanced by the sensitive hearing of their broad ears and the sound-ranging capabilities of their melodious voices. Their personalities tended toward the effervescent side of the spectrum, and the music they created was ideal for expressing joy and delight. The most popular performers and composers tended to be Cree, and even if a song were written or popularized by a member of some other species, it was usually a Cree who recorded the version the worlds thought definitive.

When the musical expression of magnificence, joy, splendor, and dance became a province of other species, the Terrans had been left with tragedy, with the music of loss and sadness. Other species found something fascinating in the Terrans' straightforward utterance of despair, in standing to face the truths that were unendurable. Even the Shaa approved. They found the idea of tragedy ennobling, and perfectly in tune with their own stern ethic, their own belief that all but their own ideas were transient and mortal . . . and if people like Lear and Oedipus came to grief, it was only because of an insufficient understanding of the Praxis.

Derivoo was simple—one singer, a few accompanists, and absolute purity of tragic expression. It had none of the Daimongs' grandeur, or the burbling joy of the Cree. What derivoo possessed was the confrontation of one soul with darkness, a soul resolute in the knowledge that darkness will triumph but willing nevertheless to shout the fact of its existence into the face of the howling cosmic wind.

Sula listened enthralled. The singer's presence was magnificent, and the musicians knew how to accent her effects without spoiling her simplicity. The urgency of her voice and the purity of her emotion closed on Sula's heart like a fist. She seemed to hear the words pulsing through a veil of blood. Death, to Sula, was not a stranger.

She had helped to carry *Delhi*'s dead from the scorched control room, crew curled into charred husks that weighed no more than a child, that left a dust of charcoal mortality on her hands.

She had killed two thousand or more Naxids at Magaria.

When she was young she had killed a grown man, had him thrown into a river.

She had once killed an unhappy, confused young girl.

Mortality wove a web through the air around her, warranting that her spark, too, was brief, that she, too, was dust on the hands of fate.

Assured of this, she felt a smile draw itself onto her lips. She knew where she was.

Sula was home.

* * *

There was a brilliance in Sula's face that evening, a rising of color in the cheeks and an unearthly glow in the green eyes. The derivoo had transformed her. Martinez watched in fascination as the singer's spirit entered Sula, and he was so overcome by the ivory and roses of Sula's complexion glowing in the soft light of the club that the only reason he failed to fling himself on her and feast with his lips on that perfect countenance was that he was afraid he'd spoil it, that her beautiful trance would be broken. . . .

He didn't dare kiss her until after they'd left the club, until he felt her shiver in the chill of the night air and he could wrap her in the warmth of his arms and press her lips with his own.

"That was *wonderful*," she said after a moment. He felt a brief disappointment that she spoke of the derivoo and not his kiss.

"She's one of the best," Martinez said. He took her arm and walked with her down the street in the general direction of the funicular. The door of a bar opened and cast a warm glow on the pavement. Music thumped out from clubs.

"You're cold. Would you like to stop in one of these places and take the chill off?"

"I'm not cold. I'm all right." She forced a smile. "I don't want to hear any other music tonight. It wouldn't measure up."

She turned to him, the color still high in her face. Her smile was brilliant. Martinez maneuvered her into the recessed doorway of a shop and took her in his arms and kissed her. For a moment he enjoyed the warmth of her breath on his cheek, the softness of her lips, the taste of a citrus-flavored soft drink on her mischievous tongue, and then he drew back. Sandama Twilight whirled in his senses. His heart was beating thickly, to a strange lurching rhythm, and his mind seemed to be lurching as well, incongruous thoughts and impressions flashing from its dim recesses. He forced it into the channel he wanted.

"You know," he said, "I wasn't joking when I said I wanted to join your family."

Her smile was bemused. "I suppose I could arrange to adopt you. Though I hadn't planned on being a mother quite so young."

"There's an easier way I could join," Martinez said. "We could get married."

Sula stared at him, pupils wide in her green eyes, and then an expression of suspicion crossed her face. "You're not joking, are you, captain?"

"N-No." Martinez fought the stammer that seemed to have suddenly possessed his tongue. "Absolutely not."

Sula's face was dazzling in its sudden brilliant splendor. Further words seemed suddenly unnecessary. His lips took their answer from hers.

A moment later, mind whirling, he was walking with her down the street, aware of the idiot's grin on his face and the bloom of happiness in his chest.

"Your family really thinks this is all right?" Sula asked. Earlier in the evening he'd told her what had happened to Sempronia, banished for loving a man of insufficient rank.

"They'll have plans for you," Martinez said. "They'll want to load you with a few million zeniths and buy you a showcase palace in the High City and a country estate where we can entertain." He grinned. "And if you *don't* want any of that, you'll have to be *very firm* with them."

Her eyes narrowed. "And in return for this, I'll have to do what exactly?"

"Pry open some doors in the High City that are otherwise closed to provincials."

She gave a bemused shrug. "I'm much more a blunt instrument than I am a pry bar," she said. "I could get the doors open, maybe, but I wouldn't answer for what the folk on the other side might think about it."

"Best let Roland work that out on his own."

Sula gave a sudden bright laugh and swung herself like a

child on the end of his arm, shoes skipping on the pavement. "So what happens next?"

"We could make the announcement tomorrow afternoon at the reception after Vipsania's wedding." He grinned at her. "That'll serve her right for diverting the guests' attention at *my* party." He swung her laughing on the end of his arm. "And before that, in the morning, we could pay our visit to the Peers' Gene Bank and get the paperwork out of the way."

She gave him a startled, half-believing look and dropped his hand. "The *what*?"

"Don't worry. They just take a drop of blood."

"The *what* bank?" Her voice turned insistent.

"The Peers' Gene Bank," Martinez said. "Just to get all the bloodlines on record."

She turned down the street, and he fell into step with her. He saw her face reflected in window glass, a wavy dark-eyed ghost. Skepticism invaded her face. "Is this strictly necessary?" she asked. "I never heard of this place."

"I don't suppose the Gene Bank advertises," Martinez shrugged. "But then they don't have to. It's the law, at least here on Zanshaa, if you're a Peer and want to marry. We have a gene bank on Laredo, too, though it's not just for Peers."

"There wasn't anything like that on Spannan." The planet, Martinez knew, where she'd been fostered after the execution of her parents.

"Some Peers care more about their bloodlines than others, I suppose," Martinez said. "It's a stupid old institution, but what can you do?"

They came to one of the Lower Town's canals and turned left to the bridge they could see in the distance. The scent of the canal filled the air, iodine and decay.

Sula's face hardened. "So what happens to the drop of blood once they draw it?"

"Nothing. It just goes into the record."

"And who consults the record?"

A canal barge chugged by, its running lights shimmering on the dark water. The greasy wake slopped against the stone quay. Martinez raised his voice against the sound. "No one consults it, I imagine. Not unless there's some question about the parentage of the children." He slipped up behind her as they walked and wrapped her in his arms. He nuzzled close to Sula's ear and said, "You're not planning on having children by anyone but me, are you?"

He could feel surprising tension in her shoulders, and then the deliberate attempt at relaxation. "No one but you," she said abstractly. She slowed her walk, then turned to him and gave him a quick kiss. "This is so sudden," she said. "A few minutes ago I was just a woman with a medal and no job, and now—"

"Now you're my partner for life," he said, and was unable to restrain his grin.

She looked at him with an expression he couldn't read. "You're not getting carried away in some kind of stampede, are you? How many marriages are going on in your family, anyway?"

"You and I will make three. Or four, but I'm not sure Sempronia rightly counts, and I don't know if she's actually getting married or just threatening to."

Her arms tautened around him like wire, and she pressed her cheek hard to his chest. Sandama Twilight floated through the air. "Three marriages at once," she said. "Isn't that unlucky?"

"It sounds lucky to *me*," Martinez said.

"I can hear your heart beating," Sula murmured irrelevantly. He stroked her pale gold hair. A cold gust chilled him. Water slopped against the quay.

"What's the matter?" he asked.

There was a moment's silence, and Martinez felt a wariness touch his nerves. She loosened her arms and looked up at him.

"Look," she said. "This is all very sudden. I'm not used to the idea yet."

He looked at her with the dizzying sensation that he had just stepped onto the edge of an abyss, and that a single misstep would send him spinning into the void.

"What," he said carefully, "are you trying to tell me?"

She gave him a gentle kiss and offered a tentative smile. "Can't we just go on as we are for a while?"

He looked at her. "We don't have a lot of time. I want this to happen before . . ."

A door opened ahead of them, and music boomed out. Torminel in the brown uniforms of the civil service spilled into the doorway, then stood there calling to one another while the music shouted out around them, stringed instruments shrieking in a minor key. Sula bent her head, put her hands over her ears as discordant cymbals crashed.

"I need to *think*," she insisted over the noise.

Sudden anger drew a hot slash across Martinez's chest. He found himself raising his voice over the blaring music.

"I'll spare you the trouble," he said. "A moment's thought would tell you that this is your best chance for security and the restoration of your family name, not to mention your difficulty in finding a patron in the service. So my own brief analysis would seem to indicate that your problem isn't the money or the palace or the place in the country, your problem lies with *me*. . . ."

Sula's eyes lifted to his, wide and sea-green and cold. "Spare the commentary," she said in a voice hard as diamond. "You don't know *anything* about my problems."

Martinez felt his spine stiffen under Sula's gaze. His mind raced, a dark turmoil illuminated by jagged flashes of anger. "I beg to differ, my lady," he said. "Your problem is that you lost your money and your position and all the people that you loved. And now you're afraid to let anyone love you, because—"

"I won't hear this!" Sula's voice cut like a lash. Her hands were still flat over her ears. The gold light that poured from the open door glowed in her eyes like angry fire. "I don't *need* this pompous idiocy now! You don't know *anything!*"

The Torminel were staring at them now with their huge nocturnal eyes. Cymbals, tuned to strange minor keys, crashed again and again in Martinez's ears.

"I—"

"It's not about you!" Sula shouted. *"Will you please get it into your head that it's not about* you!"

Then she spun on her heel and marched away, pale legs flashing beneath the hem of her black dress as she shouldered her way through the Torminel. Martinez stood on the pavement and watched her, a wild disbelief throbbing through his veins.

It was happening *again.*

Once before he had watched Sula walk away through the night, her heels emphatic on the surface of the street while the lights of the Lower Town gilded her hair. Once before he had stood stupidly and watched while she walked out of his life, while a cold morning wind blustered along the canal and his heart filled with a mixture of bewilderment and anger and knife-edge anguish.

Not a third time, Martinez swore to himself. His fists clenched. *Not again.*

It's not about you! she had cried. A reassurance he found pleasing.

It was all Sula's mess. Let her find her own way out of it.

Martinez let himself into the Shelley Palace, threw his overcoat over the ugly bronze Lai-own on the newel post, and made his silent way up the stairs. It was sheer bad luck that he encountered Roland, who was putting the remains of a late supper into the hallway on its tray so that a servant could pick it up in the morning. Roland straightened, adjusted his dressing gown, and gazed at Martinez with cool interest.

"Matrimonial ambitions thwarted, I take it?"

"Oh be silent for once, can't you?" Martinez brushed past Roland toward his room.

Roland's voice pursued him. "Would you like me to take up your cause?"

Martinez paused at his door as a savage laugh rose to his throat. "You? Talk to Lady Sula on my behalf?"

"Talk to *someone*," Curiosity entered Roland's mild gaze. "What's the problem, exactly? I would have thought she'd leap at the chance you offered her."

"The problem," Martinez said through clenched teeth, "is that she's crazy."

"Better to find out now rather than later," Roland said. His tone was sympathetic.

The last thing Martinez needed was Roland's sympathy, or his help either, so he bade his brother good night and went into his room. He tore off his jacket and flung it on the bed in anger, then hopped on alternate legs while he yanked off his shoes and kicked them under pieces of furniture.

She called *me,* he thought in cold fury. It had been Sula who had initiated contact after her previous flight. It was she who had come up the skyhook to meet him as he stepped off *Corona.* She had pursued *him.*

Well. The pursuit was clearly over.

Martinez glared at the wallpaper for a while, and then he found his eyes sliding to the comm unit.

Call her, he thought. Call her and *demand* an explanation.

He took a step to the comm, then stopped. She hadn't given him an explanation the first time she'd walked out on him; what made him think she'd give him an explanation now?

He stepped away from the comm, then sat on the bed, his big hands dangling uselessly between his legs.

He stood up again. Then sat down. Then he lunged for the comm.

Sula didn't answer. When the automated message service clicked on, Martinez broke the connection.

He didn't want to leave a message. A message was something she could laugh at.

Better to find out now rather than later. Roland's words echoed in his skull.

Martinez called again after twenty minutes. And again after an hour.

He knew that Sula had no place to be but at her apartment. He pictured her sitting before her comm display, contempt glimmering in her green eyes as she watched the system log one call after another . . .

Martinez went to the window and stared out at the dark, empty street, and over the sound of the wind skirling against the eaves he could distinctly hear the sound of dreams quietly crumbling to dust.

Sula lay curled on her side in the great ugly Sevigny bed and pressed a pillow to her chest as if it were a lover. The morning light shone bright through a crack in the drawn curtains. Her eyes felt hot and sore. The scent of Martinez was still faint in the bed, and the pillow was moist with her tears.

She hadn't cried in all the years since she had taken a pillow very like this one and pressed it over Caro Sula's face. That effort had wrung the last tears out of her, had made her stony, like a high, cold mountain desert. She had adopted Sula's rank and position and moved into the place that had been reserved for her, and all the while she had despised those she'd duped, those who, like Jeremy Foote, considered themselves the epitome of creation. She had seen what the High City called worldly, and known that none of those supposed sophisticates had seen what she had seen, done what she had done, or would have dared to make the choices she had gladly embraced.

But all that had ended with Martinez. At his appearance she had felt the first fall of rain on the arid wilderness she called her heart. She had greened under his touch, blossomed like the desert after the first rains.

And now the moisture was being squeezed out of her again, drop by drop, by the relentless hand of remorse.

Why couldn't I trust him? Anger curled her hands into fists, and she battered the pillow as if she were hammering the life out of an enemy.

Her alarm chimed, reminding her that she had to give her deposition in the Blitsharts trial. She doubted she had slept at all. She rose from her bed and felt a stab of pain in the stiffened, clenched muscles of her back.

Sula showered and donned her undress uniform. She made a pot of tea but couldn't bring herself to drink it. The comm display glowed at her from the desk in the front room: at some point in the long despairing hours of the night, she'd told the comm to refuse all calls and to devote itself exclusively to calling up all available information on the Peers' Gene Bank. She downloaded the information into her sleeve display and reviewed it in the taxi, and while waiting to give the deposition.

Rage began to simmer in her as she discovered the law to be just as Martinez had described it. A drop of blood was required for Peers not just on on Zanshaa, but on the accelerator ring and in the unlikely event that Peers married somewhere else in the system. She set out to find worlds where Peers did without a gene bank, and found nearly thirty, including Dandaphis, Magaria, Felarus, Terra, and Spannan, the planet of her birth.

Sula could hardly accept Martinez's proposal with the proviso that they had to travel to one of these obscure worlds for the marriage. There *had* to be an exception to the regulation, and she set her computer to seek through every available database for every rule and paragraph and picture and article ever written about the Peers' Gene Bank.

Then it was time to give her deposition, and found that the attorney for the insurance company provided a suitable target for her wrath. *"Haven't you asked that question twice already? Didn't you hear my answer the first time? Are you deaf or an idiot?"*

The attorney for the Blitsharts, though feigning disapproval, seemed to enjoy the flaying of his colleague, at least until it was his turn. *"What kind of imbecile question is that? If I had a cadet as thick as you are, I'd order him to defect to the Naxids and let him sabotage them."*

The savagery had made her feel better for an instant, and afterward empty. She returned to her apartment, drank a cup of cold tea, and ate some of the food she had acquired in the expectation of sharing it with Martinez.

As she sat alone in the silent apartment, the anguish began once more to fill her.

She should have trusted him, she decided. She could have said, "I'm not the real Lady Sula. The real Sula died and I took her place. If anyone checks the records at the Gene Bank, they'll find that out."

She could have trusted Martinez that far. She wouldn't have to say how Caro Sula had died.

But she hadn't brought herself to tell Martinez anything, not even a fraction of the truth, and now it was too late. If he'd ever been inclined to trust her, that trust must have been shattered.

Vipsania's wedding was as magnificent as the short lead time and the thinned population of the High City would permit, and was held at the palace of Lord Eizo Yoshitoshi, the groom's father. Roland delayed things by arriving a few minutes late, thus earning a frown from Lord Yoshitoshi, who had been standing amid his new in-laws in an attitude that suggested he was testing the air for bad smells.

After Roland made his apologies, the couple, along with selected representatives of their families, convoyed to the Registrar, where the brief official ceremony was performed by one of the Yoshitoshi cousins who wore the scarlet and white sash of a Judge of Final Appeal. By the time they returned the reception was in full swing, with a Cree band playing its witty way through old standards and Lai-own waitrons in stainless white satin jackets circulating with drinks and canapes.

Martinez had approved of the trip to the Registrar because all he was required to do at the ceremony was stand in silence and watch, and the reception earned his annoyance because he was required to be civil to everyone present.

He hoped that Sula would arrive to throw herself at his feet and beg forgiveness, her garments rent in penitence and her knees bloody from walking to the palace on her patellas, but it didn't happen.

He tried avoiding contact by feigning interest in the palace's architecture, but unfortunately the building had been constructed during the heyday of the Devis mode, with long clean featureless lines, and had been furnished and decorated in much the same style. There was little to observe in clean featureless lines once one had observed how clean and featureless they were. The walls were mostly bare except for an occasional painting, and the paintings were mostly blank white canvas except for an intricate swirl of color slightly off the painting's geometrical center. One particularly daring canvas was avocado-green, but the off-center swirl of color looked much the same as the others.

"The height of restrained elegance, don't you think?" The voice in Martinez's ear was that of Roland.

"Warships come out of the builders' yards with more interesting decor," Martinez said. He turned toward the bustling reception—more and more people were fleeing the High City for the safety of other systems, but the wedding of the Yoshitoshi heir had still managed to draw five hundred of the most elite Peers in the empire. "Here they all are," Martinez said. "All the great names come to Vipsania's wedding. Your triumph."

"I'll feel the triumph when I see all these people at *our* place," Roland said, and he sipped from his glass of white wine. He turned to Martinez. "I'm sorry to have scandalized the Yoshitoshis by turning up late."

"I'm sure you were late for a good reason."

"In fact I was." He looked sidelong at Martinez from narrowed, catlike eyes, as if he were reluctant to face Martinez head-on. "I hope you'll appreciate my efforts."

"I will if you got me a job." Martinez was in little mood for Roland's games.

Roland offered a slight smile. "In a manner of speaking, I did," he said. "I've arranged for your marriage."

Martinez answered with a cold, murderous stare. Roland looked out across the crowded room and lifted his glass in salute to a Lai-own in convocate red.

"You *did* put yourself in play, Gareth," Roland said. "And I *did* say I would take up your cause."

"I hope," Martinez said, "you are prepared to grovel in apology to the poor woman's family, or better yet marry her yourself."

Roland raised his eyebrows, all mock innocence. "Don't you want to hear her name?"

"I was rather hoping not to."

"Terza Chen." And, in the shocked surprise that followed, Roland said, "You have no idea how hard I had to pressure her father. He's been willing to take millions of our lousy provincial zeniths, but a provincial son-in-law was another matter." Self-satisfaction gleamed in his eyes. "Still, I managed to convince him that our alliance really was for the long term."

Martinez found his tongue. "Terza Chen? That's insane."

Roland's mock innocence returned. "Really? How?"

"For one thing, she's in mourning."

"Lord Richard Li is dead."

Lord Richard Li? Martinez thought. *One of the Fleet's brilliant rising stars? That's who she was in mourning for?*

"He's *very recently* dead," Martinez pointed out. "She can't have got over it."

Roland took Martinez by the elbow and leaned close to

his ear. "With grieving widows, it's best to strike quickly. I assume it's much the same with grieving fiancés."

Martinez shook off Roland's hand. "Forget it." His eyes searched the crowd. "Lord Chen has to be here, somewhere. I'll find him and tell him the marriage is off."

"If you must." Roland affected a shrug. "While you're at it, you may as well tell him you won't be taking your new appointment, either."

Martinez gave Roland another cold stare, but a surge of warmth beneath his collar told him the stare lacked conviction.

"Oh, did I forget to mention that?" Roland's smile was that of a well-fed predator. "Squadron Commander Lady Michi Chen needs a tactical officer aboard her flagship. And later, of course, as she rises in the service she will be in a position to offer you one choice posting after another."

And then, in the silence, Roland leaned close again, and his soft voice was a silken purr in Martinez's ear. "You know," he said, "I *thought* that might compel your attention."

NINE

Martinez wandered through the Yoshitoshi Palace in a kind of daze, his mind unable to manage thought, exactly, but swept instead by erratic surges of pure feeling: black anger followed by weird hilarity, detached irony by profound disgust. The disgust and the irony tended to predominate, passions so strong he could taste them.

Irony tasted like used coffee grounds, and disgust like copper.

Behind the grace and the fine manners, he thought, behind the tailored uniforms and the brocade and the seams sewn with seed pearls, there was nothing but the circle of fat, hairless animals, molars grinding, jowls running with the thick juices of the common trough.

He wanted to shriek at them. *Shriek.* But they wouldn't listen, wouldn't hold off their gorging even when the Naxids loomed and threatened to knock down the whole foul sty.

Martinez found Terza standing by a Devis paper screen, white with one panel of pale blue. Her gown was a radiant contrast to the austerities of the Devis mode, in the ornate high style so popular since the war had begun, deep gold with a pattern of green vegetation and brilliant scarlet flowers, all flounces and fringes, and slashed to reveal the satin underskirt. Terza's hair was bound with white mourning thread, and covered with an intricate net of tiny white starflowers. She was with a group of her girl friends, and listening to them with what appeared to be careful attention.

Martinez hesitated at the sight of her, then made his way to her side. She turned to him, and her lips parted in a shy smile. "Captain Martinez," she said.

"My lady," Martinez answered. He turned to her friends. "I'm afraid I must beg your pardon for taking Lady Terza away from you."

He drew her away, down a side corridor. His nerves flared with contrary impulses: to laugh, to whimper, to tear off his clothes and fly screaming down the hall. Instead he asked, "Has your father spoken to you?"

"Yes." Her voice was soft. "Just before we left home."

"You got the news before I did." Terza moved with perfect grace in her elaborate, rustling gown. Martinez tried a door at random, found it opened on a kind of bed-sitting-room, a somber bed in white and black and a desk of pale cinder-colored wood with paper, glass calligraphy pens, and a stick of ink ready for use. He drew her inside and closed the door.

"I'm sorry about the mourning threads." Terza's hand made a vague gesture by her hair. "I knew I shouldn't be wearing mourning when we're engaged, but my father only talked to me after I'd dressed."

"That's all right," Martinez said. "From everything I've heard about Lord Richard, he was someone worth mourning."

Terza looked away. There was an awkward silence. Martinez took a grip on his thoughts.

"Look," he said. "If you don't want to do this, we'll call it off. And that's that."

Faint surprise marked her features. "I—" Her lips shaped a word that she failed to utter. Her eyes darted to Martinez. "I don't object," she said. "I know families arrange these things. My engagement to Lord Richard was arranged."

"But at least you knew him. You moved in the same set. You barely know me."

Terza gave a fluid nod. "That's true. But—" A kind of tremor passed across her eyes, a reflection of some inner thought, and she looked at him. "You're successful and reliable. You're intelligent. Your family has money. So far as I can see, you're kind." Her gown rustled as she raised a hand to touch his sleeve. "Those are good things, in a husband."

Martinez felt the world spin in giddy circles about the small room with its writing desk and austere little bed. He looked at the young woman standing before him, the perfectly schooled body with its willowy grace, the elegant hands, the lovely serene face and smooth skin, and he wondered if what he beheld was entirely art—if it was the trained response of a woman who knew her duty to her clan and who was doing it regardless of any distaste she might feel, or if by any chance there was some genuine feeling behind her words. If beneath the brocade and elegance she was one of those nightmare creatures he had seen clustered around the trough, or was what she actually appeared, a beautiful and gentle human being.

But even if she were the former—even if there was avarice and calculation behind the mask—what did that matter? It was only fit in that case that Martinez should shoulder his way to the trough and seize what he could for himself, the appointment under Michi Chen being only the appetizer.

And if Terza were actually what she appeared, then that was even better, and he was lucky. Sula had once called him the luckiest person in the universe. Certainly he had been lucky enough to escape Sula. Perhaps Terza Chen was another great piece of luck.

Distantly, the dinner gong rang. The wedding guests would begin their progression toward the ballroom, where the tables had been set.

He looked at Terza and put his hand over hers. "Just remember," he said, "you've had your chance to run away."

Conscious of the light touch of her on his arm—the touch not of the woman he loved, but of a stranger—Martinez turned and walked with Terza toward the fate that awaited them.

* * *

Sula's research on the Gene Bank uncovered no loopholes in the regulations that governed the place, and after a while her view of the display began to shimmer with tears. The chime of the comm made her gasp in surprise. She swiped at her swollen eyes with the back of her hand and answered. A few minutes later she signed for a packet of orders from the Commandery.

Her leave was now officially over, and on the morrow she was to join the staff of Fleet Commander Ro-dai, who headed something called the "Logistics Consolidation Executive," run out of an office building in the Lower Town.

Sula reheated the morning's tea and stirred cane sugar syrup into it while she stared at the orders printed on the Commandery's crisp bond paper. *You are required and directed to present yourself at 09:01 hours at Room 890 of the Dix Building* . . . It was the reality of it, the creamy paper, the sharp outlines of the letters, the absolute directness and clarity of the Commandery's wording, that somehow made up Sula's mind.

She would walk around the corner to the Shelley Palace and see Martinez. She would force an interview, if necessary, by claiming to have orders from the Commandery—she had the envelope and paper in hand, after all. She would tell Martinez that she was not the genuine Lady Sula but an imposter who had taken her place, and throw herself on his mercy. *Hit me, spit in my face, denounce me to the authorities . . . or marry me.*

His choice.

The idea was so dangerous that she felt a welcome rush of adrenaline, and the hairs on the back of her neck prickled. A wild wind of liberation began to sing through her. To give up her secret seemed intoxicatingly like freedom.

Sula washed her face and applied cosmetic. She put her orders back in their envelope and tried to reattach the seal, then decided it didn't really matter. They weren't really Martinez's orders, after all.

The wind of hope blew strong in her heart. She squared her shoulders and put on her uniform cap and left the apartment with the crisp envelope held in her left hand. A drum rattled in her mind as she marched down the pavement in proper military style, executed a precise right-turn at the corner, and paraded to the front door of the Shelley Palace.

Her ring was answered by one of the Martinez sisters' homely maidservants. "Captain Martinez, please," she said. "Orders from the Commandery."

The servant was a little flushed, and the laughter that tried to tug at her face hinted that Sula had interrupted her in the middle of a good giggle.

"Captain Martinez isn't in, my lady," she said. "I believe he may be with his fiancée."

"Lord Gareth, I mean," Sula corrected, "not Lord Roland." And far too late thought, *Roland's getting married?*

The servant appeared a little surprised. "It's Lord Gareth who's getting married, my lady. To Lady Terza Chen. We've all just been told." She seemed surprised at Sula's shock. "If it's urgent, you might try the Chen Palace, miss."

"Thank you," Sula said. "I will."

The door closed.

"Ah. Ha," Sula said.

Military reflexes came to her rescue. Despite knees that were suddenly without strength, Sula managed an about-turn, a right-angle turn at the street, and another turn at the corner.

On the way to her apartment she clawed the envelope and its contents to confetti.

Bitch. Bitch, he was mine.

"Congratulations on your new son-in-law," said Lord Pezzini. "Now I see why you were so assiduously promoting his career."

Lord Chen looked at Pezzini, his thoughts sour, his countenance bland. "Thank you, my lord," he said. "Though I believe any assistance I've attempted to render Captain Martinez has been based entirely on his merits."

Pezzini's lips quirked into a condescending smile. "Of course," he said.

Lord Chen considered what an open-handed slap might do to Pezzini's smile, and kept that picture in the forefront of his mind as he walked with Pezzini toward the somber quiet of the Control Board's meeting room.

Pezzini was hardly the first to smirk at the news. When the announcement of Terza's engagement to Martinez had been announced the previous afternoon at the wedding banquet, the applause and congratulations had been civil, but he'd seen the looks exchanged by the guests, the surprise followed by condescension, pity, and contempt. *Another* great old family fallen to the parvenu Clan Martinez. Ngeni, Yoshitoshi, and now Chen. What inducements could Lord Roland have possibly offered to persuade Lord Chen to agree to such a hasty, ill-advised alliance? And what rustic swarms of country-bred, knuckle-dragging Martinez cousins and nieces and nephews would soon be swarming into the High City to despoil the great families of their sons and daughters?

The inducements offered by Roland Martinez had been many, in fact, and so had the discreetly-veiled threats. It had taken all the entire morning for Roland to finally batter his way through Lord Chen's defenses. At one or two points Chen had been on the verge of calling the servants to have Roland flung from the house.

Even now he could barely believe that he had given away his daughter—no, he corrected ruthlessly, not given. *Sold.*

To a man who was no doubt laudable in his way—*ingenious,* that was the word for him, a clever sort of person who had done well in his chosen sphere—but who was in no way worthy of marriage to a Chen. Just because a man was *useful* didn't mean that he was entitled to father the next clan heir. Who were his ancestors, after all? How many palaces had they owned in the High City, and for how many centuries?

Terza had taken the news well, simply tilted her head, pondered for a moment, and said "Yes, father," in her soft voice. The sight of Terza in her room, given such news while she sat in her elaborate gown with the mourning ribbons for Lord Richard still in her hair, had almost broken Chen's heart.

Lady Chen had been far less reasonable. She had screamed, wept, and threatened, and when none of that worked she shut herself in her room and refused to go to the Yoshitoshi wedding. Lord Chen had the feeling that it would be all he could do to get his wife to her own daughter's nuptials.

It was a matter of luck, Lord Chen thought as he took his place at the board room's broad midnight-black table. The Martinez clan was lucky, and Clan Chen was not. He needed the Martinezes' luck.

But some day, he swore, the luck would change. Clan Chen would be restored to its former glory, able to stand on its own without assistance.

Then his daughter would be free. She would no longer be a hostage to his ill fortune, and would then be able to rid herself of her embarrassment of a husband, and to have a life worthy of the heir to one of the great families in the empire.

This Lord Chen promised himself. And, in the meantime, if Captain Martinez failed to treat Terza with the utmost respect, if he treated her ill or raised a hand to her or caused her misery, he would see Martinez dead.

There were still a few things a high-born Peer could arrange. There were clients of Clan Chen whose occupations were less than legitimate, and who would be willing to do favors for the clan head. A son-in-law, dead by mysterious means—it would be easy to arrange.

He took note of the other board members as they entered the room. He had been quietly lobbying them for the adoption of the plan to evacuate the capital—the plan of that *use-*

ful man Martinez—and Chen had made headway with his peers. There were three besides himself who were willing to urge the plan on the Convocation, but three wasn't enough. They were balanced by the three votes that Lord Tork could count on.

That would produce a tie vote. If Lord Saïd would only appoint Lady San-torath's successor, then the issue might be resolved, but the Lord Senior seemed in no hurry to do so. The delay made Lord Chen grind his teeth. He could almost feel the pressure wave of the advancing Naxids on the back of his neck.

Lord Tork entered, and with him a group of three Fleet officers in full dress uniforms. The leader was a Lai-own in the uniform of a senior captain; the others were aides, a Terran and a Torminel with heavy dark spectacles comforting her large eyes.

Lord Chen studied the newcomers carefully. Black collar tabs, he thought, that meant the Intelligence Section. Before the war the Intelligence Section had been perhaps the smallest division of the Fleet—there was no enemy, after all, on which to gather intelligence, and the section's rival, the Investigative Service under Lord Inspector Snow, which investigated criminal activity within the Fleet, had thrived at their expense. But the Investigative Service had received a black eye in their failure to discover the rebels' plans, and the Intelligence Section had found a new purpose and new funding. It was trying to come up with imaginative ways to monitor the enemy and even to insert spies into Naxid-held territory, but most of its work at this point consisted of analyzing rebel capabilities. The board regularly received briefings from the Intelligence Section and the other intelligence services, but the group that had entered with Tork contained none of the usual faces.

The two aides softly closed the doors, leaving the Fleet Control Board and its guests isolated in the hushed, dimly lit room. The board's Cree secretary took up his stylus and cued recorders that would transcript the meeting for history. The Torminel aide removed her spectacles.

The scent of dying flesh wafted from Lord Tork as he took his place at the head of the table. His unblinking eyes looked left and right as if he were slowly counting the members present, and then he rapped the table with his pale knuckles.

"My lords," he said, "I should like to introduce Captain Ahn-kin, of the Intelligence Section, who yesterday sent me a report that I realized was of profound consequence. The captain has made a discovery with grave implications for the war, and I decided to bring him here before you so that we may respond as a body to this information."

Ahn-kin stepped forward—he was not offered a seat— and adjusted his sleeve display so as to send information to each of the board members' desk displays. Lord Chen looked at the desk before him and saw, glowing in the ebony surface of the table, a document with the title *Analysis of Premiere Axiom and its Role in Rebel Force Structure.*

Premiere Axiom? he thought. He had heard the name before, but he couldn't remember where. Ahn-kin soon refreshed Chen's memory.

"Some of you may remember Premiere Axiom as a shipping company created by rebel plotters in order to secretly move resources from one place to another prior to the rebellion," Ahn-kin said. Without any clear place at the table he was hovering awkwardly above Tork's left shoulder, shifting his weight from one leg to another in his discomfort. "Premiere Axiom was created in the Year of the Praxis 12,477, four years before rebellion, and is privately held. Its principal shareholders include Lady Kushdai, Lord Kulukraf, Lord Aksad, and other rebels. Lady Kushdai serves as chairman." Chen's display showed the company's organizational structure.

"On the day of the rebellion," Ahn-kin continued, "three Premiere Axiom cargo ships were inbound to Magaria."

Names and manifests flashed across Chen's displays. "We believe they carried personnel sufficient to crew the ships captured by the Naxid rebels on that first day, thus enabling their subsequent victory at the Battle of Magaria. Nineteen other ships had been purchased over the years by Premiere Axiom, and probably carried legitimate cargo in addition to any cargoes intended to aid the rebels. At the time of the rebellion most of these were in five other inhabited systems in the reaches between Naxas and Magaria."

Chen's display showed planetary systems, all systems that hadn't been heard from since the rebellion had begun. Ahn-kin shifted from one foot to the other, then continued his briefing.

"We suspect these ships held soldiers that captured critical sections of the ring stations, possibly with the help of rebels already on the station. Though we have heard nothing of any of these Premiere Axiom cargo vessels since the rebellion began, presumably they continue to serve the rebel cause."

Lord Chen jumped as Ahn-kin gave a convulsive explosion that Chen only belatedly realized was a sneeze. The poor Lai-own stood directly behind Lord Tork, Chen realized, and was breathing in the scent of Tork's perpetually decaying flesh with every inhalation.

"I beg your lordships' pardon," Ahn-kin said, and took a few steps to the side, where the odor was not so strong. He took in a deep breath, then continued.

"Our investigation into enemy capabilities initially concentrated on military equipment, organization, and facilities, and then only gradually began to take in civilian facilities and capabilities as well. Approximately a month ago we became aware that Premiere Axiom had commissioned ten new cargo vessels from civilian yards on six different worlds, all of which were in one stage or another of completion at the time of the rebellion. We assumed the Naxids wanted to add carrying capacity to their fleet, and these new ships were added to our estimates of rebel inventory. It was only in the last few days, however, that our analysis unit acquired a specialist in ship construction, Lieutenant Kijjalis here"—the Torminel braced, chin high—"who was able to examine the vessels' plans in any detail, and we reached," he took another deep breath, "certain conclusions."

Ship schematics, data from the Imperial Ship Registry, flashed on the board's displays. Lord Chen, who owned ships, leaned closer to take a careful look. A lean merchant craft, he saw, with small capacity for cargo. It would be useful, he supposed, for carrying high-value, high-priority cargo, but otherwise could scarcely be operated at a profit.

Built to carry urgent war materiel, he thought, from one base to another, and given the capacities of the engines, to carry it fast. The cargo would be missiles, perhaps, or key replacement personnel, or information so critical that it could not be trusted to the usual channels . . . and at that point his imagination flagged.

"It was the limitations of the new vessels that intrigued me," said Lieutenant Kijjalis. The Torminel was no doubt very warm with his full uniform over his fur, and there were probably hidden cooling units in his tailoring.

"The ships' cargo capacity is small," she said, "and the engines large for such a small ship. And their modular construction, which would enable the owners to reconfigure their crew and cargo areas, is unnecessarily expensive. And then I realized that the ships were never meant to be cargo vessels."

Chen's heart gave an unexpected lurch as he looked again at the schematics. It would take a relatively brief stay at a dockyard to strip away the modular cargo and crew sections, he saw, and to replace them with missile batteries, expanded crew quarters, and action stations with enough radiation shielding to insulate them from the blasts of antimatter missiles.

Lord Chen looked at the Torminel lieutenant in a fever of

sudden calculation. "And how many of these ships did you say there were?"

"Ten, my lord."

"Ten warships."

"Yes, my lord," Ahn-kin interrupted, taking the reins of the discussion. "Once they are retrofitted with weapons and crew, we estimate they would be the equivalent of a medium-sized frigate, with twelve to fourteen missile launchers, one or two pinnaces, half a dozen or so point-defense lasers, and a crew of approximately eighty."

"Ten *frigates* . . ." breathed Lord Mondi. For once the Torminel forgot his careful diction and lisped like a child.

Frigates were the smallest class of true warship, certainly, but once they were added to the formidable enemy fleet concentrated at Magaria, the implications were horrific.

"Do you realize what this means?" Lord Pezzini demanded. His face was red. "This means . . ."

"*My lord,*" interrupted Lord Tork forcefully. "I must ask everyone here to refrain from speculating in the presence of these officers. Until the briefing is finished, please confine your remarks to questions and comments related to Captain Ahn-kin's presentation."

There was a formidable silence, broken by Lady Seekin.

"How certain are you?"

The officers from the Intelligence Section looked at each other, hesitant to make too definite a commitment before this august audience. It was Lieutenant Kijjalis who answered. "I am absolutely convinced that my analysis is the correct one. But insofar as I must admit the possibility that I may be in error, let me say that my confidence is on the order of ninety percent."

"I concur," said Ahn-kin.

"And so do I," said Lord Chen. The board members looked at him. "I own ships," he pointed out, "and I'm familiar with ship design." He tapped the display in front of him. "These are warships in everything but armament and

proper shelters for the crew, and a Fleet dockyard can remedy that in a short time." He looked at Ahn-kin. "Do you
have an estimate for the completion of these vessels?"

"At least two should be complete by now," Ahn-kin said.
"These would be the two building at Loatyn, which were
undergoing trials when the rebellion broke out. Since
Loatyn submitted to the enemy soon after, I think we can
safely say that these have almost certainly completed their
refit and joined the enemy fleet. Probably three more should
be joining any day now." Estimates flashed on the screen.
"The remaining five could be completing about now, but
since three of these would have to fit out at Naxas, they're
still two months or more from the main enemy concentration at Magaria."

Lord Chen felt a chill in his blood as he thought suddenly
of Lord Saïd's deception strategy, the phony messages from
dissidents that the Lord Senior was confident were delaying
the rebel attack. Whether the Naxids believe the messages or
not, it wasn't the alleged conspiracy that was delaying their
attack, they were delaying because they were waiting for the
ten newly minted frigates that would give them overwhelming power against the defenders.

The Naxids would soon be able to bring forty-five ships
against the twenty-five defending the capital, and the number of attackers rose to fifty-three if the eight ships from
Protipanu were included. No matter how brilliantly Lord
Fleetcom Kangas maneuvered, he could not hope to win
against those odds. The loyalists would be overwhelmed and
annihilated.

There were a few stunned, hopeless questions from the
board before the officers from the Intelligence Section were
sent away, and then a long, numb, despairing silence before
Lord Tork spoke.

"My lords," he said slowly, "I think it is now obvious that
we can't hope to hold Zanshaa. We must adopt another
plan."

"The Martinez Plan?" Chen said pointedly, and felt a mean little stab of satisfaction at seeing Pezzini wince.

Lord Tork turned his pale face toward Chen. "Lord Saïd, when he spoke to me about your visit the other day, referred to it as the Chen Plan. Perhaps it should retain that designation."

Lord Chen, who now realized that Tork knew that he'd gone behind his back to the Lord Senior, resolved that he refused to be embarrassed by the knowledge.

"Your lordship gives me too much credit," he said.

Lord Tork's mournful face turned to the others on the board. "I shall demand an immediate interview with Lord Saïd," he said. "I trust you will all attend?"

Lord Chen, as he rose from his chair, thought back to the desperation of the last few days, his frantic lobbying efforts aimed at getting the government to adopt the plan that Lord Tork and the other die-hards had just accepted without question . . . and then it occurred to him to wonder:

The Martinez luck. Is it working already?

Walpurga walked through her wedding with a half-curious, half-thoughtful expression on her face, as if she were observing with considerable interest the quaint rites of a tribe of Yormaks.

PJ Ngeni, on the other hand, looked as if he were attending his own funeral.

At the climax of the marriage ritual Walpurga sat on the edge of a bed, her legs dangling over the side, while the groom sat on the floor with her feet in his lap as he removed her slippers. Perhaps in most homes this ceremony took place in an actual bedroom, but in the Shelley Palace—as in the Yoshitoshi Palace two days before—a large bed had been moved into a drawing room for just this purpose.

The guests at Walpurga's wedding were a small fraction of those at Vipsania's. The circumstances of the marriage seemed to call for a smaller celebration, and each family had invited only intimates, a total of about fifty people.

The ribbons of one slipper untied, PJ paused, his long face drawn with melancholy, to permit pictures to be taken. Lord Pierre Ngeni stood near his cousin, arms folded on his chest, to make certain PJ went through with it. Roland, rather more confident of the outcome, smiled easily in the background.

Martinez, watching with more sympathy than he'd perhaps intended, wondered what expression the picture-takers would find on his own face, at his own nuptials two days hence.

PJ completed the ritual to polite applause. Walpurga's toenails had been lacquered a brilliant shade of crimson to compliment her wedding gown of red and gold tissue. The two rose and kissed, again as cameras hummed about them.

A sudden anger flashed through Martinez. Let *my* wedding not be such a farce, he violently thought.

Afterward, after Walpurga put on her slippers once again and the crowd began to disperse, Martinez approached Terza, who had been watching with a kind of serene smile that Martinez would have found eerie had he not, already in their brief acquaintance, learned that this was an habitual expression of concealment.

Terza saw him walking toward her, and her gaze shifted to him while the smile altered, he hoped, to something more genuine. He had been trying to spend as much time as possible with his bride-to-be, though with so many last-minute arrangements on the part of both families this had amounted only to a few hours. With her father occupied exclusively with the Convocation and the Control Board, her mother refusing to have anything to do with the proceedings, and many of her relatives fleeing the capital, Terza was forced to plan her own wedding, and on only a few days' notice.

You've got to get her pregnant, Roland had urged him that morning. *Tell her you want children right away, that she should get her implant removed and take Progestene or something to induce ovulation.* And when an annoyed Martinez had asked him why in hell he should do that, Roland had patiently explained. *When the Chen family's back on its feet after the war, Daddy Chen may try to make his daughter divorce you. I want you to have fathered a couple of bouncing baby heirs by that point—and if Chen tries to disinherit them in favor of children by some other parent, Clan Martinez will serve him with a lawsuit that will nail his ears to the wall.*

It had not cheered Martinez to discover that Roland was already thinking ahead to his divorce.

"Shall we walk in the garden?" Martinez suggested.

"Certainly."

The garden in the Shelley Palace courtyard was old and overgrown, shadowed by the rambling structure of the palace, which had been built over many centuries and in different styles. The two stood for a moment before an allegory of The Triumph of Virtue over Vice, the two central figures so old and weathered that their faces had become nearly identical abstractions, corroded blind eyes over hollow, mournful mouths.

"Who is that person?" Terza asked, indicating an elderly Terran woman in a light summer frock who walked amid straggling forsythia. "She's not dressed for a wedding."

"I'm not certain who she is," Martinez said. "But we have only the front part of the palace, you know. Shelley relatives and clients and pensioned servants live in the back—there's a regular crowd of them, and I haven't been here long enough to know them."

"Sometimes I have the same problem at our properties," Terza said, "though of course I'm supposed to know them, they all work for us."

Martinez took Terza's arm and drew her away from the corroded statues and along an old, uneven brick walk, where the sound of their heels was muffled by moss. "I imagine it's hard work being the Chen heir," he said.

"Not yet," Terza said. She glanced at him. "My father's given me some of his clients to look after, and some properties. But it's nothing like real work—I have plenty of time for my music and for a full social schedule."

"Perhaps he wants you to enjoy your freedom while you're young."

Terza looked thoughtful. "That might be part of it. But I think he wanted to know who my husband would be before he charted my course, so that he and I could compliment each other in the way of our goals."

Martinez looked at her. "That's odd."

"How do you mean?"

"You'll be Lady Chen one day. Your husband will be Lord Chen only because of you. He should fit himself to your ambitions, not the other way around."

Her heavy silks rustled. Terza gave a close-lipped smile and looked down at the moss-covered walk. "That's a generous thought. So if I elected to pursue a career in the Ministry of Works, you'd resign your commission to join me in my postings?"

Martinez felt his heart shift into a faster, far more uneasy tempo. "Let's hope neither of us ever has to make such a decision," he said.

Her downcast smile widened. "Let's hope not." She turned her cool brown eyes to his. "But in all seriousness, you wouldn't object to my having a career?"

"No, not at all. But isn't being Lady Chen a career in itself?" His own father had never worked at anything other than being Lord Martinez of Laredo, and it had seemed very much a full-time job.

"I suppose," Terza said. "But some administrative experience would come in handy, for dealing with family enterprises and clients, and later for the Convocation."

She wouldn't have any anxiety on that last score, he knew. The head of Clan Chen was always coopted into the Convocation, along with the heads of around four hundred other families, a fact of history that less privileged Peers like Lord Martinez had always resented.

"And of course we're at war," Terza added. "I want to do what I can to—oh."

"Hold still." Martinez went down on one knee and disentangled her trailing gown from an intrusive hydrangea. He looked up at her.

"Thank you," she said.

"You're welcome."

There was a moment's silence as Martinez knelt at her feet, and then Terza gave him her hand and helped him rise. He could feel the warmth of her hand through the soft, paper-thin leather of her glove as they continued along the garden path.

"Perhaps I'll try for a post in the Ministry of Right and Dominion," Terza said, naming the civilian ministry that, under the Fleet Control Board, governed and supported the Fleet and smaller, related services. "That way I could aid both my father and my husband."

"That's a . . . worthy idea," Martinez said. She heard the hesitation in his tone and raised an eyebrow.

"You don't quite approve?"

"No, not that." Martinez searched his mind for the best way to phrase the thought that had flown on chill wings into his mind. "Perhaps you should choose another ministry, that's all," he said. "If the Naxids win, they might be more likely to . . . leave you alone."

Sadness touched Terza's lips. "I've decided it's useless to guess what the Naxids might do," she said.

A chord sounded plangent along his nerves. Ah, Roland, Martinez thought, have you considered we might be getting this girl killed?

They came to another statue grouping, representing an allegory harder to read than the first. A woman poured water from a jug into a pool, and a man with a mustache and tall peaked hat watched while strumming a bulbous stringed instrument. The figure of a large, self-satisfied bird perched on the woman's left shoulder. In the air floated the freshness of water and the moist scent of mosses and lilies.

Before the statuary Martinez took both Terza's hands. He could see the pulse beat in her throat. She looked up at him for a moment, her eyes inquiring, and then she tilted her face toward him to be kissed. Her lips were warm and pliant.

He hadn't kissed her before, not really. There had been formal kisses when the engagement was announced, but that had been for the benefit of an audience. This was for the two of them alone.

Martinez couldn't help but think of the excitement he'd tasted on Sula's lips, the way her kiss had always seemed to promise fire and passion . . . That fervor was absent here—instead there was a gracious acquiescence mixed with a kind of hopeful curiosity.

He decided that this was not a bad place to start. He put his arms around her. He breathed the warm scent of her hair. Water splashed and chuckled from the stone woman's jug.

His sleeve comm chimed. He gave an apologetic laugh, disentangled himself, and answered. He looked at the display to see the face of Vonderheydte, *Corona*'s former junior lieutenant.

"My lord," Vonderheydte said.

"Lieutenant," Martinez said in surprise. "How are you doing?"

"Very well, my lord, thank you." Vonderheydte paused, licked his lips, and then broke into a bright grin. "In fact, my lord, I'm getting married tomorrow. I thought I'd extend you an invitation."

Laughter burst from Martinez. The marriage motif was being repeated a few too many times. Solemnity, then farce, followed now by parody. At this rate his own nuptials would barely rate a footnote.

A sobering thought struck Martinez. "Just a moment," he said. "Haven't you been married twice before?"

"Yes," Vonderheydte admitted, "but Daphne is different. This time I've found the right woman."

"I'm pleased to hear it," Martinez said. "I would be honored to attend, if I can."

"Empire Hotel, lord captain," Vonderheydte said, "Empyrean Ballroom, 16:01 hours."

"Very good," Martinez said. "I'll be there unless something urgent calls me away."

Martinez blanked the screen and looked at Terza. "One of my officers," he said, then corrected, "my former officers."

"So I understood," Terza said.

"Would you like to join me at the wedding? Perhaps we'll pick up some useful ideas."

Terza smiled. "I have to organize our own wedding for the following day, remember. I don't think I'm going to have the leisure to attend anything between now and then."

"Ah." He looked at her. "Would you like me to assist? I'm rather good at organizing things."

"Thanks, but no. I'd lose too much time explaining everything."

A gust of wind found its way into the courtyard and rustled leaves. A sudden impulse seized him, and he took her hand. "Terza," he said.

"Yes?"

"Could we have children—a child—right away?"

She was surprised. "I—I'd have to schedule time to get the implant removed, and—" She looked at him. "Are you sure?"

His mouth was dry. "I might die," he said.

Her look softened, and she touched his cheek. "Yes," she said. "Yes, of course."

Terza put her arms around him and kissed him. His mind whirled. He couldn't tell whether this paternal impulse was his, or Roland's. He hated the fact that he didn't know, that he himself couldn't tell whether his genes were truly clamoring for offspring or whether he was becoming an unwitting expert at emotional blackmail.

Disgust, he recalled, tasted like copper.

This time it was Terza's comm that chimed. With a peal of apologetic laughter she dug into her costume for a hand unit and answered. The voice that came from it was that of her father.

"Is Captain Martinez with you?" he asked.

Lord Chen, though he treated Martinez in person with courtesy, hadn't yet brought himself to address him by his personal name.

"Yes," Terza said. "He's here."

"Then I'll tell you both," Chen said. "This morning Lord Saïd addressed a closed-door session of the Convocation and recommended the evacuation of Zanshaa. The measure passed on a voice vote with very little opposition."

Martinez felt, in his muscles and nerves, the easing of a tension of which he had been unaware; and he looked into Terza's face and saw the relief that was mirrored in his own. "Excellent, my lord," he said loudly, in hopes that Lord Chen would hear him.

Terza turned up the audio for the benefit of Martinez's straining ears. "Two Fleet cargo vessels are being requisitioned to bring the Convocation to another location—we haven't worked out where. The Martinez Plan will be adopted, though Captain Martinez should be warned that Lord Tork's decided it should be called the Chen Plan."

Chen's poached my idea, Martinez thought with a spasm of annoyance. "It doesn't matter what they call it, my lord," he said, "so long as it contributes to a successful outcome of the war."

As he uttered this blatant falsehood Martinez saw amusement crinkling the corners of Terza's eyes, and his irritation increased.

"Good of you to feel that way," Chen said. "You should also know that the board has agreed to my sister's request that you serve as her tactical officer. You'll be ordered aboard her ship as soon as suitable transport can be arranged."

Which, since Martinez was on Zanshaa and Míchi Chen was currently orbiting Zanshaa's system at enormous velocity, was a more complex task than it sounded.

"Thank you, my lord," Martinez said.

Terza laughed. "Do you have anything to say to *me*," she asked, "or should I just hand the comm to Gareth?"

Lord Chen lowered his voice so that Martinez had to strain to hear the words. "Just that I'm sorry not to be with you now," he said. "Things are moving too fast. I wish we could spend more time together."

"So do I," Terza said.

"I love you." There was a hesitation, and then, "I'll see you tomorrow."

"See you then. Bye."

Terza put her comm away.

I love you, Lord Chen had said. Martinez had not yet told Terza this, for the simple reason that Terza, an intelligent person, would have known it wasn't true. He had thought about saying it for form's sake, or even out of politeness; but something restrained him from beginning his marriage with a lie. Nor did he want to start with an embarrassment of candor: *I love another* was hardly the best way to approach a relationship.

He sensed that, for both himself and for Terza, a veil was being drawn very carefully over their private feelings. Not simply because truthfulness would be unwelcome, or even because in their situation it was irrelevant, but because it could wound. For Martinez to mention his involvement with Sula would not simply be to voice an awkward truth, it would be to draw a weapon. A weapon that either he or Terza could use in time, and use to draw blood.

And so, silence. He took Terza's hand and kissed her cheek. And in the bright afternoon light he drew her farther into the garden.

"Walpurga looked lovely," Terza remarked. "Don't you think?"

Irony, Martinez was reminded, tasted like old coffee grounds.

Martinez knelt before the battery of cameras with Terza's feet in his lap and smiled out at posterity. The actual marriage had occurred some hours earlier, in an office at the Registrar before Judge Ngeni of the High Court, and since then there had been a number of popular rituals of which this, the symbolic consummation, was the last.

Above him Terza sat in the canopied bed that had been assembled in one of the parlors of the Chen Palace. She was dressed in a scarlet gown so laden with glistening gold brocade that it creaked. Martinez wore full parade dress, with silver braid and jackboots and—at least for the ride to the Registrar and back—a tall leather shako and a long cloak that draped to his ankles. He had carried the baton of the Golden Orb as well, which meant that Judge Ngeni had to begin the ceremony by snapping to attention and baring the throat ready to be sliced by the sickle-shaped, ceremonial knife Martinez wore at his belt . . .

Martinez began to undo the red ribbons that laced Terza's brocade slippers. The cameras whispered as they came in for a closeup. Martinez unlaced both slippers, then drew one off after the other. The audience applauded. Terza's feet were small and delicate and the soles were warm to his touch.

The last ritual complete, one of Terza's friends handed Martinez a stylish pair of shoes, red leather and bows, which he drew onto Terza's feet. He stood and helped Terza, awkward in her brocade and tall heels, to rise. They kissed, and again the cameras whispered.

"You're beautiful," he murmured.

"Thank you." She smiled and kissed his ear. He could feel the warmth of her cheek against his own.

Nor were his words anything less than the truth. Terza was lovely in her brocade, with her black hair worn loose past her bare shoulders. She had carried herself all day with perfect grace and composure. The wedding, which she had organized in all its complexity, had gone without a hitch and spoke well for her managerial skills.

Surrounded by the ritual and Terza's perfect presence, Martinez found in himself the flicker of a growing hope. Much better than black self-disgust he had experienced last night, which he had spent with Amanda Taen.

That had been the end result, perhaps, of an excess of bonhomie occasioned by Lieutenant Vonderheydte's wedding. The bride, Lady Daphne, had been a young, plump, good-natured redhead, completely unlike anyone Martinez had envisioned as the partner for Vonderheydte in the long-distance delectation that Dalkeith had described.

It was then that Martinez recalled that Vonderheydte's video lover had been someone named Lady Mary.

Oh, he thought.

Martinez began to relax amid the company of his former shipmates. Vonderheydte had no relatives on Zanshaa and so had called in the Fleet for support: every officer and cadet of Vonderheydte's acquaintance had been invited. All *Corona*'s officers were present, except for Shankaracharya, who Martinez assumed was still in hiding.

Martinez was no longer in command of them and he could be at his ease. The young officers were in high spirits, and their merriment rang through the ballroom. The hot punch tasted innocent enough but reeked of brandy fumes. At some point in the afternoon Martinez began to realize that, as an officer at least two grades senior to any other present, his presence was becoming an inhibition to the verve of his juniors. He was perfectly at home among them, but the feeling was not quite reciprocated. He began to fear that at any moment he'd overhear one of them refer to him as "the Old Man." Saddened by this, he raised a glass of punch and offered the bride and groom a final toast, and then made his way out.

Alcohol swam through his head as he descended the

broad hotel stair. The evening was young and there was nowhere for him to go—he could go to the Shelley Palace and watch his brother in triumph; he could visit Terza while she was organizing their nuptials and annoy her by getting in her way.

The ringing chant of the "Congratulations" round from "Lord Fizz Takes a Holiday" began to sound from the Empyrean Ballroom upstairs. A desperate sadness began to creep into Martinez's thoughts. This kind of joy was beyond him now.

For all that he'd burned for promotion, he had enjoyed his career as a junior officer. The responsibility had been light, the companionship for the most part pleasant, and the nights had been his own.

Those carefree nights were gone, especially now that he was about to become annexed to the Chen family. One Chen would be his superior officer, another his wife, another his patron on the Control Board—and Roland, in charge of the Martinez family checkbook, would pay for it all. After tomorrow he could scarcely take a step without their combined approval.

That was when the disgust had begun to overwhelm him. It was his own ambition that had led him into this trap, a marriage to a woman he barely knew, and to whom he was likely to bring only pain. If he could bring himself to dislike Terza he might find relief—he could simply use her then, use her with a clear conscience, and know that she deserved to be used. But knew Terza well enough to know that she deserved well at the hands of any husband, and deserved as well a better husband than he.

Dancing through his thoughts was the tempting impulse to flee. Run as Sempronia had run, and take his chances.

But Sempronia's example showed him what he could expect. His allowance cut off, his patronage in the Fleet turned to outright enmity . . . Instead of enjoying a private income like that of most officers, he'd have to live on his pay while administering whatever obscure rathole of a supply depot or training camp to which the enmity of the Chens condemned him.

Martinez took a detour into the hotel bar and dwelt on these matters for the space of two drinks. By the time he'd finished the second the vision of Amanda Taen had risen in his mind. A final night of bachelor revelry seemed the very least he could offer himself, a last blaze of freedom before the velvet night of captivity.

When he called Amanda he discovered to his surprise that she had no plans, and was amenable to dinner and a visit to a club afterward. She was as full of fun as he remembered— joyous, uncomplicated, uninhibited—and when he bedded her she was delight itself. It was only afterward that she mentioned his upcoming marriage, which she'd seen, of course, in the society reports.

"I don't do married men," she said. "So from this point on, you're on your own."

"I'll miss you," Martinez said, with perfect sincerity.

"I'm glad I'm not rich or a Peer," she sighed. "I can marry whomever I want."

A bubble of sadness burst in Martinez's heart at the truth of these words, and he felt the tentacles of Clan Chen drawing him toward his destiny.

Now—the tentacles wrapping him head to foot—Martinez made his way with Terza through the throng of guests and to the car that waited outside. He shook Lord Chen's hand, and the veteran politician gave what Martinez somehow knew was a perfect imitation of a heartfelt smile. Lady Chen allowed him to touch one frozen, clenched knuckle. Roland offered him as triumphant thump on the shoulder.

Followed by Alikhan, who wore an immaculate uniform and who carried the Orb in its case, Martinez and Terza descended into their open-topped car. Alikhan joined the driver in the front, and the car carried them away to the Hotel Boniface, where Martinez had rented a suite in which they could enjoy married life for as long as the Fleet permitted.

The car cruised down the Boulevard of the Praxis. The breeze threw back Terza's hair, revealing the curve of her throat. It was still early evening, and people on the street were going to their entertainments. Martinez gave a start at the sight of white-gold hair gleaming beneath a streetlight—but as he stared he realized this wasn't Sula, but a shop clerk trudging her way to the funicular and her home in the Lower Town.

Terza's maidservant Fran was waiting for her in the suite. While Fran looked after Terza in the dressing room, Alikhan turned down the bed, laid out Martinez's dressing gown and pajamas, then helped Martinez out of his jacket and boots.

"Thank you, Alikhan," Martinez said. "You've been splendid tonight."

Alikhan beamed from beneath his spreading mustachios. "I wish you every happiness, my lord."

Alikhan withdrew: servants were stabled in another part of the hotel. Martinez stripped off the remainder of his uniform. He stared for a moment of incomprehension at the pajamas, then threw them in a drawer. He donned the dressing gown and stepped into the bathroom to brush his teeth and comb his hair. He returned to the bedroom and wondered whether he should get into the bed, or wait for Terza.

He turned down the lamp to a modest glow and smoothed the bedcovers. Hope and resentment warred in his thoughts. He mentally added the hours he'd actually spent in Terza's company, and found them to be less than eight.

There were several women, he recalled, that he'd taken to bed on less than eight hours' acquaintance. Why should this occasion be any different?

And yet it was. The other women he need not have seen ever again, but he would be with Terza for the rest of his life, or at least until her father ordered her to divorce. Tonight would have lasting consequences, and those other nights had not.

He turned at the sound of a door opening, and saw Terza enter. She wore a silk nightgown of deep blue, a bed jacket of a lighter blue with gold lacework and a collar of golden fur, and slippers with pompoms.

Her black hair was drawn back over her left ear, and there, shading the ear, she wore a large white orchid. A necklace of pale flowers draped her bosom.

Martinez paused, frozen by the sheer beauty of it, feeling the unexpected impact of this vision on his nerves, on his tingling skin. Terza paused in the doorway and offered him a shy smile.

Martinez walked toward her, took her hand, and kissed it. "You're beautiful," he said. "I've never seen anything so lovely."

A memory of Sula's translucent skin came to his mind, the way the blood flushed to the surface at the touch of his fingers, and he suppressed it. Instead he put an arm around Terza's waist and kissed her pliant lips.

"You're not tired?" he asked.

"Of course I am." She raised a hand to touch his cheek. "But some things are worth missing a little sleep."

He kissed her again. Her lips parted warmly and a sudden desire fired his blood. Her arms went around him. Martinez kissed the bared neck, and the scent of her perfume touched his nerves. His blood ran cold, and he drew back.

"What is that scent you're wearing?"

She gazed up at him in all innocence. "Sandama Twilight," she said.

"I—I'm sorry," he said. "But could you wash it off?" He managed a delicate cough. "I'm—sort of allergic. I'm sorry."

Terza's eyes widened in surprise. "Of course." She gave him a swift kiss, and left his arms. "I'll be right back."

Martinez walked to the bed and sagged against the heavy wooden footboard. His heart lurched to an uncertain rhythm, and he felt a sudden prickle of sweat on his forehead.

He stepped to the window and opened it and inhaled the night air, scouring his throat of Sula's perfume. His head cleared. Panic faded. When Terza returned, her poise unruffled and her person veiled in the scent of lavender soap, Martinez smiled and took her again in his arms.

He drew her to the bed and sat with her on the edge of the mattress. He untied the satin ribbon that closed her bed jacket, and he drew the jacket off. She looked at him, face calm, pupils broad and deep as oceans in the dim light.

"I had my implant removed this morning," she said. "The doctor said there's no need for Progestene—she said that the month after the implant is removed, chances of pregnancy are far above normal." Her fingers touched his hair at the temple. "Chances are I'll conceive soon, if that's what we want."

Martinez felt his skin flush as he was overwhelmed by a silent explosion of unexpected joy. "How wonderful," he said, his tongue suddenly thick. As he kissed her he made a quiet resolution to himself. He would not treat this marriage lightly, or as an imposition. Terza was lowering herself in order to marry him, let alone to conceive his child, and he owed her the maintenance of her dignity. If he were to be a husband, he would be as sincere a husband as he could manage. His own self-respect demanded no less.

He drew the flowers from about her neck and kissed her throat and shoulders. Her skin was warm against his lips. He drew her down on the bed. Her face was pale amid the black flower of her hair. She watched him through half-veiled lids as he caressed her.

Sula was fire and passion, Amanda laughter and joy. Terza was something deeper, perhaps more profound. There was a center of serenity and poise that seemed to recede from him even as he reached for it. That was training, certainly, though perhaps it reflected as well her own essence, a kind of acceptance that was at the very heart of her.

Everything he did, he did to bring her pleasure. He strove

with his hands and lips to unsettle that composed tranquillity
that he had seen in her since that first day in the courtyard of
the Chen Palace, and he found his reward as her breath
quickened, as she gave an involuntary cry.

The sound inflamed him: so the core was not all composure after all. He increased his efforts; he matched his breath
to hers. Her fingers dug into his arms, his shoulders, his
back. She cried out again, the cry of the lost soul alarmed to
find itself wandering in darkness, and he helped her find her
way back to the light, where he waited for her, the partner of
her bed and breath, her husband. . . .

The singer's whitened hands floated in the air like lovers
whirling on the dance floor. Her voice clashed like swords,
soared like eagles, or bled like a wound. The audience hung
breathless on her every word, and thrilled at the controlled
fury of her black-eyed stare.

Sula sat alone in the back of the club, a drink untouched
on the table before her. She was seriously contemplating letting alcohol into her life.

She knew that Martinez's wedding had gone off that afternoon; the society reports were full of it. Martinez and Lady
Terza were abed by now, and Martinez was playing with his
bride the same games he had played, only a few nights ago,
with Sula.

Because the Chen family obviously handled the guest list
without consulting the bridal couple, Sula had even been invited to the nuptials, though her work furnished her with an
excuse not to attend. She had sent a nicely wrapped present,
however, the pair of matched Guraware vases that Martinez
had given her.

The Logistics Consolidation Executive, under the command of a Lai-own fleet commander called out of retirement
for the duration of the war, was intended to resolve conflicts
between various wartime demands on limited resources. Decisions had to be made concerning which arm of govern-

ment was to have first call on assets, and those decisions were made by the executive.

The work was uninteresting and required long hours. Sula had no problem with that. The more hours she spent with work, and away from her thoughts, the better.

Sula picked up the little glass and felt the smooth chilled surface against her fingertips. Her nostrils flared with the sharp herbal scent. She had ordered iarogüt, a liquor made by fermenting a root vegetable of Lai-own origin, then flavoring it with a kind of lemony weed. The result was faintly purplish in color and about fifty-five percent alcohol.

Nasty stuff, iarogüt, but cheap and readily available. It was the liquor of choice for most of the serious alcoholics in the Fleet, all the crude old crouchbacks with the blackened eyes and the skinned knuckles and the broken veins in their noses that Sula, when she'd been assigned to her ship's military constabulary, had rounded up from local jails and marched back to their ships for punishment.

If she were to drink, Sula thought, there was no point in starting on the high road, with the choice wines and the sweet liqueurs. The gutter was what she was after, and iarogüt was what could take her there.

The derivoo singer gave a cry, a keen of anguish that broke off into a sob. Her man, the father of her children, had gone. The singer raised a hand, fingers curled as if around the hilt of a dagger. She was considering cutting the throats of her children in order to make her husband suffer.

Sula returned the glass to her table. The liquor trembled, lapping at the rim of the glass as if it were eager to escape. The invisible dagger seemed to gleam in the air.

Martinez had been playing a double game, that much Sula saw with perfect clarity. He'd always had Terza in reserve; and when Sula had balked, he'd shifted to his backup plan without missing a step.

But what, she wondered as she tapped the marble table with a fingertip, had Martinez *really* been after? Perhaps his father would raise his allowance if he married. Maybe there was some choice appointment that depended on an officer having a wife.

Whatever the reason, it couldn't have involved money or prestige or patronage in the Fleet, otherwise Martinez would have made Terza his first choice, not his second. There had to be some reason why he'd approached Sula first.

And then it occurred to her that there need be no reason other than a nasty little game that Martinez chose to play with the hearts of women. Months ago, the cadets in the duty room had told her of his success in love—was it possible to be a seducer without despising the object of seduction? Perhaps Martinez played Sula for his own amusement. It was Sula who resumed contact with Martinez after months of separation, and now she wondered if Martinez had viewed this as an opportunity for seducing one woman while quietly courting another.

The musicians struck a decisive chord: Sula's eyes leaped to the stage. A moment of decision had been reached. The singer lowered the dagger, her hand trembling. Tears glittered in her eyes. Her lips caressed the names of her children.

Then the singer called out the name of her man, and the dagger flashed high again as another chord rang out.

And perhaps, Sula thought, the game had been Terza's as well. Terza had seen Sula socially—had said she *admired* Sula. During that time, had Terza been aware of negotiations for the Martinez marriage? Or perhaps even initiated the negotiations?

Sula's hand on the table formed a fist, the knuckles white. The tension in her arm made the liquid in the chilled glass tremble. Suppose, she thought, it was all Terza's fault.

In Sula's mind there formed the vision of a sumptuous bed, satin sheets, limbs interwoven and glowing in candlelight. For a moment she entertained the fantasy of bursting in the door, of committing massacre . . .

Another chord rang from the stage, and the singer's hand

lowered again, trembled, and then drove the imaginary dagger into her own belly. The derivoo cried out, stumbled, and died in song, with the name of her man on her lips.

The singer took her bows as applause rang out. A cold smile played across Sula's lips. There was a difference, she thought, between truth and melodrama, and the singer had crossed it.

So had Sula.

She raised the chilled glass to her lips, inhaled the harsh fumes for a moment, then slammed the glass to the tabletop. Liquid splashed her fingers.

Sula rose, put money on the table, and walked out into the night.

TEN

That the Convocation was to take Wormhole 2 to Zarafan was a coincidence: Zanshaa's place in its orbit currently made Wormhole 2 the closest of Zanshaa's eight wormholes, and thus the Convocation was much more likely to be out of the system by the time the Naxids arrived.

But Zarafan was only ten days' hard acceleration from Zanshaa, and too close for the Convocation's safety: a Naxid expeditionary force might just decide to venture that way. It was then that Lord Chen fully earned every septile the Martinez family was paying him, by standing in the Joint Evacuation Committee (which included the Fleet Control Board) and moving that the Convocation simply keep on going once they reached Zarafan and continue all the way to Laredo.

Laredo was three months away at reasonably comfortable accelerations, and tucked into a fairly obscure corner of the empire. There were many more likely places for the Naxids to search for the Convocation than Laredo, and if the enemy moved in that direction they would have to make a significant commitment of resources, there would be plenty of warning, and the Fleet would have time to counter the enemy advance.

In addition, the small squadron of frigates being built at Laredo shipyards by Lord Martinez should be complete by then, and able to aid the Convocation's defense. The Convocation would be withdrawing toward its supports.

Lord Chen's motion was passed by the committee. Lords

Saïd and Tork insisted on secrecy, even from other members of the Convocation; and it was Lady Seekin who suggested that false rumors of the Convocation's destination should be spread.

So it was that the next day the Convocation found itself voting to evacuate to a destination kept secret even from them. There was a good deal of grumbling, but a rumor that the Convocation was due to convene on Esley, with its spectacular vistas and luxurious resorts, helped to reconcile the lords convocate to their collective exile.

At Lord Saïd's urging, the Convocation voted to evacuate in three days' time, and to declare that any convocate who remained behind would be declared a traitor. Each convocate was allowed two servants or family members, and the rest of the household would have to find their own transport.

To Esley. Or to Harzapid, headquarters of the Fourth Fleet. Suddenly there were *two* rumors.

Lord Chen, fortunately, had no worries about losing Terza in all the confusion. She would be flying to Laredo on her own, on Lord Roland Martinez's family yacht, unaware of the fact that her father would probably arrive ahead of her.

It was on the day prior to departure, during a debate on finance, that Lord Chen managed his own personal triumph. The evacuation of Zanshaa meant that the war wouldn't end soon, with a huge battle that would crush the Naxids and reestablish order throughout the empire. Instead the war would continue, along with the appropriations necessary to keep it going. Thus far the empire had kept running through a series of emergency spending measures backed by currency reserves and special issues of bonds. But the reserves were gone, the price of bonds had crashed after the news of Magaria became general knowledge, and the government was now simply creating money on a day-by-day basis to meet its obligations. No revenue was expected from the third of the empire controlled by the Naxids. Inflation was heading toward double-digit levels. Once the empire was informed that the government had fled Zanshaa, who then was going to accept its currency? The bonds might well be worth more as wallpaper than at their face value.

In normal times the government was run on a relatively small budget. The Peers took care of most minor matters at their own expense. The rest was paid for by rental of government property, distribution of energy from ring stations and other sources, sale of antimatter to private shipping, a tax on telecommunications, and an excise tax on interstellar commerce.

All this was clearly inadequate, and had been from the first day of the war. But the alternative was to tax those who actually possessed wealth, and these were for the most part Peers and Peer-owned enterprises. Peers had always been reluctant to tax themselves; and for the most part they saw no reason why mere civil war should alter this condition. They pointed out that they already spent a great deal of capital in the public interest, maintaining roads, creating water and sewer projects, managing charities, sponsoring theatrical events, and the like. The lords convocate became desperate to raise money by any means other than direct taxation, the result being an erratic series of consumption taxes—on salt, on beverages, on use of warehouse space in government-controlled ring stations.

That last intrusive decree had driven Lord Chen into a frenzy. As a shipowner he was already subject to a flat fifteen percent tax on the value of any cargo he discharged onto a ring station—to have to pay *again*, to store the same cargo, was ruinous.

Yet most of the Convocation were not shipowners, and in their desperation tried to double the excise tax to thirty percent. At this rate of taxation interstellar commerce was simply unprofitable: no ships would fly. Lord Chen and every other convocate with shipping interests pointed this out repeatedly, and in the end staged a filibuster that managed to talk the subject to death.

The impending evacuation of Zanshaa had removed the last of the die-hards' excuses for believing the war would be a short one, and in the Convocation's last session before its departure from the capital, a bill was placed before the house to pay through the war by means of an income tax of one percent. Traditionalists insisted that this was worse than revolution—even the Naxids, vile as they were, would not be so vicious and so radical as to place a tax on equity. Lord Saïd assured the lords convocate that the measure was a temporary one only.

He pointed behind him with his ceremonial wand, through the transparent rear wall of the Hall of the Convocation to the terrace, from which rebel Naxids had once been hurled. "If we do not find a way to pay for this war," he said, "we might as well throw ourselves from that cliff, because it will be a more merciful fate than what the Naxids will give us."

With the arch-conservative Lord Senior speaking for the measure, the tax passed with margin of sixty-one percent. One of the dissenters—a toothless old Torminel—thumped an angry fist on her desk and growled that, as the Convocation had forsaken the principles of civilization, she might as well remain on Zanshaa and wait for the Naxids, who seemed to have a clearer idea of decency and order than the members of the house.

The Lord Senior politely suggested that perhaps the lady convocate had forgotten that such an action, as the Convocation had decided only two days before, constituted high treason. "I would regret extremely the necessity of ripping you limb from limb and hurling you from the High City," Saïd said, "but alas, my lady, we are the servants of the law, not its masters."

Lord Chen barely heard this exchange: he was too busy rejoicing. Just a few hours ago, in committee, one of his ship-owning colleagues had slipped a rider onto the revenue bill abolishing the excise tax on cargoes. Very suddenly his business was profitable again, and even at the cost of one percent of his income he could expect colossal profits. Admittedly most of the money would be going to the Martinez family for the next five years, but after that Lord Chen could look forward both to increased profit and the end of his relationship with Clan Martinez.

And, he thought in triumph, all those annoying revenue officers on the ring stations that had so harassed his captains and agents would now descend to the planets below, to harass everyone else.

Even at the cost of one percent of his income, Lord Chen thought, this was welcome news.

"Well, Gare, as it happens you've got a choice of transport."

Lieutenant Ari Abacha raised to his lips one of the Commandery's tulip glasses, with white and green stripes, and sipped his cocktail. He was a long-limbed man of superior social connections and a perfectly majestic brand of indolence, and he and Martinez had become acquainted when they were both on staff at the Commandery. Abacha was still on staff, as the red triangles on his collar showed, and now as Michi Chen's tactical officer, Martinez once again wore the red tabs himself.

"I say, Gare, it's decent of you to take me to the senior officers' club," Abacha said. He glanced over the barroom, his social antennae twitching, and then he leaned close. "That's Captain Han-gar over there, you know. Rumor has it that these days he's pissing on the doorstep of Squadron Commander Pen-dro . . ."

"A dangerous business," Martinez murmured. His eyes were fixed on the display glowing in the table, showing him one small Fleet craft after another.

Not that one, he thought, that was nearly a pinnace. He didn't want to be strapped into a coffin for all that time.

"It's dangerous only if his wife finds out," Abacha said. "But Pen-dro has a habit of rewarding her lovers. Look what happened to Esh-draq."

Martinez did not encourage this line of conversation, being instead more interested in the variety of craft that might be employed in the task of uniting him with Michi Chen's squadron and his new appointment. With forty or fifty days of very nasty acceleration in the offing, he wanted at least a little comfort.

"Say, Ari," he said, "what do you think of this one?"

The vessel in question was one of the craft that had been conscripted to defend Zanshaa in the aftermath of the Battle of Magaria. Optimistically called "picket ships," they had consisted of a variety of small craft hastily outfitted with missile launchers and sent to patrol the system in the hope that they might somehow score a hit or two on the enemy before being annihilated. Once Chenforce had arrived to defend the system, the picket ships had been withdrawn.

"Ah," Abacha said as he looked at the design. "Nice boat. That was one of Exalted Flower's corporate yachts, built to shuttle their executives around their mineral concessions in the system. Nicely appointed. Said to have an excellent kitchen. A pity you won't have one of their chefs aboard."

The boat, which had retained its original corporate name of *Daffodil*, had docked with the ring station two days earlier and discharged what no doubt had been a highly relieved crew of four. After routine maintenance that would complete in four days, *Daffodil* would be available for further use, which would include taking Martinez to Michi Chen's flagship.

"I'll take this one, then," Martinez said. "Thanks very much for giving me the choice."

"Think nothing of it," said Abacha. "I'm happy to help out a friend from the old days." An expression of distaste crossed his face, and he leaned closer to Martinez. "All sorts of new people here now," he said. "Rude, useless, ignorant . . . always bustling about and ruining one's day. Do you know, since the war's started, some days I'm here eighteen hours straight!"

Martinez widened his eyes. "I'm shocked."

Abacha's eyes grew fierce. "And now that we're evacuating, it's going to get worse. I'm only allowed three trunks and one servant! Regulations clearly state I'm entitled to five trunks and two servants!" He gave the table an angry thump. "I've finally got my two boys trained to starch my collars exactly as I want them, and to serve me a Hairy Roger at just the right temperature, and now I have to let one go. Who knows what the Fleet will do with him? Turn a fine valet into a machinist or something."

"I'll take your extra," Martinez said. His rank entitled him to four servants, but he'd never had more than Alikhan. Since his escape with *Corona*, his life had been speeding so fast that he'd never had time to search the ranks for servants, and if he were to serve on a flagship he should probably acquire someone more polished than his ex-weaponer.

Abacha looked disapproving. "I promised my boys they'd never have to do ship duty."

"If they're evacuating," Martinez pointed out, "they'll have to spend time on ships anyway. Unless they'd rather stay on Zanshaa and wait for the Naxids."

Abacha sipped his drink and made a face, as if he'd just tasted lemon juice. "I'll ask them. But whatever happens, they're going to be vexed."

"Tell them they'll be on a flagship. That's something."

Abacha only shrugged, but then he cheered. "By the way, Gare, we're having some rare parties these days. Since we can't take it with us, everyone's drinking up their finest stock. You'd be welcome to join us in our revels, if you like."

"My calendar seems to be quite full these days," Martinez said.

"Oh yes!" Abacha beamed in approval. "Newly married and all. You've got quite a catch in the Chen girl."

"Thank you," said Martinez.

"You know," Abacha laughed, "I thought that Lady Sula would be your next conquest."

Martinez felt a counterfeit smile cleave to his face. "You did?" he asked.

"I was duty officer in Operations, remember . . . I saw the logs that showed all those messages you were sending each other during the Blitsharts business. I felt certain you were . . ." Abacha searched for a word. ". . . building an intimacy." He shook his head. "I guess nothing came of it. Pity. She's a lovely girl—very suited to you, I thought."

"As you say," speaking past the tension in his jaw, "nothing came of it."

"Still," Abacha said, "it ended happily, yes?" He gave an appreciative smack of his lips. "Lady Terza Chen! How perfect for you! You're a lucky man, you know it?"

"Yes," Martinez said. "I've been told." He reached for his drink, and a cool frumenty fire poured down his throat.

Ari Abacha was still in a contemplative mood. "You and Caroline Sula," he mused. "Who'd have thought that you'd become so famous? You have to wonder how such a thing could happen."

"War," Martinez said into his glass. "All it took was war."

A cold wind was blustering around the High City, carrying with it the smell of rain, so Martinez took a cab from the Commandery to the Shelley Palace, where he would join Roland and Walpurga for dinner. He was spending the day without Terza, who was joining her parents on the ride to the skyhook, and wouldn't be back till late.

This was the day fixed for the Convocation's evacuation. Though no announcement had been made and there were no reports in the media, all the High City seemed a part of the secret. The Boulevard of the Praxis was filled with trucks taking household goods into storage, and several of the larger palaces were being shuttered. Another element that made up so much of the capital's distinctive style was abandoning Zanshaa, and no one knew what would come, with the Naxids, to take its place.

Shutters weren't going up on the Shelley Palace yet, but it was only a matter of days before they would. Personal possessions were being packed, to be shipped up the skyhook and received aboard the *Ensenada,* the Martinez family yacht, to be carried to Laredo along with the family. They would leave as soon as Martinez brought his honeymoon to an end by leaving for his appointment with Michi Chen's squadron. Martinez supposed it was nice of them to wait, but he thought it was asking a lot of Terza to endure three months' daily exposure to Roland, Walpurga, and PJ.

Daffodil would be ready in four days, which meant Martinez's marriage would be seven days old before he and Terza were parted, certainly for many months, possibly a year or more. Conceivably forever, if things went wrong.

The first days of marriage had been tranquil: the serenity that seemed to surround Terza had embraced Martinez in its calm, scented arms. He and Terza spent most of their time in the hotel suite, having their meals brought in, and aside from chance encounters on their short walks they saw no one.

They opened their wedding presents. Martinez managed to conceal his shock when the Guraware vases were unwrapped. *She hates me,* he thought, in sudden desolation.

He sent the vases straight into storage, where he hoped they would remain forever.

They sent thanks to wedding guests. Fresh-cut flowers had been sent to the room every day, and Terza arranged them into gorgeous displays that radiated color and scent in every corner of the apartment. Thankfully she never remembered Sula's gift, and Martinez never had to look at Terza's flowers arranged in Sula's porcelain.

Terza and Martinez discovered a mutual liking for the plays of Koskinen: Terza enjoyed the sophisticated portrayals, and Martinez the cynical epigrams. They called up *The Sweethearts Divided* onto the parlor's video wall and watched it with great pleasure.

Martinez missed the intensity he'd shared with Sula, the

way their minds had seemed to leap suddenly into the same channel, the intense, often unspoken mental collaboration they'd shared when they devised the plan for the evacuation, or even—the minds leaping across star systems—when they'd created a new system of tactics.

Terza was all tranquillity and excellence—self-possessed, considerate, alert to his wishes, efficiently arranging their time together. But there was an unearthly quality to this tranquillity, and sometimes Martinez suspected he was watching a performance, a brilliant performance of the highest order, and he wondered what it concealed.

Martinez found something of an answer when he watched Terza play her harp. As her fingers drew music from the strings the habitual calm and serenity were replaced by an intensity that bordered on ferocity—*Here is fire.* Martinez was intrigued. *Here is passion.* He saw her breathe with the music; he saw the determined glitter in her eye, the throb of the pulse in her throat. Her engagement with the music was total, and the sight of it a revelation.

Martinez tried to carry the music with them to bed, to kindle the same passion there, in the bower she filled with rainbows of flowers. He flattered himself that he was successful. In the music of limbs and hearts Terza soon found her rhythm. Her trained musician's fingers, sensitive already to nuance, learned to caress him and draw forth any timbre she desired, piano to fortissimo. She was not shy. In between moments of love there was a sweetness to her that he found touching.

But somehow his time with Terza failed to equal other, recent experience. With Sula the play of love had been more brilliant, more brittle, its peak a moment of realization, a knowledge of self and other and the whole blazing, brilliant universe beyond. In Sula he found the confirmation of his own existence, the answer to every metaphysical quest.

Martinez failed to find this with Terza, and furthermore he knew perfectly well that it wasn't Terza's fault. At a loss for any other options, he strove simply to please her, and it pleased her to be pleased.

The problem, Martinez thought as he paid the cab, was that he simply didn't know on what footing the marriage stood. He couldn't be certain if it was a business arrangement, a piece of practical politics, a folly, or a farce. He couldn't tell if he and Terza were a man and woman bought and sold, or simply two inexperienced people trying to make the best of what fate had handed them, aware that at any moment fate could declare the whole arrangement nothing more than a joke.

Martinez opened the door to the Shelley Palace and saw PJ standing irresolute in the hall, and he thought, at least my marriage isn't *that*.

"Oh," PJ said, his eyes widening. "I was thinking of, um . . ."

"Taking a walk?" Martinez finished. "You don't want to. It'll rain soon."

"Ah." PJ's long face was glum. "I suppose I should have looked." He returned his walking stick to the rack.

One of the maidservants arrived to take Martinez's uniform cap. "Shall I tell Lady Walpurga you've arrived?" she asked.

"Not just yet," PJ said, and turned to Martinez. "Let me give you a drink. Take the chill off."

"Why not?"

Martinez followed PJ into the south parlor, where he saw a glass already set out on a table, the sign that this was not PJ's first drink of the day.

"Terza's well, I hope?" PJ asked as he made a swoop for the mig brandy.

"She's very well, thank you."

"Would you like some of this," holding up the brandy, "or . . ."

"That will be fine, thanks."

They clinked glasses. Rain began to spatter the broad windows, and outside Martinez saw people leaning into the downpour and sprinting to their destinations.

PJ cleared his throat. "I thought I should let you know," he said, "that I've decided to stay."

"Stay?" Martinez repeated. "You mean on Zanshaa?"

"Yes. I've spoken to Lord Pierre and, ah—well, I'll be staying here to look after Ngeni interests while everyone's àway."

Martinez paused with the brandy partway to his lips, then lowered the glass. "Have you thought this out?" he asked.

PJ gazed at Martinez with his sad brown eyes. "Yes, of course. My marriage to Walpurga is . . ." He shrugged. "Well, it's an embarrassment, why not admit it? This way Walpurga and I can part and . . ." Again he shrugged. "And no one can criticize, you see?"

"I see," Martinez said. He swirled his brandy as he considered PJ's decision. "But Lord Pierre is a loyalist convocate," he said, "and the Naxids must have him on their list of people they'd very much like to . . ." He searched for an appropriate euphemism. "*Interview*. And I can be reasonably certain that I'm also on the list, and now you're related to·*me* as well." He looked at PJ carefully. "I don't really think you'd be safe."

PJ flapped away the danger with his hand. "Pierre thinks I'll be all right. I'm only a cousin, after all. And it's not as if I *know* anything . . ."

"There may be a great deal of discomfort before the Naxids find that out. And besides, you could be held hostage."

PJ put down his glass and straightened his jacket. "As if anyone in the empire would alter their course of action on the chance that *I* might be killed."

Martinez had to concede that PJ probably had scored a point.

"Gareth," PJ said, "it's the only way I can help. It's *war,* it's critical that I do . . . *something.* If all I can accomplish in the war is to look after some property and some farms and pensioned-off servants while Pierre is away, then that's what I'll do."

Martinez narrowed his eyes. "You haven't volunteered for anything else, have you?"

PJ blinked. "What do you mean?"

"You haven't volunteered to work for the Legion, or the Intelligence Section, or some similar outfit?"

PJ seemed genuinely surprised, but then turned thoughtful. "You think they'd take me?"

I hope not, Martinez thought. "I shouldn't think so," he said.

PJ reached for his glass and took a long, morose drink. "No. I'll just be living in a wing of the palace while the rest of it's closed up, and making sure that my old nurse and a few hundred other folk are looked after."

To Martinez, it seemed as if PJ was genuinely determined. "Well," he said, raising his glass, "here's luck to you."

"Thank you, Gareth."

As Martinez touched his lips with his glass, the front door boomed open and a gust of wind riffled papers on the side table. Martinez glanced through the pocket door to see Roland in the hall wiping rain water from his jacket.

"Damn it!" Roland called. "I wish I'd thought to take my overcoat. It was sunny when I left. Is that brandy?"

He strode into the parlor, water droplets clinging to his hair, poured himself mig brandy, and took a deep drink.

"Sempronia's married," he said. "I just came from the ceremony, such as it was."

"I thought we weren't speaking to Sempronia," Martinez said.

"We're not." Roland took another drink. "But I was required to sign the papers permitting the whole thing to take place. Which I *had* to do, because Proney was threatening either to travel with Shankaracharya as his mistress, or to join the Fleet as a common recruit and serve as his orderly."

Martinez concealed a smile. "She hasn't lost her spirit, I see."

"No. She has her young man thoroughly under her thumb, from what I could see." There was a cynical glimmer in Roland's eye. "In ten years, she'll look brilliant and he'll look fifty."

Martinez looked at his brother. "Now you're the only one of us unmarried," he said. "And you're the oldest. It hardly seems fair."

Roland smiled into his brandy glass. "I haven't found the right woman."

"Why not?" Martinez said. "I'm surprised you didn't try to marry Terza yourself."

PJ, with his recent marital wounds, seemed uncomfortable at a question concerning the rational organization of matrimony.

Roland waved a hand. "I prefer to keep my arrangements with Lord Chen on a business basis," he said, then shrugged. "Besides, I'd make Terza unhappy, and you won't."

Martinez gazed at Roland in pure curiosity. "How do you know that?"

Roland patted Martinez on the shoulder. "Because you're a decent person who gives everything his best," he said, "and I'm a cad who would put Terza aside the second I'd fathered an heir on her and could find a better match."

Martinez found himself absolutely at a loss for a reply. Roland finished his brandy and smiled.

"Shall we call Walpurga and have our supper?" he said. "Signing away a sister makes me hungry."

Supper was in the smaller family dining room, a place with yellow silk wallpaper and elaborately carved furniture inlaid with bits of white shell. PJ and Walpurga dined in amity, though without any expressions of affection beyond Walpurga's offhand, "Pass the sauce, dearest." Roland discoursed on political events. Martinez, when asked, said that he found marriage surprisingly congenial, something he would have said even if it weren't true.

When Martinez returned to the hotel he found Terza lying on the bed still in the light trousers and silk jacket she'd worn to her tropical destination, curled around a calla lily she'd plucked from one of her arrangements. There was a satisfied, rather secretive smile on her face.

Martinez paused in the doorway and absorbed this sight. "What are you thinking of?" Martinez asked.

Pleasure twitched at the corners of her mouth. "Our child."

He felt a shimmering warmth in his blood. He crossed the space between them in a few steps, sat on the mattress, and touched her arm. "You can't know you're pregnant already, can you?"

"No. In fact I'm reasonably certain I'm not." Terza looked up at him, and shifted to place her head in his lap. "But I think I will be before you leave. I have a . . . sense of impending fertility."

Martinez stroked the fragrant mass of her hair. Her cheek was warm against his hand.

"Four days," he said.

She sighed. Her dark eyes sought his. "Thank you," she said. "You've been very good to me."

He was puzzled. "Why wouldn't I be?"

"The marriage wasn't your idea. You could have taken any resentment out on me—I was the one available, after all." She took his hand and kissed it. "But you've tried to make me happy. I appreciate that."

And are you happy? That was the next question, but Martinez hesitated to ask it. There was an air of truth that hung in the room at the moment, and he didn't want to tempt fate.

"I can't imagine wanting to hurt you," he said.

She kissed his hand again. "Four days," she said, and smiled up at him. "We're lucky to have so many."

"We are." He stroked her cheek as a warm tenderness rose in his blood. "I'm a lucky man."

The luckiest man in the universe, he thought, remembering Sula's words.

He wondered if Sula would say the same now.

The day after the Convocation left Zanshaa, the new Military Governor, Fleet Commander Pahn-ko, announced that, as a safety measure, martial law was to be imposed on all of Zanshaa and that the accelerator ring was to be completely evacuated within the next twenty-nine days. As the ring that circled the entire planet possessed an enormous internal volume that housed nearly eighty million citizens, this announcement created something of a logistical challenge.

It could have been worse, Sula thought. The interior spaces of the ring, enormous but lacking in charm, were the natural habitat of the poor. Yet the authorities hadn't wanted a critical installation like the Zanshaa ring, with its port and military facilities, its administrative centers and its quantities of dangerous antimatter, to house unstable social elements, and these elements tended to lurk among the lowly. Rents had been artificially kept high and the inhabitants relentlessly middle-class, drawn to the ring by certain privileges, such as excellent educational facilities for their children and the chance to profit as middlemen on interstellar trade, or as contractors for military or civilian transport. Most of the ring was in fact empty, with no water, power, or heat available for anyone trying to live on the cheap in the uninhabited space.

Now the solid citizens of the ring were going to come down the skyhooks to the surface of Zanshaa, millions every day, each with a bag of possessions and a built-in requirement for food and shelter. If they weren't poor and needy now, they would be soon.

The brilliant minds of the Logistics Consolidation Executive were put to work on the problem. "Nearly three million every day for a month!" cried Sula's Lai-own boss. "Impossible!"

"Perhaps we could just chuck them off the ring and let them get down on their own," Sula suggested.

The Lai-own glared. "I would prefer *useful* suggestions, if you please," he chided.

Sula shrugged. She had found that when she began work on the problem that the evacuation actually made things simpler. The only things going up to the ring were critical personnel leaving Zanshaa, these and engineers getting ready to blow the ring apart. Once the ring was stripped of all the useful cargo and supplies, the giant cars that normally contained cargo could be converted to carry personnel. If enough acceleration couches couldn't be manufactured in time—and it looked as if they couldn't—the passengers could be sandwiched between narrow, heavily padded partitions.

It wouldn't be pleasant, and they'd bounce around a bit, but it could be done.

"How are we going to find places for them once they're here?" the Lai-own cried.

"We've got three billion people on the planet as it is," Sula said. "Eighty million more is just a drop in the bucket."

She began to work on the problem, buoyed somewhat by this evidence that the administration had adopted her plan for evacuating the government and the Fleet and then blowing the ring to bits. It would have been nice, she thought, if someone in authority had acknowledged her contribution. Another medal would have been welcome. Even "thank you" would have been nice.

No thank-you came. She wondered if Martinez, that bastard, had pinched her share of the credit.

Her self-destructive impulses had not survived the night she'd heard the derivoo. Homicidal impulses were entertained briefly, then dismissed as unworthy.

Nothing important, after all, had changed. A man Sula hated had married a woman she barely knew—and why should that matter to her? Her own position was barely altered: she had the same rank, the same distinctions, and lived with the same knowledge of her own danger as she had a month ago. Nothing fundamental had altered.

All this she argued to herself successfully, and only doubted these truths at night, alone in the giant Sevigny bed, when rage and loneliness and her own desperation stormed through her.

She was thankful for work, and delighted her chief by the long-burning hours she worked on the evacuation. She was even more thankful when a call for volunteers was broadcast through the Fleet. Hazardous duty, the announcement said, and a chance for glory and promotion while upholding the Praxis.

Sula reckoned she knew what the call was for. The plan that Martinez submitted to the Control Board called for an army to hold Zanshaa City against the Naxids. It was getting a little late to raise an army, but she supposed late was better than never.

She considered her situation—she knew that the entire Logistics Consolidation Executive was scheduled for evacuation in ten days. She could spend the rest of the war in her niche, shuttling supplies around, and let others concern themselves with victory.

That would not give Sula patronage, of course—she'd lost that chance with Martinez. She had her medals and her lieutenancy and a degree of celebrity, but that wouldn't guarantee further promotion.

The best chance of earning her next step would be to hazard her life against the Naxids. It made sense to claw out of the war as many chances for advancement as she could.

The possibility of death was not a significant consideration. She was good at argument, but hadn't yet managed to construct for herself a convincing reason why her own life was worth preserving.

Or anyone else's, for that matter.

Besides, ever since she'd heard the news of Martinez's engagement she'd felt like killing something.

Sula submitted an application, then was called for an interview before a Daimong elcap. Since some of the questions had to do with her experience with firearms and explosives, she decided that her guess as to the nature of the duty was correct. But since her answers to those questions were "basic proficiency" and "none at all," it wasn't clear whether she'd be suitable for the duty or not, and she returned to the Logistics Executive, where she was assigned to the problem of feeding and clothing the eighty million refugees from the ring.

It took only a brief glance at the data to assure her that feeding the strays wasn't going to be a problem. The planet of Zanshaa, in accordance with the dictates of the Praxis, was self-sufficient in basic foodstuffs.

But it wasn't self-sufficient in *all* foodstuffs. There were climactic and soil conditions, as well as economies of scale, that made Zanshaa less efficient at producing certain crops, and turned it into an importer of some and an exporter of others. Zanshaa's old, stable, relatively flat continents produced ideal grazing for herd animals, and Zanshaa exported beef, portschen, fristigo, lamb, and dairy products. But its tropical areas lacked certain nutrients in the soil, and this made it a net importer of other foodstuffs.

High-quality cocoa came only from off-planet. So did coffee.

So did tobacco.

Shit in a bucket, Sula thought. *Tobacco.*

Sula loathed tobacco, but a determined minority of the human race and even some Torminel and Daimong were devoted to it. Sula remembered from school that there had once been health problems associated with the weed, but medicine had solved those, and now tobacco was merely another minor air pollutant. The Shaa had disapproved of tobacco, just as they'd disapproved of alcohol or betel nut or hashish, but they'd never actually banned any of these substances, just made certain that the products were regulated and taxed and turned to the profit of the government.

She dived into a frenzy of research on commodities pricing, interrupted only when a courier came with her orders. She'd been accepted, with remarkable speed, into the still uncertain duty for which she'd volunteered, and was ordered to report in two days to the Villa Fosca, an establishment near Edernay a couple hours from Zanshaa City by train.

On her noon break Sula raced to her bank. Her previous advisor, Mr. Weckman, had left, gone off to Hy-Oso, and his replacement directed her toward the commodities desk. The prices for off-world cocoa, coffee, and tobacco had risen slightly, but the markets didn't know that the ring was going to be destroyed and that nothing would be coming cheaply from orbit for years. Sula considered futures contracts, but realized that when the Naxids came, it might be difficult for someone on their Shoot on Sight list to collect on her speculation, and decided it would be better to have the actual products under her control. With a certain amount of amazement at her own daring, she used half her fortune to purchase goods that were still in orbit, on the ring.

Once back at her desk at the Logistics Consolidation Executive, Sula issued orders for those very same cargoes to be sent down the skyhook in the next few days, and to be sent to warehouses in Zanshaa Lower Town.

Having accomplished this, she sat back at her desk with an unfamiliar sense of wonder and pride. She felt more than just a profiteer.

She felt like a Peer.

On her last day in Zanshaa she returned to the High City and the La-gaa and Spacey Auction House. The *Ju-yao* pot was still for sale, nobody having offered the minimum bid of twenty thousand at the auction.

"I'll give the owner fourteen for it," Sula told the polite young Terran who greeted her. "But I'm shipping out and I've got to have it today."

Either the woman's shock was genuine or she was a good actress. "But my lady," she said, "it's worth—"

"Fourteen, today," Sula said. "Less, tomorrow."

The woman blinked. "I'll have to contact the owner."

"By all means."

Fourteen thousand would clean out Sula's bank account, but she suspected that her bank account wouldn't do her much good under a Naxid regime anyway.

The saleswoman returned from her call with a calculating look in her eye. "He'll want the money today," she said.

"Right away, if he likes. But I want you to pack that pot in the most secure container you've got. I may have to put it through some gravitational stress."

The woman nodded. "We can produce a foam package for you that will include a pressure-sensitive balloon to support the interior."

"Very good."

Sula held the vase for a moment before it was packed away, letting her eyes dwell on the subtle shades of the blue-green glaze while she brushed the crackle with her fingertips. Then, like a nursing mother reluctantly parting with her newborn, she allowed the vase to be taken away and packed.

The next day she reported to the Villa Fosca, a pink stucco palace set amid green rolling farmland, and while cities filled with refugees and her supplies of cocoa and tobacco were sent down the skyhook and began to appreciate in value, Sula was put through a course in communications, weapons, explosives, and hand-to-hand combat by engineers, military constabulary, and members of the Intelligence Section. The tenants of the villa were Terrans only, which implied that volunteers belonging to other species were being trained at other facilities.

Life in the villa was odd. In the mornings the trainees

slogged through ditches and waist-high fields of rye in full body armor, afternoons were devoted to class work, and in the evening the enlisted went under tents while the officers wore full dress for supper and behaved as if they were at a summer resort. Almost all the officers were young—even their commander, Lieutenant Captain Hong, was under thirty—and that encouraged a lighthearted style. There was a lot of drink and music and horseplay around the pool, and at night, Sula suspected, a great deal of cohabitation. Sula, who at the formal suppers wore more impressive medals than anyone present, was treated with respect even as she declined offers of alcohol and sex. The others forgave her these eccentricities on the grounds that she was a hero and entitled to her crotchets.

Other officers were scandalized that she didn't have a servant, and though she protested that she had organized her belongings exactly as she wanted them and that anyone else could only disturb her arrangements, they insisted on procuring an orderly from the ranks. Sula had never in her life interviewed a servant and was intimidated by the prospect, but the others had already organized themselves into an informal committee and carried out the interviews themselves, while Sula sat in their midst and nodded as if this were the sort of thing she did every day. Before long she had an orderly named Macnamara, a tall, curly-haired, clean-cheeked youth who had volunteered from the military constabulary. He was one of the stars of the personal combat courses, and Sula felt a growth in confidence knowing he'd be guarding her back.

Sula gathered that Martinez's idea of defending Zanshaa with an actual army had been deemed impractical, but the government didn't want to abandon the capital entirely. Sula was to be part of a stay-behind team intended to gather intelligence and to participate in sabotage and the assassination of traitors.

Near the end of their twenty-day course, the teams were

inspected by Senior Captain Ahn-kin of the Intelligence Section, and Ahn-kin paused before Sula—braced at the salute, in immaculate full-dress uniform, with her combat gear laid out on the peristyle before her—and gave her a long stare.

"You are Lieutenant the Lady Sula, are you not?" Ahn-kin asked.

"Yes, my lord."

Ahn-kin leaned forward intently. "Why are you here, my lady?"

Surprised, Sula stammered out something about wanting to defend the Praxis.

"That isn't what I mean," Ahn-kin said. "I meant that you should not be here at all. You are one of the most recognizable Terrans on this planet. How can you hide in an enemy-occupied city and expect not to be recognized?"

For a moment Sula could think of no reply that was not obscene. Her own stupidity, and the imbecility of those running this operation, had just been driven home with the simplest of questions.

Disgust stung her throat like the taste of bile.

We're just playing soldier out here. For all the good we're doing, we might as well be playing hopscotch.

"I'll change my appearance, my lord," she said finally.

"I hope you will," Ahn-kin said severely.

The next day she went to a cosmetician in Edernay and had her hair bobbed severely, and dyed a deep jet-black. Recalling that her only civilian clothing consisted of a simple black party dress, she acquired a modest collection of civilian clothes, and wore some of these on her return to the villa. The consensus of opinion was that her pale complexion, contrasting with the black hair, made her even more striking than before.

"But do I look like *me*?" she demanded.

There was a collective hesitation. "Perhaps you could do something with the eyes."

Cosmetic contact lenses were easy enough to procure. And carotene supplements would darken her complexion, at least if she didn't overdo them and turn bright orange. Sula made a note to procure a supply of these items.

After the twenty-two days of the course were run, the group was assembled by their commander, Lieutenant Captain Lord Octavius Hong. He was a young man with hair that had gone prematurely gray, and he projected the vigor and clean enjoyment of the sportsman. Clearly he had volunteered for the job because he thought it would be a way to leapfrog over the heads of the many elcaps senior to him, a fast route to promotion and distinction.

Hong stood on the veranda and addressed the trainees ranked on the lawn below. He spoke quickly, incisively, and without notes, while making vigorous gestures with his black-gloved hands. Sula had to admit that whoever had taught Hong rhetoric and public speaking had done a good job.

"Lord Governor Pahn-ko has authorized me to inform you of a number of developments that may be of interest to you," Hong said. "Lord Saïd has ordered changes in the administration of the empire in order to assure a continuation of order in the event of a loss of the capital and the absence of the Convocation."

In the event? Sula wondered if any one of Hong's audience didn't know that one of these things had already happened, and that the other was inevitable. . . .

Hong made a chopping gesture with one gloved hand. "Each of the lords governor has been ordered to establish a General Council, composed of members of all loyal species and of all sectors of society. This council will aid each governor in administration, and provide support to the Convocation and to the successful conclusion of the war. . . ."

And to keep an eye on each other, Sula thought. And as for "all sectors of society," she thought she could name a few that wouldn't be seen among the councils of government.

"Each governor is also instructed to appoint a deputy gov-

THE SUNDERING • 275

ernor, a loyal citizen who will act in his stead if the governor is forced to surrender to the enemy. The deputy governor is authorized to appoint a secret council to aid him in this endeavor, as well as to make military appointments. The deputy and his aides will fight on in the event of any Naxid occupation."

And will keep an eye on the General Council, Sula thought. The knowledge that the councillors were being observed by secret appointees, some with guns, would no doubt have a chilling effect on any attempts to get cozy with the Naxids.

"On Zanshaa, however, the arrangement will be slightly different." Hong marched to the front of the verandah and gazed down at his command with his hands clasped behind his back and his chest thrust out, a picture of confidence and mastery. "Zanshaa is *already* under a military governor," he said. "When the Naxids come, Fleet Commander Pahn-ko and his entire staff and council move into a secret facility now being prepared for them. The fleetcom will remain in command of our units and much of the civil administration. So you can rest assured that any order you receive from *me* will have the *direct authority of the governor.* And you should know that your efforts on behalf of the Praxis will be brought to the lord governor's attention for commendation and promotion."

He withdrew a fist from behind his back and brandished it, waist-high, to emphasize the importance of this statement. Sula hadn't actually been worried on this score, but now she began to think that worry might have been the appropriate reaction all along. It was unclear how an elderly fleetcom in hiding was going to control all these elements of society without making himself conspicuous, especially considering that the Naxids were going to be looking for him anyway.

Let's hope Pahn-ko never meets anyone face-to-face, Sula thought. Let's hope they have all the codes worked out. Let's hope that nobody up the line has a complete list of all of us written out with our names and addresses.

Thus inspired by Hong's speech, the trainees were then given a false backup identity, and then left the Villa Fosca for Kaidabal, a city of two million south of Zanshaa. They were split up into three-person Action Teams, eleven of which made an Action Group—Sula was amused to see that the organization charts manifested the old Shaa love for prime numbers. Sula's Action Team 491—another prime— consisted of herself as leader, Engineer/1st Shawna Spence as technician and demolition specialists, and Macnamara as a runner and general backup.

The city was distracted by the First Fruits Festival, and amid the crowds of celebrants the teams experienced no difficulty as they took on their cover identities and practiced hiding, infiltrating, communicating through cutouts, and assembling at certain places, at certain hours, in order to conduct mock operations. The pace was somewhat more relaxed than at Villa Fosca, and Sula took a few days to travel to Zanshaa and create a small, privately held company under her cover identity, one that dealt in used machine parts. Ownership of her crates of cocoa, tobacco, and coffee were transferred to this company, and the crates themselves shifted to new warehouses. En route the labels on the boxes were changed, and now read: *Used machine parts—for recycling.* She couldn't think of any label less likely to raise curiosity or encourage theft.

No one recognized the businesslike, dark-haired, dark-eyed woman as Lady Sula. Not even when she put on her uniform, took off her dark contacts, put the black hair under a uniform cap, and went to her bank to withdraw all her remaining funds in cash. The bank clerk, no doubt used to cash withdrawals by now, stifled a yawn as she handed Sula her money.

It was then that Sula produced her special warrant from the military governor. "Now," Sula said, "I want you to erase my thumbprint from your records." Anyone on an Action Team was authorized to order any critical records erased—loans, bank accounts, lines of credit, and especially the thumbprint that would present conclusive and legal identification.

The clerk blinked. "My lady?"

"I'm closing the account. You have no reason to retain my print, and I'd like to see you erase it. In fact," showing her special warrant, "this *requires* you to erase it."

"That's not our procedure," the woman said. "We keep everything."

"Do it *now*," Sula said, but the clerk had to call her manager, who viewed Pahn-ko's order and then shrugged his shoulders.

Sula watched as Caro Sula's old print vanished into electric oblivion, and took comfort that another piece of the past was safely buried.

The Action Group moved to Zanshaa City, where they continued to conduct exercises. A rather amazing amount of specialized assassination equipment and explosive went into storage lockers all over the city. Team 491 was placed in a middle-class corner apartment in a Terran district of the Lower Town, a neighborhood called Grandview. They were on the top floor of a four-story building, with a small terrace and windows looking out over two street. It was a pleasant enough place, plainly furnished, and once all the gear was tidied away to Sula's satisfaction, the furniture rearranged, and the place given a general cleaning, she began to feel a growing optimism about her mission.

The Naxids rather obstinately did not come. Sula wished she'd known they would take their time: she would have managed a much less chaotic evacuation of the Zanshaa ring.

One morning the door chimed, and Sula answered to find the concierge, an elderly man named Greyjean. Both his upper incisors were missing and he suffered from a consequent habit of misplacing certain consonants.

"Are you finding everything suitable, my lady?" he asked.

"Everything's fine." Sula, remembering her cover identity, added, "You don't have to call me 'my lady.' I'm a commoner."

The old man seemed surprised. "My mistake, miss. I got a different impression from the constabulary."

A warning bell sang a clear note in Sula's mind. "Constabulary?" she asked. "What constabulary?"

"The military constabulary who evicted the previous tenants," the concierge said. "They said they needed this apartment for some Fleet VIPs."

Sula stared at the old man. "Ah. Ha," she said.

We are in such fucking trouble, she thought.

ELEVEN

Steadied by the arm of the rigger who helped him rise, Martinez dragged himself out of the boarding tube into the airlock, then braced briefly to answer the salute of the lieutenant who stood before him. She was nearly as tall as Martinez, and had a heart-shaped face and brown hair drawn into a knot behind the head and twined around a pair of gold-enameled chopsticks.

"Captain Martinez reporting aboard *Illustrious,*" he said.

"Welcome to *Illustrious,* lord captain," she said. "I'm the premiere here, Lady Fulvia Kazakov."

"Pleased to meet you." Martinez offered her his hand, and she took it.

Alikhan pulled himself out of the tube behind Martinez, placed his feet carefully on the deck, then braced in salute. "My lady," he said.

"This is Alikhan," Martinez said. "My orderly."

Kazakov briefly returned the salute, and nodded to the rigger. "I'll have Turnbull here show your servants to their quarters, and to yours," she said. "But I know that the squad-com would like to meet you now, if that's convenient for you."

"Certainly," Martinez said. If it hadn't been for the month of acceleration, his transit to *Illustrious* aboard the *Daffodil* might almost have been pleasant. *Daffodil* had been designed to pamper high company officials, and there were showers, a laundry, private cabins, a large range of entertainments, and a full kitchen stocked with delicacies by Perry, the recruit who had been forced to leave Ari Abacha's service, and who had joined Martinez despite the ominous prospect of ship duty. Perry had done the cooking, and judging by the exclamations of the others had done it extremely well.

"The others" constituted Martinez's full allotment of servants. The third, Espinosa, was a rigger, and the last, Ayutano, a machinist. Martinez hadn't intended to use these two as servants at all, and they had been brought more or less as a gift to *Illustrious*'s captain, as Martinez had observed that ships that had been away from the dockyards for a while could always do with extra machinists and riggers.

After leaving the airlock Martinez followed Kazakov up a companionway toward officers' country. The heavy cruiser *Illustrious* had six times the volume of Martinez's old *Corona,* with nearly the four times the number of crew. The quarters were more spacious, with corridors broad enough for four humans to march abreast.

From the first sight of *Illustrious* framed in *Daffodil*'s ports, it had been clear that the captain had spared to no expense to turn his ship into a masterpiece of style. The exterior hull had been painted with a complex geometric pattern in pink, pale green, and icing-sugar white. Inside, the corridor walls had been tiled with a distinctive, complex pattern, golden-yellow and dark red accented with white and black. Occasionally the tile pattern would open to reveal a trompe l'oeil niche or window painted with a scene from nature, a riot of greenery in which capered fanciful beasts or birds.

The rooms which Martinez passed on his way to Lady Michi's quarters were each distinctively designed, with abstract patterns which favored turquoise and red and yellow ochre, or with more trompe l'oeil, cabins painted so that they seemed to be opening to some fantastic landscape, or to a series of elaborately decorated rooms. The style and scale of it made the aesthetics of *Corona*'s old captain Tarafah, with his football motif, seem like those of an amateur.

All this, Martinez knew, had been created, supervised, and paid for by Lord Gomberg Fletcher, the captain of *Illustrious*. Martinez had never encountered Fletcher, but he knew that this offspring of the highly-placed Gomberg and Fletcher clans was not only considered the Fleet's leading aesthete, but was the owner of one of the empire's greatest art collections, some elements of which were on display in *Illustrious*'s more public areas.

And furthermore it was all immaculate. Martinez's practiced eyes saw no dust, no grime, no scars. The crew he encountered were spotlessly turned out and alert, leaping out of Martinez's way as soon as they saw him, braced against the walls, chins high.

"As long as we've passing by my office," Kazakov said, "Let me take care of your captain's card."

Kazakov's office seemed to be the wardroom, the walls mellow with scenes of men and women reclining on couches while eating and drinking. One of the lieutenants and a steward leaped to the salute as Martinez entered. "As you were," he told them.

There were computer displays along one wall, and Kazakov dropped into a chair and took Martinez's captain's key. Martinez wondered briefly why Kazakov was working in the wardroom, and then realized that it was because he, himself, had probably taken her actual quarters for himself.

A ship's tactical officer was normally a lieutenant assigned the duty by the captain; but in a flagship the squadron tactical officer was appointed by the flag officer and considered a part of her staff. Such an officer was usually still a lieutenant, if a favored one, but it wasn't completely unknown for a staff officer to have higher rank.

As a full captain, however, Martinez was the third most senior officer on the ship, and the premiere lieutenant had probably had to shift her quarters to make room for him. This would have created a cascade, with each officer bumping the one below.

There was nothing like kicking every junior officer out of bed to make a favorable impression. Martinez hoped he hadn't made the junior lieutenant bunk with the cadets.

Kazakov handed him his captain's card. "You're in the ship's computer now," she said, "though you'll have to get the lady squadcom to give you the passwords for the tactical computer. I'm sending a map of the ship to your mail buffer, where you'll be able to download it to your sleeve displays." A bit of printout whispered from a slot, and Kazakov handed it to him. "There's the combination to your safe. I'd change it if you want to be absolutely secure, since there's at least one officer aboard who knows it."

"I'm sorry if I've taken your quarters," Martinez said.

Kazakov smiled. "I'll manage, my lord. Put your thumbprint here, please, and sign."

Martinez did so, and Kazakov led him on to the squadron commander.

Lady Michi Chen's office was a masterpiece of bronzed, fluted ornamental pillars, walls painted with a fabulous landscape through which floated classically balanced, lightly clad Terrans, and a pair of genuine bronze statues, smiling naked women holding out overflowing baskets of fruit.

Squadron Leader Chen did not greatly resemble the bronze fruit girls who flanked her desk: she was a handsome, middle-aged woman, somewhat stocky, with graying black hair cut short at the jawline and in straight bangs over the forehead. Her complexion was sallow, though that was probably a result of her spending months aboard her flagship without a jot of genuine sunlight.

Martinez braced to the salute. "Captain Martinez reporting, my lady."

"Captain Martinez," she said, rising. "Welcome to the family." His spirits rose, and he took the extended hand.

"I'm very happy to be here," he said.

"Terza and Maurice are well?"

"Yes. Both getting used to shipboard life, last I heard."

"You can catch up shortly, I've been getting your messages for the last several days." She resumed her seat. "Please take a chair, lord captain." She glanced up at the senior lieutenant. "Thank you, Kazakov." The premiere withdrew.

Chenforce was no longer in the Zanshaa system: once the two great transport ships carrying the Lords Convocate had vanished into Wormhole 2, the fleet guarding the system had followed, leaving the system to the mercies of the Naxids. Chen's squadron had remained with the Convocation until their escape could be declared certain, then separated from the rest of the fleet and swung through a series of wormhole gates to arrive at its present location, the Seizho system.

Martinez's journey had been more direct: he was able to head from Zanshaa straight to Seizho, accelerating all the while, and found Chenforce waiting for him there, and decelerating at a modest one gravity.

Given that the squadron was in Seizho, Martinez thought he could guess why Chenforce was reducing its velocity.

Time would tell if he was right.

"I imagine you're tired," Lady Michi said, "and that you'd like to square your gear away and get some rest, but I wanted to greet you and to invite you to join me for supper tonight."

"I would be honored, my lady," Martinez said.

"Why don't you give me your captain's card," Lady Michi said, "and I'll get you into the tactical computer."

For the second time, Martinez gave up his captain's card. Lady Michi slotted it, gazed for a moment at the display, then tapped at her display.

"Thumbprint and signature please, Captain Martinez," she said. "Supper will be at 25:01."

"Thank you, my lady."

Martinez took his card, braced, walked to the door, and hesitated.

"You cabin will be to your right," Lady Michi said. "Your name will be on plate by the door."

Martinez thanked the squadcom and made his way out. It wasn't difficult to find his cabin: his orderlies were still in the process of installing his baggage. Martinez supervised this task, particularly the stowing of the various wines and delicacies that had been brought across on *Daffodil*.

Afterward Martinez inspected his four servants' own quarters, and made certain they had no complaints. Though it was very unusual for captains to decorate the rooms of the enlisted—usually a slap of new paint would do—the crew quarter of *Illustrious* were, like the rest of the ship, a work of art. Martinez slipped Alikhan enough money to cover any dues for the petty officers' lounge, then headed one deck forward—or "above," in the current deceleration—to his own quarters.

At the top of the companionway he was surprised to encounter an old friend, but then he saw that Chandra Prasad was accompanied by an older man in the uniform of a senior captain, and Martinez snapped to the salute, staring the recommended hand's breadth above the captain's head.

"Captain Martinez, lord captain," he said.

Senior Captain Lord Gomberg Fletcher took his time about replying. "Yes," he judged. "Apparently you are he. You may stand at ease."

The Fleet's most celebrated aesthete was a thin-faced man with carefully waved silver hair and ice-blue eyes set in deep, craggy sockets. His uniform was soft and well tailored and immaculate, and the silver buttons gleamed.

"Captain Martinez," Fletcher said, "may I present Lieutenant the Lady Chandra Prasad?"

"Her ladyship and I are already acquainted," Martinez said.

"Ye-es," Chandra said. There was a mischievous gleam in her long brown eyes, and Martinez did his best not to respond to it. He and Lady Chandra had done a two-month communications and cipher course some years ago, on a long hot summer on Zarafan, and the summer had been all the hotter for the two of them being together.

Chandra's hair had gone auburn in the years since—Martinez recalled it being brown—but the pointed chin and the full, amused lips were exactly as Martinez had stored them in his memory.

Martinez dragged his eyes away from Chandra, and decided that the situation merited the tribute direct. "My lord," he said. "Please allow me to compliment you on the appearance of your ship. It's the most complete vision I've ever seen."

Fletcher accepted the praise with easy tolerance. "You should have seen my old *Swift*. It was a much smaller ship, so I was able to make use of mosaic."

"That must have been exquisite," Martinez said.

Fletcher smiled graciously. "It was a worthy effort, I believe."

"I understand you've married," Chandra interrupted. "My congratulations."

Martinez turned to her. "Thank you."

The mischievous gleam still burned in her eyes. "Are you enjoying it?" she asked.

Surprise at the question caused Martinez to hesitate a fraction of a second. He knew better than to express any vacillation over his marriage, particularly to this woman, particularly on a ship with a Chen on board. "Marriage is delightful," he said. "Have you tried it yet?"

Now it was Chandra's turn to hesitate. "Not yet," she said finally.

Fletcher's blue eyes scanned like a receiver dish from Martinez to Chandra and back, searching for the source of the intimacy that smouldered beneath their words.

"Well," he said finally, "my congratulations on your nuptials, captain. I hope you find your stay on *Illustrious* a pleasant one."

"Thank you, my lord. Ah . . . I should mention that I've brought a full complement of servants, and that these include a rigger and a machinist. As I don't need four servants in my current situation, I'd be happy to offer these two for any purpose *Illustrious* requires."

Fletcher received this with a frown. When he spoke, it was with solemn gravity. "I believe you will find, my lord, that an officer of your stature requires a full complement of servants to uphold his dignity."

Martinez blinked. "Yes, my lord," he said.

With an enviable mixture of ease and eminence, Fletcher began to move away down the corridor, Chandra in his wake.

My *stature*? Martinez thought. My *dignity*?

"Oh, Captain Martinez, one more thing." Fletcher had paused, and turned to speak over his shoulder. "We wear full dress for dinner aboard *Illustrious*."

"Very good, my lord," Martinez said automatically. Chandra lifted a cynical eyebrow at Martinez, then followed the captain on his way out.

Martinez went to his cabin. Four servants to uphold his *dignity*? For a moment he pictured his four orderlies hustling him down the corridor in a sedan chair. Then he shrugged and went to his quarters.

For all that it was intended for a lieutenant, Martinez's sleeping cabin was twice the size of the captain's cabin on *Corona*. On the walls were murals that seemed a deliberate contrast from the trompe l'oeil he'd seen elsewhere: against a lush tropical background of greens and turquoise were objects—people, furniture, vehicles—painted to seem two-dimensional, as if the artist had worked from photographs. It was an amusing enough idea and Martinez probably wouldn't get tired of it, unlike the decor of his office, which featured a motif of chubby, naked, male Terran children, unaccountably winged, who struggled to make use of a collection of ancient weaponry, swords and helmets and armor, that had been designed for grownups. It was unclear whether the children intended to massacre each other or had some other idea in mind. Whatever their purpose, Martinez suspected he would grow to hate their sweet faces and plump buttocks before very many days had passed.

The art, Martinez saw on closer inspection, hadn't been actually painted on: it had been created in a graphics program, run off on long sheets, and installed like wallpaper.

As an antidote to the treacle on his office walls, he installed a picture of Terza in his desk display, an image of her in a long high-necked white gown, sitting in front of a vast spray of flowers that she had arranged. The picture would glow there at all hours, migrating in silence from one corner of the display to the next, a reminder of the marriage that still eluded his comprehension.

Michi Chen had kindly suggested that Martinez would need rest, but in fact he'd had plenty of relaxation aboard *Daffodil* during his transit, and he didn't feel particularly sleepy. He paged Perry for a cup of coffee, settled himself at his desk, and contemplated his discomfort at the memory of Chandra Prasad.

Chandra was as provincial a Peer as was Martinez himself, and from a less distinguished family on her home world. She'd told him that she joined the Fleet out of a desire to escape her home, and indeed restlessness seemed to be her greatest trait. During their months together, she and Martinez had mated, quarreled, reconciled, and then done it all over again. Chandra had been spectacularly unfaithful to him, and as a result he made it a point of honor to be unfaithful to her. Two months of this had left him feeling as if he's done ten rounds with a prizefighter, and had been more than a little thankful that their connection had come to an end.

Martinez had no intention of becoming involved with Chandra again, especially on a ship with one of his in-laws aboard. He would take that glimmer he'd seen in Chandra's eye as a warning, and stay clear.

He wished, now that he had time to consider it, that he'd had more practice at being a husband. All his social reflexes were aimed at making himself pleasant and available to any eligible woman in his vicinity. Sexual continence was not a virtue he'd ever felt the need to practice. He was going to have to guard himself against the well-honed gallantry that had been practiced for so long that it amounted to a reflex.

At this point he remembered that he had messages waiting, and with a degree of relief at the mental change of subject he slotted his captain's key into his desk and called them up. There were several from Terza, the latest from four days ago, and he keyed them.

Most were brief. Life on the *Ensenada*, speeding toward Laredo, was without care but hardly a gay round of social excitement. Roland was consistently beating Walpurga and Terza in games of hyper-tourney. The several hours spent each day at two gees weren't causing her any discomfort. Terza read a great deal and had a lot of time to practice her harp.

Martinez found himself warming at the sight of her face, at the lovely moment, just before speaking, when her eyes first lifted to the camera. Once she spoke he detected a slight hesitation in her manner. They hadn't spent enough time together to develop complete ease in one another's company, let alone while talking over a distance of light-days. Martinez wondered if his own discomfort showed in the audio and video he'd sent from *Daffodil*, and thought he might try writing letters in reply. It would let his manner develop more naturally, without the hesitations of video.

He triggered the latest of the messages and saw Terza on a loveseat in her quarters dressed in a high-collared blouse of blue silk moiré, her hair an asymmetric waterfall over one shoulder. He sensed a slight flush in her cheeks, and perhaps an elevated pulse rate as well, though how he knew that he couldn't imagine.

"I was right," Terza said in her soft voice. "I told you I

felt fertility coming on, and I was correct. I've known for twenty or more days that I was pregnant, but I know a lot of accidents can happen early on, and we were dealing with acceleration and so on, so I didn't want to tell you until I was certain that . . . well, that it would last. It looks as if there's no going back now." Her lips turned up in a smile. "I'm very pleased. I hope you are as well." She put one of her long, exquisite hands over her abdomen. "All sorts of magical hormone things seem to be happening to me right now. I wish you were here to share them. Please stay safe for the two of us."

The message ended. Martinez let out the long breath he'd been holding, and then played the message again. Sensation surged through his blood; he could feel his skin warming.

He was going to be a father. The realization was so staggering that Perry had to knock three times before Martinez heard it and called his steward in. Perry appeared in full dress, with white gloves, with a pot of coffee on a tray. Martinez looked at him in surprise.

"Has someone told you to put on your number ones?" he asked.

Perry placed a cup and saucer before Martinez and poured. "The other servants told me that full dress was customary aboard *Illustrious,* my lord."

"I see."

Perry replaced the coffeepot on the tray and stood back. "I'm sorry your coffee was delayed, my lord. I should let you know that there may be a problem with our meals."

Martinez had been sufficiently wrapped in his thoughts that he hadn't realized that his coffee had taken longer than expected to turn up "Yes?" he said. "Why's that?"

"It's because you're in the premiere's cabin, my lord. The squadcom's cabin has a kitchen, of course, and so does the captain's. The wardroom has a kitchen for the lieutenants, and of course the enlisted have their mess. But the first lieutenant's cabin has no kitchen facilities."

"Ah. I see."

Martinez should have anticipated this. Lady Michi had her own cook, of course, as did the captain. The wardroom was a kind of club for the lieutenants, and the tactical officer, normally a lieutenant, would under normal circumstances mess there. But as a full captain Martinez couldn't impose on his juniors for his meals, and in order to dine with either Fletcher or Michi Chen, he'd have to be invited.

On all of *Illustrious*, there was no place for Perry to prepare his meals. He nodded at the coffeepot.

"Where's you get this?"

"The wardroom steward very kindly lent it to me, my lord." Perry's face darkened. "This was after the captain's steward refused to let me into his kitchen."

"Well, that's within his rights." For a moment Martinez pictured himself living out of boxes and cans for the length of his posting, and then he laughed. "Have a talk with Lady Michi's cook," he said, "and with the wardroom steward again. Perhaps something can be worked out."

"Very good, my lord."

"And if all else fails," Martinez said, "there's always *Daffodil*." Since the Fleet hadn't provided a pilot to take the commandeered yacht away once it had delivered Martinez, the boat, with its full kitchen, would remain grappled to *Illustrious* for the foreseeable future.

Perry cheered at this. "That's true, my lord."

"I've been invited to supper with the squadcom tonight, so there isn't any urgency."

Perry left, and Martinez returned his attention to his video display, where Terza's image remained frozen, her lips parted in a soft smile, her hand touching her abdomen as if protecting the child.

A child . . . An unfamiliar sensation shivered through Martinez, and to his immense surprise he discovered that it was bliss.

He needed to respond to the message at once, if he could manage it without babbling.

Martinez told the display to record a reply, and began the babbling at once.

"This isn't a spy ring," Sula said to Lord Octavius Hong, "this is a fucking holiday association. Dreamed up by the same people who join the Fleet because they think it's a yacht club." She snarled. *"Everyone in the neighborhood* knows by now that Fleet personnel are living in our apartment. When the Naxids come, they're going to be on us in three minutes."

"Steady, Four-nine-one," her superior murmured. "I don't think it's as bad as all that."

They had met in a sidewalk café after Sula had stuck a strip of tape on a lamppost in the Old Square, the sign for an immediate meeting. In the balmy weather of early summer Hong had draped his jacket over the back of his chair and sat at the table in his shirt-sleeves. His face bore an expression of handsome, quiet confidence as he set about dismembering a flaky pastry.

He had showed respect for procedure by calling Sula by her code name, though because they'd trained together he knew her real name perfectly well, just as she knew his despite the fact that, as head of Action Group Blanche, she should refer to him as "Blanche." Awarding code names had come rather late in the training, and by that time they'd all got used to one another's genuine identities. Another aspect, Sula realized now, of the amateurishness with which this operation had been set up.

"You're based in a Terran neighborhood," said Lord Octavius. "If you were living with Naxids, you might have cause to worry, but your neighbors will have no reason to betray you."

"How about money or favor?" Sula said as she stirred

292 • Walter Jon Williams

more honey into her tea. "What if the Naxids offer a cash reward for turning us in?"

Hong gave her a stern look. "Loyal citizens—" he began.

"I want backup identities for my whole team," she said, stirring. "And everyone else in your group should get them, too." She raised her spoon and licked it, the flavor of warm clover honey bursting on the tip of her tongue.

For the first time in their acquaintance Hong's face displayed a moment of doubt. "I'm not sure that's in the budget," he said cautiously.

Sula raised her cup of tea to her lips. "Oh, for all's sake, Blanche," she said. "Our side *coins* the money."

Hong's decisive look returned. "I'll push a memorial up to higher authority, shall I?"

"I'll do the work myself," Sula said. It was an offer, and also a decision.

She still had her special warrant from the lord governor. Sula used one of the cameras with which the Intelligence Section had equipped Team 491 to take pictures of herself and her group, then put on her uniform and took the funicular to the High City. She flashed her warrant in the Records Office and took advantage of a slight ambiguity in its wording—"require cooperation in the matter of records"—to get herself a desk and the passwords necessary to do her job.

The passwords, strings of long numbers, she recorded with her sleeve camera while no one was looking.

Thus enabled, her task was simple enough that once she had her three backup identities, she saw no reason to stop. By the time the office closed at the end of day, each member of Action Team 491 had four false identities, counting the ones they'd started with.

Sula collected the last of these, the heavy plastic card still warm from the thermo printer, the seal of the government embossed on its surface.

That evening, she memorized the codes she'd printed, destroyed the printout, and thought, I must remember to use these powers only for good.

She told Hong that joke at their next meeting. He frowned, brows knitting. "You'll do well to remember, Four-nine-one," he said, "that in the military, irony proceeds from the *top*."

Sula straightened. "Very good, my lord."

"Don't call me that here."

"That's all right. It was irony."

Hong grunted, eyes fixed on his plate. As was his custom, he had chopped his pastry up into several pieces, which he now commenced to eat with military efficiency, last of all sweeping up the crumbs and devouring those as well.

The day was rainy and he and Sula met indoors. The café was crowded and smelled of damp wool, and the door banged loudly whenever anyone went in and out.

"Still," Hong admitted, "that's a good use of initiative, I suppose. You'll have to give me a list of those names, of course."

"No," Sula said. "Absolutely not."

Hong looked at her in surprise. "What do you mean, no?"

"You don't need to know our backup identities. We'll have secure means of communication no matter what names we're using, so the only people inconvenienced will be the Naxids, when they arrest you and interrogate you and you can't tell them where to find us."

Hong didn't seem annoyed, which Sula might have understood, but rather deeply and sincerely concerned, as if he'd just learned she'd come down with a serious illness.

"Are you all right about this?" he asked. "You're not having second thoughts about our assignment, are you?"

"None whatsoever," she said flatly, and held his eyes until he dropped them.

Second thoughts about *you,* she said to herself, are another matter.

* * *

That evening, out of more than merely idle curiosity, Sula used the display and touch-keypad in the surface of the old desk in a corner of her apartment's front room, and logged onto the archives at the Records Office to see if her passwords still worked. They did.

But she knew they wouldn't work much longer: passwords of this sort were changed frequently as a matter of routine, and when the Naxids arrived they might well demand exclusive control of the system.

"Ada," she said to Engineer/1st Spence, calling her by the cover name assigned her by the Fleet. "I can use your advice."

Spence brought a chair to where Sula worked, and sat. She was a short, sturdy woman of around thirty, with short straw hair and a pug nose. "What do you need?"

"I'm in the Records Office data system. And what I'd like is to make certain that I can keep my access even after they change the passwords."

Spence was surprised. "Is that legal?"

Sula suppressed a laugh. "I have a warrant," she said, and hoped her face was straight. "The problem is that the Naxids aren't going to honor it."

Spence considered the display. "Can you get into the directory?"

Sula gave the command, and a long list, thousands of files, began rolling across the desktop.

"Apparently I can," Sula said.

"System: halt," Spence ordered. "System: find file *Executive*."

Two file names glowed in Sula's display, one a backup of the other.

"There you are," said Spence. "You want to rewrite the executive file to give you permanent access."

"Will it let me?"

"I don't know. Whose passwords are you using?"

"Lady Arkat," Sula said. "She's the head of System Security."

Spence laughed. "You'd think the head of security would have thought to change her passwords the second you were out the door."

"She's rather old. Maybe she's a creature of habit."

"Or maybe she's, well, on our side."

Sula thought that the elderly Torminel was not as sympathetic as all that, but conceded she might be wrong.

"System," she ordered, "open file *Executive*."

The file sprawled out before her, thousands upon thousands of if/then statements. Sula gave a low whistle.

"How good are you at programming?" she asked.

"I *use* computers," Spence said, "I don't program them."

"My programming courses were a while ago," Sula said. Though she did some programming now and again, her skills were hardly first-class.

"Back up everything," Spence advised, "go very slowly, and make use of any help files."

"Right," Sula said, and backed up the executive file first thing, both onto the Records Office computer and into the system in her desk. She made herself a pot of strong, sweet tea and prepared for a long night.

"I'm very good at puzzles," she reminded herself.

It was the copy on her desk that she worked with. Fortunately the actual changes that she wanted to make were minor, even though they had far-reaching implications. *Whenever you change the password, send me a copy.* How complicated could such an order be?

She told the computer to send the copy to her hand comm, the one she carried with her. After a few catastrophic syntax errors, the program seemed to run, at least in Sula's desk.

Sula took a deep breath and scrubbed her palms on her thighs, drying any hypothetical sweat. She would now have to load her altered program back into the computer at the Records Office. She pictured the thousand consequences of this attempt going wrong, Hong's fury at one of his secret team being exposed, official reprimand, scathing reports in her file.

She sent her altered program to the Records Office and held her breath. Nothing happened.

Sula slowly let her breath out, then reached for her tea. It had turned cold, and the thick liquid was like a stripe of molasses on her tongue. She went to the kitchen for a few moments to reheat her tea, and when she came back, nothing had changed.

She sent herself some simple mail—"hello"—using the Records Office computer, and opened her hand comm to discover the mail waiting for her.

The next test was to see if she could create a set of identification. If she succeeded, she could simply mail the documents to herself here at the apartment. She began work, but stopped when an incoming message icon blinked onto her hand comm. She triggered it, and a text message appeared on the small screen.

My Lady Arkat,

We have detected an attempt to rewrite the Executive File of the main computer at the Records Office. This attempt occurred at 01:15:16. We will erase the corrupt copy and reload the Executive File from backups.

You have been assigned a new, temporary password: 19328467592.

Please change your temporary password to a permanent password of your choice as soon as you arrive at your desk in the morning.

In service to the Praxis,
Ynagarh, CN5, Assistant Data Administrator

Words leapt to Sula's lips, words that would disconnect her at once from the Records Office computer.

She didn't utter them.

Instead she tried to work out what had just happened. Though the intrusion had been detected almost ten minutes ago, she was still inside the computer. If the administrators had bothered to check to see who was connected remotely, they would have found her to be Lady Arkat, their own chief, a fact that would have made them reluctant to disconnect her.

Whatever the case, she still had access to the Records Office computer. She had Lady Arkat's temporary password, which would be good for the next few hours, until Lady Arkat arrived at the office and changed it. But after that Sula would be frozen out, because the executive file that Sula had ordered to send copies of the new password had been erased.

As long as Sula stayed connected to the computer, she was still able to make changes, at least as long as she avoided whatever error it was that had caused her altered program to be detected in the first place.

She took another sip of her tea, jasmine and citrus honey gone tepid, and wondered what her error could have been.

Sula looked again at the error message. *01:15:16.* They had her intrusion down to the *second.*

That gave her the first clue. Some rummaging in administration files revealed no less than six automated messages that had been sent to Assistant Administrator Ynagarh, each stating that the executive file had been replaced by one of a later date.

"Ah. Hah," Sula said.

It had been the file's date that had given her away. But in that case, why six messages, and not one?

The automated system had sent six messages because she had been detected in no less than six different ways. A second mentioned that the file size had changed. The other four informed Ynagarh that a change in the "hash signature" had been detected.

What the hell are *those*? Sula wondered. She turned to ask Spence if she knew, but Spence had long since gone to bed.

First things first, Sula decided. Dates were something she understood.

She checked the date on the executive file that had been loaded over her altered file, and found that it had last been changed nine years before. *Nine years.* The file itself had been created over *six thousand years* ago. It was obviously stable and required very little tweaking. No wonder her executive file had set alarm bells ringing.

Sula reheated her tea again and drank a cup while she contemplated the problem. Could the answer be as simple as changing the date on her file? She had the very high privileges that came with Lady Arkat's account, and found that it wasn't a problem: she changed the date on the file to nine years before, and when she made a backup file onto her own computer, the altered date didn't change back to the real one.

And a message would go to the administrators if the file's size changed: that was clear from Ynagarh's messages. The program that she loaded into the Records Office computer would have to be the exact same size as the one there now.

She clenched her fists in a cold frenzy. Now she was going to have to go through the program line by line in hopes she could pare out enough redundant programming to make up for the lines she'd added. This was *maddening* . . .

Rather than even contemplate this task, she dug for a frantic hour through Lady Arkat's help files and searched through the program's architecture, and in time discovered what a hash signature was.

The ancient executive file was compiled into a binary form that, in addition to performing its various tasks, was itself an integer. By performing a calculation that was very easy to do in one direction, but difficult to backtrack—say dividing by *pi* and using the first thousand digits of the remainder—the resulting arithmetical signature—the "hash"—could identify even tiny changes in the file's size.

Sula opened the file again and let the lines of code scroll in front of her bewildered eyes. She was too tired to think properly. She rose from her chair, stretched, and flapped her arms in hope of bringing a surge of blood into her weary mind. She stepped to the window and gazed down at the street below, the busy life of day much subdued now, the haunt of street cleaners and Torminel.

Sula's eyes lifted to the eastern horizon, soon to turn pale green with rising of Shaamah. She had bare hours in which to perform her calculations. Somehow, she had to reverse-engineer the calculation that produced no less than four wildly different hash signatures, without knowing what the algorithms were or where they could be found.

She dragged her weary feet back to her desk. The executive file was *ancient,* she thought. It was so old it might have been written by the *Shaa* . . .

And then she stopped dead, as she remembered the fondness of the Shaa for prime numbers . . .

All weariness sizzled away as she made a galvanic leap into her chair. A list of prime numbers was available in a public database, and she disregarded the first thousand as too small, then seized the next nine thousand and ran them against all values in the executive file.

One . . . The first match appeared in the display.

Two . . .

Three . . .

Four.

All the hash numbers were located in the same part of the program, which was clearly the part of the program having to do with alarms and security. She couldn't have found the alarm program with a month of random searching.

The Shaa weren't so damned smart, she concluded.

Sula scanned the program with great interest. There were the access codes, which were the key, and the alarm files, which were the lock, and there were the log files that recorded all changes in the system, which was a record of which key went with which lock, and when.

What she had to do, it turned out, was change both the

lock *and* the key. And then the records had to be changed to read, *This has always been the lock,* and *This has always been the key.*

In the next hour Sula added extra code to the executive file. In order, this set permissions on the log files to unwritable, which would prevent her manipulations from being detected, deleted the last line of the log file, which otherwise would have included her previous command, sent a copy of any new password to Sula's comm, and then set permissions on the log file back to writable, which returned everything to normal

She prepared all the hashes for the alarm files.

Then Sula created a new program that would load her own executive file into the computer at the Records Office, something that would manage the whole procedure a lot faster than could Sula by giving orders or typing commands.

The program had a number of familiar commands, and some that were new: it set permissions on the log files to unwritable, deleted the last line of the log file, engaged all diagnostic programs, updated size and hash information on all alarms, copied her executive file over the old one, altered the dates of creation and modification on her new file to those of the old one, then ended all diagnostic programs and reset permissions on the log files to writable.

She tested the operation several times in her own computer. Then, holding her breath, she triggered her new program.

Sweat prickled on her forehead as she looked at Assistant Administrator Ynagarh's messages, and saw no message alerting him to anything amiss with his computer.

She let out a long breath. It seemed that she'd got away with it.

Dawn was greening in the east. Sula made a last, obsessive scan of everything once more, just to make certain the file was as she left it, and then broke the connection. She told the apartment's system to wake her in the morning just before the Records Office opened for business, so that she could be sure to get into the computer on Lady Arkat's temporary password before it was changed.

As she prepared for bed Sula looked at herself in the mirror and was appalled. Her eyes had deep shadows under them, her hair was stringy, and there were blooms of sweat under her arms. She couldn't abide sleeping in such condition, so she took a thorough shower. She went into the bedroom she shared with Spence, groped her way to her bed, and fell into it.

For once, oblivion did not take long to reach her mind.

It seemed as if she took only a few breaths before the alarm chimed her awake, and she threw on clothing and ran to the desk. It was broad, brilliant daylight. Spence was making herself breakfast, and Macnamara had already left on his morning errands—as the team's courier, his task was to check certain public places to find if any messages had been left for the team, and he'd been provided with a two-wheeled vehicle for the purpose.

Sula called the Records Office and used Lady Arkat's temporary password to gain access to the main computer. Spence silently brought to her desk a cup of heavily sweetened coffee, shortly followed by a toasted muffin and a pot of jam.

The question was how long it would take Lady Arkat to turn up at her desk. If she were like many of the Peers in the civil administration, she might turn up at midmorning, or even after a long luncheon.

Sula opened her hand comm and put it on the desk in front of her. She ate her muffin and asked Spence for another.

She ate her second muffin. She paced. She made more coffee. She emptied her bladder. She brushed her teeth and combed her hair.

She tried to keep from screaming aloud.

Spence stayed very much out of her way.

Lady Arkat turned out to be one of the midmorning Peers. It was just after midmorning, at 13:06, when Sula saw that the head of security had checked in and viewed her morning's messages.

A few minutes later, Sula's hand comm chimed. She checked the message, and found Lady Arkat's new password waiting for her.

She leaped up from her chair to give a shriek of exultation. Then she deaccessed the Records Office and bounced joyously around the apartment, tidying the breakfast things.

Macnamara returned from his errands and walked into the apartment carrying a bag of provisions. "No messages," he reported. Then, seeing Sula's state, he asked, "Something happened?"

"I've become the Goddess of the Records Office," Sula said.

Macnamara thought about this for a moment, then nodded. "Very good, my lady," he said, and went to the refrigerator to put away the groceries.

TWELVE

Lady Michi's dining room was large enough for the formal dinner parties that were part of the service life of a squadron commander, and was made to seem larger by ornate mirrors fashioned out of highly polished nickel-iron asteroid material, and by the murals that made the room seem to open up into a series of other rooms, each with windows that looked onto a distant horizon.

Martinez wore full dress—which he would have done in any case—and found the squadcom dressed likewise. From her table, set for two, she looked up at Martinez with an expression of relief.

"Oh, good," she said, rising. "I wanted to be the first to invite you to a meal, so that I could warn you that they're all formal here."

"Lord Captain Fletcher told me."

"You spoke to him, then? Please sit down, by the way."

Martinez placed his gloves on a side table, then sat in the chair that one of Lady Michi's servants held for him. "I encountered the captain, along with one of the lieutenants, Lady Chandra Prasad."

A private smile touched the squadcom's lips. "Yes. Well. I'm somewhat less formal than the lord captain, but he sets the style on the ship, so I thought you should be warned." She looked up at the servant, an older, dignified, broad-faced woman. "Could you bring in the cocktails, Vandervalk?"

"Yes, my lady."

After Vandervalk made her way out, Lady Michi leaned across the table and lowered her voice. "I should let you know about Prasad, by the way. In normal circumstances I'm not one to repeat gossip, but I wouldn't want you to put a foot wrong here. It's reported that Lady Chandra and the captain are, ah, intimates."

The sensations produced in Martinez were dominated by relief. "Ah—thank you, my lady. Not that I would, in any case, be . . ." Martinez paused as he tried to work out exactly how to tactfully reassure Lady Michi that he had no intention of cheating on her niece with the captain's mistress, or indeed with anyone else.

This road of virtue was proving a frustrating one, and not simply in the matter of continence. When interviewing servants, he'd found a young woman machinist who would have been perfect for the post, and he had been on the verge of taking her into his entourage when he realized that she was quite attractive and that everyone would assume he'd brought her along as his lover. With ill grace he had passed her over in favor of Ayutano.

"Quite so," Lady Michi said. "I just wanted to give you a warning just in case the . . . undercurrents . . . became a little troublesome."

Martinez knew all too well how troublesome the undercurrents around Chandra could be, and he was grateful for the news. "I thank you. And—as it happens—I have news of the family."

Lady Michi was delighted to discover that Terza was pregnant, and when Vandervalk returned with glasses and the cocktail pitcher, she was the first to offer a toast to the new Chen heir.

Over dinner they talked of family and other innocuous matters. Martinez knew that Lady Michi was divorced, but not that she had two children at school in the Hone Reach, children whose liberty had been guaranteed by the Battle of Hone-bar. She drew out of Martinez a description of the fighting, and her questions were shrewd enough so that Martinez began to believe that here, at least, was a commander who knew her job.

"And apropos the war," Michi said at the end of the meal, "I may as well acquaint you with your duties." She called up the wall display and flashed onto a map of the empire, Zanshaa in the center with the wormhole routes woven like lace around the capital.

"As you've probably guessed," she said, with a sidelong look, "the Fleet has adopted what I believe is now being called the Chen Plan."

Martinez tried not to sigh too heavily. "Naturally, my lady," he said, "I support the plan fully."

Michi smiled. "My brother Maurice sent me an early copy of the plan," he said, "when it still had your name on it—yours and Lady Sula's, I recall. How is she, by the way?"

"We've lost touch."

The squadron commander raised an eyebrow, but chose not to pursue the matter. "Maurice tells me, by the way, that it was Lord Tork who insisted on changing the name of the plan. Lord Tork seems to think that you've gained more celebrity than is proper for someone of your station."

Martinez attempted without success to restrain his indignation. He protested to himself that he didn't even *know* Lord Tork. He'd only met Tork briefly, at an awards presentation. Why the hell had the chairman of the Fleet Control Board taken against him?

Martinez spoke through clenched teeth. "Has Lord Chen any idea why Lord Tork has . . . has—"

"Lord Tork is a person of fixed ideas and strong prejudices," Michi said. Her tone combined amusement and sympathy.

Martinez looked at her. "Does your ladyship have any notion how I might improve in his lordship's opinion?" he asked.

Lady Michi's amusement grew. "Avoid any distinction for the rest of the war, I suppose," she said.

Martinez decided not to pursue this annoying topic, and he turned to the wormhole map displayed on the wall.

"And our part of the plan, my lady?" he asked.

Lady Michi suppressed her smile and turned to the map. "Once the Naxids are fully committed in the Zanshaa system," she said, "Chenforce will leave Seizho by the Protipanu wormhole gate for raids into enemy rear areas, destroying commerce and any warships we encounter."

Protipanu. This was the destination Martinez had suspected when he'd heard that Chenforce was still decelerating after detaching from the fleet. Aside from being the place where the hitherto obscure Exploration Service Warrant Officer Severin had physically moved the wormhole out of the path of a Naxid squadron, Protipanu was an old brown dwarf with a highly reduced solar system: the shrunken state of the system's gas giants made slingshot maneuvers and changes of course more difficult, and maneuvering in the system would require low initial velocities.

"What's the rest of the fleet going to be doing while we're raiding?" Martinez asked.

"That information is secret, even from me," Michi said, "but from the hints I've been receiving from my circle of acquaintants, I believe your old Squadron Fourteen will be on a raid similar to ours. I've received no indication that Dofaq and Kangas are going on the offensive, so possibly they won't be doing anything other than keeping between the Convocation and the Naxids."

Under the table, Martinez clenched a fist. If only the Control Board hadn't insisted on his leaving *Corona,* it would be he who led Squadron 14 against the enemy.

"The Control Board has allowed me a remarkable degree of latitude," the squadcom said. "I'm not to go near Naxas, Magaria, or Zanshaa, but otherwise I'm permitted to choose my own targets." She spoke a few words to the video display, and a route traced in red along the wormhole map.

"This is the preliminary route I've chosen. I would appreciate your comments when you've had a chance to study it."

"Very good, my lady." Martinez's eyes were already busy tracing the route. Protipanu, Mazdan, Koel, Aspa Darla, Baido, Termaine . . . the first three systems were obscure or underinhabited, but the route then debouched into a series of highly industrialized, heavily populated systems. Aspa Darla's wealth came from two small, dense, heavy-metal-rich planets and equally rich asteroids; Bai-do's accelerator ring had huge shipyards that were probably adding to the strength of the Naxid fleet; Termaine produced . . . well, Martinez wasn't sure exactly *what* it produced, his astrography lessons were long ago, but he knew the system was rich.

"Based on these targets, I'll want you to create exercises . . . no, I believe the word is now 'experiments.'" Michi gave him a conspiratorial smile, and Martinez felt a rising exaltation. Michi reached for her cup of coffee. "We want the best chances of disrupting the Naxid war effort while avoiding large-scale damage to civilian populations—we have to assume that most of the population is loyal, and we don't want to drive them straight to the Naxids."

"True," Martinez said, though in the end it hardly mattered what the population thought. No matter what their convictions in regard to the war, civilian populations would in the end have to submit to whichever fleet held the high ground above their worlds.

Michi frowned at the display. "I'll also want exercises based on encountering opposition in these systems. We don't know where all the Naxid fleet elements are, particularly those eight ships that were in Protipanu, and in any case the Naxids may send formations after us once they figure out what we're up to. So I'd like you to devise exercises based on any contingency."

"Very good, my lady," Martinez said. "I'll start working that up immediately." This was the sort of assignment he could do easily, and his mind was already abuzz with the kind of diabolical complications he could introduce into these scenarios.

She turned to him. "Do you have any questions?" she asked.

"When would you need the first exercise?"

"Shall I give you tomorrow to rest, and the day after to work it up? Say in three days."

"I'm sufficiently rested, my lady. Let's say two days."

Michi nodded thoughtfully. "Very well, captain. If you're confident in your estimations. Any other questions?"

Martinez considered for a moment before answering. "Not at present, my lady." And then one occurred to him. "By the way," he said, "what happened to my predecessor? I assume you wouldn't have left Harzapid without a tactical officer."

Sadness crossed Lady Michi's features. "Lieutenant Kosinic was off the ship when the rebellion broke out, and in a part of the ring station hit by an antiproton beam. He was wounded—some head injuries, broken ribs and a broken arm—but when we departed Harzapid he insisted he'd recovered sufficiently to join us. But he died, unfortunately." Michi looked away. "A sad business. I quite liked the young man."

Martinez felt his spine brushed by an eerie sense of responsibility. Sula had claimed he was the luckiest man in the universe, but he'd never thought his luck would reach out and strike down a complete stranger just so Martinez could have his job.

The dinner ended shortly afterward, and Martinez returned to his cabin, where Alikhan waited with a cup of cocoa. "What do you think of *Illustrious*?" Martinez asked him.

"A taut ship," Alikhan said, "and a well-trained crew. The noncommissioned officers know their jobs. But no one understands the captain at all."

Martinez gave Alikhan a sly look. "Isn't an officer supposed to keep up an air of mystery?"

"Is he, my lord?" Alikhan, as he brushed Martinez's tunic, gave the strong impression that no officer had ever been mysterious to *him*. "The captain's a complete puzzle to the crew. And I don't think they're fond of him."

The heavy scent of cocoa rose in the room. Martinez reached for his cup.

"If he painted little winged children all over *their* quarters," Martinez said, "I wouldn't blame them."

One morning Sula took her team shopping for clothing. She wanted clothes less suitable for the neighborhood in which the Fleet had put them, clothes a little more loud, a little more worn. She didn't know the Zanshaa milieu well enough to know exactly what she was looking for, but thought she'd recognize it when she saw it.

First she took her group on a long reconnaissance. The Terran neighborhood she chose backed onto a pool filled with old boats and canal barges that were being repaired by something called Sim's Boatyard. The ripping noise of pneumatic hammers and riveters sounded in the air. The apartment buildings were prefabricated and old. The streets were crowded. There were people wandering over the worn paving who had obviously been sleeping on the streets, and the look of some of them made Macnamara hover protectively off Sula's shoulder.

Except for the clothing, this was very much like the Fabs, in Spannan, where Sula grew up. In the Fabs the mode involved stockings, felt boots, chunky ceramic jewelry, and puffy jackets sewn with rows of little silver chimes. Here, she saw, the style featured a brightly colored shirt with the collar worn outside a short jacket that belted tightly across the midsection, pegged trousers that belled out around the ankles, and shoes with thick wooden platform soles ornamented with carvings.

Sula stepped into a used clothing store and began to page through the racks. Macnamara was dubious when Sula handed him the outfit she'd chosen for him. "I don't know if I can carry this off," he said. "I'm from Kupa. From the *mountains*. We'd make our money off the winter sports, and in the summer I'd herd my uncle's sheep."

"I've seen you wear stupider stuff than this," Sula said.

Macnamara decided Sula had scored a point, and went to the changing room. When he came out, he looked like a shepherd with a very unusual style sense.

Sula sighed. "Put on your regular clothes. You'll have to be my hick cousin from the country till you can get used to wearing something like that."

Macnamara seemed relieved. Sula, remembering how he'd seemed perfectly at ease after a long hike across muddy fields in combat armor, decided that all this was going to take was practice.

Engineer/1st Spence looked more at home in the local fashion. She had at least lived in a city most of her life, and accessorized with some gaudy costume jewelry and a tall velvet hat that looked as if it had been deliberately sat on— the damage was a little too perfect to be accidental.

Sula wobbled a little on her platform shoes as she clacked out onto the pavement. Military life had accustomed her to flats.

Spence had a good eye, she decided. Sula spotted a number of the crumpled velvet hats in the next street.

"Uhh, Lucy?" Macnamara said from over her shoulder. Sula's current ID, one she had made for herself, listed her as Lucy Daubrac, and the team were supposed to use the cover names and not ranks or titles.

"Yeah, Patrick?"

"You know, you walk like an officer in the Fleet. Spine straight, shoulders back. You should try, like, slouching more."

She flashed him a smile from over her shoulder. Her hick cousin, the unemployed shepherd, wasn't so stupid after all.

"Thanks," she said, then she stuck her hands in her trouser pockets and slumped her shoulders.

Sula called up a list of apartments for rent on her hand communicator—her jacket didn't have a sleeve display—but the one she chose was found by a sign in the window: TWO BEDROOMS, FURN., W/TOILET.

Her sense of self-respect and order demanded, at the very least, a toilet she didn't have to share with strangers.

There was no concierge, let alone a doorman, just an elderly Daimong janitor who lived in a basement flat, and who let them view the apartment. The place smelled of mildew, the furniture sagged, some child had scrawled over the face of the wall video, and there was a creepy purple stain on the walls.

"If we take it," Sula said, "will you paint the place?"

"I'll give you some brushes and paint," the Daimong said. "Then *you* paint the place." With apparent satisfaction the Daimong peeled a swatch of dead skin from his neck, then let it drift to the worn carpet.

"How much is it again?"

"Three a month."

"Zeniths?" Sula scorned. "Or septiles?"

The Daimong made a gonging noise meant to indicate indifference. "You can call the manager and argue with him if you want," he said. "I'll give you his number."

The manager, a bald Terran, insisted on three zeniths. "Have you *seen* this place?" Sula asked, knowing full well he hadn't in years, and probably not ever. She panned the hand comm's camera over the room. "Who's going to pay three zeniths for this wreck? Just *look* at that stain! And let me show you the kitchen—it's *unspeakable*."

Sula argued the manager down to two zeniths per month, with a two-zenith damage deposit and three months paid in advance. She paid the janitor, dragging the cash out of her pocket and counting out the durable plastic money repeatedly, as if it were all she had, and she then insisted on his giving her a receipt.

The Daimong ambled out, leaving behind the sweet scent of his dying flesh, and Sula turned to look at her team. Neither Macnamara nor Spence seemed happy with their new home.

"Uhh, Lucy?" Macnamara said. "Why did we take this place?"

"Some cleaning and paint and it'll be all right," Sula said. "Besides, did you notice we have a back door off the kitchen? It leads right onto the back-stairs landing—it's our escape route, if we need one."

"But the *neighborhood* . . ." Spence ventured.

Sula went to the window and looked down into the busy street. The sounds of the crowd floated up to her, hawkers crying, music playing, friends hailing each other, children running and shrieking.

It was like going back in time.

"It's perfect," she said. "You can disappear into a neighborhood like this." She fished in her pocket again and came up with a couple septiles. "Here," she said to Macnamara. "Take this to the liquor store across the street and get as many bottles of iarogüt as this will buy. The cheapest stuff you can find."

Macnamara took the money with reluctance. He returned with six bottles, all opaque plastic with labels pasted on, some crooked. Sula put one bottle on the shelf, opened five, and emptied them into the sink. The harsh bite of the liquor filled the air, the uneasy mixture of grain alcohol and herbal extracts. Sula put the empty bottles into the bag that Macnamara had brought them in, then put the bag with the bottles outside the door, in the hallway, for trash pickup.

"If any of our neighbors have questions about us," she said as she stepped back into their apartment, "this will tell them all they need to know." She tilted her head back to look at Macnamara. "You're on bottle duty till further notice," she said. "I want anywhere from three to five empties put in the hall every night."

Macnamara's eyes widened. "So many? For just the three of us?"

"A serious alcoholic can drink three bottles of hard liquor per night, easy," Sula said. A fact she remembered all too well. Through the memory she forced a smile. "We're only *partly serious* drunks. Oh," she added, as another thought struck her. "You know some of that hashish-scented incense? We should buy some of that. The smell wafting under the door will only add to the verisimilitude."

"By the way," Spence said, "how do you do that with your voice?"

"My voice?" Sula was puzzled.

"You're talking in some kind of local dialect. It's like you've lived here for years."

"Ah." Surprise tingled through her. She shrugged. "I'm a good mimic, I guess. I didn't even know I was doing it."

She remembered amusing Caro Sula with her accents, pretending to be her identical sister Margaux, from Earth. She hadn't done her Earthgirl accent in a long time.

She'd spent the last seven years imitating Caro Sula instead.

The next few days Team 491 spent adding to their wardrobe and painting and cleaning the apartment. They bought food from stands on the streets and began to learn the neighborhood.

The apartment was finally arranged to Sula's satisfaction, everything painted or scrubbed, the carpet cleaned, the stove gleaming, the toilet and other bathroom fixtures fresh-scented marvels of modern sanitation. It didn't look like a place inhabited by alcoholics, but Sula couldn't bring herself to live amid squalor.

She had once. She wouldn't again.

Sula bought a spider plant in a large cream-colored epoxide pot, one that would show clearly through the window overlooking the street. She went to the south window and put it on the right-hand side of the windowsill.

"This means *no one's here, be cautious.*" She moved the pot across the sill to the opposite side. "This is *someone's here, and it's all clear.*" She placed the pot on the right side of the northern windowsill. "This is *immediate meeting.*" Moving the pot to the opposite side of the window meant *message waits at mail drop.* She turned to look at her crew. "If the pot's not here at all, or if it's in the kitchen window, that means *Unsafe. Use safe procedure to reestablish contact.*" She looked at them. "If it looks as if you're going to be arrested here, try to break away long enough to knock the pot off the sill. Make it look as if you're trying to jump out the window."

Macnamara and Spence nodded. "Very good, miss," Spence said.

"From now on," Sula said, "we use this apartment only for meetings. We each get our own place, one that none of the others knows, and we use another set of ID there."

Her two team members gave each other uneasy looks. "Does the new place have to be in this neighborhood?" Spence asked.

Sula had to think about her answer. "Your new place needs to be someplace completely anonymous. It needs to be private. It needs to have more than one exit. And you need to pay your rent with cash." She gave them a thin-lipped smile. "If you can find a setup like that in a better neighborhood, then by all means."

"What's our budget?" Macnamara asked.

"Remember, we want *anonymous.*" Sula considered. "I'll go above three a month for someplace that's got a lot of advantages, but otherwise try to stay within that." She gave them each ten zeniths in change. "Remember, you can't whip out a ten-zenith piece and just hand it to someone. People don't carry that kind of money in cash, not if they're . . . the kind of people who are above suspicion."

She sensed resistance in Macnamara as his hand closed over the money.

"Yes, Patrick?" she said.

His tone was stubborn. "I don't like the idea of you being alone in this neighborhood," he said. "Or, uh, Ardelion, either." He used Spence's code name, presumably because he'd lost track of which alternate ID she was supposed to be inhabiting at the moment.

Sula laughed. "We've just been through a *combat training course*," she said. "It's the rest of the neighborhood that has to watch out for *us*." And as his troubled expression didn't fade, she patted him on the arm. "That's a good thought, Patrick, but really, we'll be all right." And then, as she felt the powerful muscle in his arm, another thought occurred to her. "You grew up in the country, yes?"

"Well. A mountain village. But yes, more or less."

"Did you learn any handicraft skills? Carpentry, say, or plumbing, or . . . ?"

Macnamara nodded. "I'm a fair carpenter," he said. "And I can stick pipes together."

Sula smiled at him. "So you can build, say, secret compartments."

Macnamara blinked. "I suppose I can," he said.

"Good," Sula said. She looked around the apartment again, this time with a new eye.

Perhaps they weren't done fitting out this place after all.

The old and new apartments soon boomed to the sounds of saws and hammers, and the air was laden with the scent of glue and varnish and fresh paint. Useful items were secreted here and there, in furniture, in cabinets, and under floors, where Action Team 491 could lay hands on them at need. Sula, who was not so filled with the majesty of an officer that she disdained the use of her hands, learned some useful carpentry skills.

In another couple days Sula found her own apartment in the new neighborhood, a small room with a toilet, a shower, and an alcove for her bed. She subjected the room to the same merciless regime of scouring and painting that she had the other places, and carried to it some furniture that Macnamara had modified. In the furniture's hidden compartments she hid the same useful items she had stored elsewhere.

On the first night, as she lay on her narrow, newly purchased mattress, her neighbors obliged her by having a screaming fight. Through the thin, prefabricated walls she heard the sounds of bellowing, of shrieking, of furniture being hurled against walls.

How many nights, she wondered, had she lain awake as a child, and listened in fear to the shouts and screams and rage in the next room? The thunder of a chair being smashed into the wall, the crack of a shattering bottle, the smack of fist against flesh? Now in the darkness she listened to those childhood sounds again, and found her heart strangely calm.

Physical violence no longer frightened her, and it wasn't because she'd just spent the better part of two months learning how to disembowel people. It was well before the course at the Villa Fosca that she had learned how to deal with that particular fear.

She had dealt with her fear by smashing him in the head repeatedly with a chair leg, then having him tied to a heavy object and thrown in the Iola River.

It wasn't violence that frightened her now. What she feared was failure, and exposure, and the truth. The truth that lay in those samples of human DNA in the Peers' Gene Bank, and the truth that had been in the print of her right thumb before she'd burned it off—the truth that her name had once been Gredel, and that she'd grown up on Spannan, in a prefabricated apartment building just like this one, where she had lain in the dark and listened to violence thunder against the fragile wall between herself and her own fear.

The next day she left to meet her team at the other local, communal apartment. As she stood on her building's stoop blinking in the morning light, she heard a suggestive voice at her elbow.

"Hello, beauteous lady."

She turned to find a young man lounging against the wall of the building, a catlike smile on his face and a crumpled velvet hat on his head. He had the most brilliant, liquid, suggestive black eyes she had ever seen, and she decided there was no reason she shouldn't bask in their attention for a few moments more.

"Hello, yourself," she said.

He straightened slightly. "I haven't seen you here before, beauteous lady."

"I've just come down from the ring."

"You lost your home then, hey?" He sidled toward her and stroked her hand in what was supposed to be sympathy. "You need One-Step to show you around Riverside, don't you? I'll take you to all the nice places, buy you some pretties."

"You've got a job, then?" Sula asked.

One-Step narrowed those remarkable black eyes and held out both hands in protest. "I'll spend my last minim on you, beauteous lady. All I want is to make you happy."

"Why's this neighborhood called Riverside? I haven't seen a river."

The young man grinned and tapped the pavement with one platform sole. "River's under our feet, beauteous lady. They built the neighborhood over it."

Sula thought of cold, slow water moving in shadow beneath her feet, dead things rolling in pale silence on the turbid bottom, and she gave a shiver. If she'd known about the river she might well have heeded her team's doubts about the neighborhood.

One-Step sensed her change in mood, and once again

stroked her hand. "You're from the ring, hey, you don't have any rivers up there, I understand. Don't worry about falling in the water, everything's safe. Flood happens, they blow the tocsin."

Sula smiled and liberated her hand. "I've got an interview," she said.

"Well hey, I'll walk you to the train."

"I know where the train is." She spoke the words with a smile, but with finality. One-Step gave up his attempt to recapture her hand.

"Good luck with the interview, then, hey," he said. "You want me to show you around, just come here to my office any time." He threw out his hands to indicate his piece of pavement.

"I will. Thanks."

Sula felt herself relaxing as she moved down the streets that had become almost familiar. *You can disappear into a neighborhood like this.* She could disappear into what she had once been, and forget the long, grinding impersonation that had been her life.

Early on Martinez's first morning aboard *Illustrious* Perry arrived with a breakfast of salt-cured mayfish, fruit pickled in a sweet ginger sauce, and a fresh muffin. He had worked out an arrangement with Lady Michi's cook: the two shared the squadcom's kitchen and the duties of cooking for both officers. As he lingered over his coffee, Martinez called up the tactical computer and began creating an exercise for Chenforce based on encountering an enemy force at Aspa Darla.

The exercise, run the next day, was a success. However obscure the workings of his mind, Fletcher knew his job: *Illustrious* performed throughout with efficiency and precision, and so did the rest of the squadron. Martinez found himself envying Chenforce's trained, disciplined crews, and wished he'd had these people aboard *Corona* when he was in command.

Of course, Chenforce was composed of crews that had already won a victory, on the day of the rebellion, in the vicious battle waged at point-blank range with antiproton beams by ships mostly in dock. It gave the crews a certain grim esprit, and a confidence that whatever they encountered next, it couldn't be as bad as what they'd already overcome.

Chenforce also employed the new looser tactical formations that Martinez had developed, and with apparent success. Do-faq, Michi Chen confided, had sent her a complete recording of the experiments he had conducted, and she'd begun experimenting with them on her own.

Buoyed by this expression of confidence, Martinez created a more elaborate experiment for the following day. Chenforce again performed well. The third day there was no exercise, since Captain Fletcher chose the day for a personnel inspection so comprehensive that it took most of the day. Martinez, who was not under Fletcher's command, was not subject to the captain's keen eye; but that night, with his meal, he received a report from Alikhan, who had been present when his own compartment was visited by the captain.

"The lord captain's quite an enthusiast for musters and inspections, my lord," Alikhan said. "*Illustrious* is given a full inspection every six or seven days, and one department or other is mustered and examined on a daily basis."

"Does the lord captain find much?" Martinez said.

"A surprising amount, my lord. Dust in corners, untidy personal gear, bits of his murals getting chipped off . . . he's very thorough."

"I imagine the chipped murals must annoy him."

Alikhan was quite expressionless. "He keeps a painter on his staff, my lord, to make repairs."

"*Upholding his dignity,*" Martinez muttered to himself.

Alikhan raised an eyebrow. "My lord?"

"Nothing," Martinez said.

The fourth day, after another successful exercise, Martinez was the supper guest of the wardroom. The lieutenants were eager for a description of *Corona*'s escape from the Naxids on the day of the rebellion, and of the Battle of Hone-bar, and Martinez—who'd had a degree of experience in these anecdotes by now—obliged. Fulvia Kazakov, with a new pair of ivory chopsticks thrust through the knot of hair behind her head, was a meticulous hostess, satisfying her lieutenants' curiosity without giving Martinez the sense he was being overwhelmed by a pack of eager juniors. Chandra Prasad, to Martinez's surprise, was quiet—he remembered her as boisterous in gatherings. When he permitted himself to look at her, he saw her studying him with her long dark eyes.

Toward the end of the supper, Chandra received a page from Lord Captain Fletcher, and quietly excused herself. There followed a moment of awkward silence, in which the lieutenants scrupulously avoided one another's eyes, and then the conversation continued.

When he and Chandra had met, Martinez reflected later, they had shared the same problem: neither had any patronage in the Fleet. Martinez had found himself benefactors in the Chens, but he suspected Chandra hadn't found anyone to take this role—no one, perhaps, except Senior Captain Lord Gomberg Fletcher.

While there was no outright regulation against relations between a captain and one of his officers, service custom was dead against it. Aside from concerns about sexual exploitation, everyone dreaded a captain who played favorites among his subordinates, and a sexual relationship was favoritism of a particularly tangled kind. If an officer couldn't do without companionship for the length of a voyage, he or she was usually at liberty to bring a comely servant on board for the purpose.

Well, Martinez thought charitably, perhaps it was love.

He decided to forego video and wrote letters to Terza daily. In order that she might know what to expect at her destination he wrote his reminiscences of Laredo, where *Ensenada* was bound, along with descriptions of his parents, their homes, and the history of his family. He hadn't seen Laredo in nearly twelve years, but the memories rose to his mind with surprising clarity: the summer home Buena Vista on the lower slopes of the Sierra Oriente, surrounded by the maples that turned to flame in the autumn; the palace of white and chocolate marble in the capital, with its water gardens; and the tall fieldstone home set in the subtropical delta of the Rio Hondo, where the family spent its winters, and its magnificent alley of massive, twisted live oaks on which Martinez climbed as a child. His father, an exuberant man with a collection of custom aircraft and cars, and his mother, who read romantic poetry aloud to the family at night.

The letters, transformed to digital images, took days to reach Terza through the wormhole relays, but once she started receiving them she began responding in kind. Through her neat calligraphy he learned of her harp teacher Mr. Giulio, with his sharp nose and heavy knuckles; the pyramid-shaped Chen villa in the Hone Reach, built by the first Chen to reach convocate rank; and her reaction to an old Koskinen drama, a recording of which she'd found on *Ensenada.* She spoke of her pregnancy and the changes that were embracing her body.

Martinez pictured her on the love seat in her room, bent over a notebook with her hair thrown back over her shoulders and a calligraphy pen in her long, graceful hand.

He wrote that he missed her, and that she shouldn't be concerned if his letters suddenly stopped for a while. That didn't mean a battle, necessarily, that just meant he was busy or the squadron was moving.

He wrote *Love, Gareth* at the end of his letters, and found that the words didn't seem awkward. He was surprised at that, and then, as one letter followed another, the surprise began to fade.

Martinez finally rated a dinner with the captain, though this was in the context of Lady Michi and her entire staff being invited to dine. The murals in the captain's suite had actually been painted on, instead of being mounted like wallpaper. Fletcher was a gracious host, and kept up a flow of light conversation for the entire evening. Chandra Prasad was not in evidence.

Martinez dined with Michi regularly, and was a frequent guest of the wardroom. He began to feel that he should return this hospitality, and received the squadcom's permission to use *Daffodil*. He invited Lady Michi, and then the lieutenants, and finally the lieutenants along with their captain. Espinosa and Ayutano stood by the docking port with white gloves to help the guests onto the yacht. All but the captain praised Perry's cooking, but even Fletcher praised the wine, the vintages that had actually been shipped from the Chen cellars by Terza, and which Martinez had blindly loaded aboard without even looking at the labels.

After that *Daffodil* became a kind of club for the younger officers. Martinez frequently invited them for drinks or games, events where they wouldn't have to wear full dress. Despite the informality Martinez made a point of never being alone there with Chandra, or indeed with any female crew member.

Illustrious fell into routine. The Naxids seemed unaccountably tardy in seizing the capital that had been abandoned to their mercy. When Martinez had first come aboard, the Naxids had been expected any day. But the days rolled past, and the Naxids refused to show themselves. *Illustrious* went on with its series of drills and musters and inspections. Martinez suggested to Lady Michi that the number of drills be cut back: he didn't want the crouchbacks to overtrain and lose their edge. She agreed, and a drill was now scheduled for every third day.

Still the Naxids didn't come. Martinez could feel boredom twitching at his nerve ends. One day he encountered Lord Captain Fletcher in the corridor, walking with Chandra. Martinez braced in salute.

"Ah, Hoddy," Fletcher said amiably. "I call you Hoddy."

"My lord?"

Fletcher waved a hand in a vaguely beneficent gesture. "You are Hoddy. Hoddy I call you, and Hoddy you shall be."

Martinez blinked. "Yes, my lord," he said.

The captain and Chandra passed on, and Martinez hurried to his cabin, where he called up a dictionary and looked up "Hoddy." He found no entry, not even in the collection of slang.

Fletcher never called him Hoddy again. The incident remained a mystery.

Another heavy cruiser joined Chenforce, one damaged in the mutiny at Harzapid and since repaired. Chenforce now mustered eight ships, half of them heavy cruisers. The new arrival was worked into the tactical system through a series of exercises, but beyond that nothing changed. After forty days aboard *Illustrious*, Martinez and Chenforce seemed to have fallen into a pleasant trance, a wide orbit about Seizho's primary that might well last forever. The Naxids became a distant, receding dream.

The dream ended one afternoon while Martinez was writing to Terza. He answered a call, and found Lady Michi's grim face looking out of his sleeve display. "They're moving," she said. "My office at once."

Martinez sprang to his feet, dodged around his desk and dashed into the corridor, only to find Captain Fletcher ahead of him, moving at a saunter. Martinez tried not to tread on Fletcher's heels in his impatience as he followed the captain to Michi Chen's office.

"I've just received a flash from Zanshaa," she said, as they braced for salute. "Wormhole stations report the flares of forty-three ships leaving Magaria and accelerating toward Zanshaa. Considering the length of time it took the message to reach us, the Naxids should reach Zanshaa wormhole Three in about two and a half days. At ease, by the way."

Martinez relaxed only slightly. "Forty-three," he said. "That leaves a few unaccounted for."

"We can hope the others are guarding Magaria and Naxas," Lady Michi said. "And if not, and if we encounter them"—she shrugged, and Martinez saw a surprising, superior smile touch her lips—"we'll fight and we'll win. I have every confidence in our crews."

"Thank you, my lady," Fletcher said, as if he'd been personally responsible for all the crews in question.

Michi looked at the map she'd called onto the surface of her desk. "I'll want everyone suited up for the change of course to Protipanu," she continued, and then looked up. "Captain Martinez, there will be time for a squadron drill between now and then. Let's sharpen our sword one last time, shall we?"

"Yes, my lady."

The squadron commander looked over her shoulder and called into the next room. "Vandervalk?"

Michi's orderly came in with three small glasses on a silver tray. Golden fluid shone through a sheen of condensation on the glasses. Michi, Fletcher, and Martinez each took one. Martinez passed the glass under his nose and scented Kailas, a buttery-sweet dessert wine.

Michi raised her glass. "To our hunt, my lords."

Martinez felt the pull of a feral smile on his lips. On the back of his neck he felt the cold fingers of some primal ancestor, some forebear who crouched over his prey and raised stained hands to the sky in a celebration of blood and death.

"To our hunt," he said, and raised his glass.

* * *

Less than half an hour later, the ships of Chenforce swung onto a new heading and fired their engines. Gee forces began to build.

Martinez felt a growing exultation even as he felt the weight piling on his ribs.

Our hunt. The Martinez Plan was under way.

THIRTEEN

As Goddess of the Records Office, Sula worked to cover her every track that she could find. Her primary identity, the Jill Durmanov who inhabited the cozy apartment in Grandview, had been so thoroughly compromised by the Military Constabulary that Sula decided to make Jill Durmanov less substantial. Durmanov was the proprietor of the company that owned crates of cocoa and coffee, and Sula altered the records to make the proprietor Lucy Daubrac, the woman who lived in the communal apartment in Riverside. Sula made the change retroactive: Lucy had *always* owned the company, and Sula backdated the company itself, changing the record to indicate that it had been in existence for twelve years.

While she was at it, she had the Records Office send password updates to Lucy's hand comm, not to Jill's.

Change the key, change the lock. And write on the lock the words "This has *always* been the lock."

The next night she was back in the Records Office computer. She had realized that if another intrusion into the executive file were detected, or something else went amiss with the file, it would be reloaded from a backup and she'd have to act fast so as not to lose her access. Lady Arkat's passwords gave her access to the backup file, and Sula—using the same tricks she'd used with the primary file—successfully wrote her own executive file over the backup.

Summer grew warm and the heat rose in waves from the

pavement. Flowers trailed in red and orange cascades from window boxes, and the streets remained crowded well into the night. The Naxids declined to invade. Sula wondered if they'd lost their nerve.

With no enemy to fight, she and her team wandered over the Lower Town, listening. They entered cafés and bars and markets and spoke to whoever would speak to them. Sula wanted to learn what she could about the people around her.

The results were not encouraging. Most people thought that the flight of the Convocation, and the departure of the Fleet, marked the end of the war. They didn't find the prospect of domination by the Naxids particularly threatening. In any case they were willing to give the Naxids the benefit of the doubt. "You think they could be worse than the Shaa, beauteous lady?" as One-Step remarked.

"There are a lot more Naxids than there ever were Shaa," Sula answered him. "Billions. They're going to get all the top jobs—and the best middle jobs, too."

One-Step shrugged. "You got to have a job for any of that to matter, lovely one."

As the summer wore on the most popular song was "Season of Hope," by the Cree performer Polee Ponyabi, a song about giving up one's cares and anxieties and returning to a simple life of love and joy. Sula heard the soulful but catchy melody from windows, from vehicles, from clubs. The inhabitants of Zanshaa seemed willing to follow Ponyabi's advice: the restaurants and clubs were jammed, lines waited outside theaters for tickets, and the war seemed very far away.

Thus it was that when the enemy came, they seemed to come from the depths of some half-remembered dream. While taking a siesta on a hot afternoon, the windows open to bring a drift of sultry air over her skin, Sula felt the atmosphere throb with the deep basso rumble of the tocsin, the automatic horns that were normally blown only in case of flood or extreme weather. Sula jumped from her bed and told the video wall to turn itself on.

A grave announcer informed the population that news had flashed along the chain of wormhole relay stations, and it was now known that the Naxid fleet was coming. It would be another day before they arrived in the Zanshaa system, and the public was urged to remain calm. All clubs and theaters were ordered closed until further notice, and all other businesses were ordered closed after noon on the following day.

Just enough time for some fine scenes of panic in the food stores, Sula thought, and so it proved. The local Covered Market was open well into the night, and closed only because every item had been sold.

Her own supplies had already been laid by. Thoughtfully she stroked the finish of a bookcase that Macnamara had made for her, then touched the trigger that opened the secret compartment and revealed the butt of a pistol. She drew the pistol out and felt its firm solidity in her hand.

No, not a dream. The Season of Hope was about to come to an end.

A short while later she found herself in the communal apartment, where Spence already waited as the video wall repeated the same news over and over. Macnamara drifted in shortly thereafter. It was as if they all wanted each other's comfort as the world turned to night.

The next afternoon they moved onto the roof, which had an unobstructed view of the Zanshaa ring. Sula kept her hand comm on, tuned to a news channel. There were a few people there already, sitting in chairs with drinks in their hands, and the numbers grew as the day waned until it seemed the entire population of the city had become refugees, taking shelter on the roofs from an advancing flood. Sula saw even the building's Daimong janitor on the roof, pale-skinned and sinister among the drifting tide of Terrans.

The tocsin moaned out again in the late afternoon as the Naxid fleet flashed into the system, drowning out Sula's hand comm and the words of Governor Pahn-ko, who broadcast an assurance to the invaders that neither the ring nor the planet of Zanshaa would offer resistance.

The same was not promised of the horde of decoy missiles that still orbited the system, and as night cloaked the city Sula could see bright flashes amid the early stars that marked the decoys' annihilation. The scent of hashish drifted from one roof to the next. The crowds cried *aah* and *ooh* as if they were watching a fireworks display. With intoxication and night and the crowds, the roofs began to take on a kind of party atmosphere. A few young people began dancing to music.

It was then that Governor Pahn-ko came onto Sula's comm, and hers was one of many voices that call for silence.

"Naxid missiles have been fired in the Zanshaa system," the governor reported. He was an elderly Lai-own, his head nearly bald over his orange eyes, his muzzle bright with implant replacement teeth. He wore the deep red uniform of a convocate, with the ribbon of his office across his keel-like breastbone.

"We have reason to fear for the Zanshaa ring," Pahn-ko said. "I ask all citizens to remain calm in the event that the ring is attacked. In the event that the ring is in danger of destruction, I have ordered engineers to demolish it in such a way as to prevent any danger to the inhabitants of the planet."

"Brilliant," Sula breathed into the sudden fearful silence of the stricken crowd. Without actually saying so, the lord governor had implied that if the ring were to be destroyed, it would be the Naxids who were at fault.

"I thank you for your loyalty in the past," Pahn-ko went on, "and I have every trust that you will remain loyal in the future. Remember that the Convocation will return, and any who cooperate with the criminal Naxid government will be brought to account."

And how many believe *that*? Sula wondered.

About twenty minutes later the tocsin sounded for the third

time, and the Zanshaa ring was destroyed, mourned by the groaning horns seemed to rumble from deep in the protesting bones of the earth. Bright flashes illuminated the night along the great arc of the ring; strobe-light painted the upturned faces of the population with silver. Sula heard a scream, and sobs, and she watched in fascination as the last-ditch plans of the old, long-dead engineers came to fruition, and the broken remnants of the ring began slowly to separate.

She had not actually believed they would destroy the ring, not until she saw it happen.

The upper ring must have been braked and locked down, because its remains didn't separate and fly away. What happened instead was that the ring fragments rose in slow, stately silence into the night, so slowly that the fragments' separation wasn't apparent for some time. The fragments wouldn't leave Zanshaa altogether, Sula knew, they didn't have nearly enough energy; but they would rise to a higher orbit, dragging their cables behind them. Much of the fragments' mass, eventually, could be scavenged in the event the ring was rebuilt.

The tocsin fell silent, and the crowd watched, sickened and suddenly sober, as the great symbol of Zanshaa's prosperity and dominion floated from their reach.

When the Zanshaa ring had been built, the human race had been divided into primitive nation-states whose populations were happily engaged in bashing each other over the head with lengths of iron. Now that great monument of civilization and peace was no more.

Zanshaa was on its own.

Lights began to go out over the city. Much of the planet's electricity was generated from matter-antimatter reactions on the ring and sent to Zanshaa on the cables, or beamed by microwave to great rectenna fields in deserted corners of the world. Sula, as an employee for the Logistics Consolidation Executive, had arranged for large quantities of antimatter to be taken to the surface for power generation, but no more antimatter was coming, perhaps for years, and electricity rationing was an inevitability.

People began to drift away in the pale glow of the few remaining emergency lights. Sula remained, gazing upward, catching out of the corners of her eyes the bright flashes as more decoys were destroyed.

And then the deep awe she felt in her soul began to be replaced by swelling satisfaction.

Her plan. They had carried out *her plan.*

What can the Naxids be thinking now? she wondered.

FOURTEEN

The day after the ring was destroyed Sula took the *Ju-yao* pot out of storage and carried it to her little apartment. She placed it on the bookshelf in the alcove by the window, where the northern light could illuminate the fine crackle of the glaze with fine threads of silver.

This place was her home, she thought, the first she'd ever had. The apartment in the High City didn't count: she'd acquired that place not for herself, but for Martinez. This little room, in contrast, was all her own.

She sat crosslegged on her mattress and gazed at the pot, the little ancient survivor brought to live in this incongruous, raucous neighborhood. Cooking smells floated through the window from the stalls outside, mixing with the scent of paint and varnish.

The scent of home. *Home.* The small, fresh-scented room she shared with the old pot, the venerable survivor of fallen dynasties.

She hoped that was an omen.

"Oh, I forgot. You don't drink. Four-nine-one, shall I have Ellroy make you some tea?"

"No thanks, Blanche," Sula said. "I'm perfectly all right."

"Well. If you're sure, then."

"Blanche"—Lieutenant Captain Hong—took a small glass of mig brandy from the tray that his servant was passing around the company.

Hong was scrupulous in his use of code names, but at the moment this seemed unnecessary. He was meeting with his eleven team leaders in his own apartment, a spacious penthouse with a terrace and garden, and of course they had all trained together and knew one another's names perfectly well.

"My lords and ladies," Hong offered, "I drink to the Convocation."

"The Convocation," the others murmured, and sipped their brandy. Sula, who hadn't realized a toast was coming, offered a smile as the others drank.

"What I called you together to discuss," Hong said, "was the matter of taking action against the Naxids when they first arrive on Zanshaa. Now that the ring's gone, they're going to have to come down on large landing strips, using shuttles with chemical rockets."

The chemical rockets were a necessity: antimatter engines would sterilize rather too much ground.

"There are only two airfields of sufficient size near the capital," Hong went on, "and only one of these has suitable facilities for maintenance of ground-to-orbit craft, and that's Wi-hun. We can be reasonably certain that's where the Naxids will land." He smiled. "They won't know that the spacecraft maintenance facilities will have been dismantled before they arrive."

He called up the wall display, and a map appeared of the area between central Zanshaa and the landing field at Wi-hun.

"Once the Naxids secure Wi-hun," Hong said, "we expect they'll advance on Zanshaa and occupy the seat of government in the High City. There are three plausible routes." These flashed on the map in green. "Our Action Group has been assigned the Axtattle Parkway. When the Naxids begin to load up, we'll receive the word from our sources, assemble, and strike the enemy as they enter Zanshaa. We'll then retreat to the city and lie low till the next action."

One team leader raised a hand. "How about a truck bomb?" she said.

"Very good," said Hong. "We can park it along the boulevard and wait till the Naxids are adjacent before setting it off. From vantage points in the buildings alongside, we can open fire, shoot down as many of the surviving Naxids as we can, and then fade away in the confusion."

The planning began. Hong was meticulous and assigned several of the officers to examine possible sites for the ambush. Another was told to requisition a truck from the Fleet motor pool. Sula was ordered to work out escape routes once the actual ambush site had been decided.

"We'll meet tomorrow to receive reports and make our final plans," Hong said. "Please leave one by one so you don't attract attention."

That afternoon Sula took a stroll along the Axtattle Parkway. The road was broad, six lanes wide, and lined on either side by rows of ammat trees that shaded the pedestrian walks with their long, spear-shaped leaves. The neighborhoods on either side of the road were Terran, which explained why Action Group Blanche had been assigned this particular corridor. Along the road were medium-sized businesses or apartments, the buildings old but well maintained, with gables and mansard roofs. The district had a prosperous air.

Axtattle Parkway was a high-speed artery feeding Zanshaa's heart; the roadbed was elevated above other roads, and access to the highway limited. Only a few major roads connected with the parkway—the smaller streets in the residential areas led away, not toward, the ambush site. The pursuers would be stuck on the limited-access highway, with no way into the neighborhoods except on foot, a fact that would make escape easier.

Sula smiled. Blanche would be pleased.

FIFTEEN

Warrant Officer Shushanik Severin thought of the cooking oil in the lifeboat's galley. There were several kinds, each in its own high-gee-resistant resinous container, and each type was one hundred percent fat.

He thought about lifting a container of cooking oil to his lips and drinking the contents like the finest wine.

Fat. Fat was good. *Fat makes warmth.*

Severin was visualizing the sensual pleasure of licking the cooking oil from his lips when the alarm rang, and he bounded from his rack to the door of his sleeping quarters, and pushed off for the control room, flying easily in the microgravity of Asteroid 302948745AF.

With his hand he scrubbed frost from the displays and gaped. *Engine flares.* After all these months, warships had finally come through the torus-shaped Protipanu Wormhole 2. And they had come in hot, because the radar detector was chirping out the message that the lifeboat was repeatedly being hammered by blue-shifted radars. They were looking for an enemy.

What they didn't know was that the enemy was about to give them more than they were ready for.

There were crashes and flailings of arms and legs as the rest of his crew of six arrived in the control room. Severin batted away a floating thermal blanket that had come adrift from someone's shoulders, and said, "Take your places."

To his second-in-command, Gruust, who was strapping

himself into the acceleration couch before the comm board, he said, "Gruust, prepare for transmission."

And then he turned to his chief engineer, and could not stop the blissful smile from breaking out on his lips. "Begin the engine startup sequence. And let's get some heat in here."

The squadron commander led Chenforce from her own hardened Flag Officer Station more or less at the cruiser's center of gravity: she was the fulcrum of the ship literally as well as metaphorically. Martinez, as her tactical officer, sat facing her in a separate acceleration cage: another cage behind her held her two signals lieutenants and a fourth a warrant officer who monitored the state of the ship.

Two bulkheads separated the squadcom from Captain Fletcher, who sat in a separate command station forward, with a full staff of lieutenants and warrant officers to control *Illustrious* and its weapons. Auxiliary Command, aft, was in the charge of Lieutenant Kazakov, who would only be called upon to issue an order if her captain were killed.

Fletcher had done his best to ornament the unpromising material of the Flag Officer Station: he'd made the little boxy room seem larger by employing murals that made the station seem to be part of a vast pillared hall through which citizens of the empire, dressed in antique fashions and armed with nets and spears, pursued fantastic animals. The illusion, however, was spoiled by the large surface area that had to be devoted to the various navigation and weapons displays, and around which the little sentients and beasts were forced to vault or climb. In all, the room had to be considered one of Fletcher's lesser efforts.

Ignoring the hunters and prey on the walls, Martinez kept his eyes fixed on his tactical displays, for all that there was very little on them. Protipanu was a brown dwarf so faint as to be nearly invisible to human eyes, and earlier in its history, as a red giant, had consumed its inner planets and demolished others through gravitational stress. The result was a lot of asteroids, with the four surviving planets quite far out, and at the moment widely scattered. These were gas giants, with some of their outer atmosphere blown away but with their heavy cores still intact.

Chenforce was heading toward the nearest of these, Pelomatan, intending to swing around it on the way to another planet, Okiray, and on to Wormhole 3 and the transit to Mazdan. It had been possible to plot a course directly from one wormhole to the next, but both Martinez and Lady Michi had rejected that notion because the roundabout route gave more options in the unlikely event that any enemy warships were still in the system. Because Chenforce had decelerated so much since leaving Zanshaa, the transition to the next wormhole would take nearly eight days.

"Message!" The astonished cry came from Coen, the red-haired signals lieutenant. "Incoming message!"

"Where from?" Michi demanded. "The wormhole station?" The squadron had just blasted past the station, which had been out of touch with its counterpart at Seizho since the wormhole had been moved out of alignment. It was barely possible, Martinez supposed, that the Naxids had ignored the useless station and that loyalists were still occupying the place.

"No." Coen put a hand to the side of his helmet, as if it would help him hear better. "The message is coming by comm laser from an asteroid, and it's in the clear. It's supposed to be from a Warrant Officer Severin of the Exploration Service."

"Let's hear it," Martinez said, and then winced for forgetting he wasn't in charge and anticipating his commander.

Coen didn't wait for Michi to confirm the order, but sent the message to everyone in the Flag Officer Station. A miniature Severin appeared in a corner of Martinez's display, a shaggy-haired, bearded man in the blue uniform of the Exploration Service. Martinez enlarged the image as the man began to speak.

"This is Warrant Officer First Class Shushanik Severin to any incoming warship," the bearded man said. "My crew and I were assigned to the station at Wormhole Two when the rebellion broke out. When the frigate *Corona* transited the system to Seizho, Captain Martinez warned me that a Naxid squadron was following within hours. I therefore ordered the wormhole moved seven diameters off the plane of the ecliptic, and then loaded my crew into the lifeboat and grappled it to an asteroid. Since that time, we've been powered down and keeping the enemy under observation."

The bearded man leaned toward the camera, and his voice took on urgency.

"My lords, *the Naxids never left Protipanu!* The original eight warships have been reinforced by two more, and they have scattered approximately a hundred and twenty decoys throughout the system. Our observations have been updated every hour, and I am appending a standard navigation plot with the latest information. The positions are a bit approximate, since we'd give ourselves away if we used radar, and have been forced to use our visual detectors to look for engine flares and then do a bit of interpolation, but we've been accurate in the past."

Martinez could see that Severin's breath turned to mist as it left his lips. "We will be standing by to answer any questions, though we request permission to leave for Seizho as soon as possible because, ah, the Naxids are bound to notice us now, and we are unarmed and helpless.

"We are standing by. This is Warrant Officer Severin."

"Message from Captain Fletcher, my lady." This was Lady Ida Li, the other signals lieutenant and a distant relation of the Lord Richard Li who had been engaged to Terza before the war. "The captain suggests the message may be Naxid disinformation."

"I don't believe so, my lady," Martinez said. He looked at the image of Severin, who was now wrapping himself in a silver thermal blanket. "I remember Severin from *Corona*'s passage through the system. This is the man."

He's had his ass frozen to that rock for five months, he thought in disbelief. And I believe that is frost I see on his mustache.

"Tell Captain Fletcher," Michi told Li, "that Captain Martinez has encountered Mr. Severin before, and vouches for him."

Which was not quite what Martinez had said, but Martinez knew better than to correct his superior.

"Comm, reply to Mr. Severin's message," Michi said. "Acknowledge, and tell him to stand by."

"Acknowledge Severin's message," Coen repeated. "Tell him to stand by. Shall I give him permission to evacuate the system?"

"Yes," Michi said. "Why not?"

"I've checked the attached file," Coen said. "No viruses or other sabotage software."

Martinez loaded Severin's file into the tactical computer, and the near-empty Protipanu system blossomed with bright images, all attached to little identification labels giving course, speed, and class of vessel. There were far too many to take in at once. Martinez decided a virtual display would be more useful, and at his command the vast spaces of Protipanu's system blossomed in his mind. He sat at the central point of the brown dwarf and looked with care at the distant fires that orbited him.

The supposed enemy squadron was two-thirds of the way across the system, partway between the Olimandu and Aratiri gas giants. It was moving in the same circle around Protipanu as Chenforce, and if it accelerated, it would eventually come up on Chenforce from behind, perhaps after four or five days.

Other icons identified as decoys were scattered throughout the system, some orbiting Protipanu in one direction, some in the other. All of them were echeloned to look like enemy squadrons, and if Severin's estimates were correct Chenforce was going to be encountering one of them head-on in about fourteen hours.

The problem was that there was no real confirmation for any of this. Chenforce's radars had yet to reach any targets and return with information. If Severin's information were in fact Naxid disinformation, Martinez had no way of knowing.

Martinez let the virtual solar system fade from his mind and delivered his analysis to the squadron commander.

"If we increased acceleration we could probably make Wormhole Three before the Naxids could stop us," he said.

Michi shook her head. "No. I'm not going to strike out on this mission with an enemy force right on our tail. I want to beat them right here, at Protipanu."

Martinez looked into her dark eyes and felt a stirring in his nerves. *To our hunt.*

"Very good, my lady," he said. He looked at the plot on his display, then put it on the wall display for both of them to see. "If Severin's right about the location of the enemy it will be days before we engage, but I can see one decision we're going to have to make fairly soon." He manipulated a pointer on the display to indicate the supposed decoys they would encounter in fourteen hours. "Do we behave as if we already know these are decoys, or as if they're real ships? We'd use a lot more missiles on real ships."

Michi's eyes narrowed. "What's the advantage to putting on a pretense that we think they're real?"

"I'm not sure yet," Martinez admitted. "It depends on how they plan to use their decoys."

Michi considered. "We have some hours to think about it," she said. "Let's see if Severin's information is confirmed."

"Transmission!" Coen called. "Radio transmission, from Wormhole Station Two." He frowned at his display. "What we're getting is fragmentary and low quality. And it's coded."

Sent by radio instead of powerful communications laser, the message was having a hard time getting through *Illustrious*'s radioactive tail. The Naxids in the wormhole station were broadcasting to everyone in the system rather than to an individual ship.

"Send the message to cryptographic analysis," Michi said. "It'll give them some practice." She looked at Martinez. "Which raises another issue," she said.

"Yes, my lady?"

"We've got to destroy all three wormhole stations. I don't want any information getting to the Naxid fleet command about the tactics I'm going to use."

There was a brief silence as Martinez thought of the crews of the stations watching the missiles racing toward them, the speeding death they could do nothing to stop. "Very good, my lady," Martinez said. "Shall I ask Severin to confirm that the relay stations are all occupied by the enemy?"

"Blow Station Two first," Michi said. "They've *already* shown they're the enemy."

"Yes, my lady." Martinez transmitted the order to Husayn, Fletcher's weapons officer, and then—when Fletcher broke in asking for confirmation—informed the captain that the live-fire order had come from the squadron commander.

Martinez enlarged the communications board on his display, with its picture of the bearded Severin puffing out steam as he sat at his acceleration couch waiting for his engine start-up sequence to conclude.

"Mr. Severin," he transmitted, "it's very good to see you again. This is Captain Martinez, tactical officer for Squadron Commander Chen. I would advise you to remain at your present location until the plasma cloud near Wormhole Two has dispersed, and in the meantime to get your crew into their hardened shelter. Right now, however, I'd like your confirmation that all wormhole stations have been occupied by the Naxids."

Severin was already several light-minutes from the

squadron, so it was some time before Martinez saw him turn from a conversation with someone off-camera, and stare with quick attention at the incoming transmission. At first there was a moment of pleased apprehension—Martinez assumed he'd been recognized, and felt a touch of vanity at Severin's reaction. Then Martinez saw Severin's moment of puzzlement, followed by alarmed concern. Severin gave a quick glance to another display, presumably to confirm that the missile was on its way—which in fact it was, though it wouldn't have shown on Severin's display as yet.

"Captain Martinez," he said, "welcome back to Protipanu. The pleasure of this meeting is all mine, believe me. Your message is understood and we'll take shelter. All wormhole stations were occupied by the enemy, so far as we can tell. We'll stand by for any further—" His eyes darted to the other display again. "I can see your missile has been fired. We've got to halt our countdown and get all our spare rations and gear out of the hard shelter, so good luck to you and yours. We'll remain standing by."

Martinez smiled. The tiny radiation shelter on a lifeboat was designed to hold the crew in very close quarters during a solar flare emergency, not a very likely occurrence in the vicinity of a brown dwarf like Protipanu. Apparently Severin had been using his shelter as a butler's pantry.

There was quite enough time to clear the shelter out. *Illustrious*'s missile had to counter the momentum imparted to it by the squadron before it could begin to claw its way toward its target, and everyone involved was going to have plenty of warning, even the Naxids.

Martinez called up his weapons plots, and let the computers calculate trajectories for a moment. Then he turned to Michi.

"My lady squadcom," he said, "Station Three is clean across the system and it's probably too early to start shooting at it. But we can most likely take out Station One before the Naxid squadron learns the missiles are on the way and takes effective countermeasures. The station is relatively close to us, and if the enemy are where Severin says they are, they won't have time to fire countermissiles. They're going to have to use lasers, and at that range, if our missile is jinking, they'll have to be very lucky to hit it."

Michi nodded. "Transmit the order, then. Let's make it two missiles, just in case."

Martinez contacted Husayn again and gave the order. There might be enough warning, he thought, for the Naxids to escape through the wormhole if they had a lifeboat like Severin's, and then he wondered at his squeamishness at killing the station crews. They were rebels, of course, and deserved death almost by definition. At Hone-bar his orders had killed thousands of enemy, and it hadn't occurred to him to hesitate. Yet something in him shrank at the thought of the crews' helplessness, at the fact that they'd see their death coming for hours in which they could do little but watch their oncoming extinction.

So, he asked himself, he would feel better about killing them if they could only shoot back? There did not seem a high survival value attached to this strategy. The entire empire had been built on using massive force against helpless populations, and was now convulsed by a civil war in which thousands, millions, even billions could die. Martinez told himself that he should get used to it.

Lady Michi didn't seem troubled by these considerations. She unbuckled her webbing and rolled her cage forward to plant her feet on the deck.

"It doesn't look as if anything very exciting is going to happen for several hours," she said. "I'm going to stretch my legs and get something to eat. Lieutenant Coen," to the signals lieutenant, "tell the squadron that this would be a good time to feed crews in shifts." She looked at Martinez. "Monitor the situation till I return, Captain Martinez. Let me know if there's any change."

"Very good, my lady."

He let the thoughts go and busied himself with his displays. Over the next couple of hours flights of vehicles winked into existence on the screens as the *Illustrious* radars began to confirm elements of what Severin had told them. Severin's data indicated these were all decoys, though their behavior didn't prove anything one way or another.

Before Lady Michi returned, Station 2 was engulfed by an antimatter fireball. Martinez decided that this didn't qualify as sufficiently exciting news to disturb her, though he reported it verbally, half an hour later, when she returned.

"Thank you," she said, showing little interest. "Anything else?"

Martinez showed her the displays. "The Naxid squadron should be realizing we exist about now." He looked at her. "Do you suppose they've been ordered to Zanshaa, to meet the advance from Magaria? Or to Seizho to block the hypothetical escape of our hypothetical Home Fleet? If that's the case, we may just exchange places like a couple of dancers and then go about our business."

Lady Michi seemed intrigued by this idea. "When will we find out?"

"They'll burn past Aratiri in twenty minutes or so. Either they'll carry on toward Wormhole Two, or swing toward Pelomatan after us, but we're not going to get to see what they do for a hundred or so minutes after that."

"Interesting." She put a hand on her acceleration cage and lowered herself into her couch. "Have we heard from Mr. Severin?"

"No, my lady, but he was well outside the deadly range of the blast."

"I want to put him in for a decoration. Freezing out here for five months was a brave and noteworthy thing, and he did it on his own initiative."

"Yes, my lady." Martinez considered this. "But how are we going to let the Fleet know of the recommendation?

We'll be out of touch for months. Severin may have to carry his own recommendation home with him."

Michi frowned. "That won't look good, will it? Showing up at the Seizho ring station and saying, 'By the way, I've earned a medal'?" She let go of the acceleration cage and let the couch swing to its neutral, reclined position. Somewhere a bearing squeaked. She pulled down her displays to the locked position in front of her.

"Well then," she said. "Since the Exploration Service is under Fleet control for the duration of the war, we may as well take advantage of the fact. Inform Mr. Severin that he's just received a field promotion to full lieutenant." She turned to her signals lieutenants. "Li, call up the appropriate document. I'll sign it and send a facsimile to Severin."

Martinez watched this display of privilege and patronage with surprise and a degree of awe. Severin was a commoner, and commoners were rare in the officer corps. Rarer still was a field promotion. Martinez didn't think there had been one in centuries.

Martinez triggered his comm display. "Mr. Severin," he said, "this is Captain Martinez. Squadron Commander Chen wishes me to inform you that in return for your gallantry and enterprise you have just received a field promotion to full lieutenant." The *gallantry and enterprise* was his own addition, but he thought it sounded good.

He smiled. "Allow me to be the first to call you 'my lord.' Your lieutenancy is very well deserved. Have a pleasant return journey. End transmission."

He raised his head from his displays and saw Lady Michi smiling at him. "Why don't you take a break?" she said. "I'll let you know what the Naxids do around Aratiri."

"Very good, my lady. Thank you."

He unwebbed and got to his feet, and as soon as he began to move realized how badly he'd stiffened from his hours on the couch. He hobbled toward the door, and as he went he slaved the tactical screen to his sleeve display.

No sense in being out of touch.

Severin turned to his crew. "Would any of you care to be the *second* person to address me as 'my lord?' " he asked.

There followed a moment of profound stillness.

"Right," Severin said. "Let's get on with the diagnostics, then."

Though Severin hoped the radiation hadn't touched the crew in their little shelter, some stray gamma ray from the destruction of Station 2 might have damaged the lifeboat's electronics, and so a check was clearly in order.

As the diagnostic programs ticked along, Severin considered how his future had just changed. The Exploration Service was small, and he'd just made the leap to its elite—and furthermore, the rank carried even more weight now that the service had been militarized. He could now give orders to Fleet personnel—he could give orders to Fleet *officers,* provided he outranked them, and as a full lieutenant he now outranked all sublieutenants and full lieutenants with less than—he checked the chronometer—two minutes' seniority.

He could give orders to *Peers.* And despite lieutenants being called "my lord" as a traditional courtesy, he wasn't a lord, and wasn't ever going to be.

He wondered how the lords were going to like that.

Maybe I won't be invited to their lawn parties, he thought. Though he suspected the situation was going to be a little more complicated than that.

But come to think of it, he had a more immediate situation at hand. He and his people had all been enlisted crew together, and their relations had been informal. Though Severin had been in charge, he rarely had to give an actual order: usually he'd simply point out that something needed to be done, and generally the thing was done without his having to pay more attention to it. When he'd come up with the idea of remaining in the Protipanu system to gather intelligence on the enemy, he'd consulted the crew first, to make certain they agreed—he hadn't wanted to be stuck on an asteroid for months with people who didn't want to be there.

Now he was no longer an enlisted man. He was an officer, and even in the small Exploration Service there was a great gulf between officers and crew. He was a lord and a commoner at the same time.

He didn't even know how to think of himself. What was he, exactly?

Severin realized it was growing warm in the balmy air of the control room. The frost that coated the instruments was beginning to melt, in the asteroid's low gravity forming nearly perfect spheres on the displays. He shrugged out of his overcoat.

"Engine diagnostics nominal," the chief engineer reported.

"No sense in hanging around, then," Severin said. "Release grapples."

Electromagnetic grapples were released, and for the first time in five months the lifeboat was no longer moored to 302948745AF. Through the melting spears of frost on the view ports the Maw glowed red.

"Pilot," Severin said, "maneuver us clear of this rock."

A wild joy surged through him as the maneuvering jets fired and he felt the tug of inertia on his inner ear. Liberation at last.

"Pilot," Severin said, "take us to the wormhole at a constant one gravity."

There was a momentary flicker in the pilot's eye. "Yes, my lord," he said.

Yes, my lord. Severin felt an unexpected thrill of pride and delight at the words.

The engine fired, and Severin's pleasure in his new status was doused in a rain of ice-cold water that flew off the displays and hit him in the face.

Laughter broke from his lips. He wiped water from his eye.

Welcome to the officer corps, he thought.

Ships' cuisine tended toward stews and casseroles when a battle or maneuver was at hand: the items could be kept in the oven for hours without significant harm. Perry had brought from Lady Michi's kitchen a bowl of bison meat stewed with potatoes and vegetables, along with some hard bread that savored of the metal can in which it had been stored for, no doubt, a great many years.

Martinez ate without interest, his eyes fixed on the tactical display on his office wall. The display was framed by several of those annoying winged children who all stared at it as if something astonishing and wonderful were being revealed. Whether the enemy squadron racing toward Aratiri qualified as astonishing and wonderful was yet uncertain.

Engines flared on the display. Numerics flashed. Martinez pushed his bowl away and watched and tried to remind himself that he was watching an event that had occurred over an hour ago.

The formation that Severin had identified as the Naxid squadron raced around Aratiri, and then steadied on the course for Pelomatan.

A long, reflective sigh passed Martinez's lips. It would be battle, then. Naxid missiles would be flying up Chenforce's collective tailpipe, or they would unless he could work out a way to stop them.

His sleeve display chimed. "Yes, lady squadcom?" he anticipated.

Michi gazed out of the display without surprise. "You've seen it, then?"

"Yes, my lady."

"We'll still have hours and hours to make plans. I'd like you to join me for supper."

"I would be honored, my lady." He looked at the screen

and frowned. "According to Severin the enemy received two ships as reinforcements. I wish I knew which ships they were, it would make planning easier."

"Oh." The squadron commander blinked. "I should have told you. They're most likely the frigates the Naxids were building at Loatyn—average size, twelve or fourteen missile launchers."

Slow surprise rolled through Martinez like a tide. "They were building frigates at Loatyn?"

"Yes. I'm sorry I didn't tell you. You weren't authorized to receive that information unless"—she made an apologetic gesture—"Unless it became relevant."

Which stifled Martinez's next question: *how many other ships were the enemy building?*

"Very good," Martinez said. "Thank you, my lady."

She ended the transmission and Martinez returned to his contemplation of the screen. What, he wondered, were those little painted children seeing that he wasn't?

The reinforcements were the smallest class of warship: that was something to be thankful for. The original eight were a light squadron from Felarus, frigates with a light cruiser serving as flagship. The total offensive punch for the enemy was just short of two hundred launchers, as against Chenforce with two hundred and ninety-six launchers. That was a comfortable margin in offensive power, but it was balanced somewhat by the fact that the enemy had a couple more maneuver elements, and it still didn't mean the enemy couldn't hurt the loyalists badly enough to seriously compromise Michi Chen's mission.

Or even kill all of Chenforce, if someone like Martinez made a serious enough mistake.

The Naxid torches, he saw, remained at a high intensity. They were really piling on the gee forces. He ran some figures and discovered they were accelerating at a steady twelve-point-one gees.

Everyone in the enemy squadron was probably unconscious by now. The Naxids didn't take constant gees any better than Terrans.

Martinez reached for his coffee and breathed in its fragrance
while he considered the Naxids' tactics. He decided that
knowledge of the enemy commander would be useful, and so
he called up the enemy Light Squadron 5 in his database and
looked for the captain of *Gallant,* the light cruiser that had
served as the flagship for the squadron before the mutiny.

Gallant was too small to carry a flag officer, so the whole
squadron would be under its commander, a Captain
Bleskoth. Bleskoth had graduated first in his class at the
Festopath Academy, and was of a distinguished family—
there had been a Lady Bleskoth in the Convocation, at least
until she'd been thrown off the High City on the day of the
rebellion. He had edited the academy journal and was captain of the lighumane team.

After graduation he had risen quickly. While still a lieutenant he had commanded the frigate *Quest* for several
months, its captain being absent on other duty. He'd been
promoted to full captain only nine years after graduation.
Almost all of his time had been spent on ship duty, the only
exception being the three years he'd spent as aide to Fleet
Commander Fanagee, one of the great lights of the rebellion
who had led their forces at Magaria. He owned a yacht, the
Blue Shift, and had won the Magaria Cup two years running.
He was clearly on a fast course to higher command, and his
appointment to command *Gallant,* and with it command of
Light Squadron 5, had come over the heads of a number of
other officers.

Bleskoth had been a part of the rebellion even then, Martinez thought. Fanaghee had recruited him: the young Naxid
had gone to Felarus *knowing* he was going to blow the other
ships of the Third Fleet to bits with his antiproton beams.

Martinez considered the enemy captain as he sipped his
coffee. Bleskoth was young, decisive, and committed. He

led a team at lighumane, a sport that combined long-term strategy with sudden, aggressive violence. He hadn't hesitated at Felarus. He was a yachtsman, used to hard accelerations and last-minute, decisive actions.

Martinez returned his coffee cup to its saucer. He had his answer.

"They're trying to convince us that they're decoys," Martinez said later, as he reported to Lady Michi at the Flag Officer Station. "They're going to do a prolonged acceleration and deliberately take some casualties in order to convince us that they're a badly managed set of decoys and that we don't have to worry about them."

Lady Michi drummed her gloved fingers on the armrest of her couch. "That implies they want us to believe some particular set of decoys is in fact the real squadron. Which one?"

Martinez frowned. "I haven't worked that out yet."

"Have they worked out that Severin's given their whole game away?"

Martinez, standing by Michi's cage and looking down at her, felt a touch of vanity at his answer. "I checked the timing. Everyone on their ships must have been unconscious when the light from Severin's torch reached them. When they wake up they'd have to go back through the records and look for it."

"Unless," Michi pointed out, "they have an automatic alarm set to alert them to any new ships in the system."

"They *should* have set such an alarm, yes," Martinez conceded. "But they weren't expecting us, so in their surprise and haste they may not have." Michi looked dubious, but Martinez had prepared his report thoroughly, and he restrained the impulse to tick off the points on his gloved fingers. "And even if they *do* see Severin creeping off, they may not necessarily think he's been in the system for five months—he may look like a pinnace pilot we sneaked into the system a few hours ahead of our arrival, and who may not have observed a great deal. And if they *have* set an alarm, it would make sense for the alarm to alert the flagship to cease acceleration to give the commander time to work out if the new arrival is a threat, and if that happens we'll be able to see it in, oh, twenty minutes or so." He had to stop and take a breath. "If they *are* alerted but *don't* stop to evaluate their situation till the end of this long acceleration, then it will be too late, because they'll be already committed to their strategy."

Amusement tweaked the corners of Michi's lips. "You've certainly got your facts in order."

Martinez shambled into as decent an approximation of a salute as his vac suit permitted. "I do my humble best, my lady."

She raised an eyebrow. "Humble? Really? You may take your seat, captain."

Martinez saw the two signals lieutenants try to suppress their smiles, and suppressed his own as he shuffled to his acceleration couch. A superior who appreciated his moments of conceit was a welcome change from commanders of the past.

The couch rocked beneath his weight as Martinez lowered himself into it, the hoops of the acceleration cage vibrating with little metallic shivers. He reached into one of the seat compartments and pulled out a med injector, then held it against his carotid and touched the trigger. A carefully calculated cocktail of pharmaceuticals entered his system, one that would regulate his blood pressure during acceleration and strengthen his blood vessels, keeping their walls supple and whole against the danger of acceleration. Then Martinez put on his helmet, reached above his head, and pulled his displays to the locked position in front of him.

"Reminder from Captain Fletcher, my lady," said Li, from the comm board. "Twenty-six point five minutes till our acceleration around Pelomatan."

"Acknowledge," said Michi. She turned to Martinez, then

waited for him to finish webbing himself into his place before speaking.

"Captain, you mentioned the advantages of having the Naxids think that we're fooled by their decoys."

"Yes." Martinez paused a moment to collect his thoughts. The decoys were self-guided missiles small enough to be fired from a warship's missile tubes. The warships, with their resinous hulls, were not good radar reflectors, and it was possible to configure a small decoy missile to give off as large a radar signature as a warship. The decoys' exhausts had also been modified to give off the broader tail of a larger vessel. In general a decoy was less convincing the closer it got to an observer, and the longer an observer had a chance to study it.

"We have some decoys heading right for us," Michi said.

Martinez's fingers brought up his tactical displays. "We should destroy them, of course. The question is how. If we knew they were decoys we'd let them get quite close. But if we suspect they might be real, we'd open fire early and use a lot of missiles."

"I don't want to waste missiles," Michi said. "Not when we've got a real battle coming on, followed by a long campaign." Her fingers again drummed on the arm of her couch. "I'll order the squadron to open fire with lasers on that oncoming group as soon as it's even remotely possible. If we get lucky and hit one, that will prove to everyone's satisfaction—including the Naxids'—that we know the squadron are decoys and can treat them as such."

Martinez nodded. This was as reasonable a plan as any he'd been able to devise himself. "Very good, my lady," he said.

He watched the tactical displays for the next several minutes. The Naxids' frenzied acceleration continued without cease, even after the light from Severin's engine flare reached them. They had not set an alarm, at least not one that could be triggered by a small vessel such as the lifeboat.

Martinez became aware of the sound of deep breathing in his earphones. He checked the comm board first, to make certain no one had broken into the channel he shared with the squadcom, and then looked up to see Michi Chen lying on her couch with her eyes closed, asleep with a pleasant smile on her lips.

Sweet dreams, he thought. He felt a stab of envy for a commander who could relax so completely on the eve of battle.

This was clearly not an ability he had acquired himself. If he snatched a few hours of sleep within the couple of days, he'd be very pleased. And he wasn't even in charge of the squadron.

Alarms clattered as the ship prepared for weightlessness, and Martinez saw Michi start awake. She looked at her displays, saw nothing had changed, and closed her eyes. Martinez heard the deep breathing start again as the ship went weightless and rotated about its sleeping center of gravity as it prepared for the burn around Pelomatan.

Another alarm rang, this one for heavy gravity. The engines roared into life, and gravity swung Martinez's couch to a new attitude. As he was pressed deep into his seat he heard Michi's breathing grow labored as the gravities began to stand on her ribs with their leaden boots.

Martinez felt his own breath burn as it fought its way through his constricting throat. His vac suit clamped gently on his arms and legs. The ship cracked and groaned as the gravities built. In succession, as the engine vibration reached the frequency of different elements of the ship, Martinez heard the metallic keen of one of his cage bars as it vibrated in sympathy with the ship, the song of a metal washer on his console, and the hum of one of the room's recessed light brackets.

Darkness began to flood his vision, and he clenched his jaw muscles to force blood to his brain. The darkness continued to advance: the last thing Martinez saw was a scarlet stripe on his tactical display, and then the stripe twisted, spun into a narrowing spiral, then faded like a dying spark into the night. In his headphones he heard a snarl as Michi Chen fought for consciousness.

He thought he hadn't actually passed out. Dimly he heard the call of the zero-gee warning, and then the sudden release as the engines cut. He gasped in relief as he floated free in his harness, and he saw a dim tunnel in front of him, a tunnel that slowly brightened and widened until he saw the control room before him, the other officers blinking and blowing their cheeks as they looked at the world reborn.

Illustrious rotated through a brief weightless arc, and then an alarm rang and the engines cut in again, their ferocity tamed in a modest one-gee acceleration.

Martinez checked his displays. Bleskoth and Light Squadron 5 were still coming on under fierce acceleration, ready to round Pelomatan in another eight or nine hours and overtake Chenforce somewhere on the far side of Okiray.

There was a blinking light on his display, a reminder, and he looked at it to discover that missiles had destroyed Wormhole Station 1 while the squadron was thundering its way around Pelomatan. The crew hadn't evacuated, either because they didn't have a lifeboat or because they decided to remain in case Bleskroth had any stirring messages to send on to Naxas. He reported this fact to Michi.

"Excellent," she said, and yawned.

Another set of lights flashed on Martinez's display. These pointed to the fact that eight of what Severin had identified as enemy decoys, which had been preceding Chenforce on its loop around Protipanu, had just begun a course change and acceleration. They were going to cut inside the next planet, Okiray, and intercept Chenforce on the other side.

"There they are, my lady," Martinez said as he drew attention to this on the wall display. "These are the decoys that Bleskoth wants us to think are his real squadron. They're maneuvering as if to bring on an engagement on the far side of Okiray, cutting right across our course, and conveniently staying out of range until that point." More lights flashed. "Ah. And other sets of decoys are setting up to support them." Admiration for Bleskoth began to shimmer in his mind. "It's pretty clever, actually. He's got another set of decoys between us and his real squadron, and if we feel any threat in our rear it's going to be there, not his actual squadron."

It was an ingenious way of minimizing Bleskoth's tactical disadvantages. To an omnipotent observer, sitting far above Protipanu's north pole, it would look as if the Naxids were chasing the loyalists down and about to fly up their tailpipes.

From Bleskoth's perspective, however, he was flogging himself and his crew senseless in a desperate acceleration right into the muzzles of two hundred and ninety-six missile launchers. If he could keep those missile launchers firing at decoys right up until the critical moment, he had a chance of bringing off a victory.

Martinez made a note to himself that if he ever found himself defending a star system in the future, he should remember these tactics. If, that is, he could be sure there was no one like Severin to give his game away.

Hours passed. Martinez's mind buzzed with tactics, trajectories, calculations, and occasional flashes of deep paranoia, suspicion that a Naxid, just off camera, had been holding a gun on Severin for their entire conversation. Martinez kept the computer busy calculating possible courses, accelerations, and intercepts. Michi gave the order for the whole squadron to open fire with their point-defense lasers on the decoys rushing toward them from Okiray. The range was impossibly long and the targets were doing some dodging, but perhaps it relieved the squadron's weapons officers of any tension that might have built up during the long hours of waiting.

With the lasers still firing, Michi announced time for supper. Command of *Illustrious* passed to Lieutenant Kazakov as Captain Fletcher joined Martinez and Michi at her table. White-gloved formality was preserved, but the custom of not discussing Fleet business at meals was not. Michi was determined to weigh her officers' ideas.

"I'm concerned with what to do after we pass Okiray," she said. "Should we head straight for Wormhole Three, or swing around toward Olimandu and a complete circuit of the system? If we make a circuit we guarantee an engagement, but delay our exit from Protipanu by days. If we head for the wormhole, we give Bleskoth the opportunity to break off the fight, or just to pursue us at a distance."

Fletcher stirred his soup with a delicate motion of his spoon, releasing the fragrance of ginger and the fried onion that substituted for scallion. "I agree with you, my lady, that we must beat them here. A victory would be of enormous value to the government and to loyalist morale, particularly after the fall of the capital."

"How would the government find out we'd won?" Michi asked. "We'd have to send someone back to carry the news."

"A pinnace pilot could do the job," Fletcher said. He turned to Martinez with a lofty look. "Perhaps we could send someone back in *Daffodil*," he said. "Less discomfort for the pilot, and we don't lose a pinnace that way."

"I wouldn't recommend sending anyone back as long as there are still some of those hundred-odd Naxid decoys in the system," Martinez said. "We don't know how they're programmed—any boat we send back would be defenseless against them."

"Not if we make a complete circuit of the system," Fletcher continued. "We'd launch the boat after we pass Aratiri, and from there it's a straight flight to Wormhole Two."

"With all respect to Lord Captain Fletcher," he said, "I think we should go straight for the exit. Bleskoth isn't putting himself through that homicidal acceleration just to let us fly away. He *wants* a fight. It's not in his character to let us get away without one."

"His character?" Fletcher repeated. His voice was strangely dreamlike. "Are you personally acquainted with Captain Bleskoth?"

"Not personally," Martinez said, "but I've looked at his record. He's young, he's a yachting champion, he was captain of the lighumane team. He destroyed our fleet at Felarus very effectively. Everything points toward his being an aggressive, decisive commander. Just look at the way he's coming after us."

Fletcher stirred his soup again. "I ask because I *do* know Bleskoth. He was a lieutenant in the new *Quest* when I had *Swift*. He wasn't very aggressive then—he toed Renzak's line pretty severely, and toadied the squadcom dreadfully, the way those Naxids do."

Martinez saw the edifice he'd built begin a slip toward an abyss, and he made an effort to snatch it back. "How did he do at the yachting?" he asked, rather hopelessly.

"Middling, as I remember. I don't really follow the yacht scores."

An idea struck Martinez. "Who was the squadron commander?"

Fletcher tasted his soup before answering. "Fanagee."

"Ah." Martinez turned to Lady Michi. "Fanagee passed over a good many officers in order to put Bleskoth in command at Felarus. I think he must have been part of the conspiracy even then."

Michi nodded. "That's plausible." She turned to Fletcher. "How well did you know Bleskoth?"

"I dealt with Captain Reznak regularly. Bleskoth was there fairly often, dancing attendance."

When Naxids danced attendance they really *danced,* Martinez knew; their little bobs and twitches in the company of a superior would seem funny if they weren't so eerie. *Please ignore this unworthy person,* the body language seemed to say, *but while you're ignoring me, please take note of the excellent qualities of my cringing and the sincere tone of my supplication.*

Michi looked thoughtful. "We've got quite a lot of time yet before we need to make any decisions," she said. "But if Bleskoth keeps up this pursuit, I'm inclined to Captain Martinez's opinion."

Fletcher shrugged. "As you choose, my lady. But Captain Martinez's approach allows for the possibility that the enemy may escape. Mine does not."

"Very true." Michi savored her soup, clearly still considering her options. Martinez tasted his own, peeled bean curd off his teeth with his tongue, and then decided to bring forward another element of his plan.

"Whatever scheme we use, we'll be engaging on the far side of Okiray. We're both going to pass through Okiray's gravity well in order to help make the turn for the next objective. But what that means"—he called up the wall display and showed a graphic of the planet with the long, flat curves that represented potential trajectories—"is that Okiray is a choke point. However dispersed the Naxid squadron is, they'll all have very limited choices concerning where to pass the planet. So my thought is to have a lot of missiles waiting for them right here, at the choke point." He flashed a bright cursor onto the display, at the ships' closest approach.

Michi studied the display with interest. "They'll see the missiles coming. They can blanket the area with their own countermissiles."

"My lady," Martinez said, "they need *not* see the missiles coming. There are eleven decoy missiles between us and Bleskoth, all pretending to be an enemy squadron. If we launch our own missiles at them, we can provide a screen that will prevent the enemy from detecting another set of missile launches."

Fletcher looked as if he were about to object, but Martinez, who thought he knew what the objection would be, spoke on quickly. "Our missiles are going to have to burn a good long time, first to counter our own velocity and then begin an acceleration toward the intercept point. Normally that would give the enemy plenty of time to detect them, but in this case *we can hide them behind the planet.*"

There was a moment of concentrated silence. "Tricky timing," Fletcher observed. "Very tricky timing."

"Yes, my lord." Martinez's answer was heartfelt. "Very tricky timing indeed."

Fletcher pursed his lips and looked reflective. Michi narrowed her eyes in thought.

"Perhaps we need to flesh out this plan with a little more detail," she said.

Two hours later, with the crew strapped in after their meals, the warning for zero gravity blasted out, and acceleration ceased. Chenforce rotated, and began a constant one-gravity deceleration in place of the acceleration they'd been maintaining to this point.

Tricky timing indeed . . . Martinez wanted to make sure all the elements in the tactical display, all the graphics with their little arrows of velocity and direction, were going to be pointed in the right direction at the right time.

Chenforce also fired a barrage of sixteen missiles toward the decoys coming toward them from Okiray. The squadron's laser batteries hadn't manage to hit a one of them, and Martinez wanted the Naxids to think that Chenforce's deceleration was to gain a little time to study the oncoming force and to prepare to receive them in the event they turned out to be warships.

After that, Michi stood the crew down from action stations and resumed normal rotation of watches. It would be hours yet before the missiles reached their targets.

Martinez remained in his place, however, to see what happened when Bleskoth's force detected the missile launch. The Naxids broke off their heavy acceleration and reduced to half a gee while they confirmed whether or not the missiles had been fired at them personally, or at something else. Precisely twelve minutes later, the acceleration resumed.

The telling discovery, though, was that all other Naxid elements behaved in exactly the same way. When the light from the missile flares reached them they decelerated abruptly, waited exactly twelve minutes, and then resumed their previous behavior.

Bleskoth had programmed them cleverly. If Severin hadn't warned Martinez which of the Naxid formations were the actual warships, Martinez would have been hard-pressed to work out the answer for himself.

Martinez left the Flag Officer Station for his cabin, where Alikhan helped him out of his vac suit and then poured his nightly cup of cocoa.

"There's a good feeling in the ship, my lord," Alikhan reported. "The crew are convinced we're going to win."

"I'll try not to disappoint them," Martinez said.

Alikhan bowed slightly. "I'm sure you won't, my lord."

Martinez showered off the polyamide scent of his suit seals, then got into bed for what turned out to be a lengthy struggle between sleep and his own imagination, each making ingenious sallies, excursions, and flanking attacks to thwart the other. Very little was resolved in those hours, except that Martinez realized that his goals had changed.

He wasn't simply going to win the battle. He'd known he could beat the Naxids for some time.

The trick was to beat Bleskoth without compromising Michi Chen's mission. And that meant that Chenforce could take no hits, lose no ships, suffer no casualties.

At Hone-bar he had managed exactly that, but at Hone-bar he had an entire friendly squadron to produce, like a magician, from beneath his cloak. Here he had no such advantage.

In the darkness of his cabin, he swore he would produce such a victory.

And then, turning on the lights and lighting the tactical screen, he began to make the victory real.

In five hours the oncoming Naxid decoys, unable to defend themselves except by acceleration and weaving, were destroyed by twelve of Chenforce's sixteen missiles. The remainder continued to accelerate, taking separate, meandering courses to their destination, Wormhole Station 3. The relay station needed to be destroyed before Martinez unveiled his tactics around Okiray.

Martinez watched the decoys destroyed on the ceiling display above his bed. Afterward, reasonably content, he managed a few hours' sleep.

After breakfast the Naxid squadron, preceded by the group of eleven decoys, made a screaming turn around Pelomatan and fell into the wake of Chenforce. They dropped their acceleration to two gravities while they considered the tactical implications for the loyalists' deceleration, then increased to eight gravities, which would leave them merely miserable instead of unconscious, crippled, or dead.

Very tricky timing . . .

A quiet, eerie normality continued for the rest of the day. The crew weren't called to action stations, not even when another missile barrage was fired at yet another group of decoys rounding Okiray. The Naxids paid more attention to the missile firings than Chenforce did: once again every enemy ship and decoy cut its acceleration for twelve minutes as the flares from the missiles reached them.

Aboard *Illustrious* officers and enlisted were all employed as the service required, the normal cleaning and polishing and routine maintenance, and Captain Fletcher mustered the divisions responsible for suit-and-seal maintenance and for mechanical repair, and gave their workrooms a thorough inspection, awarding the usual demerits for untidiness and grime.

The senior petty officers, somewhat more practical, devoted extra time to inspection and maintenance of the powerful damage-control robots, which, remotely controlled by operators in armored crew compartments, would effect repairs in the event *Illustrious* was damaged by enemy action. Martinez quietly had a few words with the division chiefs, and they gladly accepted Alikhan, Espinosa, and Ayutano as auxiliaries within their commands.

Martinez figured he wouldn't be needing them to uphold his dignity in an actual battle.

He found himself wandering the ship, with no goal in mind other than a reluctance to stay in any one place for very long. He had never been good at waiting, and the wandering helped keep him from checking the figures on his plan over and over again.

The crew, he found, were remarkably quiet: it was as if they were *listening,* going about their duties but extruding invisible antennae that strained the aether for information from the officers, from each other, from the vacuum beyond the cruiser's hull. Even after the captain ordered the spirit locker opened and the crew served a ration of liquor with their supper, the good cheer was subdued and the drinking thoughtful.

Walking in his stiff-collared dress tunic to the squadcom's suite, Martinez encountered Chandra Prasad, dressed with equal formality, on her way to a private supper with the captain. She braced at the salute, but then a broad smile broke out on her face and her stiff posture softened.

"Three years ago," she said, "who'd have guessed?"

He looked at her. Apparently they were going to have the conversation that he had been doing his best to avoid.

The moment awkward, he thought.

Chandra shook her head, a disbelieving smile spreading across her face. "Golden Orb," she said. "Hero of the empire. Marriage to the Chen heir . . ." Amusement flashed in her eyes. "The captain thinks you're a freak of nature, you know that?"

The feeling's mutual, then, Martinez thought.

"It's a violation of Fletcher's aesthetic to hear clever ideas spoken in your accent," Chandra said. Then, as annoyance raced along his nerves, she reached out and patted his arm. "But he *does* believe you're clever. He thinks it's a shame you weren't born to the right family."

"He should know the right family," Martinez said, "if anyone should."

Chandra offered a cynical smile. She spread her hands and glanced down at herself. "And look at me. Nothing's changed. Still scraping along looking for a patron."

You haven't found one? Martinez wondered. What was Fletcher, then?

She looked at him. "There wouldn't be a Chen to spare, would there?"

"Lady Michi has a boy at school, but you'd have to wait." He tried to make a joke out of it, but there wasn't any laughter in Chandra's dark eyes.

"Really, Gareth," she said. "I'm desperate. I could use some help."

"I can't promote you, Chandra," Martinez said. "Not till I get flag rank, and I don't think that's going to happen anytime soon."

"But you're going to get command of a ship before long. And that ship will need a first lieutenant. And if you do something brilliant with your ship, the way you do, your premiere's going to get a promotion." She folded her arms and gave him a searching look. "I'm putting my money on you, Gareth. You always seem to come out on top."

Frantic alarm bounded like a rubber ball along the inside of Martinez's skull. He really didn't want Chandra as a first lieutenant. It wasn't that he minded her ambition, but he'd want a premiere less tumultuous, and besides he didn't want her close to him. Yet he felt sympathy for her position—eight months ago, he'd been in the same situation, a provincial officer with no patronage and scant chance for promotion.

"I'll see what I can do," he said. "But look—we're going to beat the Naxids here. And that will mean notice for everybody on the flagship."

Disdain curled her lip. "It'll mean notice for *you*. And for Chen, and the captain, and promotion for Kazakov—and isn't she smug about it, the bitch!" She shook her head. "There isn't going to be much notice left over for the little provincial who's been waiting for seven years for her next step."

Martinez found whatever sympathy he'd retained oozing away. "There's nothing I can do now," he said. "I'll see what I can do"—he gave a hopeless shrug—"when circumstances change."

"I know you will." She put a hand on his arm again, then leaned forward to softly kiss his cheek. Her scent whirled in his senses. "I'm counting on you, Gareth."

She turned from Martinez and went to her meeting with the captain. His head spun left and right, like that of a frantic puppet, until he made certain that the kiss had been unobserved.

This is going to be trouble, he thought.

Supper with the squadcom was surprisingly relaxed. He presented the latest version of his plan, and received her approval.

"I'm going to head for the wormhole gate, by the way," she said. "I agree with your analysis of Bleskoth's character."

Martinez felt a little tug of pleasure somewhere in his mind. "Have you told Lord Captain Fletcher?" he asked.

"I will in the morning."

That night he might have managed a few hours' sleep. He was up well before his usual time, walking about the ship, nodding to any crew he encountered but not speaking. He tried to make the nods brisk and confident. He hoped the thought, *We're going to thrash the enemy* was shining out of his eyes.

When he found himself nodding, brisk and confident, to the same crewman for the third time, he realized how absurd was this behavior and he returned to his cabin. Silence grew around him as he sat at his desk. In the semidarkness the faces of the winged children seemed unusually grave.

He looked down at the surface of the desk and saw Terza, the image he'd installed there on his arrival, and the sight reminded him that he hadn't written her since leaving Seizho. He picked up a stylus and began.

In a few hours we're going into battle. You can spare yourself any suspense in regard to the outcome, because you won't be receiving this unless we win.

And then the words stalled. After that opening sentence, his usual queries about her health and the memories of his boyhood on Laredo were going to seem banal. Going into mortal action alongside thousands of comrades seemed to call for some degree of profundity and introspection.

The problem was that introspection was not his strong point, and Martinez knew it.

He began by describing the silence of the ship, the way the vibration and rumble of the engines seemed to fade into white noise . . . how the crew were dutiful but quiet, waiting and watching . . . how he thought the battle would go well, and that he was hoping to win it without Chenforce taking any casualties.

I was called 'clever' the other day, he wrote. *It's a word people use to describe a kind of intelligence of which they do not entirely approve, and I have been called clever before. I am inclined to resent it, but suppose I should take whatever compliments come my way. At least they don't call me stupid.*

Martinez looked at the lines and thought that, before he sent the words onward, he should find out whether it was Michi or the captain who censored his correspondence.

His stylus hovered over his desk as he wondered what to

write next. *An old lover kissed me yesterday, but I didn't want her.*

Not the most reassuring of sentiments. His stylus didn't move.

He looked at Terza's picture, and he tried to remember her voice, the way she moved. Only vague memories came to him. The time they'd spent together seemed like a half-remembered dream.

Without invitation, pictures of Sula came to his mind. He remembered the flash of her emerald eyes, the silken weight of her golden hair on his palm, the taste of her flesh on his lips. It was as if he could reach out and touch her.

The scent of Sandama Twilight stung his sinus. He felt the weight and thrust and agony of a long steel sword as it drove through his heart.

An old lover kissed me yesterday, he thought, *but she was the wrong old lover.*

The pain will go, he told himself.

I delight in your letters, he wrote, *but send a little video with your next message, so that I can see what you look like now.*

And then he signed, *Love, Gareth.*

He didn't send the letter on to whoever would censor it, but instead saved it in memory, and then blanked the desktop.

He secured the stylus in its gravity-proof holder and looked up to see winged children leering at him from the walls.

Three hours before *Illustrious*'s closest approach to Okiray, Lady Michi gave a dinner for the cruiser's officers. Alcohol was not served. Chandra Prasad was not present, being officer of the watch and in command of the ship. Martinez wondered whether Fletcher had made special provision for that.

Michi was an accomplished hostess, making certain to include everyone, even the most junior, in the conversation.

Captain Lord Gomberg Fletcher, reflected multiple times in the mirror-bright asteroid material that decorated the walls, presented a series of magnificent pictures with his silver hair and patrician manner, so elegant and imposing that he seemed almost to be a host rather than a guest. Martinez, his eye on his sleeve chronometer, drank much coffee, ate whatever was put in front of him without tasting it, and said little.

At the conclusion of the dinner, Michi rose to offer a toast, raising her crystal glass of water. "To victory," she said.

"Victory!" they all chanted, and for the first time that day Martinez felt his heart surge. Tongues of flame seemed to flicker on his skin. He was going to win this battle, and he was going to make the victory total.

"Action stations, my lords," Michi said. "Now, if you please."

Martinez returned to his quarters, took off his dress uniform, and used the toilet thoroughly before donning his vac suit. Helmet under his arm, he marched to the Flag Officer Station, encountering other crew on their way to their places. As they braced to let him pass he saw smiles on their faces, nods of greeting. Their absolute confidence buoyed him. He began to feel the pulse of victory surge through his veins.

Michi had not yet arrived at her station. Martinez made a point of circling the room and shaking the hands of Coen and Li and Franz, the warrant officer who monitored the status of the ship. Lady Michi arrived, saw what Martinez was doing, and made the rounds herself.

"Luck," she said, clasping Martinez's hand.

He looked at the brown eyes beneath the straight bangs, and smiled. "And to you, my lady."

He webbed himself into his couch and the displays brightened around him. Forty-six minutes till their closest approach to Okiray, and six minutes till the next missiles were launched. All the squadron had already received their orders, and Martinez restrained his impulse to contact all the ships and confirm.

The six minutes ticked slowly by, and then two missiles leaped from each ship in Chenforce, and after igniting antimatter engines hurled themselves toward the eleven decoys that flew between the squadron and Bleskoth's warships.

Martinez hunched forward and stared at the displays as anticipation hummed in his nerves. He was very interested to know if Bleskoth would behave as he had twice before, cutting his acceleration for twelve minutes whenever Chenforce fired missiles. Martinez thought that Bleskoth didn't have any choice—his decoys were all programmed with that twelve-minute pause, and if he didn't want to give himself away he'd have to follow suit.

Which was exactly what happened. Martinez took a deep, relieved breath. Bleskoth had just saved him the burden of recalculating a lot of trajectories at the last minute.

The ship rotated and the engines began the Okiray burn. Martinez tensed and growled and fought for breath, blackness closing in on his vision as he fought a losing war against the growing force of gravity. Eventually he passed out, and so missed the moment when the squadron's tactical computers launched a hundred and twenty-eight missiles, all to be guided by a pair of cadets in pinnaces who—unconscious, like everyone else—were launched into space after them.

Gravity eventually ebbed, and Martinez gasped for air and clawed for his displays, trying to bring them close to his dimmed vision. Failing, he lunged forward against the reluctant webbing and slammed the rim of his helmet on the display, staring unblinkingly until the bright icons of the missiles flared into being at the darkened center of his vision. They were on their way, and were keeping the mass of the planet between themselves and the advancing enemy. Triumph blazed in his mind as Martinez sagged back into his seat.

Minutes later, the sixteen missiles fired at the eleven decoys, located most of their targets, and created a brilliantly hot screen of expanding, overlapping plasma spheres between Bleskoth and Okiray, preventing the enemy commander from seeing the last missile launch.

Bleskoth had no way of seeing the doom that was waiting for him in the planet's shadow.

"All ships, increase deceleration to three gravities at 18:14:01," Martinez signaled the squadron.

"*Imperious* acknowledges," Coen reported. "*Illustrious* acknowledges. *Challenger* acknowledges . . . all ships acknowledge, my lady."

The force of the engines punched Martinez back into his couch. Chenforce was no longer content to wait for the Naxid pursuit: now they would increase the rate at which the two forces converged.

Minutes ticked by. The nearest Naxid decoys maneuvered like real squadrons, adjusting their velocities to that of Chenforce. Other decoys, making no pretense that they were warships, came screaming at inhuman accelerations from remote corners of the system, and would be used as weapons. Bleskoth's squadron punched through the cooling plasma screen and for the first time saw that the loyalists were headed for Wormhole 3, not a circuit of the system, and that Chenforce was inviting a fight.

The Naxid force dropped its acceleration while it considered its options. No doubt Bleskoth wanted to clear his head and think. Martinez gave a shout of pure rage while he beamed course and speed changes to the missiles approaching Okiray, to keep them hidden from Bleskoth's radars.

When the Naxids' engines flared again, Martinez was ready. Another set of course changes were sent to the missiles, and then Martinez looked up at Lady Michi.

"Permission to starburst, my lady?" he asked.

She nodded. "Permission granted, lord captain."

"All ships," Martinez sent, "Starburst Pattern One. Execute at 18:22:01."

Coen chanted off acknowledgments from the other captains. Acceleration abruptly ceased and sent Martinez's stomach lurching unexpectedly into his throat. *Illustrious* reoriented, Martinez's cage swinging gently with the movement, and then the acceleration resumed and his couch crashed violently in a direction that was suddenly "down." The elements of Chenforce began to separate, moving in a seemingly random pattern determined by the bit of chaotic mathematics that Caroline Sula had built into the new Fleet maneuvers, gliding along the convex hull of a dynamical system.

Bleskoth's squadron reoriented for its burn past Okiray. No matter what they saw Chenforce do, it was too late for them to change their intended course now.

"All ships," Martinez sent, "fire by salvo."

"*Illustrious* acknowledges. *Challenger* acknowledges . . ."

By the time a hundred and sixty missiles and another pair of pinnace pilots leaped into space and began their burn for the enemy, all Naxids were unconscious from the high gravities they were pulling on their approach to Okiray. They would have to deal with the salvo after they woke up.

And if Martinez was lucky, they wouldn't wake up at all.

The rebel Light Squadron 5 hurled itself into Okiray's gravity well. And the hundred and twenty-eight missiles that had been lurking in the planet's shadow flashed forward to intercept them.

On his displays Martinez saw little but a sudden roil of angry antimatter energy, a concentrated burst of gamma rays and energetic neutrons that poured from the heart of the expanding plasma. It was clear that the Naxids' automated laser defense systems had caught a number of the attacking missiles, and that these had probably blown up other missiles arrowing to the same targets. But surely, Martinez insisted to himself, some must have got through.

There was a strange crunching noise in Martinez's ears as he searched the displays for any sign of the enemy. At some point he realized that the sound was the grinding of his own teeth. He relaxed his jaw muscles through a deliberate effort.

Seconds passed, and then his heart sank as he saw ships flying out of the expanding, cooling plasma cloud. *Two,* he counted, *three, seven.* No more.

Ten had flown in. His ambush had accounted for almost a third of the Naxid strength.

It should have been more, he thought in a sudden burst of passion, and then his head snapped up at the sound of Michi Chen's voice.

"All ships," she said, "fire by salvo." Coen at the comm station transmitted the order to the other ships.

Another hundred and sixty missiles launched, their precise paths guided by the individual ships' weapons officers. Martinez felt a surge against his spine as *Illustrious* made a course shift, all in accordance with Starburst Pattern One.

One of the Naxid ships, he saw, was on a diverging course from the others. Its engines were no longer firing. But he saw missile flares appear near the single ship, and knew it was still in the fight.

The other six had all fallen into *Illustrious*'s wake. Martinez had been right. Bleskoth had planned all along to hang on to Chenforce's tail until one side or another was beaten.

The six Naxid ships ceased acceleration. Missiles leaped off their rails. Then the warships rotated and began a fierce deceleration burn, trying to slow the rate at which they were overtaking Chenforce. They knew they were in trouble.

Martinez felt a wild grin distorting his features. It was all working brilliantly.

"Another salvo," said Michi Chen.

The enemy spat out missiles at a fantastic rate, many intended as countermissiles, the rest flying to the attack. The

Naxid decoys, receiving new orders, began to home in on targets. Individual ships' captains and weapons officers ordered countermissile fire.

Martinez watched it all, surprised by the comparative silence and order of the Flag Officer Station. In his previous battles he'd been in Command, a hive of energy as sensor operators called out their findings, signals traffic flashed back and forth, weapons officers fired missiles and worked out their plots, the officer at the engine controls repeated course and acceleration orders, and he himself shouted his own commands into the din.

Here there was very little sound, only the rumble of the engines, Lady Michi's occasional orders, and the signals lieutenants calling out other ships' acknowledgments. Now that the battle was fully joined, Martinez was little more than an observer. He could offer advice to Lady Michi, but she seemed to be doing fine on her own.

Throwing out too many missiles for his taste, but in general doing well.

Enemy lasers began to rip into the oncoming missile salvo. Expanding plasma shells brightened the darkness. Soon the Naxids vanished from the displays, their very existence concealed behind the plasma screen.

But the plasma bursts were closer to the enemy than they were to Chenforce, and the Naxids were racing toward the plasma screens that baffled and confused their sensors, while the loyalists were increasing their distance. Martinez felt triumph hum in his veins at the thought of the screen moving closer and closer to the enemy until it enveloped them, leaving them prey to missiles they couldn't even see.

Chenforce's own point-defense lasers began their fire at oncoming enemy missiles, joined shortly thereafter by the bright lances of the antiproton beams mounted on the heavy cruisers. The mutually supporting fire wove patterns through the darkness like swords clashing in the night, impaling oncoming missiles with high-energy fire. Plasma flares dotted the night. A blazing curtain seemed to have been flung across half the universe.

Martinez shifted to a virtual display so that he could better study the developing situation, and found, as the system blossomed in his skull, that he now seemed to be sailing in serene silence amid a hellish scene of unspeakable violence. He shifted his perspective so that he seemed to be closer to the enemy, just in front of the advancing plasma screen. He had moved back in time as well, the time it took for light from this point to reach *Illustrious*'s sensors. Missiles leaped out of the screen on wild, frenetic dodging paths. Lasers quested after them. A pillar of light blazed off Martinez's right shoulder as several incoming missiles were hit at once, a line of fury pointing like a long arm toward the frigate *Beacon*. Martinez realized that he—or rather his position in the virtual display—was about to be engulfed by blazing plasma and his view of the action turned to electromagnetic hash. He pulled back to zoom across space, and up time's axis, in pursuit of Chenforce.

"Fire by salvo," said a woman's voice.

The flashes were continuous now, a curtain of sparks winking against the cooler background of expanding plasma. Against the pulsing background lights it was difficult to perceive one area as different from any other, and so it took him a few moments to see the looping coil of missiles that were again in pursuit of *Beacon,* all jumping out of the long arm of cooling plasma that he had noted earlier. It took another moment or two for Martinez to perceive that *Beacon* was in genuine danger.

His pulse thundered suddenly in his ears. Martinez banished the virtual display with an angry wave of his hand and jabbed with his thumb the bright square on his display labeled *transmit, all ships*.

"All ships: concentrate defensive fire to aid *Beacon*! *Beacon* is the subject of a focused attack!"

No sooner had defensive weapons begun to weave a pattern of protective energies near the frigate than *Beacon*'s own lasers struck an attacking missile a slightly off-center blow that sent it tumbling, spilling out a spray of antimatter that flung itself into space like beach sand being flung from the hand of a child. The result was a sheet of blazing particles drawn across the night, a sheet that completely obscured a pack of attacking missiles from the ships that were trying to aid the frigate.

Beacon was on its own, and its trained Daimong crew destroyed four missiles before the fifth and sixth engulfed the frigate within their fireball. Martinez gave a roar of pure rage and smashed his couch arms with both fists. *"No!"* he shouted, then chanted, "damn-damn-damn" before realizing he was still transmitting to all ships, and angrily punched at the display to give himself a moment of private, scorching fury.

He had promised himself a one-sided victory like Honebar, where the loyalist forces suffered no casualties, and now he had broken that promise. The fact that he had not spoken the promise aloud in the presence of another person made no difference: the most important promises are those one makes to oneself. He wanted to seize Bleskoth by the throat and shriek, *You made me break my word!*

It was the absence of *Beacon* within the squadron's defensive fire pattern that caused the next casualty. Through the gap came one of the Naxid decoy missiles, now turned to an attacker with an overlarge radar signature. In spite of its being a seemingly easy target the missile led a charmed life, darting and rolling by pure chance behind plasma screens created by less lucky attackers.

Martinez wasn't aware of the intruder until it got perilously close to *Celestial,* when it was destroyed by the light cruiser's concentrated defensive fire at the last instant. Hard radiation slammed the ship, and the superheated fireball flashed toward its hull. Martinez shrieked out another long, frustrated string of *damns* as the cruiser disappeared into the burning plasm, and he turned his attention to the enemy with thoughts of revenge on his mind.

It was only then that a new realization dawned, that there seemed to be many fewer missiles in the display. The defensive batteries were picking the attackers off: no friendly ship was under immediate threat.

No new aggressor missiles had flown out of the plasm screen in the last couple minutes. *Why have they stopped firing?* he wondered, and then the answer dawned.

"My lady"—Martinez began, and then remembered he'd shut down his comm line. He called up the private channel between himself and the squadcom. "My lady," he said after he made the connection, "I think the fight's over. We've won. They're all dead."

His words coincided with one of the random course changes dictated by Starburst Pattern One, and as the engines cut and the cruiser rotated, Michi and Martinez stared at one another in the sudden weightlessness, floating in their cages, eyes locked, amid the sudden silence.

"Congratulations, my lady," Martinez said. "It's a victory."

Lady Michi held his gaze for a moment, and then touched her transmit button. "All ships," she said. "Cease offensive fire."

Martinez went to the virtual view, and the first thing he saw was *Celestial* sailing out of the cooling plasma sphere, its engines still a brilliance in the night. A silent cheer rose in Martinez's throat. The cruiser hasn't been destroyed after all, and the propulsion systems, at least, still worked.

"Comm: message to *Celestial*," Michi said. "Ask Captain Eldey for a status report."

Martinez turned his attention to the Naxids. Their ships should be flying out of the cooling plasma cloud at any second.

The Naxid squadron didn't come. There was one Naxid ship only, the cripple that had lost its engines on the approach to Okiray and was flying on a different trajectory from the rest. All the other Naxids had been wiped out, and Chenforce hadn't even noticed when it happened.

The single surviving Naxid ship wasn't capable of maneuver and wasn't firing missiles—probably it had used them all up, except perhaps for a handful to be used defensively. It might well drift on forever into the cold gulf between the stars, like Taggart and the *Verity*.

A suitable punishment, Martinez thought in his anger. Let them starve to death.

"All remaining missiles," Lady Michi said, "target on that lone ship."

From her tone Martinez knew she, too, was in the mood for vengeance, but that she thought starvation too good for the Naxids. Orders pulsed out to the remaining missiles from the last salvo, and these reoriented and began a furious burn for the sole remaining enemy.

The Naxids had to have known the fate that awaited them. Apparently they had no missiles, or at any rate no missile launchers that worked. Their point-defense lasers flashed out and the missiles began to die. Michi simply fired more. The lone survivors of Light Squadron 5 died a good half-hour after their comrades, after fighting with a bravery and skill that no other Naxid would ever see or celebrate.

Martinez watched the ship die without finding in himself the sympathy he'd displayed for the crews of the wormhole stations. The enemy warship was nearly as helpless as the relay stations, but it had helped kill a lot of his comrades, and he watched its death agonies with bitter satisfaction.

"All ships reduce deceleration to one-half gravity," Michi ordered. "Prepare to retrieve pinnaces and remaining missiles."

"Message from *Celestial,* my lady, by radio," reported Coen. "Lieutenant Gorath reporting." *Celestial* had remained silent since Michi's initial query, though since the cruiser had continued to maneuver according to the dictates of Starburst Pattern One, it had been clear that there were survivors and that there would probably be communication as soon as the means were restored.

"Lieutenant Gorath believes that four forward compartments are breached," Coen reported, "and that Captain Eldey and everyone in Command is dead. The ship is maneuverable. Lost sensors are being replaced. Communication and point-defense lasers non-responsive. One missile battery is believed destroyed, but it's too hot to go out there right now to make certain."

"Signal Lieutenant Gorath—Well done," Michi said. "Tell her we stand ready to provide any assistance she may require." She turned to Martinez. "Captain Martinez, please tell all ships to make a complete visual sensor survey of *Celestial* and send the results to Lieutenant Gorath."

"Yes, my lady." Locked in Auxiliary Command, the Torminel officer had nothing but remote sensors to inform her of the state of her ship, and most of the sensors had probably been knocked out. Pictures would undoubtedly help.

The squadron ceased deceleration, rotated, and began acceleration again toward Protipanu Wormhole Three, still nearly five days away, and then the crew stood down from action stations. The few surviving missiles were retrieved by the ships that had fired them. Of the fourteen pinnace pilots that had been shot into space to shepherd missiles toward the foe, eight weathered the battle, one of them *Beacon*'s sole survivor. These returned to their ships, all save for the deeply traumatized Daimong cadet who was brought aboard the flagship to replace a pilot who had been killed. The cadets' berth would smell less sweetly, but Martinez suspected the cadets would not complain. They would know how easily *Illustrious* itself could have been reduced to radioactive dust cooling in the solar wind.

Martinez knew he would not enjoy seeing the *Beacon* cadet's pale, startled face, though not on aesthetic or olfactory grounds. The Daimong would be a reminder of his own failure to protect the *Beacon* and fulfill his promise to himself of another victory without casualties.

Martinez left the Flag Officer Station, returned the vac suit to its storage closet in his quarters, showered, and dressed. The comm chimed with an invitation to dine with the captain, and he accepted.

In his head he kept seeing the arm of fire reach for *Beacon*. If he had been able to keep his mind properly focused on its significance he would been able to foresee the missiles that would have raced out of it, and had the squadron's defensive fire ready to concentrate in that area.

Bleskoth, you bastard, he thought. The Naxids' destruction of the *Beacon* was a personal affront. It was a deliberate attack on the value that Martinez placed on the quality of his own mind.

There was a soft chime from Martinez's comm, and a light flashed on the display. It was a reminder he'd set for himself, and normally he would remember what it was, but now he was too tired for the recollection to come into his mind. He ordered the comm to deliver its message and was told that Wormhole Station 3 should at this moment have been destroyed, though it would take ten hours for the light from the explosion to reach *Illustrious* and confirm the kill.

The wormhole station had been destroyed hours before any of the light from the battle would have reached it. No observer would be able to send the results of the combat on to Naxas or to the Naxid fleet. They would have to wait for Chenforce to pop out of the other side of the wormhole at Mazdan, and even then they wouldn't know *how* Bleskoth's squadron had been destroyed.

With two of their squadrons annihilated, here and at Hone-bar, maybe the Naxids would start to suspect that the loyalists had developed a new superweapon that could stamp out large forces at a single go. Martinez tried to console himself with the grim hope that the Naxids would spend a lot of time and money trying to figure out just what the weapon was.

Alikhan arrived, full of praise for the behavior and skill of *Illustrious*'s petty officers and weaponers, then he helped Martinez change into full dress for the captain's supper. At Fletcher's table Martinez was placed between Michi and Chandra Prasad. Relief and victory made the talk loud and joyous, a joy fueled by wine and toasts offered by the officers. When it came time for Martinez to raise his glass, he offered briefly, "To our comrades on the *Beacon*," and for a moment the cheer at the captain's table ebbed.

For the rest of the supper he remained silent unless spoken to, and without difficulty ignored the press of Chandra's leg against his own.

After the meal, Martinez returned to his room and tossed each item of clothing to Alikhan as he removed it. "The ship's doctor brought something for you, my lord," Alikhan said, and indicated a packet on the tabletop.

Martinez opened the packet and rolled a thick capsule into his hand, a sleepsniff. "Why did the doctor bring this?" he asked. "I didn't tell him to—"

"He brought it on the squadcom's orders, my lord," Alikhan said. "She wants you to get a good night's sleep. She told me I'm not to disturb you in the morning until you call for me."

Martinez looked at the object in his hand.

"You and Lady Michi, I think you're a good team," Alikhan said.

Without words, Martinez raised the sleepsniff in his two hands and broke the capsule under his nose. The bitter taste of the drug coated the back of his throat as he inhaled.

"You've been very busy these last days, my lord," Alikhan said as he collected the broken capsule and dropped it in the cabin's waste slot. "I'll bet you haven't even taken a look at the Maw."

"The Maw?" Martinez repeated dumbly. He could already feel the drug stealing over his mind.

"I've always found it an impressive sight," Alikhan said. "I'm sure you remember from when *Corona* was in the system." He turned on the video over Martinez's bed and switched the overhead tactical display to the feed from the cruiser's outside cameras. "There we are, my lord. Sleep well."

"Thank you," Martinez said. He slid into his bed and Alikhan turned off the room lights as he made his way out.

Martinez stared up at the Maw, the ruddy luminous circle of supernova ejecta that dominated Protipanu's sky. The picture feed was fantastically detailed, and he could make out details of the Maw's architecture, luminescent swirls, mysterious dark clouds, smoky pillars.

He closed his eyes, and saw the faint glow of the red ring on the insides of his eyelids.

Much better, he thought, than seeing *Beacon* die all night, over and over.

It was his last thought for many hours.

With the red light of the Maw leaking through the view port, Lieutenant Shushanik Severin sat in the hushed silence of the control room and watched the Naxid squadron destroyed in ripples of distant fire. Knowing approximately when the battle was about to take place, he had brought his crew and his lifeboat back to the Protipanu system, drifting through the wormhole with engines dead and every passive sensor combing the darkness for the signs of combat.

When he'd left Protipanu three days earlier he'd steered straight for the Seizho wormhole station. The station had been abandoned, but it was still full of supplies, and for two days his crew had luxuriated in warm beds, unlimited hot showers, shaved chins, and giant meals.

His superiors on Seizho, Severin suspected, didn't quite

know what to do with him. He had disobeyed orders when he moved the wormhole, and so they would be justified in instituting disciplinary action; but on the other hand his action had prevented the system from being attacked by a Naxid squadron, and he had returned to Seizho with a load of intelligence and a field promotion from no less than Squadron Commander Chen. They decided, apparently, to follow Lady Michi's lead, and sent congratulations and a series of commendations. Severin was to be awarded the Explorer's Medal, and his crew the Award of Righteous Conduct.

Other news was less encouraging. The Naxids had taken Zanshaa.

His crew was surprised that, with the fall of the capital, the war would actually continue, but as soon as Severin heard the news he realized at once what Chenforce was hoping to accomplish: a massive raid into the enemy heartland while the Naxids were pinned down defending the capital. Severin approved. The plan had a devious flair that he found very much to his taste.

Returning to Protipanu had been his own idea. He hadn't asked permission, merely informed Seizho that he was going. He would be on the other side of the wormhole before any objections reached him.

Now, as the sensors showed him ten enemy ships vaporized and seven loyalist survivors burning for Wormhole 3, Severin was pleased that he'd made the decision. He could inform the empire of another loyalist victory, ten enemy ships destroyed at the cost of a single warship. It might not reverse the blow that was suffered by the loss of Zanshaa, but it might help to boost the morale of the population and give any defectors second thoughts.

And Chenforce had used some interesting tactics to accomplish its victory. Severin was going to have to think about those.

Severin made certain that the lifeboat's computers had

successfully saved and duplicated the recordings of the battle, and then ordered the maneuvering jets to turn the lifeboat's bow toward the wormhole, then the engine startup countdown resumed.

While he waited for the engine to fire he sent a message to the loyalist squadron. Knowing there were no longer any Naxids in the system to overhear, he used radio and sent his message in the clear.

"This is Lieutenant Severin to Squadron Commander Chen," he said into the camera, and allowed a grin to break out on his face. "Congratulations on your sensational victory!" he said. "I'm in the system temporarily as an observer, and as soon as I return to Seizho, I'll transmit a full record to the authorities." He paused, his grin fading, and then added, "I hope you'll forgive my presumption in mentioning this, my lady, but I suggest that you double check the location of Wormhole Three as you approach. The Naxids may have moved it, the same way I moved Wormhole One.

"I'll have left the system by the time this message reaches you. My best wishes for the success of your mission go with you. Message ends."

The message was sent flying into the darkness just as the engine fired, and Severin instinctively raised a hand to keep his face from being splashed by a rain of cold water. There was no splash of water: the condensation had evaporated days ago.

Severin laughed. Life wasn't simply good, it was interesting. And *interesting* was the best thing of all.

SIXTEEN

Ten days after the fall of the ring, the first message came to Zanshaa from the Naxids. Sula stepped over the empty iarogüt bottles in the hall and entered the backup apartment at Riverside to find Spence and Macnamara watching the wall video.

"It's been going on for most of the last hour," Macnamara said. "The Naxids are changing the administration of Zanshaa."

The video showed a Daimong announcer, who was reading the same announcement over and over. The choice of a Daimong was a good one, Sula thought—that fixed face couldn't show emotion, and if there were emotion in the voice, only other Daimong would detect it.

"Lady Kushdai, Governor of Zanshaa under the Committee to Save the Praxis, has given the following orders," the Daimong said. "A series of appointments are now commanded. Lord Akthan is appointed vice-governor, and will proceed at once to take possession of the Lord Senior's quarters, and to form a government for Zanshaa until Lady Kushdai can take up her post in person. Lord Akthan will have full powers to appoint and dismiss officials. Lady Ix Jagirin is appointed to command the Interior Ministry. Lord Ummir is appointed Minister of Police. Lady Kulukraf is appointed head of the Ministry of Right and Dominion, with power to command all Fleet resources in the Zanshaa system . . ."

"Now we know the conspirators on the planet," Macnamara said grimly. His hands flexed as if it were closing on a Naxid windpipe. "These are the traitors we've had among us all along."

Sula considered this. "Not necessarily," she said slowly. "These are all prominent Naxids who have been in the civil service for years. Some of them had high office before the rebellion, but were dismissed since. Lady Kushdai might have just appointed people she thought could keep things going until she arrived."

Kushdai had probably thought she was going to come down from the ring and simply take over, Sula thought. The fact that the ring had been destroyed and the takeover delayed had been transmitted to Magaria, and the decision to create an interim administration transmitted the other way.

"I think we should kill them before they can organize protection for themselves," Macnamara said.

"We'll see what Blanche says about it," Sula said. Even if those called to their posts were innocent of any conspiracy against the government, a few of them probably *should* be gunned down, just to make any others think twice.

The Daimong went on with his announcement. "The following individuals are to turn themselves in to the police, or face arrest. Former Governor Pahn-ko. Former Lord Commissioner of Police Lord Jazarak . . ."

Suspense hummed in Sula's nerves as the names continued, and then the list came to an end and Sula's name had not been mentioned. Neither had Lieutenant Captain Hong, or anyone in Group Blanche.

All records of the stay-behind groups, along with all *other* Fleet records, had allegedly been erased from the computers at the Commandery, the space they'd taken in storage turned into strings of random numbers. Any official trail that led to Action Group Blanche was supposed to have left the planet when the Commandery was evacuated.

It seemed as if Sula and her comrades, for the moment, were safe.

* * *

"The lord governor left the High City successfully, before the Naxids could move against him, and is now in the hidden seat of his administration. We still have a legitimate government on Zanshaa. The chain of command still functions."

As Hong spoke, his servant Ellroy still circulated among the guests with refreshments, but in somewhat more cramped circumstances. When the Naxids were called to power by the authority of the fleet that now occupied the system, Hong had left his conspicuous life and quietly moved to a smaller apartment under his primary backup identification.

He also complained about no longer being able to visit his clubs. Sula was relieved to know Hong was taking at least a few precautions.

"Blanche," Sula said, "we now have a group of Naxids who are supposed to be running the planet on the behalf of their Committee to Save the Praxis. There's nobody to protect them except some Naxid police, and we know a lot more about guns and explosives than the police do. Shouldn't we make an example of some of these people before the enemy can give them proper protection? That should deter others from following their example."

Hong nodded. "That's a possibility, Four-Nine-One," he said. "Some of our people are keeping a few potential targets under surveillance. But the lord governor has decided that maintaining civilian morale is the best deterrent against people cooperating with the Naxids. We must inform the population of the existence of the secret government, and countering enemy propaganda, so the first priority has to be the distribution of the first issue of *The Loyalist*."

The Loyalist was the less-than-inspiring title of the covert newssheet that the government intended to distribute in Zanshaa city. Newssheets were normally distributed by electronic means, and printed locally either by subscribers or at a news café. Unfortunately a covert newssheet could not be distributed this way, for the simple reason that the entire electronic pathway from the publisher to the subscriber was under the direct supervision of the government.

Computers were ubiquitous in the Zanshaa environment: they were in furniture, in walls, in floors, in kitchen appliances, in ducts and utility conduits, in clothing, in audio and video receivers, in every bit of machinery. Not all of these computers were very intelligent, but still they amounted to a couple hundred computers for every citizen. The Shaa had been perfectly aware of the potential for mischief in a computer network that they didn't control absolutely, and so every computer built over the last ten thousand years was hardwired to report its existence, its location, and its identity to a central data store under the control of the Office of the Censor. A copy of every text or picture transmission went to the same place, where it was scanned at high speed by highly secret algorithms that attempted to determine whether or not the message had subversive content. If such content were found, an operator could determine the route of the transmission—which computer had sent it, which had received it, which computers had played its host en route. Officers of the Legion of Diligence could be sent on their way to make an arrest within a matter of minutes.

The Legion of Diligence had been evacuated along with the government, but it was only reasonable to assume that the Naxids would soon have its equivalent, and that meant *The Loyalist* could not be distributed by electronic means. A printing press had been procured somewhere outside the capital, and stocks of paper, and a distribution network set up into Zanshaa. An entire branch of the secret government, Action Group Propaganda, was devoted to this purpose.

So assassination was out. Playing news agent was in.

And, Sula thought, who was to say that the Lord Governor wasn't right? Even if the Action Group managed to kill a few of the newly appointed administrators, who would know it? The Naxids controlled all media, and if they didn't choose to inform the population, no one else would. Not unless the distribution channels for *The Loyalist* were working.

"The first number of *The Loyalist* will have important news," Hong said. "A Midsummer Message from the Lord Governor, of course, but also news of a victory. Chenforce has destroyed ten enemy ships at Protipanu."

The other officers gave a cheer while Sula's heart gave a sudden lurch at the knowledge that Martinez had been present at the battle.

Ten enemy ships. Martinez was making a habit of knocking them down by tens. Maybe he liked round numbers.

Sula suppressed a sudden, foolhardy burst of laughter. It was ridiculous how thoughts of Martinez could turn her perfectly organized mind into a seething, useless stew of anger and undirected passion.

"Were any of our ships lost?" someone asked.

"There were no losses reported," Hong said, which did not quite answer the question. Sula suspected that if it had been another bloodless victory, as at Hone-bar, the news would have been trumpeted to the skies. There had been loyalist casualties, then.

Sula was confident that Martinez hadn't been among them. She could trust his luck that far, at least.

The bastard.

The rest of the meeting was devoted to discussing strategies for distribution of the newssheet. Sula contributed little, just sat on her chair, drank the excellent coffee that Ellroy passed out, and nibbled anise-flavored cookies handed round on a platter.

If Hong knew of this victory over the enemy, she realized, if details were to appear in the newssheet, then that meant that Hong, or the governor, or someone in the chain of command had a means of contacting the government, and receiving information from them. Since the accelerator ring was gone, and since the Naxids couldn't be expected to permit messages through whatever normal channels remained, then they had to have managed it some other way.

Sula let a bite of the anise cookie melt on her tongue and considered how it could be done. You could reprogram some of the communications satellites in orbit so that they could send messages without the authorities knowing. If the signal was strong enough, and the transmission accurate enough, they could go through the wormhole without having to use the wormhole repeater stations.

But at that distance, a laser signal would be subject to some scatter, and the wormhole station might well detect the message. So to avoid that, you'd send your signal to a satellite constructed so as to be invisible to radar and placed somewhere near the wormhole, not between it and Zanshaa like the relay station but well out to one side, perhaps even on the other side of it. The satellite would receive a message from Zanshaa, then retransmit it across the wormhole, as it were, the beam moving at an oblique angle to another satellite similarly placed on the other side. If the satellite were placed correctly, the message would be undetectable.

And if such a means were used, what the head of Action Group Blanche would require in order to report directly to the Fleet Intelligence Section would be a laser transmitter and receiver, and an apartment with a south-facing balcony.

Sula noted the summer sun streaming in through the balcony doors, and afterward, when the team leaders left individually or in small groups to avoid attracting attention, Sula remained to the last and took a stroll on the balcony. And there was the transmitter—Hong hadn't even taken it indoors after his last transmission, just packed it in its case and put the receiver under a chair, and leaned the laser attachment, in its waterproof case, in the corner behind a potted dwarf pear.

The object didn't seem worthy of comment, so Sula didn't mention it when Hong joined Sula on the balcony. Sula thanked her superior for his excellent coffee, and asked him how much he had left.

"Not much," he said, and shrugged. "I can always buy more, though the price is going up."

"I have a contact," Sula said. "Let me see what I can do."

While the summer burned on and newly appointed Naxid bureaucrats settled into their offices, Action Group Blanche and the other action groups were involved in the old-fashioned business of picking up newssheets and distributing them around the city. This required more time and organization than one might expect: Action Teams 211 and 369 found private garage space for the Group Propaganda trucks that moved the sheets from the printing plant, and then the amazingly heavy crates—labeled "fruit preserves," with two layers of genuine fruit preserves packed around them in case anyone checked—were unloaded, and bundles of newssheet were passed on to the other action teams. Sula, whose team had been provided a Hunhao sedan, filled the car with so many papers that it sagged on its suspension.

In their garage Sula and Team 491 filled briefcases, shoulder bags, and rucksacks with papers and tottered away on their errand of distribution. Piles of sheets were left on the doorsteps of bars and cafés, where patrons could pick them up, some sheets were placed on benches in parks, some taped to lampposts. Each newssheet bore the plea, "Please reproduce this sheet, and share it with loyal friends. It would be dangerous to transmit its contents through electronic means."

The tension was unending. It was a simple enough mission but it called for a high degree of alertness, Sula moving along the streets with dangerous documents under her arm, scanning for police, for Naxid silhouettes, for anyone that might be following her. Getting arrested for something like this would be inane. One of her team paralleled her, moving on the other side of the same street. The third kept watch, and as they moved, their roles switched in rotation.

Every time the team disposed of its sheets, they returned to the sedan for another pile. It was three days before Team 491 finally disposed of all its copies. Towards the end Sula, feet and back aching, wanted to take a stack of sheets to the top of a high building and hurl them to the four winds. For some reason she didn't.

The sheets seemed to have some effect. The news reported a decree from Lady Kushdai that anyone caught distributing subversive literature would be subject to extreme penalties. She overheard people discussing the battle at Protipanu in cafés where she stopped for refreshment. Three times Sula saw obvious facsimiles of *The Loyalist* stacked in various public places. She knew they were copies because the quality of the paper was superior to the original.

Aching and exhausted, Sula retired to her private apartment and caught up on the messages from the Records Office. She wasn't surprised to discover that Lady Arkat had been retired as head of security. She had been allowed to send a graceful message of farewell to her subordinates, thanking them for their years of service and wishing them the best. She had then turned over her access and her passwords to her replacement, a Lieutenant Rashtag of the police force, and the altered executive program promptly sent copies of Rashtag's new passwords to Sula.

Rashtag began his new administration in bombastic mode, issuing a series of new decrees having to do with security and threatening dire punishments for infractions. New passes would be issued, and police would check them at the door. Anyone not at his station during working hours would suffer reprimand or worse. All intrusions would be reported immediately. The watchword was *Efficiency!* The next day the watchword was *Security!* After that, *Loyalty!*

Sula recognized Rashtag's style, which was common enough in the Fleet, and a look at his file, which was available to anyone with Rashtag's passwords, confirmed her judgment. He'd been a police sergeant for the last eleven years, and had just received his step to lieutenant in the last few days, as a consequence of being born a member of the right species. A bully promoted beyond his ability, he would be pleased by those who flattered and truckled to him, and offended by pride or even quiet competence. He would promote the flatterers and drive out the capable. Records Office security would soon be tied in its own regulations and ineptitude, and be less use than ever.

She'd had captains like that. She should make a note never to target Rashtag: he was too useful to the loyalist cause.

Following Rashtag's amusing orders came something of more interest. The Administrator of Records, the senior civil servant in the Records Office, had been replaced by a Lord Ushgay, and Ushgay had ordered an immediate search through the records to find buildings in certain locations, all to be requisitioned by the government. A large hotel in the High City was to be acquired, with first-class appointments—not that in the High City there were any other kind—plus a number of palaces, preferably those belonging to traitors who had fled Zanshaa with the outcast government.

Other buildings in the Lower Town were also to be requisitioned. Hotels or whole apartment buildings in the vicinity of the main railroad terminus and the funicular railway, plus warehouses as close to that area as could be found. The machine shops of the railway were to be requisitioned, as was the nearby government motor pool and repair shops, including hundreds of transport vehicles suitable for Naxid drivers and passengers. Enough to transport nearly two thousand Naxids.

Sula gave a low whistle. Now *this* was interesting.

That evening, Sula made a diagonal chalk mark on the streetlight on the northeast corner of Bend and 134th Street, the signal that she wished to meet with Hong in front of the Pink Pavilion in Continuity Park at 16:01 the following afternoon. She found Hong beneath one of the old elms, and they approached each other with bright smiles fixed to their faces, as if they were old friends encountering one another by chance. Hong took her arm and began to stroll with her along one of the paths.

It was a bright summer day, and the park was full. A group of Torminel flew kites, preparing for the Kite-Flying Festival in a few days; and young teams of Naxids played lighumane in fields fenced off by bright alloy uprights.

"This is a hand comm," Hong said, as she felt something drop into her shoulder bag. "We'll use it only for the Axtattle operation—when that operation's over, destroy the unit or otherwise dispose of it."

Elms rustled overhead as Sula nodded her understanding.

"Our sources," Hong continued, "have told us that Naxid police have been ordered to clear five airfields of all non-Naxid personnel. All of them are on this continent, more or less in a circle around Zanshaa City. One of the fields is Wi-hun, so we're still betting that's where the rebel main body will land." He gave a grim smile. "From now on, your team is on alert. I want you all sleeping in your apartment, with your equipment ready. When Naxids begin to land, I'll send you a message on the hand comm announcing that your cousin Marcia's given birth. If I mention birth weight, these are the number of shuttles landing each hour. If I say it's a boy, that means shuttles are landing at Wi-hun and the Axtattle plan is on."

"Understood."

"Once Marcia gives birth, nobody is to be more than two minutes away from your apartment. When I hear the Naxids are getting ready to move into the city, I'll send a message telling you when to meet me at a restaurant. You'll get your team to the Axtattle site by that hour."

"Understood. It looks as if we'll have a fair amount of warning, because they're requisitioning transport from Zanshaa City." Sula dropped into Hong's own shoulder bag an envelope containing a data foil with a summary of the Records Office intercepts, and then she gave him a brief recapitulation of its contents.

"The hotels and apartments near the funicular will be barracks," she said. "The other buildings will hold their gear, supplies, and transport. The new elite will be in the palaces in the High City, and the officers and administrators in a High City hotel. My guess is that will be the Great Destiny Hotel, which has a lot of Naxid-suitable rooms and a restaurant that specializes in Naxid food."

"Very plausible," Hong nodded.

They paused near the fountain, great white moving columns of water that obscured, then revealed, the park's famous statue, The Unsound Regarding Continuity with Awe. Continuity looked remarkably like one of the Great Masters, the Shaa. An irony, considering that the Shaa as a species had not Continued.

"No matter what happens on the Axtattle Parkway," Sula said, "I think we ought to plan the destruction of the Great Destiny Hotel. Make a second truck bomb, drive it in the lobby some night, and blow every middle-rank administrator into low orbit. And the fuckers won't be able to hide *that*—half the city could look out their windows and see it go up."

A gust of wind brought a fine spray of water into Hong's eyes. He blinked and held up a hand. "Difficult to get that stuff into the High City, with only the funicular and the one road."

"That's why you prepare the truck now," Sula said. "I know you have teams in the High City, yes?"

Hong looked opaque. "You're not to know that, Four-Nine-One."

Sula, who had heard Lieutenant Joong complain that it was vexing to live around the corner from his old smoking club without being able to visit for a puff on the old hookah, simply shrugged.

Cool mist fell on her face. She and Hong moved out of the fountain's range and Sula handed Hong a package.

"Coffee," she said. "Highland, from Devajjo."

Hong was impressed. "Where did you find it?"

Sula offered a private smile. "Military secret. But let me know when you need more."

Through the modest scattering of radioactive dust that had once been a wormhole relay station, Chenforce passed from the Koel system into that of Aspa Darla. Koel was a bloated red giant, cool and eerily luminous, that squatted in the middle of its system like a tick swollen with blood, and the system was uninhabited except for the crews of the relay stations, all of whom had died in the last few days from the missiles fired by Michi Chen from Mazdan, before her ship had even entered the Koel system.

The reason the crews had to die involved Koel's position as a hub, with four heavily trafficked wormhole gates. Squadron Commander Chen had decided she didn't want the Naxids to know which wormhole she planned to use to leave the system, and so all means of communication between Koel and the outside were eliminated.

Martinez appreciated Lady Michi's cold-blooded logic, but he regretted the wormhole stations. Not so much because of the Naxid crews, though he would have spared them if he could, but because the stations were in their own way vital.

It wasn't just that the stations knit the far-flung empire together with their high-powered communications lasers, but they also kept the wormholes themselves from evaporating. Wormholes could destabilize, or even vanish, if the mass that moved through them was not eventually balanced by a similar mass moving the other way, and the wormhole stations were built around powerful mass drivers that could hurl through the wormholes colossal asteroid-sized chunks of rock and metal that would serve to balance the equation.

The stations' function as a communications relay could be filled by parking a ship equipped with sufficiently powerful communications gear in front of a wormhole, but the act of balancing mass against mass was a problem not so easily solved. People were going to have to be careful moving through Protipanu and Koel for fear of endangering their route home.

That also was part of Michi Chen's intent. Even though Chenforce had moved on, commerce through the wormhole junction would slow to a crawl as planners worked frantically to balance mass.

Chenforce's accomplishments in Koel showed that the empire was more fragile than Martinez had suspected. The civil war could change its landscape permanently.

Not that any of Koel's wormholes were in immediate danger. Chenforce had found sixteen merchant ships in the system and destroyed them all to prevent them from contributing to the Naxid economy and war effort. Some of the crews, seeing the missiles coming, had escaped in lifeboats, and some hadn't.

There were going to be more ships in Aspa Darla, and a bounty of other targets as well. But there was no reason to destroy Aspa Darla's wormhole stations, as Aspa Darla had only two wormholes. Everyone would know that Chenforce was headed from here to Bai-do.

As soon as Chenforce flashed into the system, *Illustrious* broadcast Michi Chen's message to the ring stations on the two metal-rich planets Aspa and Darla.

"All ships docked at the ring station are to be abandoned and cast off so that they may be destroyed without damage to the ring. All repair docks and building yards will be opened to the environment and any ships inside will be cast off. Any ship attempting to flee will be destroyed. Your facilities will be inspected to make certain that you have complied with these orders. Failure to obey orders will mean the destruction of the ring."

Four pinnaces were launched, and raced toward Aspa and Darla to perform these inspections in advance of the arrival of Chenforce. It would be some hours before the squadron received a reply, and in the meantime Martinez, strapped securely on his acceleration couch, watched the sensor displays in case a Naxid squadron turned out to be in the system.

The ships in the system were using radar, a sign that Chenforce wasn't expected here, and there were already a vast number of details appearing on Martinez's displays. Many ships flying in and out, all soon to be targets, and no fleet formations to be seen.

Martinez began to relax. This was likely to be a one-sided affair, another triumph, and triumph was all he asked of fate.

He glanced at his own displays and saw the seven ships of Chenforce grouped in a tight cluster—a standard, old-fashioned formation, as neither Martinez nor Michi saw any sense in revealing their dispersed tactical formations unless lives were at stake. At the center of the formation, protected by the others, was the damaged *Celestial*. The Torminel crew, aided by damage control parties from other ships, had performed prodigies of repair, and had surprised everyone by rescuing Captain Eldey and the others trapped in Command and believed dead. *Celestial* was able to maneuver with the rest of the squadron, but had lost one of its missile batteries, much of its defensive armament, and about a quarter of its crew.

Another message flashed from *Illustrious*'s transmitters.

"This is Squadron Commander Michi Chen to all ships in the Aspa Darla system. All crews are to abandon ship immediately. All ships in this system are to be destroyed. We will not fire on lifeboats."

Missiles began firing shortly thereafter, to reinforce this order.

Time passed. It was becoming clear that the Naxids had no warships in this system.

"Message from Captain Hansen of *Lord May*, my lady," said Lady Ida Li. "He . . . seems rather irate."

Martinez saw a tight smile on Michi's face. "Very well," she said. "I'll hear him."

Lord May's captain was a composition in scarlet: red hair, bristling red beard, red face, and bloodshot eyes that suggested Chenforce's arrival had interrupted a bout of serious drinking. "Don't kill my ship, damn you!" he boomed in a roaring voice that made Martinez wince and reach to turn down the volume on his earphones. "I *hate* the fucking Naxids, there was just no damn way to get out of their clutches till now! I'm heading for Wormhole One—just tell me where the fuck to go from there!"

Lord May was in fact the closest ship to Chenforce, outbound from the system to Koel, and looked right down the throats of the oncoming missiles.

Martinez watched the smile play over Michi's lips. "I'll answer that one," she said, and then touched controls on her comm display and looked into the camera pickup. "Captain Hansen, you will set a course Koel-Mazdan-Protipanu-Seizho. If you deviate from this you will be destroyed. From Seizho you may wish to continue into the Serpent's Tail, as Seizho is dangerously near the enemy. Message ends." Then she looked up at Martinez. "Captain, will you tell Command to retarget that missile?"

Martinez felt a smile break out on his lips. "At once, my lady." He had a feeling that Aspa Darla was going to be lucky for him.

Martinez's equilibrium had been restored during the long crossing of the Mazdan and Koel systems. There had been no nightmares of *Beacon*'s loss, no lonely episodes of doubt or terror. The crew were cheerful, and the officers congratulatory, and gradually Martinez's fury at *Beacon*'s loss had faded. Even Captain Lord Gomburg Fletcher invited him to dine, alone without any of the other officers present, and endured Martinez's accent for two entire hours without so much as a wince. Martinez tried to avoid being "clever," on the theory that cleverness was what Fletcher would appreciate least. For the most part they discussed sports. Fletcher, like Martinez, had been a fencer at the academy.

After it was clear that no enemy warships lurked in the Aspa Darla system, Michi stood most of the crew down from action stations. Martinez rose from his couch with a growing optimism in his heart, and then a thought occurred to him.

"My lady?" he said. "Shall we send crew mail and dispatches with *Lord May*?"

Michi agreed, and the crew's messages home, plus a brief message from Michi to the effect that they'd entered Aspa Darla after a journey from Protipanu free of incident, were coded and sent to friendly territory courtesy of Captain Hansen. Included was Martinez's long serial letter to Terza, plus briefer messages to other members of his family, all save Roland, to whom he had very little to say.

Martinez had, some time ago, asked Michi to censor his mail personally on the grounds that it might contain Chen family business, and Michi had agreed with perfect amiability. There was no Chen family business in the messages, not unless Martinez's speculation about the development of the Chen heir counted as business, but Michi did not complain, and Martinez was pleased that Fletcher wasn't reading his messages.

At Martinez's request Hansen sent recent news to *Illustrious*. The Naxid news videos trumpeted the fact that Zanshaa had fallen without a fight, though they lamented that "pirates in the employ of the renegade government" had destroyed its ring. Civil government was in the process of being established on Zanshaa, and would be throughout the empire as soon as the renegade government was hunted down and received their just desserts. The Naxids admitted to a hard-fought action at Hone-bar, but did not mention its results. Martinez found the omission annoying. Anyone used to living under the censorship would find it obvious enough that Hone-bar had been a Naxid defeat, simply from the fact no victory was mentioned.

They might at least have mentioned my name.

We are continually involved in attacking the enemy's ability to make war, Martinez began in a new letter to Terza. *There is little or no danger to ourselves, but great harm to the enemy's economy.*

I think of you constantly, and hope you are well.

Sparing *Lord May* was the only deviation from the plan that Martinez had devised for the Aspa Darla raid. The Naxid administrators of the two planets' rings, with no force to stand between them and the oncoming loyalists, obeyed Lady Michi's orders. All ships on the ring were jettisoned; the repair and construction bays were all opened, and ships under construction shoveled out into the vacuum. Antimatter missiles found all these targets as well as the ships moving in or out of the system, and by the end of the raid a hundred and three ships were destroyed. A few managed to accelerate through Wormhole 2 to Bai-do before loyalist missiles could find them, but Chenforce would catch them there.

Two pinnaces passed close to each ring, cameras trained on the open construction bays to make certain that Michi Chen's stern orders had been obeyed. The pinnaces were recovered without incident at the far end of the system.

As Chenforce flashed past, another order was given to the Naxids. "You will broadcast the following message on all communications channels every hour until we leave the system. We will be monitoring your communications to assure compliance."

The message featured Squadron Commander Chen sitting in her office, wearing her viridian dress uniform and gazing at the camera with solemn eyes.

"This is Squadron Commander Chen," she said. "Loyalist forces operating under the authority of the Convocation and the Praxis have returned to your system. Do not believe rebel propaganda claiming the war is over. Loyalist forces are advancing into rebel areas and have already destroyed two rebel fleets at Hone-bar and Protipanu.

"We will be leaving your system soon in order to fight the

rebels elsewhere, but please believe that we will soon return. Those who cooperate with the rebel government or military will be judged and punished. Those who remain faithful to the Convocation and the Praxis will be rewarded. Until the return of lawful government, good citizens will not cooperate with rebels and other enemies of the empire."

The message was still being broadcast five days later, when Chenforce left the system.

SEVENTEEN

Cousin Marcia gave birth to a boy two days after Sula's meeting with Hong. Weight was not mentioned. Sula already knew the Naxids were landing, because she'd heard the sonic booms rattle the windows as the shuttles came in, and had been counting.

The Naxids were coming down in groups of eight. If the shuttles were standard military type, each would carry eighty Naxids plus their gear, and the total would not land an armed force very quickly. They had probably brought in just enough shuttles to secure the ground termini of the space elevators so that they could send their main force down from the ring. Without the ring, this deployment was going to take quite a while.

After four trips, the sonic booms ceased. The former government had ordered the destruction of all suitable fuel stocks, and the Naxids presumably returned to orbit to refuel. Sula wished she knew how much fuel the enemy fleet brought with them.

She knew from her readings in Terran history that things such as ground-to-air missiles had once existed, and she longed for a battery of them. But the Fleet did not have such things, because the Fleet did not fight from the ground. And the police didn't have them, either, because they didn't need missiles to arrest criminals—and if there was civil disorder, well, either the police crushed the riot with their small arms or they called in the Fleet to turn the rioters into a cloud of raging plasma.

Team 491 sat in the small apartment at Riverside, the video a constant murmur in the background; news when it wasn't Macnamara watching sports. The Naxids had decreed a full schedule of summer sports, diversion for a population suffering from spot shortages and the electricity ration, and Andiron was on top of the ratings and delighting its fans. Macnamara watched the games obsessively, cross-legged before a spread oilcloth on which he disassembled and cleaned the team's weapons.

Spence stayed in the bedroom she shared with Sula and used the wall video to watch a long succession of romantic dramas. Sula tried to avoid overhearing any of the dialogue. She figured she knew pretty well how those romances turned out in real life.

Sonic booms rattled the windows again, sixteen landings altogether, and then the booms stopped. The Naxids had probably run out of whatever fuel they'd scavenged. Sula pictured Naxid constabulary pouring into some chemical refinery and demanding they alter their output.

Sula worked her way through three volumes of mathematical puzzles and a volume of history—*Europe in the Age of Kings*—before her comm chirped with a text message from Blanche for a breakfast meeting at 05:01 at the Allergy-Free Restaurant in Smallbridge, a district of the Lower Town. Sula looked at the message and felt her skin prickle hot with a sudden rush of blood. Trying to control the sudden urge to pant for breath, she rose from her seat and walked with care toward where her team waited, their eyes on her. Sula's feet seemed to sink into the floorboards beneath her feet, as if she were walking on pillows.

"It's tomorrow morning," she said. "Nine hours from now."

* * *

Mr. and Madame Guei held hands as they sat on the sofa, their eyes wide as they watched Action Team 491 turn their pleasant apartment into an ambush site. Their infant son dozed on his father's lap, and their nine-year-old daughter, having rapidly grown bored with the three heavily armed soldiers who had appeared in their quarters before sunrise, played games on the video wall.

Sula had told the Gueis that they were allowed to do nothing else with the video wall, or any other form of communication in the house. They were particularly urged not to call the police. The action team was there to fight Naxid rebels, not to interfere with their lives, but their lives *would* be interfered with if necessary.

The Gueis complied quietly. They seemed to comprehend easily enough that no one had given them a vote in whether their apartment was going to be turned into a battlefield.

The drive to the Axtattle Parkway was accomplished in the dead of night and without trouble. Due to the electricity rationing, there was very little activity on the streets at that hour. Somewhat to Sula's surprise, they even found a legal parking space half a block from their destination.

Another team had arrived before them, had awakened the building manager, shown him their warrants, and had him surrender his passkeys. They now held the manager and his family incommunicado in one of the other apartments. One of the advance team let Group 491 into the building, and their team leader let them into the Gueis' apartment, where they quietly woke the family, got them dressed, and assembled them in their front room.

Normally the teams might have taken positions on the roof, but the gabled mansard roofs common in the district did not permit such a thing. Not only was there no place to hide on the roofs, but a misstep would have pitched them all into the street below.

Once in the Gueis' apartment, Team 491 opened their duffels and began their transformation into soldiers. On Sula's head was a helmet with a transparent faceplate onto which combat displays could be projected, and she wore on her torso a midnight-colored carapace that would protect her against small-arms fire and shrapnel. Over it all was a cape that projected active camouflage: it was like a giant video screen that showed whatever was on the reverse side. The image wasn't perfect, and tended to waver with the folds of the cape, but if she stayed still it would fool the eye even at close ranges, and there was a hood she could pull over her head.

Each team member carried a pistol that fired silent, subsonic ammunition, a rifle, three grenades, and a combat knife. Each carried a gas mask in case the Naxids threw gas at them, and Macnamara assembled a large, tripod-mounted machine gun on the dining table that had been shoved under the apartment's main window, one that would blast vehicles below with a torrent of fire from the quaint gable that slightly overhung the walk below. Macnamara didn't even have to expose himself to accomplish this: he could control the gun with a remote pad, or even command it to shoot at anything that moved in a given area.

Below, as the eastern horizon began to glow with a pale jasper light, Sula looked over the ammat trees and watched the traffic move up and down the parkway, mostly heavy trucks bringing goods to the predawn city. The bridge over Highway 16 had sculpted iron railings ornamented in a bright alloy with a lobed, scalloped design that Sula recognized as Torminel in origin. The eleven Action Teams of Group Blanche were hidden in four of the buildings overlooking the ambush site, ready to pump death down on the stunned survivors of the bombing.

Sula's nerves gave a warning tingle as she saw a truck come into view directly across the parkway from her on Highway 16, a twelve-wheeler that crept slowly down the road as it dipped beneath the broad bridge, and then didn't come out the other side.

Across Highway 16 from her position, Sula knew, Lieu-tenant Captain Hong was standing over a command detona-tor. A drop of sweat trickled slowly down her face. Suddenly she wanted to tear the helmet off her head and take several long, cool breaths.

Sula saw signal lights flashing out of the corner of her eye, and she turned to see several trucks lined up by one of the parkway's exits. She looked left and right, and saw that the parkway was nearly empty, the few remaining vehicles pulling off. The traffic control computers were clearing the road.

This was worth a message to Hong, Sula thought. She trig-gered her helmet mic and said, "Comm: to Blanche. Blanche, they're clearing the parkway. I think we'll have company soon. Comm: send." As soon as the last word left her lips, her communicator coded the signal, compressed it, and sent it in a burst transmission to Hong across the parkway.

The response was just a click, no words to be overheard or decoded.

More lights flashed on the parkway, toward the city cen-ter, multicolored emergency flashers. Sula pressed her hel-met to the window to see a swarm of police vehicles coming in a dense swarm down the parkway, moving in a compact mass in all six lanes. She thought about making another transmission but decided that Hong couldn't help but see this for himself.

Sula drew back from the window as a river of black-and-yellow police cars poured past, some of them falling out, parking every few hundred paces on either side of the park-way. Sula's nerves began an unpleasant little crawl as Naxid police emerged from the parked vehicles, their scuttling, centauroid bodies unmistakable in the growing light. They wore helmets and body armor covered with chameleon-weave that duplicated their flash-patterns, the red flashes of their beaded black scales that served as a silent, auxiliary form of language. Each carried a rifle in its forelimbs. They were flashing continually at each other, one pattern after another displayed on their chests and backs, and Sula wished she could read their patterns.

Well, she thought, that's it. The truck bomb might still work, but surely the rest of the operation couldn't continue. She could count more police directly below than there were members of Group Blanche, and within minutes many more could arrive, racing down the parkway from right and left. Any second now, she should hear the order for everyone but the team with the detonator to withdraw while they still could.

The order didn't come. Sula pulled off her helmet and ran a gloved hand through her hair to comb out the sweat.

She wondered if she should transmit to Hong suggesting withdrawal, and then a picture rose in her mind, Hong's expression of deep concern, his question, *Are you all right about this?*

Sula would wait. She took several deep breaths, and then she waited some more.

She turned to scan the room. Macnamara was silent and stoic, his hands flexing as if eager to grasp his machine gun; and Spence was pale, looking as if she wished she were in one of those romantic videos of hers, the ones that guaranteed a happy ending.

It occurred to Sula that she had never led other people in combat. Everything she had done against the Naxids had been done entirely on her own, strapped in her pinnace while it shepherded a volley of missiles toward the enemy. The missiles had not possessed beating hearts or bodies of flesh, not like Spence or Macnamara or the Gueis, whose daughter was still gazing at her video game with intent eyes that might soon be called on to witness a massacre . . .

Sula realized that she would much rather be alone in this. Her own life was nothing, a breath in the wind, of no value to anyone. Responsibility for others was by far the greater burden.

More flashing lights. Sula peered out of the window and saw a pair of police vehicles moving slowly down Highway 16, then disappearing beneath the bridge where the bomb truck waited. The driver of the truck, code name 257, was still in the truck, having feigned a breakdown. He might be arrested, or decide to do something dramatic.

Shit-shit-shit . . . The word drummed its way through Sula's brain. She picked up her rifle from where it waited against the wall, and held it in her gloved hands. Taking this as a signal, Macnamara stepped to where the machine gun waited and put a hand on its stock. Sula waved him back.

"Use the control pad," she said. "Mark out everything in the street or on the sidewalk as a target."

Macnamara nodded to himself, then stepped back to perform this task. Once he triggered the gun, it would fire automatically at anything in the target area until told to stop or until its considerable ammunition reserve was exhausted. It was ideal for covering a withdrawal by the rest of the team.

The rifles held by Sula and Spence were less convenient, insofar as they needed a person to point them at the enemy and squeeze the trigger. But the view through their sights could be projected on the helmet faceplates of the operators, which meant that neither Sula nor Spence actually had to flaunt their heads in the way of enemy fire. Only their hands and forearms need be exposed, with the trigger permanently depressed so that the gun would fire automatically at anything designated a target.

She could feel her pulse beating high in her throat. She wondered if she should step back from the window if everything was about to blow up right this instant.

Sula gave an involuntary start as her hand comm chirped. She reached for it, encountered instead her camouflage shroud, and then groped inside its folds, all the while wondering why someone had called her hand comm instead of using the far safer burst transmissions of the radio.

By the time she opened the comm and pressed it to her

ear, it had stopped chirping. Voices were already engaged in a dialogue.

"What's the situation, then?" Hong's voice.

"The police tell me I've got to move the truck or get myself arrested." The other voice was two-five-seven's. "I a-told them we've got a tow on the way. I a-told them this here is a valuable piece of property and that I ain't a-going ta take the responsibility of running a twelve-wheeler on just one fuel cell, but they sez I got ta. So I told a-them what I'd do, I'd like call my supervisor like."

Sula winced. Two-five-seven was a team leader and a Peer—a highly educated and cultivated young man—and he was doing his best to speak in some manner of working-class accent, and failing miserably.

If the Naxids didn't hear something wrong in this, then they were deaf to all nuance.

Two-five-seven had done something reasonably clever, though. He'd rung a number that would contact all the teams at once, so that all would know what was going on and none would panic and try something desperate.

"Right," Hong said. "You might as well pull out, the people we want won't be here for a while. Take the first left on top of the ramp, and I'll meet you there. Four-nine-nine, are you there?"

"Yes, Blanche." Another voice.

"I need you to send me your car with a driver. Have him meet me at the truck, and have him bring all his gear."

Meaning his weapons, presumably.

"The rest of you," Hong said, "sit tight, and stick with the plan."

Sula returned her hand comm to her trouser pocket, her mind spinning with the effort of trying to work out what Hong now intended. Surely he couldn't retrieve the ambush now.

Surely the only sensible thing to do was to order his teams to leave as quietly as they had come.

Sula watched as the truck slowly pulled out from beneath

the bridge and disappeared from sight around the corner of the building. The Naxid police drew their vehicles across the road on either end of the underpass as roadblocks.

Hong's voice came over Sula's helmet phones, and Sula hastily put on her helmet to better hear him.

"Someone has to signal me when the convoy passes."

Others hastened to assure Hong they would do this. Sula remained silent.

She looked over the room again, saw the Gueis with their taut faces, the daughter still fierce in her determination to win her video game. Plopping sounds came from the video wall, and odd little cries. Apparently the game had to do with animals jumping over one another in a rather complicated arboreal environment.

More police flashers to the right, far down the parkway, away from the city center. Now that Sula had her helmet on, she turned up the magnification on the faceplate to see a wedge of police vehicles coming toward her, and behind them larger transport, visible only as they passed through the brilliant slices of dawn that fell between the buildings.

"Comm: to Blanche," Sula said. "I think they're coming. Comm: send."

"All teams," came Hong's response. "Let me know when they begin to cross the bridge."

Sula turned to the Gueis. "I want all of you down flat on the floor," she said. "When things start, I want you to crawl out of here. *Crawl,* understand?" She swiped her hand parallel to the floor in a gesture that meant, *flat on the floor.* "Take shelter in the hallway, or with a neighbor on the far side of the building."

"Yes, my lady," said Mister Guei. Sula felt a spasm of amusement: she must be good at being a Peer for Guei to call her "my lady" when no one else had. Guei and his wife looked at each other, then lowered themselves and their infant son to their creamy carpet. The daughter was reluctant to leave her game, but her mother snapped at her and dragged her to the floor by one wrist. The daughter looked as if she might cry, but then decided against it.

Sula turned back to the window. The Naxids were coming on quickly and it was less than half a minute before the first wave of police vehicles came by. They moved at moderate speed, unhurried. Behind them were sedans, then trucks and buses, all moving widely spaced in a long column. Sula couldn't see the column's tail even with her faceplate on full magnification.

"Comm: to Blanche. They're on the bridge. Comm: send." No doubt every other team leader was shooting Hong the same message.

All the vehicles were dark with Naxids. Some of the trucks were open and carried long weapons, machine guns or grenade launchers, operated by alert crews that scanned the buildings as they passed by. Sula drew farther back into the room and hoped that the grenade launchers weren't loaded with antimatter grenades.

That would be very, very messy.

"Comm: to Blanche. They're heavily armed, and there are a lot of them. I don't think we should engage . . ."

Her words trailed away as the bomb truck reappeared, booming down the Highway 16 ramp at high speed, the silent electric motors pushing each of its twelve huge wheels at maximum acceleration. Following the truck came a blue Victory sedan, presumably the car that belonged to Team 499.

At Hong's wild audacity a frenzied admiration sang through Sula's heart. The group leader was attempting to repair the flaws in his plan with sheer courage.

Sula's nerves gave a leap as the truck hit the Naxid police roadblock and flung the vehicle aside like a man waving off an insect. A piece of the police car, curved yellow metal, flew high into the air and hit the pavement with a clang that Sula could hear even through the window. A Naxid lay sprawled where his own car had hit him. Another danced aside with surprising speed and then was clawing on the pavement for the rifle that had fallen off his shoulder.

The truck disappeared under the bridge with a series of distant booming noises as its tires vaulted expansion joints in the pavement. The Victory followed. The Naxid grabbed his rifle and raised it to his shoulder, then seemed to dissolve in a shower of sparks.

Each of Group Blanche's rifles held a box magazine with four hundred and one rounds of caseless ammunition, all of which could be discharged in something less than three seconds. It looked as if the Naxid had just absorbed about half a magazine.

Then the weapon was turned on the police car, and the vehicle leaped and juddered and sparked, then sagged on its suspension as a baleful white mist rose from its punctured frame.

A few seconds later the Victory sedan reappeared, driving in reverse up the ramp at full speed. The Naxid procession continued to roll by, and seemed not to have noticed the fight or to be slow in reacting to it.

"All teams, stand by." Hong's voice, ringing with fine triumph, came over Sula's headset. "Prepare to detonate on my order."

Sula turned to her team. *"Flat!"* she said. *"Now!"*

Rather than dropping on her belly Sula squatted with her back to the outside wall, taking comfort in its solidity.

The explosion seemed to come in several rapid stages, first a great crack that made the glassware in the Gueis' sideboard rattle, then a huge boom that Sula felt pass through her like a wave, stirring each soft organ in passing, and lastly a massive crash that felt like a kick in the spine, a bass thunder that seemed to lift the apartment building off its foundations, then drop it down again with a bone-stirring impact.

Her head happened to be turned to the left, to the gable window, and she actually saw it bow inward like a bubble about to pop; but the window material was tough, and to Sula's surprise it rebounded back into the frame.

Oh well. Now they'd have to shoot it out.

She sprang to her feet as debris rattled against the side of the building. The bridge had gone up beautifully, leaving behind vast hole surrounded by a tangle of writhing girders and rebar. Above the destruction a tower of dust and smoke flickered in the dawn light. Debris was still falling onto the roadway. A sinister lick of flame rose lazily from the dark pit below.

It was difficult to tell how much damage had actually been done to the Naxids. Their convoy was widely spaced, and probably no more than one or two vehicles had actually been on the bridge when it was destroyed. If they'd ever been there, there was no sign of them now. One bus lay on the far side of the bridge more or less where the explosion had caught it, intact but capsized, its windows broken and sightless. The rest of the convoy had come to a stop. Naxids boiled off the vehicles like a swarm of dark insects.

"All teams, open fire!" Hong's sunny, encouraging voice sang in her ears. "Fire, fire, fire!"

Sula looked at her team as if through a light fog: there seemed to be a lot of suspended particles in the air. Spence was pressed flat on the floor, hands over her helmet, and Macnamara was sitting up with a stunned expression on his face.

"Up!" Sula urged, her blood suddenly alight. "Get firing!"

Fire one magazine from each weapon, she thought, then get the hell out. Even given surprise and superior position, the thirty-odd members of Group Blanche couldn't expect to hold out for long against the hundreds of Naxids in the street below.

At that instant all the windows facing the Axtattle Parkway burst inward, the material that had resisted the explosion now shattering before a torrent of Naxid fire. Sula flung herself to the floor as window shards rattled off her body armor and a sleet of laths and plaster came down from the ceiling. Over her head the machine gun spun on its tripod as rounds hit the long barrel. Macnamara rose to his feet and reached up to take control of the weapon, but Sula shouted *"Get down!"* and Macnamara, his expression startled, joined her on the floor.

"Set the gun to automatic and get out!" Sula said. Through her hard body armor she felt sharp impacts on the floor as bullets came through the windows of the floor below and drove through that story's ceiling to hit the floor on which she was lying. Holes appeared in the carpet, with little bits of pad and fluff flying up. The building shook as, somewhere, a grenade went off.

The rain of laths and plaster did not cease. Sula scurried to the door, moving in a kind of four-legged crouch, opened the door, and half-rolled into the corridor beyond. Spence was right behind her.

Sula glanced back through the door. Macnamara still knelt behind the machine gun, madly punching the pad that controlled it. His shoulders and helmet were white with the plaster coming down. "Come *on*," Sula urged him, and then her heart gave a despairing leap as he threw both arms out and fell back as a bullet took him full in the chest. Sula gave a cry and half-launched herself back into the apartment, and then she saw the scar on Macnamara's body armor, and saw that his hands were moving. She realized his body armor had repelled the attack.

"Fuck that!" she called to him. "Clear out!"

With some effort Macnamara rolled himself to a seated position and with fixed determination reached for the pad again. Sula backed out of the door as the Guei family came scurrying out on hands and knees. Blood poured from Mr. Guei's left eye socket—he'd lost the eye to a bullet, or maybe to a splinter. His wife shrieked out one hysterical wail after another, and it was the daughter who cradled the infant as she carried him into the hallway's relative safety, her face fixed with the same single-minded determination that she had displayed when engaged in her video game.

The unexpected sound of a woman's voice shouting into Sula's ear caused her to give an involuntary jump.

"Four-nine-one, this is Two-one-one. Naxid fire's too heavy. We're pulling out." Action Team 211 was the other team in this building, the one that had entered first and guided Sula's team to the Guei apartment.

Sula's head spun as she tried to remember communications protocols. "Comm: to Two-one-one. This is Four-nine-one. Acknowledge. We're pulling out, too. Comm: send."

Macnamara at last got the machine gun programmed. It tracked automatically on its mount as it found a target, depressed its barrel, fired, and promptly blew up—the barrel had been knocked out of alignment by enemy bullets, and the first round fired by Team 491 did nothing but destroy the gun that fired it.

Macnamara stared in disbelief at the ruined weapon, then reached for his rifle. *"Enough!"* Sula shrieked. "Get back here!"

Macnamara thought about it for a moment, then scuttled backward like an ungainly insect till he gained the doorway. Sula rose to a crouch, helped Macnamara rise, then said, "To the stair! *Go!*"

Spence was already on her way, limping. Sula saw that she was leaving bloody footprints in the hall. She shoved Macnamara after Spence, then followed.

Bullets still found their way into the hall, but the danger was much less than that in the front rooms. Spence reached the emergency stair, hurled open the door, and disappeared into the stairwell. Macnamara followed. Sula entered the stair last, after casting a glance back at the Gueis, the bleeding father in the arms of his screaming wife, the daughter looking after the baby with her air of intense concentration, as if trying to will away the whole situation. *Try not to hate us,* Sula thought at them mentally, and then hurled herself down the stair.

There was a snapping sound overhead, and soft rain began to fall from the building's sprinkler system.

"Fucking brilliant," Sula breathed. "Absolutely fucking brilliant." No matter how many times Group Blanche had been over the plan, no one had suggested that the first Naxid reaction to the bombing would be to randomly pump a million rounds of suppressive fire into every nearby building.

At least the stair was on the far side of the building from Axtattle Parkway, and no bullets penetrated the stairwell. As Sula's boots clattered on the risers, she realized that she should let her superior know that Team 491 was running like hell, and then it took her a moment to sort out radio protocol.

"Comm: to Blanche," she said, trying to keep her tone even. "Naxid fire is too hot. Team Four-nine-one is pulling out. Comm: send."

The response came within seconds, crisp over the sound of sprinkler water pattering on her helmet. "Four-nine-one, permission to withdraw granted."

I don't remember asking permission, Sula thought. The thump of a grenade echoed through the building. Sula could smell smoke despite the gush of the sprinklers.

A chunk of plaster banged off Sula's helmet, and she brushed wet plaster dust off her shoulder. Her team was making good time despite the water that was now beginning to spill down the stairs in little waterfalls.

The lobby was full of bewildered civilians, many partly dressed or in their night clothes. Some were wounded. The sound of wailing children echoed off the tile walls, and people sloshed in water in bare feet or slippers. There was no sign of Team 211.

"All of you clear out!" Sula shouted. She waved an arm to indicate direction. "Head back two or three streets and wait for the all-clear. If you're hurt, you can call for help there."

"What's going on?" someone demanded.

"It's the war!" shouted an angry bass voice. "The damn war!"

"But isn't the war over?" asked the first.

"Get moving!" Sula shouted. "Move back before you get caught in the crossfire!" *You idiots,* she added to herself.

She turned to her team. "Ardelion, how badly are you hurt?" Using Spence's code name.

Spence looked down at the boot that left red trails in the water. "I'm not sure. I think it's minor, but it hurts like a bitch."

"Do you need to be carried?"

Spence shook her head. "I can keep my feet. I just hope I don't have to run."

"All right, then. You and Starling pull your hoods over your heads. Rifles completely under the capes. Brush that crap off your shoulders. Move with these people till you get to the car."

She tucked her rifle under her arm, barrel downward, knocked as much plaster dust off her shoulders as she could, and pulled the hood over her helmet. A pinch sealed the hood in front, over her faceplate, but her faceplate displayed the image transmitted by the hood sensors so that she had a perfectly workable picture of where she was going.

Macnamara in the lead, the team moved with the civilians till they got outside. Suddenly the sounds of firing were much louder, and echoed off the buildings. Vertigo eddied in Sula's skull at the slight distortion in her vision, and the stuffy air inside her suit sent warning signs of claustrophobia tingling up her nerves. She had to marvel at how well the camouflage capes worked—she couldn't see anything of Spence or Macnamara except their boots and the wet footprints they left on the pavement.

Once outside the civilians dispersed, and encountered groups of other civilians. They had heard the explosion that destroyed the bridge, apparently, and come either like fools to gawk or like good citizens to help anyone injured by the blast. But the shooting and the continued explosions had made them pause, and now they just hovered in the street, uncertain, all gawkers now.

Sula moved among them and tore open her hood. "Move back!" she called. "This is the war! We're fighting Naxids! Pull back or you could get hurt!"

"Police!" someone shouted, and the whole crowd began surging back. Sula chanced a look over her shoulder, and saw Naxids in black-and-yellow uniforms scurrying around the corner of the building, having run from the parkway to cut off the retreat of anyone in the building.

"Hurry!" Sula shouted, terrified that the Naxids might decide to fire into the crowd. She and her team were sprinting when they arrived at their car; Spence's wound barely slowed her down. Sula opened a rear door and flung herself sprawling across the backseat. Macnamara, the best driver, took the driver's seat, and Spence the front seat opposite.

"Take us out slowly and as quietly as you can," Sula said. The crowd was still falling back past them, and Sula was amazed the Naxids weren't shooting at everything that moved.

"Comm," Sula said, "to Team Two-one-one. Are you out of the building? The building is being surrounded by the enemy. Comm: send."

Her mind filled with a hopeless plan for driving back toward the building and gunning down the Naxids to break Team 211 free. She'd do her best, but it would just get them all killed.

Two-one-one's voice, when it came, was breathless. "We're out, Four-nine-one! We're running like hell for our car!"

Good for you, Sula thought. The Hunhao swung into the street, its four electric motors driving the wheels in silence. Sula bit her lip: if the Naxids saw them and opened fire now . . . she remembered the Naxid police vehicle that Hong had wrecked with just his rifle.

"Ardelion," she said, "how's that leg?"

Spence was bent over examining the injury. "I can't bend over far enough in this damn armor to get a good look," she said. "But I think the bullet went right through the calf. I'll slap an aid pack on it and we'll take a closer look at it later."

Sula sat up and peered out of the back window as the car pulled away. The Naxid police were concentrating on the building, fortunately, not on any onlookers. Those yellow-and-black uniforms were now being reinforced by others in viridian Fleet body armor. She could still hear gunfire rattling away, but none of these Naxids were firing.

Suddenly there was a cry in her ears, and Sula's blood ran chill as she heard a voice crying over the rattle of gunfire. "All teams! This is Three-six-nine! We're with Team Three-one-seven! The Naxids have cut us off! We have one dead out in the street and the rest of us are wounded! We need help!"

Hong's voice came next. "All teams, this is Blanche. Assist Three-six-nine if possible! Three-six-nine, give us your location please."

Sula called up a street map onto her visor display, and her heart sank as she realized the weakness of the escape plan. She had considered it an advantage that the district was cut into quarters by the intersection of two major roads—all the teams and their vehicles could escape the scene on quiet local roads while the Naxid convoy would be on Axtattle Parkway, with only limited access to the area.

While that was all true, what Sula now realized was that the two major roads cut Action Group Blanche into four pieces, and made it virtually impossible for any of these divisions to help one another. Sula's team would have to cross both Highway 16 and Axtattle Parkway in order to get into the area where Teams 317 and 369 were pinned down, and that was going to take luck and a fair amount of maneuvering.

"Starling!" she called to Macnamara. "Drive as fast as you can! Prepare to turn left on the second street following this intersection!"

She put the sedan through a series of maneuvers that got it across Highway 16 at a dead run, but by the time she had worked out a route that crossed Axtattle Parkway the two beleaguered teams had ceased to call for help. Either they were all dead or in the hands of the enemy.

By that point, however, Team 151, who had started in the building across the parkway from Sula, was in its own fire-fight, having been caught dragging a wounded comrade toward their escape vehicle. Team 167 tried to help them but both teams were overwhelmed before Sula could get her own car back across Highway 16 to their aid. Two members of Team 499 were caught in the open, on foot, and forced to surrender—and at that point Sula remembered that Lieutenant Captain Hong had taken 499's car and driver in order to carry out his improvised plan for demolishing the bridge.

Everything was crumbling away. Almost half of Action Group Blanche had been killed or taken, and all in a matter of minutes. Through it all Hong's cheerful voice continued to call into Sula's ears, giving orders, trying to coordinate a response that would rescue his doomed teams.

There was nothing Sula could do to help any of those in trouble. She tried to keep her voice calm as she told Macnamara to slow down and drive out of the area following one of the prearranged escape routes.

Perhaps Team 491 escaped only because Team 211, who had been in Sula's building at the start, got involved in a high-speed chase with a swarm of police and drew all Naxid reinforcements away. Team 211 eventually crashed their car, and the team leader called that they would try to get away on foot. By that point they were far enough away that their radio transmissions were breaking up, and Sula, driving in another direction, heard no more from them.

Hong made a last transmission telling the remaining teams to go to ground, and then he, too, fell silent.

Sula stripped back her camouflage hood, took off her helmet, and turned off her radio comm. She took out the hand comm that had been dedicated to this mission, stripped the batteries, flung it from the car with enough force to shatter it on the curb, and then lay back on the seat and gave herself up to weariness and the sense of bitter defeat.

We're going to have to get better at this, she thought.

If we live.

EIGHTEEN

By the time they arrived in their own home area Spence's leg was too stiff and painful to permit her to walk, so Sula had Macnamara drive to the Riverside apartment they all shared. The car was parked in the alley behind the building, and Sula opened the door to the back stair, the one with the door that led from the second floor landing to their kitchen. As the laughter of children echoed down the stair, Sula helped the bandaged Spence get on Macnamara's back, and then stayed with the car and its military gear as Macnamara carried her up the stairs to her bed.

"Some kids in the stair saw us," Macnamara said when he returned. "I told them it was a boating accident, that she got her leg caught between a boat and the quay."

"What made you think of that?" Sula asked in amazement, but Macnamara only shrugged. She stuffed a pistol down the waistband of her trousers in back, made sure the weapon was covered by her civilian jacket, and left the car to Macnamara.

"Go to your private lodgings," she told him. "I'll look after Spence. Make your rounds normally tomorrow morning, but make sure you check the position of the flowerpot before coming into the aparrment." She hesitated. "If you get a signal that there's something waiting for us at a mail drop," she said, "don't pick it up yourself. Pay someone else to do it, and make sure he's not followed when he gives it to you."

Macnamara was startled. "That'll give away the location of the drop," he said.

"There are plenty of mail drops," she said. "There's only one you."

She left Macnamara to contemplate this and bounced up the stairs, past the small children who had laid out a toy tea set on the landing, and slipped into the apartment. She moved the flowerpot in the front window from *No one's here* to *Someone is here and it's safe,* and then went in to check on Spence.

Sula unbound the field dressing and inspected the wound. As Spence had suspected, the bullet had driven clean through the right calf. There was very little bleeding. The calf was swollen, the skin smooth and taut as the skin of a grape and beginning to turn blue, but the wounds seemed relatively clean, with no great amount of tearing, and Sula found no foreign matter in the wound after she cleaned it, no splinters or bits of cloth. She sprayed on antibiotics and fast-healer hormones, put another field dressing on, a dressing that contained even more antibiotics and fast-healer hormones, and then loaded a med injector with a standard painkiller, Phenyldorphin-Zed.

Spence tilted her head back, brushing the hair back from her neck, and Sula pressed the injector to Spence's carotid. Sula's heart gave a sickly throb in her chest. Blackness rimmed her vision. She realized her hand was trembling.

"Maybe you'd better do this yourself," she said.

Sula had to leave the room before the hiss of the injector came to her ears. From the front room she stared down into the busy street, seeing the vendors with their racks and carts, the people who moved along the street in thick crowds but who never seemed to be in a hurry.

Frustration scorched Sula's nerves. None of these people knew that a battle for Zanshaa had been fought and lost that day. It was very possible that none of them would ever know unless the Naxids chose to tell them.

Sula thought of Guei crawling down the hall with his eye socket pouring blood. The voices of Team 317 calling for help as bullets tore the air around them. Caro Sula, her face slack with narcotics, lying with her golden hair spread on a pillow as her best friend fired dose after dose of Phenyldorphin-Zed into her neck . . .

Sula slammed her fists down on the windowsill and marched back into the room she shared with Spence. Spence looked back at her past half-lowered, drugged eyelids, the injector still in her hands. The room smelled of disinfectant.

"Can I get you anything?" Sula asked. "Would you like something to eat?"

"Can't eat." Spence made a vague gesture at the wall. "Video, maybe?"

Sula told the video wall to turn on, and settled on her bed to help Spence watch one of her romantic dramas. The hero was an older man, a Peer, handsome and cynical; the heroine was young and astoundingly beautiful. Her beauty seemed to unlock the hero's personality, if not unhinge his sanity altogether: he disgorged a perfectly stupendous amount of jewelry, clothing, and trips to exotic climes before dismissing a long-time mistress and installing the heroine in his High City palace. The heroine seemed bewildered and faintly distressed by much of this, but she understood the meaning of the palace at least, and consented to the Peer's offer of marriage.

Sula, who had more experience with older, cynical Peers than Spence, watched the ludicrous goings-on with growing impatience. Her mother, she knew, would have loved this story, had in fact done her best to *live* it—she had spent most of her life in service to some man or other, her chief problems being that her beauty tended to attract admirers from another end of the social scale than the Peerage, and that most of these were married already.

Her mother, who she had not seen in years.

Claustrophobia began to press on Sula's mind with cotton-wool fingers. She was in the apartment waiting, and for what? A handsome Peer with a fistful of jewelry? A horde of Naxids with guns? For Martinez, to carry her off to his palace in the sky, the palace that Maurice Chen had bought for him?

Sula made sure Spence was comfortable and then went out into the streets. Laughter and chatter rose around her while gunfire echoed in her skull. The first action against the Naxids had been a catastrophe. Action Group Blanche was in ruins, and the survivors in hiding. The Naxids were doubtless installing their government in the High City at this exact moment.

Simply for a place to go, Sula went to the Grandview apartment, a walk that took her over the better part of an hour. She studied the building for a while, then decided that it was unlikely the Naxids were waiting for her as yet. There were belongings she might as well fetch out, and some preparations it might be worth her while to make.

She saw a light on in the apartment of the toothless old concierge, and an idea occurred to her. She bought a newssheet from the vendor on the corner, walked to the apartment, and stuck a head in the concierge's door.

"Mr. Greyjean?"

"Yes, miss?" The old man shuffled toward her from the kitchen, carrying in one gnarled hand a plate with a piece of toast.

"I wonder if I might ask a favor of you."

"Of course."

Sula eased the door shut behind her. "Mr. Greyjean, do you remember that when I first moved in, you thought I was a Fleet officer?"

"Oh yes, of course. Do you mind if I eat my toast while it's hot?"

"No I don't," she said, "and I *am* a Fleet officer."

"Ah." Greyjean munched toast, which caused more of his consonants to disappear than usual. "Well, I always thought so." He gave a watery glance around his room. "Would you like to sit down, my lady?"

"Yes, thank you."

She perched on the edge of an elderly, overstuffed chair; Greyjean sat on a small sofa. "I'm here to fight the Naxids, you see," Sula said. He nodded. "So," she continued, "the Naxids might well come looking for me."

Greyjean nodded. "Well yes, that makes sense."

"And if they do . . ." Sula handed him the newssheet, neatly folded into quarters. "Could you put this in your kitchen window, so that I could see it from the outside?"

Greyjean contemplated the thin plastic rectangle. "In the window, you say?"

"Yes. You could keep it by the window, you know, and then just prop it up if the Naxids come."

Light colors were recommended for these sorts of signals: the white plastic sheet would stand out well against practically any background.

Greyjean rose from his sofa and shuffled toward the kitchen, his plate in one hand and the newssheet in the other. Sula followed. Greyjean put the sheet in the window, pinning it in place with a terra-cotta pot that held a ficus.

"Will this do, my lady?" he asked.

"Yes, but only if the Naxids come."

"Of course, yes." He took the white rectangle out of the window and placed it under the potted plant. "I'll just keep it there," he said.

"Thank you, Mr. Greyjean."

Greyjean shrugged and took another bite of his toast. "My pleasure, my lady."

Sula reached into her pocket, took out a twenty-zenith coin, and put it on his plate. His eyes widened.

"*Twenty* zeniths?" he said. "Are you sure, my lady?"

He might never have held twenty zeniths in his hand in his life.

"Of course," Sula said. "You're entitled. You're working for the government now." She winked. "The *real* government."

For a long moment Greyjean considered the apparition on his plate, and then took the coin and slipped it into his pocket. "I always wanted government service," he said, "but I never had the right schooling."

Chenforce sped from Aspa Darla Wormhole 2 into Bai-do, the ships coming in hot, their radars pounding away as they began maneuvering the instant they passed the wormhole. Martinez had his eyes fixed on the displays, and in the radio spectrum found, as he suspected, a black, dead system, with the only radio sources being the system's star and its single inhabited planet. He switched to optical and infrared censors, and found rather more. Large numbers of merchant ships burned at high accelerations for wormholes leading out of the system.

"Targets," Martinez reported, and with a sweep of his fingers so categorized them on the tactical display.

"Assign targets to weapons officers within the squadron," Michi said. "Tell them to launch missiles when ready."

And in the meantime the familiar message had automatically been broadcast, and was being repeated every few minutes: *"All ships docked at the ring station are to be abandoned and cast off so that they may be destroyed without damage to the ring. All repair docks and building yards will be opened to the environment and any ships inside will be cast off . . ."*

The Naxids at Bai-do had known they were coming for days and had ordered everyone in the system to switch off their radars. It would be many hours before Martinez had a complete picture of the system. He had very little anxiety on that score, since they'd entered through a wormhole that was at a great distance from the system's sun, and any warships guarding the system would be much closer in.

". . . Any ship attempting to flee will be destroyed . . ."

For the first two days Bai-do seemed a repeat of Aspa Darla. No warships were discovered. Merchant ships in flight were destroyed, and most crews had enough warning to escape in lifeboats. No drunken Captain Hansen appeared on comm to object to the annihilation of his vessel. Large numbers of ships were cast off from Bai-do's ring, and a pair of pinnaces were launched from *Judge Arslan* to inspect the ring and to make certain orders were carried out.

A modest round of dinners and parties continued, though under strict orders for superior officers to restrain the amount of drinking as long as the squadron was in enemy space. Martinez played host to a party of lieutenants and cadets aboard *Daffodil,* and Fletcher once more had Michi and her staff as guests for a formal supper.

"Your ring will be inspected to make certain that you have complied with these orders . . ."

The crew of *Illustrious* was reasonably light of heart when they strapped into their action stations for the two pinnaces' closest approach to Bai-do. The pinnaces would pass no closer than a quarter of a light-second, but the powerful sensors on the small craft would be able to see perfectly well into the open hangar bays, yards, and docks, and relay the information to the flagship.

After supper at Fletcher's table, Martinez felt heavy-lidded and drowsy in the warmth of his vac suit, and he adjusted the internal atmosphere to a more bracing temperature. The two signals lieutenants murmured in soft voices as the pinnaces, on their approach, began feeding *Illustrious* packets of intelligence from their communications lasers. Idly, Martinez moved the pinnaces' feed onto his displays, and only then noticed the flashes in the corner of his tactical display.

"Missile flares!" Martinez said in perfect astonishment. "Missile flares from the station!"

His drowsiness was inundated by a wave of adrenaline that slammed into his bloodstream with the force of a tsunami engulfing a coral atoll. Martinez banished the pinnace feeds from his display and enlarged the tactical array. The accelerator ring had fired a pair of missiles, each clearly aimed at one of the approaching pinnaces.

"All ships!" Martinez said. "Defensive weaponry to target those missiles!"

It was an order he felt he could safely give without Michi's approval. Michi herself was shouting to her signals officers.

"Message to Ring Command! You will disable those missiles *immediately* . . ."

Too late, Martinez thought. The display showed an event that had happened twenty-three minutes ago. By the time Michi's message flashed the twenty-three light-minutes back to the ring station, the missiles and the two defenseless boats would have had their rendezvous.

It was barely possible that the squadron's defensive lasers might knock down one or another of the missiles, but guessing where a jinking missile would be in twenty-three minutes was a task better suited for a fortune-teller than a weapons officer . . .

The voices of the Terran pinnace pilots crackled into life in Martinez's headset, announcing in voices of surprising tranquillity the appearance of the missiles. They would attempt evasive accelerations, all the while continuing their automatic scan of the Bai-do ring with their sensor arrays.

Any evasion was pointless. In order to avoid the streaking missiles, the pinnaces would have to accelerate so heavily as to crush their passengers. The only hope for the pilots was that the missiles weren't actually trying to kill them, but to create a screen between the pinnaces and the ring station in order to prevent observation.

After Michi's message was sent to Ring Command, there was a sudden cold silence in the Flag Officer Station.

". . . *Failure to obey orders will mean the destruction of the ring* . . ."

The remembered words burned through Martinez's mind like fire.

The threat had been made. But a threat meant nothing unless there was the will to carry it out.

"Captain Martinez," Michi said in a new, cold, inflection-less tone, "please plan an attack on the Bai-do ring."

"Very good, my lady."

The plan had been made ages ago when Chenforce was still circling Seizho's sun, and Martinez needed only to update the tactical situation before presenting it to the squadron commander. Michi glanced at her tactical display only briefly. There was a new hardness in the set of her mouth.

"Convey the plan to the squadron, captain," she said. "Prepare to execute on my command."

"At once, my lady." He could not make himself reply with the words, "very good."

Martinez passed orders to each ship in the squadron. Michi leaned her head back on her couch support and closed her eyes. "The bastards are testing us," she said in a nearly inaudible voice. "After Koel, the Naxid command has had time to issue orders to the Bai-do ring, and to others as well. They want to find out if we'll actually carry out our threats."

"After we destroyed the Zanshaa ring," Martinez said, "why would they think we'd stick at Bai-do?"

Michi had no answer. Martinez, a sickness chewing at his belly, watched his display, saw the pinnaces standing on tails of flame in mad frenzies of acceleration as they tried to escape the fate that pursued them.

The heavy acceleration was a mercy in a way, because the pilots were almost certainly unconscious when the missiles found them.

Martinez looked for a long, terrible moment at the silent expanding plasma spheres at his display, and then raised his eyes to Michi. There was black anger in her eyes, as well as a horror at the order she was about to give.

"Captain Martinez," she said. "Destroy the Bai-do ring."

Martinez found that his lips formed an answer. "Yes, my lady." He touched the transmit pad and gave the orders.

Missiles lanced out from the squadron. The ring was a big

target and so the salvo did not need to be large. There were laser defenses on the station, not intended so much for military purposes as for destroying meteors or small out-of-control spacecraft that might threaten the ring, but these were not capable of coordinating the same sort of defense as a squadron flying in formation, and the ring's destruction was assured.

Martinez was surprised to see more missile flares from the target, a salvo of a dozen aimed at the squadron. Another dozen followed a few minutes later, and then a third. All were destroyed en route, and he received a message of explanation from Lieutenant Kazakov, who had been analyzing the data sent by the pinnaces before they were destroyed.

"There are partly completed warships on the ring, lord captain," she told him. "Three heavy cruisers and three frigates or light cruisers. Apparently one of the big cruisers has got a working missile battery."

The Naxids were going to let the Bai-do ring die in order to defend half a squadron of half-built warships that were lost anyway. Martinez clenched his teeth in frustration and anger.

The enemy frigate fired several more salvos before the end. None of the Naxid missiles proved a threat to Chenforce, and all were destroyed without undue effort. Two-thirds of the loyalists' missiles were also destroyed, but the plan allowed for that.

Illustrious was at its closest approach to Bai-do, three light-seconds, when the first missile impacted the ring. There were several more strikes after that, and each vaporized a section of the bright wheel that circled the planet.

A thing as huge as a planetary ring takes a long time to die. The upper level was still moving much faster than the lower, geostationary level, and each upper fragment separated from the lower ring and shot off on its own trajectory, each a curved airless sickle filled with corpses, brilliant in the sun, carried by its greater momentum into a higher orbit.

More horrifying, however, was the larger piece of the ring on the far side of the planet from Chenforce. This piece, nearly half of the ring, was still intact, and its upper ring never had time to completely separate from its lower before the whole mass began to oscillate and fall into the atmosphere. The cables were designed to burn up on reentry, but Bai-do was not so lucky as far as the rest of the structure was concerned. The upper ring contained hundreds of millions of tons of asteroid and lunar material used as radiation shielding. When the colossal structure broke up on contact with the atmosphere, all its great mass came raining down on Bai-do's blue and green equator.

Martinez watched as Bai-do's land mass flared from the impacts, as great shimmering golden waves rose from impact sites on the blue ocean. Smoke and dust and water vapor rose high into the atmosphere. Here and there were the distinctive sparkle of antimatter. Enough dust might be blasted into the upper atmosphere to shroud the planet in cold and darkness for years. There would be massive crop failure, and with the ring gone there would be no way to import food.

The ones who died now might well be the lucky ones.

"How many people are living down there?" The question, half-whispered, came from Lady Ida Lee.

Four point six billion. Martinez happened to know. He'd absorbed the fact when he'd planned the raid. And the population of the ring itself was in the tens of millions.

"Tell the crew to secure from action stations," Michi said. She looked ten years older.

Martinez locked his displays above his head and rose from his couch. The scent of sour sweat and adrenaline rose from his suit. He felt older than Michi looked.

As he followed his commander from the room he felt a spasm of dread.

How many more times are we going to have to do this?

* * *

Sula took the train back to Riverside, carrying a bundle of clothing from the Grandview apartment, where she had emptied her closet and made certain other arrangements as well. She found Spence drowsing with the med injector in her hand. The video wall was repeating the same announcement over and over, and the announcer was a Naxid.

Lady Kushdai, the new governor, had taken up residence in the High City, and Zanshaa would now begin a new reign of peace and prosperity under the Committee to Save the Praxis. A group of anarchists and saboteurs had made an unsuccessful attack on the government's forces that morning, but all had been killed or captured. Many civilian casualties had occurred as a result of the attackers' vicious and unreasoned assault.

The next news item was a shock: five hundred and five hostages had been taken, a hundred and one from each species under the Naxid administration, any or all of whom might suffer death if incidents of anarchy and sabotage did not cease.

Sula stared at the video in thoughtful surprise. *Five hundred and five.* And from five species, when only Terrans had been involved in the ambush.

Peace. Prosperity. Hostages. She wondered if the Naxids realized the message they were sending.

The news hummed in her thoughts as Sula went out onto the street to purchase food from vendors. The people had got the news before she had, and they were furious. Everyone seemed to know that the hostages had been pulled in off the street, at random, and that none of them were anarchists or saboteurs.

The Naxids were not making friends.

For the next three days Macnamara arrived every morning after his rounds to report that no messages were found at either the primary or backup locations. Sula burned off nervous energy by tidying relentlessly and bathing frequently. She looked after Spence, watched the news, and spent a lot

of time connected to the Records Office computer. She created new identities for everyone that she knew or suspected
had survived the Axtattle Parkway ambush. She didn't have
their pictures, but used images taken from other IDs already
in the system, images that resembled the people she had
trained with.

A new administrator had been put in charge of the Records Office, someone fresh from Naxas. Everyone in the office, and the government generally, was made to swear
allegiance to the Committee to Save the Praxis. Hotels and
warehouses were requisitioned, including—as Sula had anticipated—the Great Destiny Hotel.

Contact was not made.

On the fourth morning Macnamara came with a message.
"You didn't pick it up yourself?" Sula asked, with a glance
toward the window and the street below. If Macnamara had
been followed . . .

"I did like you told me," Macnamara said. "When I saw
the signal that there was a message at the drop, I paid a va-
grant to pick up the message for me. I told him to bring it to
the far end of an alley so that I could see if he was followed,
and then I performed a series of evasions on the two-wheeler
before returning here."

"Did you see anyone at all?" Sula, nerves humming, still
couldn't resist a glance into the street.

"No. No one."

Artemus has a new posting. The message was printed on
the inexpensive thin plastic used for newssheets and other
disposable forms of communication, and called for a meeting with Hong at the Grandview apartment the following
morning at 11:01.

Hong had never called for a meeting at Sula's apartment
before—he had always preferred a meeting in a public
place, usually outside a café, where it might be possible to
spot any observers.

Sula touched the plastic sheet to her upper lip. It was perhaps unreasonable to think so, but neither the plastic nor the message smelled like Hong.

She gave Macnamara instructions concerning which piece of equipment he'd need for the next day. Sula's own preparations had been made when she'd last visited the Grandview apartment. She left Riverside and took a taxi past Greyjean's window, where the rectangle of white newssheet stood plain to see, confirming Sula's suspicions that the Naxids had been to visit.

The next morning Spence remained in the Riverside apartment on the theory that a limping engineer would only make the team more conspicuous. Sula and Macnamara took cabs past the Grandview apartment separately on their way to a meeting three streets away. The white newssheet was still in the window. There were some large unmarked vehicles that looked innocent enough, but which might contain police.

Certainly Lord Octavius Hong was not observed lurking on a street corner, or arguing with the concierge.

Sula and Macnamara met at precisely 11:01, then walked toward the Grandview apartment on opposite sides of the street. They could see no light through the apartment windows, and no squads of Naxids in yellow-and-black uniforms lurked in alleyways.

Once the apartment was in sight, both hesitated. Sudden doubt swam in Sula's mind. Her heart throbbed in her chest. She could be misjudging the whole situation.

A sonic boom rattled windows, and Sula almost jumped out of her skin. But the sound had clarified the situation somehow, and she raised a hand to her head and deliberately combed her fingers through her short, black-dyed hair.

Across the street, Macnamara pressed the switch on the detonator in his jacket pocket.

In the Grandview apartment, the explosive that Macnamara's carpentry had concealed in the furniture went off, blasting ahead of it a storm of steel ball bearings and roofing

436 • Walter Jon Williams

436 • Walter Jon Williams

nails. To minimize casualties in nearby apartments the explosive force had been deliberately directed in a swath from the interior of each room toward the outer wall. The windows blew out in a red blaze of heat and horror, and Sula heard screams as debris rained onto the street below.

Ramps slammed down from two large gray vehicles nearby, and Naxid police charged out, racing for the apartment where flames were now lapping from the windows.

"Ah. Hah," Sula said.

She turned and walked away. Her feet seemed to sink deep into the pavement, as if it were made of soft rubber.

Hong had been captured, then, in the wake of the Axtattle fiasco, and had been forced or persuaded to give up the procedures by which he contacted his teams. Others teams besides Sula's would be betrayed. She had to assume that she and her team were now the only members of Action Group Blanche now at large.

She and her team were alone in the city, inhabiting false identities, without allies, few resources, and with no way to contact her superiors.

Caroline, Lady Sula, had limited resources to cope with this situation. What was needed was another person, with a different set of skills.

It's *my* war now, Gredel thought, and kept walking.